April - 2020
El Dorado County Library
345 Fair Lane
Placerville, CA 95667

UNDER A BRIGHT BRIGHT YELLOW SUN

THE BRONZE SWORD

S. G. MUSCARELLO

WESTBOW
PRESS®
A DIVISION OF THOMAS NELSON
& ZONDERVAN

WestBow Press books may be ordered through booksellers or by contacting:

WestBow Press
A Division of Thomas Nelson & Zondervan
1663 Liberty Drive
Bloomington, IN 47403
www.westbowpress.com
1 (866) 928-1240

ISBN: 978-1-9736-2207-9 (sc)
ISBN: 978-1-9736-2208-6 (hc)
ISBN: 978-1-9736-2206-2 (e)

Library of Congress Control Number: 2018902721

Print information available on the last page.

WestBow Press rev. date: 09/13/2018

A great chunk of the imagination that comprises this humble narrative was formed to the creak of the backyard swing during my childhood, near a town called Placerville, in the foothills of the Sierra Nevada Mountains. I hope you find the same great enjoyment in experiencing Orenea in this book as I have. I am immensely indebted to a few extremely special individuals for the production of this novel. The first in this list is God, who, as always, deserves the full glory in all accomplishments, being the origin of language itself, without which, you can imagine, the book writing process would be severely complicated indeed.

The second person on this list is my mother, whose encouragement, technical knowledge, and other aspects have played a vital role on this endeavor.

Next on this list are my father and Russell and Grace Toliver for their encouragement. I also cannot fail to mention my childhood friends Connor, Fina, Zachary, Michael, and Molly, who (in hence order) served as the base inspiration for the characters Mighty Cedar, Veenatch, Zatch, Mik, and Pona-Pow.

I would also like to thank you, dear reader, for bearing with me thus far. God bless you all.

Sincerely,
S. G. Muscarello

CHAPTER I

IT WAS AN UNUSUALLY WINDY, frosty morning in early spring. Frigid rain slowly trickled down the stained glass window on the third floor of the five-floor mansion out on the open green plain in Germany. Behind the large castle-like structure lay the hills, which sat proudly in the background. This elegant structure, which had been built long ago, was named Grasslan Manor. Presently there was a meeting being conducted in the large old-style dining room. The Fur Christus Gelflown party was awaiting their speaker.

Outside, their warmly clothed dark-bearded preacher hurried along the muddy dirt road. He was already late and was eager to be with the assembled gathering. He was not far from the manor, which was outwardly adorned with brick, stained glass windows, and a dull green hedge. The man hurried on. Finally, he stepped forward to the outer gate. A precarious-looking guard armed with a large sword and pistol patrolled alertly by the sturdy iron door.

"Name," the guard demanded in clear German.

"Pastor John Paul Pell," the preacher replied more bravely than he felt. Just simply mentioning his name could cost his freedom—or even his life.

The guard, who was standing in the shelter of the old stone arch over the gate, raised his brown curly mustache, slipped from his coat pocket a small leather-covered notepad, and recorded something in it. "I have been told of you, John," he commented cheerlessly, still keeping the small pencil to the paper. "Business?"

"I am here to speak with the brethren," John replied nervously.

The guard pulled the heavy gate open easily. Mr. Pell slipped through the iron gate, which was only slightly open, and hurried along the little path to the door. He was pleased with the red brick pathway instead of bothersome mud. The bricks on this building matched the bricks on the walk, and Mr. Pell tried to imagine how many scarlet bricks there were on the building, which had an exterior completely painted ocean blue other than the bricks, some stained glass windows, and the entrance. A few awkward domes perched proudly atop the mansion's towers.

Along the side of the building was a green hedge, which had yet to bloom. The man nervously knocked the heavy brass knocker on the great wooden door. He could not wait to behold the expression on his congregation's faces when he delivered his proposal. A well-dressed porter cracked open the creaky door and peeked out.

"Come in," the porter said, beckoning Mr. Pell to step onto an orange mat in the darkly painted entry.

Immediately two identically clad butlers entered the small, empty room. One of the men bent down and started scrubbing Mr. Pell's muddy black boots with a clean white rag.

"Lift," the butler ordered stiffly. John lifted his foot so the butler could clean the bottom of his boot. Standing on one foot, John saw the man wiping his foot and smiled. He glanced up at the iron lantern hanging from the black ceiling. Butterflies danced inside him. He hoped this would not be his last address. The butler quickly finished John's shoes and started to straighten his soaked plain clothes.

"Thank you, friends, but you may feel free to do your job lightly for your own convenience." But the butler was not paying attention. The second butler, who had remained silent until now, stepped forward.

"May I show you to your dressing room so you can change into some more suitable clothes?" John nodded, and the butler pushed open a plain black wooden door, which led down a hallway lighted by lanterns and decorated with elaborate paintings painted by the owner of the manor himself.

"I do not want to keep the brethren waiting," John insisted as they walked down the hall.

"You must be dressed appropriately to speak to that many people," the butler replied mechanically. There was a short pause.

"Do you train to serve your visitors in this manner?" John remarked, trying to create friendly conversation.

"Yes," the butler replied expressionlessly.

John could see this man was not in the mood for conversation. So he walked quietly behind the butler, who paused to open another small door and beckoned John to enter. The large room contained rows and rows of men's clothes hanging on long poles running lengthwise across the room. Different kinds of clothes were placed at different sections in the room. Wooden pegs, which stuck from the sides of the poles, indicated the sizes. So many garments! So many colors!

"What size do you wear?" the butler asked as he picked through the clothes.

"Size small," John replied. He was only five feet four.

Coming out of the mess of clothes, the butler handed John a colorful outfit. John was shown to a changing room, where he changed from soaked clothes into a lace-trimmed men's specialty suit. It was an elegant red-and-green velvet outfit with a matching cap. The small dressing room offered a large wood slab bench held up by iron chains. The butler diligently helped John button and place the small cap on his head.

"You look very handsome in that," the butler declared blandly. "I shall show you to the chamber." They walked down the hall to a pair of very large oak double doors, at which two men stood ready.

They pulled the large shiny golden rings, and slowly the heavy doors creaked open. The immense room with high ceilings was crowded with two hundred people. The eldest were seated in elaborate chairs at a long table.

Immediately, a small gray haired man, who was the owner of Grasslan Manor, scurried up to John. "You are late, John! I have hardly kept this crowd from rioting!" he exaggerated.

"I'm sorry, Herr Heinrich," John apologized.

"You know this kind of meeting is illegal nowadays. There is a fortune on your capture," Heinrich whispered.

"Yes, indeed," John replied irritably, "with this government taking more and more of our rights away."

"Indeed," Heinrich agreed.

"I was admiring your paintings in the hall," John asserted.

"Well ... thank you," replied Heinrich, blushing.

"So," John asked softly, rubbing his hands together, "are they ready?"

"Yes, yes, of course—go in," replied Heinrich.

The room was elaborately adorned with large tapestries around the gigantic fireplace, which was located at the back of the room by the tiny back entrance. A cello player produced cheerful classical music in the corner.

"Everyone clear the stage! Station five zero, halt!" Heinrich ordered. The musician immediately quit playing, and those standing on the stage began to stir. The stage was only a space of bare floor six inches above the rest.

John stepped onto the shiny wood in front of the dense crowd. "Thank you for coming," he began. "For years the Christians in Europe have been persecuted. You all are of many races. Most of you are from Scotland, Germany, Italy, Britain, or Gall. Some of you are from Bohemia, Switzerland, Spain, Hungary, and many other places. But Christians were persecuted in many of those countries." Some in the crowd nodded knowingly. "So," John continued, "you fled to Germany. Here it was safe for many years—but did you know you were breaking the law by being here at this moment? But where can we flee now? The government is growing very hostile! Alas, nowhere in Europe can we go! So we must leave Europe."

A ripple of excitement spread through the crowd.

"I have been praying much for guidance, and I have come to a decision. We must embark on an extremely dangerous mission. I know many of you cannot come with us because of responsibilities God has entitled you to. But I believe that this coming summer, year of our Lord 1501, we as a congregation should sail to the New World."

A gasp rose through the astonished gathering, and Heinrich, who was painting in the corner, cupped his stained hand over his mouth.

"What about the ships?" a man from the crowd inquired.

"I have already been looking and comparing prices, trustworthiness, and other things," John replied unsurely. "But I do know—and that is *know*—that God will provide."

"What about the language barrier?" a woman in the crowd asked.

"Ah, yes," John replied. "I know how hard it can be to learn a new language. I myself am from Venice, Italy. But I am sure we can work something out with the local natives and—"

Just then, ten German official knights barged into the room. The frightened people gasped, and John stood frozen on the stage. This was it. They had been discovered. The people were doomed. The light glistened menacingly off the knights' shiny breastplates.

"Pray tell," John inquired timidly, "who gave us away?"

Ignoring his question, the knight said, "We have come to arrest you all for the sake of our master and lord, King Maximilian, son of the great Frederick III of Germany, on the following properties concerning—"

Suddenly, a blinding light engulfed the room. John squinted his eyes shut and buried his face in his hands. Overwhelmed, he stumbled a few steps back and collapsed to the floor, trembling. Then everything went black.

John curled up in a ball and squinted his eyes shut tightly. For some reason, he seemed more comfortable and the floor felt softer.

"It's all right now," his wife, Elaine, explained softly. John suddenly realized he was no longer on the dining room floor. He slightly opened his eyes and looked around. John was lying on an elaborate bed with an embroidered canopy in a massive bedroom. He pushed back the warm covers and sat up.

"What happened? Did I fall unconscious? And ... the people ... are they safe?"

"Calm yourself," his beautiful wife whispered.

Heinrich came scurrying into the room, splattered with paint and carrying a rag and a clay bowl of water. "Oh, John, you are awake! The shock just got to you a bit, eh? Here, drink some water." He hurried handing him a gigantic cup of cool water that had been waiting on the nightstand and placed a wet cloth on his forehead.

"What happened?" John asked.

"No, no, no ...," Heinrich asserted. "You need rest."

"I cannot rest until I know what happened," John protested.

"Well," Heinrich began, "if I didn't know better, I would say it was an angel ..."

"A what?" John asked.

Heinrich shrugged. "You heard me."

John stroked his short beard. "Go on," he urged with interest.

"I can hardly explain it. The angel's light ... overwhelmed me. It was as if the presence of the Lord engulfed the room, as did the light. Almost everyone in the room curled up on the floor, as did I. Then, as quick as if one blinks an eye, that awesome light was gone. We rose frightened to our feet and found the knights dead on the floor."

"God punishes the sin of man," John remarked breathlessly. "I believe that this is a sign from God that we should go to the New World. I really don't want to go. I don't want to endanger the congregation that God has entitled me to."

Time passed. Thankfully, the German government was too busy with other matters to truly affect the little church and their leader. The seasons rolled around from late winter to spring. Despite the lovely flowers, the fresh fragrant air, and the magic of things coming alive, the Fur Christos Gelflown group had been making top-secret plans to escape Germany. Heinrich sadly gave Grasslan Manor to his son, and many other houses and possessions were sold. John, who had been diligently searching for a ship within budget, had hired four large wooden ships—one to hold provisions and three to hold passengers. The captain suggested that they take enough provisions to last the entire trip, plus enough to last about four weeks extra. However, John felt a strong conviction to take almost four times that.

"That is why I hired that fourth ship instead of three," he protested.

Other than provisions, many other obscure things were loaded onto the fourth ship. Livestock, woodwork, and a gigantic iron bell were only a few. The women set to work *making* preservable foods, and the men set to work *buying* preservable foods. The days dragged on, each day inching dangerously closer to the sailing date, July 8. March turned to April. April turned to May, and the goods that had been gathered were loaded onto the ships. The plan was that one of their preloaded passenger ships, which was currently in England, would sail into an isolated German port on the same day they would set sail for the New World. The days began to get warmer and more humid, and John knew that soon he would have to make that heart-wrenching and dangerous move. By the end of June, most of those embarking on the trip had sold or given away their residences and belongings. Some couldn't make the trip for sensible reasons.

On the morning of July 8, John and his faithful wife strolled out onto the dock. On the horizon sat an amazing sunrise—a glowing slash of orange. "If God can make that spread," John commented, "he can get us there safely."

Elaine, his wife, looked at him as if to say, *I agree.* A little black speck appeared on the horizon. The speck slowly neared and became a ship. By the time the sun had risen, the ship was near the harbor. Half-naked sailors scrambled about the ship and called out sharply to each other. An ugly patch littered the clean white sail. This was clearly the ship they had been awaiting from England.

But as soon as the ship reached the dock and was tied by long, thick ropes, the wind changed completely! Now the wind was blowing out to sea—to the New World. John and Elaine chuckled. No words needed to be exchanged.

Soon people started to arrive. The other three ships had already arrived, and with heavy hearts, the Fur Christous Gelflowns sadly boarded the passenger ships. Some of the most trusted friends and family were there to say goodbye.

Slowly the four ships drifted out to sea. The relatives and friends slowly left the dock.

For over a year, they waited and waited for the ship to return bearing news of the new colony. But the ships never returned.

Now we skip to 1624, to an early American colony we call Plymouth. But still, 123 years later, the Fur Christous Gelflowns's whereabouts remained a precarious mystery.

CHAPTER II

THE BEAUTIFUL WOODS WERE PEACEFUL and quiet this time of year just outside of Plymouth, Massachusetts. The ancient deciduous trees, which made up most of the dense woods, burst fervently with bright and vivid unreal colors atop their towering majestic ashen trunks, which seemed to slither all the way to heaven. The forest floor was matted thickly with large flesh-colored dead leaves. Bright sunlight pierced through the thick leaves of the oaks, maples, and birch to reach a short and somewhat scrawny-looking separatist boy who was collecting berries for his family. His name was Peter. The first thing you would notice about him was his bright ocean-blue eyes and fiery red curly hair. He was slight and small and almost everything about him was thin. His skin tone was like wax and bore a few little scars as marks of various illnesses and his head looked a tad too large for the rest of his body. A few of the townspeople believed that these illnesses were what had so severely stunted his growth. Some, who did not already know him, would have mistaken him for a small seven-year-old, although he was much older than that.

As Peter wandered slowly along through the gorgeous wilderness, he noticed something very ugly among all the beauty—someone he had seen too many times. Tall, sturdy Charlie Cox suddenly glanced up at Peter. Charlie was a notorious troublemaker in Plymouth and a member of the Billington Boys gang, which was a group of younger people who caused much of the trouble in Plymouth. Charlie, being somewhat immature, seemed to like nothing better than to make Peter's life as miserable as possible.

An evil smirk spread upon his unwelcome face as he arose gracefully to his feet. He began to prance meanderingly around Peter in a circle, all the while staring at him in an intimidating way. Peter was not *too* afraid because he had learned to live with Charlie's cruelty. Still, he peeked out of the corner of his eye to see if there was a plausible way of escape. Mother, who was often worried about him, would cause a great fuss if he came home with a bloody nose—again. Peter tried to be as bold as possible, bracing himself for whatever Charlie might do to him.

"So, twerp," Charlie sneered, "how are things in the nursery?"

Peter's face turned pink. "I ... I'm eleven years old," he corrected.

Charlie precariously drew back his large fist. Peter squinted his eyes shut and tensed as he awaited the blow. Charlie thrust his fist at Peter's upper cheek, stopping only about an inch from his face. Peter snapped his eyes shut and jerked back, causing him to tumble painfully back onto the soft dry leaves. The tin kettle which he had been keeping the berries in landed on the ground with a loud clang. Shakily, he jumped back to his feet. Charlie broke out into wild laughter. Peter sighed.

"So now you have had your petty little joke. May I go home now? I have work to do. And you probably do as well."

"Oh, of course. I'm sure your mother will be worried that you have escaped from your crib."

"I don't sleep in a crib," Peter insisted. "In fact, it has been many months since I have even *seen* one."

"Is that so?" Charlie shot back. "Well, wherever you *do* sleep, you sure have been spending a lot of time there. Why, not one fortnight ago you were allowed to sleep and lay down all day for four days straight. That big father of yours must not care a halfpenny how much you work. Perhaps he's not so good a man as they say."

Peter stared at the ground angrily. "I was ill … And you will not speak poorly of my—" His defense was cut short by Charlie swinging his hard fist at Peter's face once more, and this time he really did hit him. Again Peter tumbled backward, and again Charlie laughed raucously. Peter winced in pain and tenderly touched the place where he had been struck beneath his right eye. He was about to stand up when a booming voice from behind him stopped him short.

"Charles Cox." Charlie spun around to face the detention master, Mr. Snows, and another man, both of whom didn't seem amused.

"Are you supposed to be somewhere else, young man?" he demanded sternly.

"No, sir," Charlie responded innocently.

"I thought you were still in detention," Mr. Snows challenged.

"Uh … no," Charlie stammered. "That ended … um … a few hours ago."

"It did, did it?" Mr. Snows said. "Not according to your mother. Anna sent me to find you and bring you back to detention."

"Since when did you start calling my mother by her first name?" Charlie retorted disrespectfully.

"Don't talk to me that way," Mr. Snows responded calmly but firmly. "And by the way, why does Peter have a bruise on his face?"

"What bruise?" Charlie asked, not so innocently.

"You know what bruise," Mr. Snows replied. "Tell me what happened."

"He … he fell," Charlie argued.

"If he fell, why did you laugh?" Mr. Snows asked.

"I thought he was joking," Charlie lied.

The man looked down and shook his head sadly. "Come with us, Charles," he ordered sternly.

Charlie drew himself proudly to his full height and stuck out his chest. "No!" he shouted defiantly. "I'll not go with you!" He turned sneakily and attempted to escape, but the two men quickly snatched him before he had run far.

Mr. Snows marched stiffly up to Charlie, who was struggling

furiously. He dug his large rough fingers into Charles's thick brown hair and tightly grabbed it. He gruffly yanked the stubborn rascal's head back, forcing Charlie to peer directly into Mr. Snows's face. "I'm glad your father didn't live to see you behave like this," he scolded. Then he turned to the others, who were having no difficulty keeping Charlie from squirming out of their strong grasp.

"Shall I take him back to the detention house?" the second man asked.

"Unfortunately so."

The man dragged away his captive, who was still kicking and cursing wildly. Mr. Snows turned compassionately toward Peter, who was still a little shaky and his heart still pounding.

"Peter," he inquired anxiously, helping Peter to his feet, "are you well? It appears you bore a severe blow."

"It is not *that* terrible," he insisted, dusting himself off casually and trying to appear as untraumatized as possible. "I'm fine. That Cox boy is just an oversized coward."

"Perhaps, but that oversized coward should still not be allowed to lay bruises on others merely because they have less size than him."

Mr. Snows bent down and peered attentively at the swollen black-and-blue bump under Peter's right eye.

"That looks quite bad," he declared sympathetically. "Does it hurt a lot?"

"Well …," Peter replied hesitantly, picking up his kettle, "a little, I suppose, but not much."

Mr. Snows smiled warmly and patted the boy on the back. "Come on. I'll walk you home. Your mother will know how to treat that bruise."

Peter dunked the damp rag into the tin bowl of cool water on the table beside him and gently pressed it to his swollen face. He winced in pain and groaned.

"How does it feel?" his mother asked affectionately.

"A little sore," Peter complained. He slumped wearily down on the hard wooden chair he had been resting on in front of the warm fire as his mother fussed over his injury. The only furnishings in the small one-room cabin were a small fur rug, an undersized table and chairs, and an old trunk.

Mother smoothed back her long shiny golden hair beneath her stained coif and seated herself quietly beside her son. A concerned expression marked her face. She stared searchingly into Peter's troubled eyes. "Peter, I'm worried about you."

"Why, Mother?" Peter asked curiously.

"Does what Charlie says bother you?" she questioned.

Peter's face turned red, and he stared sadly down at his legs. "Um … I don't wish to discuss this right now." Mother nodded and rose to stir the large pot of soup in the large fireplace.

Suddenly, Peter's two younger sisters, Elisabeth and Rebeccah, bounced energetically into the cabin through the doorless opening. They were obviously identical twins. Their puffy sunny-blonde hair bounced against their shoulders as the two five-year olds entered.

"We played with Charlotte today!" Rebeccah announced proudly to her mother, who beamed and pretended it was the best thing in the world. Rebeccah continued to explain in detail what they had done.

Elisabeth padded softly to where Peter was sitting. "Is it better?" she asked softly.

"Yes," Peter said. He smiled at his little sister, who stared innocently back at him. Rebeccah, the other twin, bounced happily up to Peter, who placed the wet rag gently back into the water.

"I think your purple spot looks pretty," she declared. "I want to have one too."

Peter chuckled. "You wouldn't want one," he assured her. "It hurts very bad."

"I still think it looks very pretty," she said obstinately.

Just then, a knock resounded on the side of the cabin near the entrance, and a moment later, Andrew Thomas, one of Peter's friends, invited himself in. Andrew was tall and sturdy with blond spikey hair and slightly tanned skin. The Thomas family lived in the house next door and had been fast friends with the Washingsworths ever since Peter could remember. Andrew was like a cousin to Peter and was the only boy in Plymouth who would be his friend.

"Good morning, Peter," he greeted. "I just wanted to tell you that ..." He stopped dead in his tracks when he noticed the large swollen nob on his friend's face. "Whatever happened to your face?" he asked in surprise.

Peter chuckled. "I had a collision with a particular someone who happened to have escaped from detention," he explained.

Andrew understood what he meant. "Oh," he said. "I just came in to tell you that Mr. Kenelm will be telling a story for the children around the fire tonight. Will you come?"

Peter's face lit up. His favorite thing to do was sit around a cheery fire with other children and listen to Mr. Kenelm tell a story. Kenelm Winslow, whom many affectionately called "Mr. Kenelm," was the brother of a prominent citizen, Edward Winslow, and amused himself by sometimes telling the local children stories around a campfire. It was one of the few forms of entertainment in the colony.

"Yes," Peter responded excitedly, "I would like that very much."

Andrew smiled with satisfaction. "All right," he concluded cheerfully. "I will see you tonight."

The large glowing fire crackled cheerfully as the children gradually gathered beneath the setting sun. Peter waited excitedly for Andrew to arrive. Finally, just as it became dark, Andrew and his younger sister, Charlotte, wandered into the circle to join Peter and the twins. He seated himself comfortably beside Peter, who was sitting at the base of a log, and patted one of Peter's thin shoulders heartily in greeting.

Suddenly, Mr. Kenelm walked gaily to the middle of the large circle lined with happily excited children and youths sitting either on the ground or on the logs. Peter reclined back onto the log and waited for Mr. Kenelm to begin. That's when he heard some soft footsteps on the leaves behind his log. Peter glanced behind him to see a dark figure leaning contently against the trunk of an autumn stricken maple that canopied gracefully high over his head. The young native's shiny braided black hair flowed down his bare back, all the way down to his rough deerskin pants.

"Care to sit with us?" Peter asked hospitably. The boy shook his head shyly. This Indian boy sometimes listened in the background because he could understand just enough English to enjoy it. Peter would sometimes invite him to sit with them, although he never accepted the invitation. A sharp whistle suddenly pierced the cool evening air, and all eyes quickly turned to Mr. Kenelm.

"Good evening children!" he greeted joyfully. He appeared to be in a jolly mood.

"Good evening!" all the children shouted back, each apparently trying to be the loudest one there. With that, he began his story.

"Tonight," Mr. Kenelm announced, "I shall tell you all a story that happened over one hundred years ago in a faraway land ..." Everyone seemed to enjoy it.

As Peter and his friends smiled and shivered at the exciting, frightening tale, something entirely different was taking place in the meeting house, where there was an important meeting in session. About a dozen men gathered formally around a rough handmade table before a calmly burning fireplace. But the men around the table were anything but calm. They were furiously slamming the table with their fists, yelling and arguing all at once. An elderly bald man tapped a small wooden mallet on the table.

"Order! Order!" he shouted authoritatively. But the men ignored him and kept on shouting. Only a few of them waited calmly and quietly. "Order! *Order!*" he demanded. The noise gradually dissolved, and all eyes were directed toward the man up front. "We shall not get anywhere if we only argue," he scolded. "Let's take your suggestions one at a time."

"But those goods are imperative if we are going to construct the new community," someone murmured.

"It's impossible!" one younger man blurted out, waving his hand over the wrinkled hand-drawn map in the center of the table. "It's not humanly possible to transport the goods that far by the spring. It is *impossible!*"

Commotion began to rekindle, and the frustrated man at the front threw down the mallet again. "*Silence!*" he ordered. "What our brother has declared might be the unfortunate truth, but if anyone objects, he may do it at this moment—calmly."

At that moment, a short well-known gentleman stood up quietly. He was a stocky man with long dark curls spilling from beneath his worn hat. A large mustache with curled-up ends rested on his upper lip, above a short dark beard.

"Do you wish to say something, Mr. Winslow?" the man with the mallet asked.

"Yes, sir," he replied confidently. "I do believe it is possible to transport the goods for the new settlement before spring."

"How do you propose we do this?" inquired an elderly man.

"I say," Mr. Winslow began, "that we may be able to transport the necessary goods down the Quantum River to a nearby riverbank and carry them from there." He pointed instructively to the long, meandering river snaking its way through the old colorless map. All the men leaned in intently.

"Could that be accomplished?" another man asked curiously.

The one with the mallet shrugged. "We must test it and see. I do believe this might be an ingenious plan. I say let's do it. I'm putting you in charge Mr. Winslow."

"I think my brother Kenelm will do well in managing the boat's construction," Mr. Winslow suggested. "I'll ask him after he's finished telling the children a story."

"Thank you for arousing this possibility," the leader said politely. "I'll give you all some time to consider and pray about this crucial matter. But for now, session adjourned."

The fire had died down a little. Andrew and his younger sister had just departed, and the story had ended some time ago. Peter, who had enjoyed the tale very much, stood up quietly to ask Mr. Kenelm some questions. Most of the other children had gradually trickled away from the circle and had headed home for bed. Mr. Kenelm sat idly squatting, staring at the dying fire. He glanced up as soon as he noticed the small scrawny boy standing before him.

"Hello, Peter," he greeted him in a friendly tone. "How was my story tonight?"

"Good, good," Peter assured. "I enjoyed that one a lot."

"Thank you," Mr. Kenelm said cheerfully.

"I was just wondering where did you hear that story. I don't recall hearing that one before now."

"Oh, yes," Mr. Kenelm said. "That one is not very well known anymore. It used to be popular around one hundred years ago— around the time it happened."

"That actually happened?" Peter asked.

"Yes," Mr. Kenelm responded. "I just added the part about the ghost. But I believe it was told back in the old days to spook people. Quite a sad tale if you think about it. But I believe the preacher's name was … was … Oh, yes, Pell. John Pell. But to answer your original question, I just read it in an old book."

This seemed to strike a chord deep in Peter's uneducated mind. He stared dreamily into the fire. "What is it like to read?" he asked longingly. Mr. Kenelm glanced up, surprised at Peter's question.

"You mean to say," Mr. Kenelm inquired, astonished, "that no one has ever taught you your letters?" Peter shook his head sadly. "Not even your father and mother?" Peter shook his head again.

"They don't know how either."

Mr. Kenelm felt sorry for his young friend. "Oh," he mumbled. "But to answer your question ... it is somewhat like telling yourself a story ... someone else's story, I suppose ..." Before Mr. Kenelm could say anything else, Rebeccah and Elisabeth tugged impatiently on Peter's baggy sleeves.

"I wanna go home now," Rebeccah whined.

"I'm coming," Peter whispered with frustration. He smiled politely at Mr. Kenelm. "Thank you for your time."

"My pleasure, Peter," Mr. Kenelm replied as the twins half dragged Peter away with them.

When they finally skipped on happily ahead of him into the darkness, an idea suddenly popped into Peter's head. He suddenly spun around to face Mr. Kenelm. A creative, mischievous look appeared on his face.

"Do you suppose," Peter asked curiously, "that the grandchildren of those people who sailed may still be around somewhere?" Mr. Kenelm showed surprise at Peter's unusual question.

"Well ... I suppose it's possible," Mr. Kenelm guessed. "They could have been shipwrecked on an island in the middle of the ocean ... or ... I don't know."

Peter nodded thoughtfully and continued to stride briskly homeward. *Someday*, Peter daydreamed, *I just might find them.*

"Give thanks to the God of heaven—his love endures forever." Father sang the old hymn sweet and low until finally his two daughters were asleep peacefully. Finally satisfied that they were fast asleep, Father climbed quietly out of the loft and down to where Peter's small grass mat was by the fire. It was his routine every night. He would sing the girls to sleep and then pray a prayer over Peter.

His son lay on his back, staring silently up at the ceiling. Sensing that something might be wrong, Father squatted down by Peter and stared searchingly into his son's blue eyes.

"Is there something troubling you?" he asked caringly. Peter stared awkwardly down at the dull yellow blanket covering him.

"Yes," he admitted. Father flashed a look of concern and felt Peter's forehead gently. His enormous warm hand seemed to cover Peter's forehead completely. Father was everything Peter had ever wanted to be, and Peter always respected and admired his father greatly.

"Are you ill?" his father asked with concern. "I feel no fever." Peter shook his head wearily. Father knelt down by his son and sighed.

"Son," Father inquired, "does it have to do with the bruise on your cheek?" Peter squirmed uncomfortably and nodded.

"Charlie d-did it," he stammered. "I seem to be his main target— that is, when he's out of trouble." Peter paused awkwardly. "Sometimes he beats me to the ground, but more frequently he calls me names and tells me ugly things. Other children mock me for this too, but when they do it, I just pretend that I enjoy it as much as they do. I laugh and walk away to cover up how much I dislike it … when I can muster up enough acting skills to make it effective, that is. Many of them, especially the younger ones, think it's just innocent fun; they have no idea how it bothers me. But Charlie knows. Oh, how *he* knows." Large tears swelled up in the corners of his hurt eyes, but Peter quickly brushed them away. As far as he was concerned, real men did not cry.

"He makes fun of how small and thin I am and of how often I am ill. He tells me that I am dumb because I cannot read and mocks how my clothes never fit me right and how I cannot work in the field like the other boys and must help the women cook and do petty jobs instead," he lamented. "When he says these things, it hurts more than many bruises. He knows that. If only he could beat me up every day—but silently." Peter sniffed quietly.

"I just want to be like other boys, Father. Is that so great a request? I want to be able to run and play with them without getting too tired.

I want to work with them in the fields, and I want to be treated by people like I am eleven years old and not mistaken for a small child. And I don't want to be pitied by everyone all the time. I want to be big and strong and well, like you. Have you any idea what it feels like to be the one everyone pities? Why, out of all the people in existence, did *I* need to be the unfortunate one?"

Father paused thoughtfully and intently considered Peter's statement, and for a moment, Peter thought that he had forgotten to reply. Finally, he answered.

"I do not believe you are unfortunate, at least not in the way you perceive yourself as being."

"Sir?"

"Son, do you remember when you were young, shortly before we left Holland, and you worked sweeping the floor and doing small jobs for the blacksmith on Van Bloom street to earn a little extra money?"

Peter wrinkled his nose. "Yes, he was not cruel to me, but he sure didn't pay too well."

"I suppose you are right, but I'm sure you noticed that he had many different tools in his shop for his trade. There were large, sturdy tools like the anvil, the large hammer, the great sturdy chisels, and the flatters that were designed to shape great pieces of iron into different shapes. But there were also smaller less durable tools like the pump drill and many smaller hammers and chisels that were designed for more delicate work like making files and shaping smaller pieces of iron. Who is to say that the smaller hammer is worth less than the larger hammer simply because it cannot shape great hunks of metal as effectively as the larger ones can?"

Understanding what he meant, Peter paused thoughtfully and said, "I would still rather be the larger hammer."

Father laughed his deep laugh and patted his son's slight shoulder. "Who knows," he said. "Perhaps someday you will. And remember the thing I have told you many times—no matter how unfavorable your situation, *never* allow yourself to fall into self-pity. Feeling sorry for yourself is dishonorable and poisonous and will rid your life of productivity if you let it."

Peter nodded sleepily in reply to the old self-pity lecture. His father gently tucked Peter in, and after saying the same old prayer over him, he then wandered off sleepily to bed. Peter quietly felt inside his pillow, which was a rolled up deerskin. Was it still there? Yes, it was. He could still feel the hard worn hilt. It was a genuine eleventh-century sword made out of pure bronze, which Peter had inherited from his father on his tenth birthday. The sword had been passed down in Father's family for centuries, and Peter kept it a secret from everyone outside the family, except his friend Andrew, for fear that it would be stolen. He always made sure it was safe before he slept. The sword was the most precious thing he owned. None of the other boys in town owned swords—and few of the men, for that matter.

Peter pulled a worn black leather sheath from his pillow and slid the heavy sword out carefully. The long shiny bronze blade twinkled dreamily in the cheery fire's glow. Afraid to damage it, he quickly slid it back in its sheath and rolled it carefully back in the pillow. Peter might not have enjoyed perfect health, but he was lying on a clean mat in front of a warm fire with a full stomach and a loving unharmed family sleeping peacefully around him in a clean, warm, sturdy cabin. Yes, Peter was blessed.

CHAPTER III

"Son, son." Mother shook Peter by the shoulders gently. "Wake up. It's time for work. Rise and shine, Peter!" Peter opened his sleepy eyes and stretched his sore limbs luxuriously. The twins stood patiently by their mother, waiting for Peter.

Rebeccah giggled. "You have sleepyhead hair," she teased. Peter ran his hand through his curly bright red hair, which had become quite untidy during the night. He sat up sleepily. Rebeccah laughed gaily at her big brother. She had always been expressive and more likely to chatter, whereas Elisabeth had always been more quiet and solemn.

After Mother hurriedly fixed Peter's hair, she hastily handed each of her children two dry handfuls of cornmeal for breakfast and then rushed them out the door for the chores. Outside, contented hens clucked and scurried about their feet just as the people of Plymouth were bustling back and forth about their business.

The robins and sparrows chatted cheerfully in the clear autumn air in the bright jolly sunrise. Most of the other men and boys his age had already been in the fields since a quarter of an hour ago. But Peter was not strong enough. Although he couldn't work like his peers, he was made to work with the women because his parents didn't wish for him to grow lazy.

The dusty main road was lined on either side by neat long cabins flanked by flocks of contended chickens and ducks behind stick fences.

After Peter had hastily fed the family's many chickens and ducks, he joined the rest of his family seated quietly beneath a tall ancient oak facing away from the street. Peter enjoyed working out in the fresh air instead of indoors.

"Our neighbor, little Johnny Mayharvest, was playing in the raspberry thorns one too many times," Mother explained, showing him a tiny pair of shredded britches and shirt. "His mother is quite ill as of late. Sewing her son's torn clothes is the least we can do." She handed Peter the torn shirt and a tiny needle and thread. Peter sighed. It would probably take all day to finish it.

Mother handed the britches to Rachel, a dark-haired teenaged girl who was sitting quietly near him. She was Charlie's older sister but wasn't cruel like her brother; however, Peter still detested being around her because it seemed that all that she cared to do was chatter up a storm. Sometimes Rachel worked with the Washingsworths to help them with the chores (probably as a sort of retribution for all the wrongs Charlie had done Peter). Peter skillfully started to stitch one of the many tears.

"Did you hear what happened in the town council meeting last night?" Rachel asked.

"No," Peter replied, still keeping diligently to his stitches. *Oh brother*, he thought, *I hope she doesn't start gossiping again.*

"They made a new decision on the new community they are planning on building."

"From where did you hear that?" Peter inquired. "There has not even been a final call on whether or not the new community is even going to be built in the first place."

"Mary Chilton told me. She heard it from someone who was there," Rachel replied. "Anyhow, they might transport their supplies in a boat. The Winslows are in charge of it."

Peter's interest perked. "Do you suppose they could use another boy to help build it?" he inquired.

"I suppose," Rachel replied, "but I don't think its official yet."

Peter smiled thoughtfully. Perhaps he would ask Mr. Kenelm about that later. This could be his precious chance to fit in with other boys. Such opportunities were few and far between ...

Just then, he noticed Rachel and Charlie's mother strolling and chatting with Mr. Snows on an old overgrown trail in the nearby forest. Peter was becoming curious because this was not the first time he had spied them together.

"What are they doing?" Peter questioned.

Rachel glanced up calmly at him. "What are who doing?" she asked.

Peter gestured toward the couple in question. "Your mother and him," he explained awkwardly. "I've seen them together before. Why does your father let them be together alone?"

"He went to heaven during our first winter here."

"And Mr. Snows's wife ...?"

"She died too. Mr. Snows sometimes delivers firewood to our home."

Peter sighed, recalling the horrific first winter. All he could remember about it was lying helplessly on bare hard ground, cold, half-starved, and seriously ill. He had not been expected to live for more than a few days at that point. He was grateful for everything now. His family had been one of the only families in the colony not to lose a member during those cold and difficult months, in part because Mother and the then-infant twins had remained in Holland until the following spring. Peter considered himself fortunate.

"By the way," Rachel added, "I have been wondering what happened to your eye." Peter had nearly forgotten about yesterday.

"Your brother punched me," he admitted. Rachel nodded understandingly.

Peter slumped down comfortably against the pine tree and continued his even stitches. More people strolled past him. As they walked past, one of the women glanced down at Peter with pity. He was embarrassed to be seen doing women's chores out in public. Suddenly, he wished he had stayed inside today. If the boys saw him sewing again, it would become another one of the many things they mocked him about. Even Andrew sometimes risked his reputation by regularly associating with Peter. *This afternoon, Peter planned silently with a smile; I'll go join them in building Mr. Winslow's boat. Then eventually they might realize I am not too odd after all.*

A strong cool breeze brushed against Peter's face, which caused his determined eyes to water. He quickened his pace so that he would not be too late to help the other boys build. This could be his chance to fit in. Finally, Peter caught sight of some boys working hardily with some boards in the meadow. Peter tightened his long red wool scarf around his neck and braced himself nervously. He guessed what was about to happen. About ten boys were working diligently on the thick mat-like grass. Among them, Peter recognized Andrew, who was using a large hammer and nails. Others sawed boards on large upside-down washtubs, and still others soaked them in a large barrel of water to make them pliable. There were even a few Indians helping.

Andrew waved at him. All the others paused and looked up.

"Well, well ... if it isn't ole Sring Bean," one particularly cruel boy taunted meanly. Peter tried to ignore him.

"Hello. Do you know where Mr. Kenelm is?" he asked bravely. Before Andrew could answer, another butted in.

"Ya lookin' for Mr. Kenelm? Be careful, String Bean—he might step on you." All the boys except Andrew laughed loudly. Peter's face blushed bright scarlet. Dutifully, he tried to pull up the corners of his mouth in a smile, but something seemed to go wrong.

"That's not likely," another boy added, "since he has that orange rug on his head." They laughed again. Peter's face twisted in a strange expression, and he shook his head. Andrew opened his mouth in protest, only to shut it again. Peter could not really blame him. He stared angrily into the gleeful eyes of the boy who had mocked him last. Peter knew what that boy was thinking. He thought that since Peter was unable to defend himself, he could feel at liberty to jeer at him all he wanted to. Peter's fists clinched tightly at his sides. *Well, if that is what he thinks*, Peter thought bitterly, *then I'll show him that I can hold my own. Then he'll be sorry—very sorry.* Peter crouched over and prepared to charge. Just before he started at him, Peter stopped himself short. *No*, he thought, *this is not the way to go about it. Violence is wrong, and besides, it will only prove that they are right about my not being able to defend myself. I could never win in a fight against any of them.*

Peter turned away on his heel and began to wander sadly home. He could hear the pounding of hammers and the roar of saws from behind him. The cruel words of the others marched through his mind like enemy troops. Peter hung his head and squinted painfully. Heavy tears grew in his eyes. And this time they weren't from the cold wind.

Time flew like a bird in spring. Except for when he was ill, Peter did almost the same thing every day. He did not even try to go back to help with the building project. So many people willingly helped build the large boat that it was finished in only a month, and now it was carefully being tested to be sure it was leakproof, stable, and strong.

Every Sabbath the Washingsworth family faithfully attended church. Because it was harvest time, Peter was often allowed to help with some of the minor harvest tasks. One clear afternoon, Peter was walking Elisabeth through the woods to go husk some corn in the fields. Suddenly, Elisabeth stopped and picked up a fallen leaf ablaze with bright orange autumn color. She lifted it up gently to the bright sun and studied it carefully.

"Look, Peter," she explained,. "See all those lines on the leaf? Those look like many teeny tiny roads in it. And see, this other leaf has roads too. Even flower petals have roads in them."

Where does a child her age get things like that? Peter wondered.

One night a stabbing stomach pain woke Peter up. *Oh no*, he thought, *now I'll never get to sleep.* He tossed and turned, but the pain would not subside. Rain thumped steadily on the log roof. Peter moaned softly and cradled his ailing stomach in his arms. He did not worry. After all, this had happened before many times. He could hear the sounds of Rebeccah and Elisabeth's deep sleep breathing from the loft above him. Just then, he heard his parents discussing something quietly on the other side of the small cabin. Peter painfully rolled over to listen. A candle flickered cozily on the table.

"And there will be a big picnic in the meadow. Then we'll ride the boat home again," Father explained.

"But, John," Mother protested, "we'll be riding on a boat. I can only try to forget how seasick we were on the voyage over to this land."

"Edward Winslow said that one does not get seasick on a river," Father protested.

"What about Peter?"

"Why can't he come? Besides we'll just paddle there, eat, and paddle back upstream in only a day."

"But still," Mother persisted, "I am worried about the Coxes being there. Charlie, I mean. He will likely …"

"Don't worry, Martha," Father assured her. "There will be many adults around."

"Are you sure?"

"Yes, come now. It will be very enjoyable. And we still have two weeks to think it over."

Mother paused and sighed thoughtfully. "Well, all right, I suppose," Mother relented.

All of the sudden, Peter's stomach didn't seem to hurt as much anymore. He enjoyed picnics much. And on a riverboat! What an adventure!

"Come now, don't worry," Father coaxed. "The Winslows are taking every precaution imaginable. And besides … what could possibly happen?"

CHAPTER IV

"Hooray! Hooray!" Rebeccah cheered excitedly. "Today is our picnic! Today is our picnic!" She danced excitedly around the cabin.

Although Mother was still skeptical, she joined in the excitement.

Peter himself was excited to the bone. It was a rare treat to enjoy excitement like this. Impatiently he peeked into father's old pocket watch as he counted down the minutes. Adventures like this were rare and quite exhilarating for the participants.

"Can I take my dolls?" Rebeccah asked hopefully.

"You'll lose them," Mother warned.

"*Pleeeeaaaassssseeee,*" Rebeccah begged. "I promise not to lose them."

"Oh, all right, you may," Mother relented, "but keep them safe. I shall not get you any more of them."

Peter felt so much excitement trapped inside him that he thought he might blast through the ceiling. Finally, father announced that it was time to go. Rebeccah and Elisabeth hurriedly grabbed their worn dolls, and Peter carried his blanket to sit on and his pillow in case the twins grew tired and cranky. The walk was not a long one. As the family trooped through the woods to the Quantum River under a rainless blanket of clouds, Rebeccah scurried happily up to her older brother.

"I want to walk next to you," she declared, "because I love you and I want to marry you when I grow up."

Peter laughed softly. "You can't ... I'm your brother ..." But before he had time to say anything else, they had reached the river. They were early. Peter stopped short and jumped back. Because it had rained heavily in the past two weeks, the roaring, bubbling river appeared nearly twice as wide and wild as the last time he had laid eyes on it. Great billows of water gushed tirelessly around smooth jutting rocks and foamed like a rabid dog.

"John," Mother asked, clearly worried, "are you sure this is safe? I don't want us getting hurt." Father seemed to share her concern. He walked toward the Winslows, who were carefully loading the food into the large rowboat.

"Is this safe? It looks treacherous!" he shouted over the vigorous roaring river.

"Oh, yes," Mr. Winslow assured, "our native oarsmen have successfully navigated worse." Peter glanced over at the boat that was resting on the shore. It was smaller than he had expected and barely more than a simple rowboat. *I truly hope those oarsmen know what they're doing.*

"Can we go inside it? Can we go inside it?" Rebeccah chirped excitedly.

"Yes, I suppose," Mr. Kenelm agreed. "What harm could it do?"

Soon more people trickled into the large clearing by the river. Peter reclined comfortably against the rough back of the strong rowboat and smiled contentedly as the twins played quietly with their shabby but endeared, corncob dolls in the boat near him. He fidgeted impatiently.

Mr. Winslow stepped joyfully up in front of the eager crowd. "I am glad you all came to take advantage of this new vessel. My wife and a few other ladies have graciously prepared this delicious food for us to enjoy. Now, I suppose we shall be off." He beckoned them to enter the boat, which was full of a great many small crates of appealing food.

The aroma floated temptingly into Peter's nostrils. He couldn't wait to get there and start his adventures. He had heard that Mrs. Winslow was staying home with their children for some reason. He observed the faces around him. There was the Wilson couple, who had just arrived on the last boat with their newborn baby, standing to his left. On his right were Andrew, his sister Charlotte, and their father, Mr. Thomas; and beyond them were the three Coxes and Mr. Snows with the oarsmen. Peter counted silently. *That's nineteen people present.*

As people slowly boarded the boat, Peter strategically positioned himself near Father because he knew that Charlie, who was close by, would not dare bother him if he were by his big strong father, whom Charlie feared greatly. Father gently placed his muscular arm around Peter's thin shoulders and gave them a soft squeeze. Peter scooted away slightly. He didn't want it to look as if he were cuddling.

Two strong rugged-looking natives dressed in tanned deerskin grunted as they shoved the heavy crowded vessel into the raging river and then swiftly leaped into it themselves. They immediately began to oar diligently, keeping the helpless vessel from being controlled by the destructive river and keeping it from going too fast. Mr. Winslow was friends with many Indians, and he was trying diligently to evangelize them. Peter marveled at how skillfully they oared and how they could keep the vessel at such a safe speed. Rainless clouds coated the autumn sky as the jolly group rode happily down the river, laughing and chatting. Rebeccah and Charlotte began singing so loudly and out of pitch that people soon insisted they be silenced. Peter and Andrew chatted quietly about the harvest.

"We're almost there," Mr. Kenelm announced.

Peter shivered excitedly. *Only a few more minutes ...*

But Charlie, who had remained strangely silent, was secretly plotting a "harmless" practical joke. It was sure to get him into deep trouble, but he didn't care—he was accustomed to trouble and he could get himself out of it somehow anyway. Things seemed a little boring without anyone to tease. Even Peter was sitting near his intimidating father.

Charlie smirked slyly. He crept up noiselessly behind one of the oarsman and stabbed him vigorously in the back with his thumb. The annoyed man reached behind his back to shoo him away, and the oar slipped helplessly into the raging river. Before anyone knew what was happening, the oar had been swept away in the dangerous current and the other rower, being unable to control the vessel alone, soon had his oar lost to the same fate. As it turned out, this dangerous trick wasn't very well thought out because the second the oars were gone, the unrestrained rowboat shot off suddenly downstream, crashing its way through the rapids like an infuriated bull.

Peter was hurled violently against the rear of the boat. Panic and chaos soared. Playfully the river tossed the vessel amongst intimidating rocks and soggy floating logs. The boat swayed, bowed, and jerked in all directions as the river hurled it carelessly past enormous smooth black mossy boulders and through gushing rapids, foaming and raging. Peter was certain that they must have lost someone on impact, for he himself would have surely been hurled violently over the side if it had not been for his clinging to the rear board of the boat, which was sticking up. With each rapid, the boat would (or at least seemed to) be airborne for a few moments before crashing raucously back down to the water, creating a great splash that would rise much higher than the side of the boat. Peter was soaked almost instantly. Was this the end? He was sure it must be. *Oh God …*

Women screamed frantically, and children cried loudly with fright, the deafening noises of the river swallowing their helpless wails. Fear and panic gripped Peter's pounding heart. How quickly things had changed from an exciting affair to a nightmare. Peter felt sure he would die today. He screamed in terror as they whizzed past a boulder, missing it by but an inch, and crashed head-on into yet another rapid, the impact upon collision nearly throwing him overboard yet again. Water had splashed into the boat and was now a little higher than Peter's thin ankles.

The men desperately tried to use the boxes in which the food and utensils had been stored to scoop out more water than was coming in—a task that was next to impossible. The autumn trees blended in a colorful blur on the shore, which made Peter's eyes hurt to glance at. The boat jerked and sped so speedily around curves that each one nearly hurled Peter over the side. Cold wind rushed hard against Peter's drenched skin. The blowing was so severe that when he faced the wind, he could scarcely keep his watering eyes open. It was the fastest he had ever gone.

Mr. Winslow had mentioned before that one didn't become seasick on a river, which that was true ... when they were peddling slowly and steadily. Soon Peter began to feel dizzy and nauseated. He leaned his throbbing head against the side of the boat and moaned as a chilling wave of frigid water washed over him, which soaked his clothes and made him shiver. This reminded him of the Mayflower during the terrible storm. Peter leaned his head off the side and got sick. A wave of frigid water washed over him again.

Mother wrapped her arms protectively around her son from behind. "Don't worry, son," she comforted fearfully. "God will protect us. Just pray, Peter. Just pray." Such faith was something Peter could only wish to have.

For four miserable days, the small, helpless boat tossed at the mercy of the freezing river. It seemed to Peter that the hellish nightmare would never end. It was not that they didn't try to stop and dock the boat on the shore, for there were parts of the river that were less violent, but it was difficult enough to keep the little boat dry.

Peter was miserably seasick. He tried reluctantly to force down his meager rations but couldn't keep anything down. Peter constantly sat helplessly at the rear of the boat, his arms coiled around a long board at the back of the vessel. Frigid water was constantly crashing into the boat (it felt as if all the water was splashing on Peter, but he was actually at one of the dryer parts of the boat). The few passengers who were not seasick worked tirelessly, using the food crates to dump the water out. Almost everyone else was dreadfully seasick (the stench alone was enough to make anyone queasy). Peter was vomiting almost constantly. Sometimes, when he felt the most miserable, he would wish he didn't even have a stomach.

After four days, Peter was almost ready to give up praying. This much time seemed a hellish eternity to him. It began to seem as if he'd always been imprisoned on this miserable little vessel—that perhaps sleeping in a warm, dry cabin with a still stomach and without all the panic and fear had only been a fanciful dream, which he had only wished existed. Peter leaned his weak and tired head against the side of the rough splintered wood. The boat seemed to be going a little more slowly now, as if the current wasn't quite so strong or violent. Peter moaned weakly. Then, all of a sudden, Peter heard an excited commotion among the people around him. He tried to open his eyes to investigate, but the world spun before, so he closed them and moaned again loudly. His head throbbed, and he could feel every heartbeat all over. He felt Mother's warm and loving arms wrap around his shivering, feverish body. For a few minutes, Peter soaked in the warmth from Mother's arms savoringly. Mother, who seemed to recognize her son's need for warmth, continued to hold him gently.

"Look, son," she whispered in his ear, "it's beautiful."

Peter reluctantly cracked his eyes open, and the sight that he saw met his eyes like a welcoming oasis. It was now that he realized what had happened. The river had deposited them into a lake, and now they were drifting instead of being driven forward, which was something he had been too dizzy to realize at first. The majestic, calm ocean-blue lake was nestled between two tall, handsome pine-wooded mountains that towered like giants. Surrounding these two mountains were lazy rolling hills blanketed by delightful bright orange poppies and dotted by shady willowlike oaks, whose branches stooped so low that they touched the ground. Behind all of this lay a vast mountain range towering off in the distance on all sides. A thick, pale sky-blue fog line veiled the bases of these distant purple giants, making them appear to be floating in the air. All of this was set beneath an elegant blue afternoon sky dotted by pure fluffy clouds. But most of the weary passengers were either too cold or too sick to fully appreciate the beauty. Yet the sight of this new place filled Peter's weary heart with the candlelight of sweet hope. He assumed that it likely wasn't possible to return to Plymouth, but was there a new life possible for them here?

The adults immediately began to paddle the heavy boat to shore slowly, using the empty food crates, which were cracked and full of holes. Peter almost thought that he didn't feel quite so seasick anymore. But he was still dreadfully dizzy.

Finally, the base of the boat bumped loudly as it hit the rocky lakeshore. Mr. Winslow was the first to stumble out onto the soft and lumpy red clay, which was dotted by tuffs of grass and small jagged rocks. He immediately knelt down reverently and led his tired fellow passengers in a prayer of thanksgiving for allowing them to arrive safely.

While they had been on the lake, Peter's seasickness had eased, but he was still too weak to walk. So his father gently pried his arms away from the board at the back of the boat and carried his pitifully light son to shore and laid him down on a soft nest of pine needles beneath a tall fir tree. Peter's face was deathly pale, and chills raged all over him. Then suddenly an overwhelming faintness descended upon him like a tidal wave to drown him, and Peter slipped into unconsciousness.

Darkness had veiled the land by the time Peter's eyes finally opened again. A glowing white moon shot streams of blue and silver light onto his pale white face. His throat burned from having vomited so much over the last few days. Peter was aware that he was coated from head to toe in thick, putrid dirt and grime. His formerly clean and neat clothes that Mother had made for him were badly stained and soiled. He jumped a little when he felt a small cold hand on his shoulder.

"Peter," Elisabeth whispered softly, "are you awake yet?" He nodded painfully.

A chill fluttered down his back. *At least I'm no longer seasick,* he thought.

"I'm here, son," Mother whispered.

Peter looked up into the dark night and could make out the outline of Mother's face gazing worryingly down at him. "Are you well?"

"Mother?" Peter muttered in a raspy voice.

"Yes, it is I. My poor, poor son. You do not look well."

"Where is Rebeccah? She did … She did not fall into the river … did she?"

"No, no, of course not. She is here—asleep near your father. We are all safe, everyone aboard."

"Everyone?"

"God has been good."

A refreshing wave of relief sank into Peter. He tried to prop himself up, but that made him too dizzy. Peter's hollow stomach emitted a loud growl. He moaned again. "Oh, Mother," he begged, "might I please have something to eat?" He expected her to shake her head.

"Yes, son … here," Mother replied quickly. She handed him one of the soggy old plates which bore a hunk of half-cooked venison. Immediately he sat up, as much as he was able, and began to devour it with an appetite of a hungry animal. Almost out of habit, the first couple of bites went right back up, but he managed to keep the rest down fairly well. As he ate, Rebeccah curled up by her father and dozed off. Peter had not realized how hungry he really was, and he was very glad to have something in his stomach that would stay down. The food gave him a little more strength, and he attempted to sit up fully. Oh, how glorious it felt not to have the surface beneath him constantly jerking and crashing!

"While you were sleeping," Mother explained, "the men went out hunting with the rifle Kenelm Winslow brought along."

"They were able to find game so quickly?"

Mother replied, "There was a group of deer grazing nearby. They brought home enough meat for all of us to eat, but when it was time to eat, you were still asleep. I couldn't wake you, but I saved some."

"Thank you," he whispered. Peter glanced at the people around him. They were all sleeping sound as rocks on the ground. Peter lay himself back down on the ground wearily. Another chill rushed over him. "Wh-why don't they light a fire?" Peter stuttered.

Mother sighed in exhaustion. "Because they don't know whether the Indians in this area are friendly," she replied. "If we light a fire, they would know we're here."

Peter noticed a look of worry in her pale blue eyes. The bright moon made her disheveled golden hair shine. He turned his head and could make out the rest of his family sleeping peacefully beside a boulder. Father's burly arms wrapped protectively around his daughter's to keep them warm. Peter sighed deeply and laid his feverish, ghoulishly pale face in his thin hands. A thick exhaustion overcame him. The only thing he wanted to do right now was sleep. However, he knew he couldn't … not before he'd said his evening prayer. It was more important than ever tonight.

The large pure white moon glowed beautifully in the deep dark sky, commissioning bluish-silver light onto the broad lakeshore, transforming the rich silky green evergreens to silver. Its ghostly white image flickered beautifully on the bumpy restless surface of the water. Peter knelt down onto the soggy shore. His thin legs made ruts in the moist sandy clay. He began to pray effortfully. The words strained out of his exhausted mind and mouth slowly and seemingly, without much meaning. Finally, keeping his eyes pried open was just too difficult. He crawled slowly back over to where his family was and was asleep before he lay his weary head on the ground.

CHAPTER V

THE FOLLOWING ARE A FEW entries from Charlie's journal, which he had happened to bring with him to record the happenings of the picnic while they were fresh in his mind:

- Friday, October 8, 1624—It is the first morning here in this dreaded place, and I'm already sick of it. Everybody seems to hate me (especially the two savages who were rowing). They blame me for this whole mess. (Incorrect!) Last night we all slept sound as dead men until Mother woke me up. Of all the nerve. How dare she wake me up this early! She knew I was terribly tired and desperately needed rest! But String Bean (Peter), the little squirt, they let him sleep as long as he pleased. Until noon, I say! The lousy excuse they gave was that he had pneumonia. Rubbish! I would be surprised if the twerp wasn't faking. He is bestowed with a faulty degree of indulgence and is horridly spoiled. If it had been me, they probably would have woken me up first! They let many other people who were ill sleep in long too. But me? No, sir! Mr. Wilson even claimed that they had let me sleep a little longer because they didn't want to hear me complaining. Complaining? Me? Well, whoever heard of me complaining?

The men went out to set up traps today. They forced me to come with them (after they made me take a bath in the lake). Rooster (Andrew), who unfortunately was not one of the ill, was also there.

The thug is such a coward. I dared him to climb onto a high rock over the lake and leap off into the water. He said he would be a fool to do it. Rooster then dared me back. Of all the nerve! Surely he should have known that someone of such high sophistication as I would never stoop to leap off such a shabby old rock as that. I might be injured or killed! Afterward, I heard Rooster whisper something to his father. His father then whispered something back about bearing crosses. Something like "We all have our crosses to bear ..." That had *better* be a compliment.

The most unusual thing happened today. We were growing quite disappointed when we ran out of bullets to hunt with this morning. But our two Indian oarsmen declared that they would try their best to make bows and arrows out of things that they could find. But as they began to search for the materials to make these, they found a great many bows and quivers of arrows by our rowboat. No one claimed bringing them. They were neatly tied together as if gifts from the locals. Everyone, especially the two savages, was very happy about this. Not only because it could give us food, but also because it likely meant that the natives might be friendly. But it also gives me the oddest feeling. We see the smoke rising up in little pillars from the mountainside, and often we hear voices echoing from somewhere across the lake. It makes me feel as if we are trying to live secretly in someone else's house. Well, anyhow ... thankfully no one seemed to find time to punish me for making the savages drop their oars.

- Saturday, October 9, 1624—Those who are ill are doing a little better today (the fact that I am even mentioning this means that there is pitifully little to talk of). Fairy (Elisabeth) is always sitting by String Bean—as she always seems to do when he is unwell. I had a good laugh at them about this—until Mr. Snows chased me off like a chicken in the corn.

One man at a time stayed up last night to keep watch. This morning there was left at our site a large skin tent. Again, no one knows how it got there. It is embroidered quite elegantly in curious patterns of red, yellow, and purple. It has the oddest shape, somewhat like a large cone. We spent a lot of time setting this up today. Near its top, there is a curious wheel-like circular symbol with many lines in it. I don't like this tent because it is so stuffy inside. I hate it here anyway. My meat is without salt. Mother and Rachel are freakishly paranoid about me and make me do too many disgraceful tasks. They think they can push me around like a child. In fact, all the others seem to think that they can exercise unfair authority over me. Today I had another good laugh at Petticoats (Charlotte) and Baby (Rebeccah) about their childish doll play. (They brought corncob dolls). Again I was chased off most disrespectfully. Ugh! I have a good mind to run off from here. Then they will be sorry.

Today Mrs. Washingsworth offered to let Fairy (Elisabeth) take a break from sitting by String Bean. Fairy found one of the large orange poppy flowers and held it up in front of the lake. Before long, a small unusual hummingbird flew up to it. She has made the biggest fuss about it among her family. She remembered everything about it, even the colors. But she is only a small child, so her description is certainly in the wrong.

Although I still detest it, I am beginning to grow a little used to this new place already. I have a habit of adjusting well to new places. Although it is quite different, the trees and landscape are very different from that of Plymouth Colony. There are not so many colorful trees because most of them are evergreens. Even the squirrels are a grayish color.

Uh-oh, I just got more bad news. I have found reason to believe that Baby (Rebeccah) has tattled to Mr. Snows about my teasing her earlier. I am surely in trouble.

- Sunday, October 10, 1624—Sure enough, I did get in trouble. But thankfully, the most trouble you can get in here is a good paddling—and with only a rotting wedge of wood besides. People seem too preoccupied with trying to establish ourselves here that they ignore me (as if they didn't already.) If they spent more time around me, they would realize my greatness. I therefore try to make myself impossible to ignore. It is seeming to work already. Unfortunately, they have decided to hold a small service since it is the Sabbath. (And I thought there was at least *one* thing good about us coming here.) We will even have a makeshift communion ceremony with meat and wild grape juice. String Bean thinks himself well enough to sit with us. Everyone is so pleased with his recovery (I really don't care one way or the other). I suppose they thought that if he got sick after those tough days in the boat that it might drag him under. That would have sure been a good riddance. I don't know what all the fuss is about. That weakling is so childish! I could bet good money that he sucks his thumb at night.

- Monday, October 11, 1624—Not much going on. I guess all I can say is that String Bean is not quite well today but he is doing better even than yesterday. Now I suppose he can finally catch up on his chores that we have all been doing for him. Lots of the others who were ill are also doing better. There is actually some good news too. The men were talking about going on an expedition tomorrow to try to find the friendly Indians who have been leaving us gifts each day. (Today they left us a large set of baskets.) They even talked about taking some of the "older boys" with them. That probably means me and (unfortunately) Andrew too. The men will leave tomorrow at dawn and come back in the evening. I can't wait.

Peter stared blankly up at the dull tent ceiling. Pain sored wildly in his head. He winced.

"Will you be all right, son?" Father questioned with concern.

Peter nodded painfully. He was accustomed to headaches. If only this one had come another day …

"I'm sorry you cannot join us," Father apologized. Peter nodded again sulkily. "Son," he promised, "as long as you are well, next time we go hunting or on an expedition, you may come along. You would make an excellent scout or watchman, for you have keen eyes. Although it might have been just as well that you couldn't accompany us this time. There is going to be much difficult climbing, and you have been unwell lately."

"Thank you," Peter mumbled.

Father fondly patted his skinny shoulder. "Get well, please … for my sake at least."

"I'll try," Peter muttered before Father joined the other men. He stepped quickly over to the cluster of men in the dark crowded tepee. A bright sliver of golden light streamed in through the tent flap and onto Peter's pale face.

Andrew nervously joined the group who sat huddled in a tight circle on the ground discussing quietly. Butterflies fluttered in his stomach. Andrew was both excited and nervous. What would they do if they met Indians? What sorts of adventures would they have in that vast, uncharted wood?

"I think we should investigate the slope on the other side of the lake," Mr. Thomas suggested enthusiastically. "It seems more uninhabited. We never see any smoke rising from there, and it is very lush. Perhaps we shall come upon a small hunting party. We shouldn't try the rolling hills because they can easily see us there. Remember, there might yet be Indians in these parts that would rather us not be in their territory or that are afraid of us." Mr. Winslow scratched his chin thoughtfully.

Across the circle from Andrew stood the two Wampanoag oarsmen, dressed roughly in loose deerskin clothes. The taller, more lanky of the two, Cakechiwa, couldn't speak any English. But the shorter, stalky one, Shamaro, could speak it well. As the white men spoke, Shamaro interpreted to Cakechiwa.

"This is good," Shamaro declared. "It is difficult to tell the difference between a friendly or a warlike tribe. Stay away from the villages. They might hate us or they might not. This mission in and of itself is dangerous." Andrew shivered.

Mr. Winslow nodded thoughtfully. "I do think Mr. Thomas has a good idea. Let's do it." Cakechiwa whispered something to Shamaro.

"He said," Shamaro interpreted, "that we should bring our new bows and arrows for safety."

Mr. Winslow nodded in agreement. "Yes," he agreed, "that is a good idea too."

"And besides," Mr. Washingsworth suggested, "you never know when you might run into a suitable hunting site. We could bring in a good haul." Cakechiwa quickly distributed the bows and quivers, intentionally skipping Charlie.

"Stop!" Charlie shouted childishly. "Didn't you just miss someone?"

Seeming to understand what he meant by the irritation in Charlie's voice, Cakechiwa loudly proclaimed something.

"He said," Shamaro interpreted with a tiny hint of glee in his deep voice, "that this boy is too childish, plays tricks, and doesn't deserve the honor of carrying a bow."

Charlie's face glowed red, and he flew angrily at Cakechiwa, but Mr. Washingsworth swiftly seized the rebel by the shoulders and quickly drew him back. Charlie's face paled, and he sheepishly backed off. Andrew was proud to have been chosen worthy to receive his own bow and arrows. He admired them proudly as Charlie glared at him jealously.

As the men continued to plan, Andrew slowly began to grow impatient. Would it be forever before they set off? Finally, after all of the necessary decisions had been made, the small yet determined group of explorers troped out of the dark, stuffy tepee and into the bright sunshine's glare. Before he left, Andrew walked slowly over to check on Peter. He squatted down beside his friend and sighed with pity. "Hello, Peter," he greeted softly. Peter nodded slightly. "How are you? Are you feeling better?"

"Somewhat," Peter muttered grumpily.

Andrew stared at his lap disappointedly. He could imagine how miserable *he* would be if *he* had been sick like this. Andrew had been one of the fortunate ones. At least Peter had brought his blanket and pillow along for the picnic.

"I'm sorry," he said quietly. "I was truly hoping that you were going to get to come with us. After all, the only other boy coming with us is Charlie, so he and I will probably be stuck spending a lot of time together."

"Don't worry," Peter replied. "I'll get better. I'll probably be feeling a little better tomorrow."

Andrew nodded with a small smile. "Good," he replied. "Anyhow, I must leave. Be sure to get well, Peter." Energetically Andrew jumped up and rushed out of the tepee.

Outside, the men were still waiting for him. The glorious land was as beautiful as ever. The deep blue lake radiantly reflected the sun's blinding glare. The lush evergreens fidgeted pleasantly in the cool autumn breeze.

"Well, everybody," Mr. Winslow announced, clapping his hands together, "I dare say it is time to set off."

Andrew reached up with effort and clutched a rough brown fir tree trunk that was above him on the steep slope. Exhausted, he dragged himself up a few more inches. Sweat dripped off his forehead. He felt as if they must have been climbing the steep and slippery slope for hours. His tired sore feet slipped on the slick pine needles.

"I ... don't see anyone yet," Mr. Winslow panted.

"I agree," said Mr. Kenelm, who was resting wearily on a tree trunk. "It's a steep slope, and there don't seem to be any Indians around here. But remember what Shamaro said, that we might need to wait a while before we present ourselves to them. This small difficulty might be ..." His explanation was interrupted by a call from Cakechiwa, who was far ahead of the rest.

"He said he found something," Shamaro interpreted excitedly.

"Good. Almost ... there," sputtered an exhausted Mr. Snows, who apparently did not have such strong legs as the rest of them and was crawling up the treacherous slope an inch at a time, a few yards behind the rest.

Andrew, more eager than ever to reach whatever it was that Cakechiwa had found, strained himself to climb a little faster. One of the trees he grabbed on to help him climb was one of those strange orange-barked trees. He had sighted this particular kind of tree before in this new land, and he was curious about them. It had a unique wiry build that appeared too skinny to hold up its great hue of impressive bright green leaves, which were shiny and glossy. Its smooth, silky trunk and branches were a soft orange in color. However, brittle black papery bark-like flakes clung in a sticky manner to the base of it. Clusters of reddish-orange berries dangled from its smooth branches. *I wonder if they're safe to eat.*

The other cedars, pines, and firs, which were mostly small young ones, were thickly bunched together, battling for desperately needed sunlight. The taller and middle-sized ones shunned the sunlight, causing it to be shady and dark beneath their thick gothic arms. It seemed that even the sun wouldn't dare commission any bright cheery rays of sunlight to penetrate beneath them. The Indians hadn't bothered to clear this slope. Andrew plainly understood why.

Finally, his sore aching legs managed to drag him to the top. A small meadow warmly greeted him. Andrew lay down wearily on his back. The soft lime green grass proved a suitable place for gently rubbing his aching legs. The only explorers other than Cakechiwa who had reached the top were Mr. Thomas (Andrew's father) and the notorious Charlie.

A forceful roar was spreading closer in the near distance. But it wasn't the hostile growl of a wild beast but the pleasant murmur of the wind. It spread slowly from tree to tree, like a harmless plague, making them tilt and lean. To Andrew, the wind seemed like a friendly companion or a playful puppy. He smiled broadly as it barged into the meadow, brushing playfully against his freckled face. It seized a giant oak, which reluctantly released a few of its shriveled dead leaves to the mercy of the wind, which sprayed them carelessly to the ground, where many had fallen before. Few trees changed color here in the autumn as they had in Plymouth, but those that did turned either dull gold or bright yellow. None turned other colors. A new idea struck Andrew. He leaped excitedly to his feet and chased some of the falling leaves, playfully trying to catch one. This was more fun than he had thought it would be. The leaves shifted cleverly at just the last minute, as if they didn't want to be caught.

"Well, well, well, if it isn't little Rooster at play," Charlie scoffed. Andrew realized with sudden horror how silly he must have looked and how much of Charlie's teasing it would provoke later.

"Watch it," Mr. Kenelm chastened. Andrew also suddenly realized that almost all of the rest had reached the meadow (except for Peter's father, who was still below, half carrying and half dragging Mr. Snows).

Cakechiwa, who had been patiently waiting for all to arrive, motioned eagerly toward his discovery. All eyes quickly turned in his direction. There, standing silently but proudly in a shaded corner of the small clearing, was a strange tall statue. So far back into the shadows it was that at first no one else had noticed it. Its unrealistic figures were apparently carved out of a single tree trunk, one figure stacked upon the other. It was as if, although he had not noticed them before, the figures had been secretly watching Andrew with their wide wild eyes. Each brightly painted figure of an individual animal was intricately carved and painted, with the wings of one bird jutting out the sides of the sculpture. Each figure seemed so real yet so mythical at the same time. Their large haunting eyes stared at their curious observers. It was as if the clearing was suddenly engulfed by a strong sense of sacredness, and if anyone were to move, it might shatter. It was as if a real-life Indian was standing before them and they didn't know if he would attack or not. The base of the sculpture was inscribed with two odd symbols. Suddenly, a small bird glided gracefully in the clearing and landed, fearless of the humans close by. With a little shout, Shamaro quickly shot the creature with an arrow.

"Why did you do that?" Mr. Kenelm asked in a slightly irritated tone. "It had obviously been tamed."

Shamaro shrugged awkwardly. "I suppose I must have been slightly startled."

"No matter," Mr. Kenelm said. He gingerly prodded the lifeless carcass with his foot. "It's a pigeon," he declared.

Mr. Winslow stroked his chin curiously. "I wonder why it landed here."

"Look," Andrew exclaimed, pointing to something shiny attached to its small leg. Mr. Thomas bent over and adjusted his spectacles.

"It looks like gold," he declared excitedly.

Charlie stared at the pigeon with wide eyes, "We're rich!" he exclaimed ecstatically. The others ignored him. Mr. Winslow examined it carefully. It appeared to be a tiny tube of some kind. He tugged at the lid, which soon popped off. He reached inside, revealing a tiny scroll of parchment.

"Oh no," Mr. Thomas sighed. "It was probably a bird trained to deliver messages. I've heard of the same kind of thing being done in England. I hope its owner won't be angry at us for killing it. I wish there was some way to make it up to them."

"Who cares?" Charlie exclaimed, overflowing with excitement. "It's gold isn't it! I struck it rich! Imagine how much more there might be where it came from! I'll be the richest gentleman in the British colonies!"

Andrew sighed, and no one else paid attention.

"I'm sorry," Shamaro apologized.

"It's all right," Mr. Kenelm assured Shamaro. Mr. Winslow carefully unrolled the leathery parchment message, but only mysterious and meaningless symbols met his eyes. Mr. Winslow, who was fairly knowledgeable about Indians, carefully examined the note.

Charlie, who by now looked as if he was about to explode, clapped his hands together ecstatically and shouted, "It's probably a treasure map! But even if it isn't, there is still enough gold there to secure my fortune. I'm going to be rich!"

Mr. Wilson glanced distastefully at him. "You are so … Look here, that little note is much too short to be a treasure map. And that bit of gold is not going to do you much good since we are marooned out here. And besides, even if we were back home, it would scarcely buy a decent wooden chair."

Charlie frowned and muttered something about prejudice toward young people.

Mr. Kenelm glanced questioningly at the two natives. "Do you recognize this?" he asked in their language.

"No," Cakechiwa replied, shaking his head. "I've never seen anything like it."

Peter flinched painfully. Why didn't this wretched headache just leave? He was so tired of his aching head that he wished he could slice the top of it right off. He rubbed it gently and cradled it in his arms.

"Here, lie down," Elisabeth coaxed in her soft, sweet voice. She took a drenched piece of cloth out of the large clay bowl of cool water (the bowel had been left for them by the Indians that very morning) and placed it gently on Peter's pale wax-colored forehead. He smiled, but it was so slight a smile that it could hardly be distinguished as a smile at all. Just as she had often when he was ill, Elisabeth was sitting next to him. Sometimes her constant presence annoyed Peter, but today he didn't mind. All day long, she had faithfully nursed Peter in the hot airless tent. She was a most talented nurse for her age. *It would be ideal if she married a doctor one day,* Peter thought. *Goodness knows there are not many little girls who really enjoy sitting with sick people.* Many times Peter had urged her to join the other girls or prepare food in the fresh air. But she had stubbornly refused to leave him in "the dark," no matter how many times Peter tried to convince her that he was no longer afraid of darkness. She insisted on talking to Peter, singing softly to him, fluffing his large, stiff deerskin pillow, and scrubbing the dirt off his pale face.

"I'll be right back," she announced softly, slowly getting to her feet and scurrying toward the tepee's open flap. Peter assumed she was getting a drink. In truth, Peter wished she would stay outside; out in the exciting world of cool, clean fresh air, singing birds, towering majestic evergreens, delicious sweet smells, and ancient maples - the world of oaks stricken yellow with autumn and fidgeting in the soft cool wind like a young child in church. Not here in the boring and unhappy world of a stuffy, hot, dark tent that contained an unhappy older brother suffering from a headache and a bad cold.

He slowly pulled himself to a sitting position and moaned softly. Peter fluffed his large pillow, which was badly stained and worn from the journey. He fluffed it a little more. No, it was still much too stiff. Perhaps if he rolled it out and rolled it back up again it might help. So he slowly unrolled his pillow. To Peter's surprise, he discovered that when he had hurryingly snatched the pillow from his mat, he had also brought the enclosed bronze sword. Here it was sitting plain as day in his pillow, waiting to be discovered. Its bronze hilt gleamed in a long streak of golden light streaming from the open tepee flap. He had forgotten it was even inside his old pillow on account of the events of the past few days. Delighted, Peter smiled with pleasure and snatched it eagerly.

He strapped the long broad leather band around his thin waist. Because he was so skinny, Father had gouged a few more buckle holes in the worn belt for him. Peter pulled it snug around himself and adjusted it. He smiled confidently and admired himself in the reflection of the bowl of water—the reflection of a bold woodsman and a hearty settler. Approvingly, Peter decided that from now on he would constantly wear the bronze sword. If Indians attacked, he would be ready.

CHAPTER VI

PONA-POW DARTED AGILELY FROM THE new settler's tepee like a doe who had just escaped the arrow point. Cautiously glancing over her shoulder to make sure no one was in sight, she slowed her pace slightly. She occasionally enjoyed the thrilling adventure of being an *agente* for the chief but was always glad when the tensity was finally over with.

A prickly dead tree branch brushed sharply against the small eight-year-old's face, smudging the thick slimy brown-and-green paint, which thoroughly coated the top half of her face, the part not covered by her black fur mask, which extended up to just beneath her eyes. Although her year and a half of strict and difficult training had made it seem unlikely to get caught, Pona-Pow always made sure that Keoko, her faithful trainer and second highest chief of the Orenean tribe, inspected her for any exposed parts which could stand out if she were hiding in the thick brush or a dark shadow.

Although she was much more comfortable investigating these peaceful El Shaddai–fearing people, she always felt better having proper protection. Pona-Pow was proud to be able to bravely serve her tribe, even if she was only eight summers old. Keoko had well trained her to run swiftly, hide secretly, and listen carefully—but most of all to be fearless. Being fearless was so difficult to do during these times.

The Oreneans were a relatively small peaceable tribe to which Pona-Pow and her family belonged. The neighboring tribe—the Tumitatakens—were ruled by Chief Mittowan, who unreasonably hated the Oreneans. Twelve autumns ago, before Pona-Pow was even born, Chief Kitowoam of the Tumitataken tribe died suddenly. Mittowan, or "Tha Great Serpent," as the Oreneans called him, claimed the throne. This was very worrisome because the new chief had been claiming for years that when he someday became chief, he would rid his land of the Oreneans for good. You see, the Tumitatakens and Oreneans both lived on the same land. The twin mountains, Moggog and Noggog, Lake Honiton, and the surrounding soft lazy rolling Fire Hills made up the land generally known as Orenea.

Although the other neighboring tribes outside Orenea had a difficult time entering the land because of the high rocky cliff that surrounded Orenea on all sides like a giant wall, the strange quimpinita fruit, delicious sweet wild grapes, and legendary breathtaking beauty fascinated them. They traded things like gold and Orenean furs with other faraway tribes for buffalo, which they used to pull large rickety carts of grapes and quimpinitas, which were dried and traded to the other tribes to be used as sustenance on the journey back to where they came from ... or at least they used to, before the conflict, that is.

For many, many moons, the Oreneans and the Tumitatakens had lived happily in peace, even being known by others as the "twin tribes." Mittowan had wasted no time in ruining that as soon as his father died. The Tumitatakens immediately began preparing battle strategies. For all of Pona-Pow's life, this bitter and deadly struggle had been waging destructively. On and on the vicious cycle of being attacked and then counterattacking had been rolling mercilessly since the new Tumitataken chief had risen to the throne. They would hide quietly in the forest surrounding a village like a wildcat and attack it suddenly. Those captives who were not strong enough to work as slaves for their captors were brutally slaughtered on-site and left. Why under the sun would the Tumitatakens want to destroy their friendly neighbors so? Why indeed? Had their neighbors not treated them well enough? Still, the Tumitatakens were determined to have the land rid of all Oreneans.

The great serpent was growing more and more impatient to clamp his venomous fangs down on the Oreneans in one final deathblow. Thankfully, they still did not have enough force to do so ... yet.

Some Oreneans complained that the leaders of the tribe were not doing enough to rescue those enslaved to the enemies, but in fact, one of the lower Orenean chiefs had founded a secret program that silently and unnoticed snatched some captured Oreneans out of slavery. It was such a secret that most Oreneans could not be made aware that it existed, and Pona-Pow was not allowed to utter the name of the brave chief who had founded it. But although this was a successful program, it wasn't enough. There had to be a way to cleverly plug the attacks before they struck. Rescuing the captured was helpful, but it broke Chief Palkente's heart to watch them sadly bury their loved ones. A crippled brother, a blind sister, and elderly father, or a sick aunt ... In all his many years, he hadn't witnessed more evil. Finally, after a while, the chief and second chief did their part as well and pieced together a plan. The plan was vague and shaky but clever. What if someone could train to hide secretly in Mittowan's hut before he discussed his plans of attack with his warriors, eavesdrop, then warn the victims to evacuate? The rest of the lower chiefs were skeptical but finally agreed to try it.

A few Tumitatakens, who were secretly on the Oreneans side, carved out a space beneath the platform where the Tumitataken chief stood while addressing his warriors where someone could hide. Although he himself was shorter than most men, Keoko found he had some difficulty fitting inside. What about children? They're young, strong, willing, and, most important of all, small. It might be difficult, but if they were trained well enough ... So four somewhat nervous sets of parents warily allowed their children to live with and be trained by the Orenean chiefs. However, there would be those who questioned the reason why there were children living in the chief's home. So as a cover-up, the six children also served as messengers between the two tribes for the chief. Children were traditionally sent as messengers anyhow, so it would not look unusual.

Twii, her younger brother Mik, Veenatch, Zatch, his younger sister Pona-Pow, and Mighty Cedar were all sent to them. They progressed in skill as they grew older and gained strength and wit.

Although they still weren't quite as skilled as the older ones, Pona-Pow and Mik (they were the two youngest) were now well equipped for the strange, exciting life of an agente (that was what they were called by the chief). Then, just a few days ago, the exciting news was announced that they would get to investigate someone other than the evil Tumitatakens. And this was extremely relevant. For a few short moons ago, a small canoe load of seventeen white men had arrived floating in their great Lake Honiton. White men! Imagine that! With women and children too!

Their main goal in investigating these mysterious individuals was to determine whether they were a dangerous threat or not. A lower chief had kindly provided the gifts in the night to help them along, for they seemed harmless so far. And who knew—perhaps if the white men turned out to be friends, they might even call on their superiors to send men to aid the Oreneans in their battle! The careful, suspicious Oreneans were still doubtful, so they didn't dare reveal themselves to the new settlers yet. Both the agentes and the lower chiefs were occupied trying to convince the Tumitataken chief to sign agreements forcing them not to harm their visitors, for the Tumitatakens were rapidly gaining military force.

All of Pona-Pow's life, there had been growing, disturbing unrest, but never had it been so tense and fearful. The great serpent's fangs were almost sharp enough to finish off Orenea, as they had witnessed in the small villages, only on a much more vastly destructive scale all at once. It could only be a matter of months … weeks … days … All they needed was to secure the loyalty of another tribe and there would scarcely be any competition. The grown-ups always seemed to have worried expressions plastered on to their faces. But for now, all

Pona-Pow wanted was out of this tiresome hot black costume and irritating face paint.

Finally, Pona-Pow reached what she had been seeking, a broad fire trail, which was a long road-like stretch of bare dirt that was used to prevent wildfires from spreading and was often regularly used as a trail for buffalo carts. She stood leaning against a tree and waited patiently for the noise of one of the large clumsy carts down the trail.

The day was lovely. A lively blue jay chattered and fluttered in the dark green foliage of the solemn yet beautiful evergreen trees. The sky was soft blue velvet, with large white clouds gliding slowly across. The air was crisp. It was mostly quiet, but not silent. The great woods were never truly silent. There was always a twig or pine needle tumbling to the forest floor or some distant animal wandering among the untidy trees. Or just quiet little chattering and fluttering noises of unknown sources that blended in with the rest.

The hard well-trodden soil on the fire trail was rusty red in color from the thick clay from which the dirt was primarily made. It contrasted from the dull pointed tannish or gray pine needles that thickly carpeted the forest floor. A soft, weak breeze tickled the yellow autumn leaves on a towering fatherly oak.

Finally, a large quimpanita cart had made it within earshot. It was a short while before the thing rounded the bend and crawled into view. The large wooden cart creaked and groaned as it rolled slowly along on large primitive disc-like wooden wheels. The two huge awkward bison lumbered clumsily along, occasionally letting out loud grunts and bellows.

As the cart rumbled by, Pona-Pow suddenly darted forward, leaped onto the back of the cart, and swung herself quickly onto its rough back. The corners, as in many of these quimpanita carts, were coated decoratively in a thin layer of gold. The cart itself was heaped with smooth, shiny quimpanitas, which were both red and green in color. Although Pona-Pow probably could have walked quicker than the slow cart could rumble, she enjoyed the ride and the quimpanitas. It was normal for children, youths, and even some adults to conveniently hitch rides on carts carrying quimpanitas or grapes, but today she was the only one on this cart. The drivers usually didn't even care if their passengers ate some of their prized cargo.

Pona-Pow's eyes scanned the many quimpanitas near her and selected a nice large red one (these were normally the sweetest). She grabbed eagerly at it with her fur-gloved hands. It was then that she glanced up and noticed the teenaged girl who was driving the cart was staring curiously at her with a hint of fright in her wide eyes. Pona-Pow didn't blame the vexed girl. After all, it would startle her if she were to find a mysterious girl dressed completely in black riding the cart, especially in a tribe where their dress was not very diverse. She grinned beneath her furry face mask and chocked back a giggle. It was sometimes amusing to watch the curious faces. Pona-Pow pleasantly waved at the girl to show that she was not a foe. The girl nodded hesitantly and slapped the back of the bison to get them moving a little faster.

Pona-Pow yanked her face mask down, revealing the unpainted half of her small red face and sunk her teeth into the crisp, sweet, juicy quimpanita's flesh. CRUNCH, crunch, crunch... The juice dripped down her chin. Through the thick veil of rugged trees, she could sometimes make out large clearings full of neat rows of friendly quimpanita trees. Pona-Pow's ears also detected the sweet, lovely sound of children singing from within. The season of autumn had stretched its beautiful welcome wings over the small humble land. This meant that most of the Orenean children would help harvest the quimpanitas from the sprawling branches of the quimpanita trees in many orchards or harvest grapes in the many sprawling vines and load them onto carts like these so they could be dried or traded with other tribes. In fact, if Pona-Pow hadn't become an agente, she herself would be harvesting now. Pona-Pow sometimes wished she could live a normal life like other children. Their singing was very sweet too.

The cart rumbled shakily along, jarring Pona-Pow's teeth and nearly making her tumble off its rough wooden side. Finally, after about a half hour of slow riding, Pona-Pow spotted the place where she should get off. She jumped gracefully off the cart and shouted a brief thank-you to the girl who had driven the cart. After regaining her balance, she set off walking briskly through the woods. Pona-Pow scrambled down the narrow dark trail to the chief's abode. She loved the peaceful freshness of the gorgeous small winding trail.

After a few short minutes, she finally came up upon a rather large clear and peaceful pond. In the center sat two large spacious islands with a thin shallow canal of water between them, which was normally a dry path between the two in the dry season. On each island sat a small, cozy traditional cabin-like hut, which, although small, took up most of the space on the islands. On each island grew small young trees that, along with the handsome cabins, created delightful reflections in the rippling water. Ducks and geese frolicked playfully in the mote-like pond near the other end. Pona-Pow reached into her pouch and slid out a large gold-plastered wooden whistle. She blew into it loudly with all of her might. In response, a small, slender canoe paddled swiftly up to her from the smaller of the two islands. Out of it jumped a short stocky man with his long smooth black hair braided neatly down his back and a stern expression on his scarred face. It was Keoko. He always donned a depressing, pessimistic disposition, "like a raincloud on a sunny day he est," the lower chiefs often whispered behind his back.

"So ya are back early," Keoko declared solemnly. "I'spose that means ya do'a'not have any new information and will'a'not be getting any anytime soon."

Pona-Pow nodded. "Yes, Second Chief."

"But that still does'a'not mean that ya wasted time," he added. "Ya have gained experience. At least I hope ya have gained experience. Probably have'a'not gained much experience fo what i'test worth. But anyhow, hop in. I'spose that tha high chief would be worried half to death if ya do'a'not come home soon."

She eagerly climbed into the canoe as it wobbled back into the cool clear water. As the girl peered into the somewhat shallow water, she could glimpse shiny silver fish wiggling through the rocks and tiny pollywogs silently playing beneath the surface. Suddenly, she spotted a small black turtle gliding easily near the surface, minding his own business. She quickly reached into the water and captured the rough squirming creature in her small hands.

"No, no, no," Keoko scolded. "I have told ya many times already that ya already have too many pet creatures. Soon ya will have so many that ya can'a'not keep track of them all."

"But why ...?" Pona-Pow sighed and reluctantly replaced her treasure back in the water. It was true; she did have many turtles, frogs, birds, lizards, and snakes to take care of. Pona-Pow loved creatures.

Finally, the canoe's sharp edge sliced into the soft red clay of the larger island. She climbed out slowly. Things were as normal. Ten-year-old Mighty Cedar (everyone just called him "Cedar") and eleven-year-old Zatch were practicing defense techniques. Cedar, although he was a year younger than his friend Zatch, was much bigger. Zatch was a shorter fellow but was skilled at defense fighting—something that hyper-paranoid Keoko had reinforced many a time. Zatch often enjoyed drilling Cedar when he seized the opportunity, as he was now.

"No, Cedar," he corrected, "i'test'a'not like that. I like this ... see? Block it with tha upper part of ya arm or ya will'a'not be able to block it right. It will just smack ya back in tha face if ya do it tha other way." Cedar posed again and carefully redid his move. Zatch, who was Pona-Pow's brother, nodded approvingly at her as she passed. His short black hair glistened in the bright cheery sunlight.

Pona-Pow ducked under the coarse leathery hide that hung in the doorless entrance to the chief's home, above which was plastered the shiny golden wheel-like emblem of the Orenean chiefs. The chief's abode was small, as were most all of the other Orenean dwellings. An inviting fire crackled happily in the center of the small cozy room beneath a smoke hole in the thatched roof. On the dusty dirt floor squatted eight-year-old Mik, poking at the restless fire with a long slender stick. Eleven-year-old Veenatch knelt in the corner in front of a tall loom, skillfully weaving the coarse tan threads with her calloused fingers. On the rough log wall hung a massive woven tapestry of the wheel emblem of Orenea. In front of it sat Chief. He was a slight old man who was as wrinkled as a raisin. His short fleecy hair was a gray symbol of the many years he had spent under the sun. For as long as she could remember, his skinny legs hadn't been able to hold his weight.

He was sitting silently on a well-worn stool made out of a tree round, his eyes closed reverently and his bony arthritic fingers bumping along the woven tapestry as he fingered it. His lips moved silently ... Chief often prayed faithfully for his endeared people, pleading with the Great El Shaddai for their safety. "Hello Number Six," Mik greeted. Each agente had a number, and for his safety, he was required to identify himself and his fellows by their number when they were still in uniform. Chief, who had just awakened to the fact that the girl had entered, glanced up slowly with his kind wise eyes.

"Ah, Number Six," he said in his old husky voice, which crackled like a small fire. "Ya have returned, I see. Why do'a'not ya sit down and tell me what ya have found out about it? Oh, but first go change into ya normal clothes."

"Yes, Chief," Pona-Pow responded politely. "But I do not have much to tell."

Chief cocked his old head. "I'spose that est good news. A few more visits to these new neighbors of ours and I think we might be ready to trust them."

Eager to remove her hot, scratchy attire, she tugged off her headpiece, revealing long smooth rippling black hair that flowed down her young back like water.

After she had quickly changed her clothes in a private corner and scrubbed off the paint, she sat down by Mik. The young boy was painfully shy and quiet, especially around strangers. "Hello," he muttered.

"Hello," Pona-Pow returned. There were a few minutes of silence.

On the wall were little pegs on which hung glittering gold medallions with the Orenean wheel design on them. Only chiefs, important officials, and warriors were allowed to wear them.

Suddenly, Twii-Wa, Mik's older sister, bounced into the hut energetically. Her name was Twii-Wa, but to her that sounded too "kissy, kissy," so she was always called Twii for short, except for by the chief, who preferred to call her by her full name. She was tall, but not as tall as her friend Veenatch. Unlike her brother, Twii had a notorious reputation for her talkative nature and a snarky sense of humor. As usual, her hair was braided in messy pigtails. Twii stopped beside Pona-Pow.

"Hello, Pona-Pow. Where under tha …? Oh, never mind. There she est."

She hurried briskly over to where Veenatch was weaving and plopped down beside her. "Poor Zatch," Twii mused.

"What under tha sun est wrong with Zatch?" Veenatch asked curiously.

Twii leaned in. "He est being sent to deliver a parchment to tha Tumitataken chief. He will likely be gone all day."

"I'test already midmorning. I'test'a'not as if there est all day left to waste," Veenatch pointed out.

"Welllll, there est still a lot of tha day left. I'test'a'not *that* late."

At that very moment, Zatch wandered dejectedly inside and slumped down against the wall. "May I wait until tomorrow? I do'a'not want to go now. I must set some traps fo quails today."

Chief shook his head disapprovingly. "A job pushed until tomorrow est a job not done at all."

"But …," Zatch started to argue, but he then thought better of it.

Mumbling sourly, Keoko started to smudge the paint neatly onto Zatch's smooth red face in stripes of alternating colors. Zatch bit his lip and sighed.

"Why under tha sun are ya complaining? I'test'a'not *that* terrible, est it? Ya do'a'not have to train all day! *We* must stay here and practice our soft walking … fo tha tenth time since last Sabbath. I would rather deliver a message to tha Tumitatakens than stay here any day," Twii declared.

"No, ya would'a'not," Zatch snapped irritably.

"Yes, I would."

"That est easy fo ya to say. Ya have never been to Mittowan's home in ya life. I'test'a'not a game."

Veenatch's dark brown eyes grew wide. "Listen to him." She added, "I once waes sent to help Cedar deliver a message to Mittowan many moons ago, and it waes one of tha most terrifying things I ever did. He est *very* frightening."

"Yes," Zatch added as Keoko finished half of his face. Twii shrunk back somewhat humiliated.

Zatch held his face perfectly still as Keoko smudged the dull paint on the other side of his face. "Watch there," Zatch warned irritably. "It tickles."

"Well fo goodness' sakes, do'a'not talk," Keoko scolded. "Ya almost ruined it!"

Zatch groaned. "Why under tha sun do we have to be tha ones to do this job?" he complained. "Everyone hates this, and this face paint est ugly and embarrassing."

"Listen," Chief explained, "someone must do it. And ya are well prepared. I think that est enough purple, Keoko. Anyhow, I wish I could go myself. I feel silly making somebody else do it. But I am'a'not as young as I once waes."

Keoko hastily brushed off Zatch's deerskin clothes.

Why under tha sun do I have to look my best to meet a tyrant? Zatch thought.

Chief slowly lifted his shaky old hands to give Zatch the large parchment scroll that he would be delivering to Mittowan. "This est very important. Be very careful with it," he instructed. "Do'a'not lose it."

"Yes, Chief," Zatch promised. "What under tha sun est it about this time?"

"Ya shall see," Chief sighed wearily. "But I will tell ya this—he est probably not going to agree on this one."

"When under tha sun *has* he agreed on one of ya treaties?"

"Good point, but this one est'a'not exactly a treaty," Chief corrected drowsily with a yawn. "I'test ... Well ... ya will see. Oh my, I think I will have a bit of a nap fo now."

Suddenly, Twii, who had been playing with Pona-Pow's pets around back, scrambled clumsily back into the cabin.

"Someone est coming!" she exclaimed. "I think i'test one of tha lower chiefs ... and he brought his own canoe!"

"Shhhh," Chief shushed in a rushed voice. "We do'a'not want them to hear ya. If i'test who I think i'test, he will'a'not be pleased that ya are here. He est opposed to tha idea of having messengers here in tha first place, and ya can bet ya right hand that he will sure give us all much grief. Quick, Keoko, blow tha whistle. Tha rest of ya go ... Well, I'spose ya know where to go. Oh, and Veenatch, on tha way, put away tha paint and hurry."

Zatch hastily opened part of one of the long round log beams in the wall and squeezed into the small hidden opening before Keoko quickly helped him replace the part of the wall. Cedar, Mik, Pona-Pow, and Veenatch rushed back inside and crammed themselves into more of these cleverly placed nooks and crannies hollowed out of the log walls.

"These bothersome old grouches," Twii muttered as she clumsily slid into another compartment in the wall.

Zatch squirmed awkwardly. The space, which had been sized for a smaller child, was very tight. Only a few of the highly trusted lower chiefs knew about the agentes' secret job, and this wasn't one of them. Everyone had already assumed who had arrived. It wasn't difficult to guess, as only one lower chief always showed up uninvited: Manasseh. He wasn't that foul a fellow, other than the fact that he did not take pleasure in many things … especially other people. Zatch was actually pleased that he had shown up, for it meant that he wouldn't need to deliver his parchment scroll to Mittowan right away. A simple glance into the Tumitataken chief's hateful, evil eyes and the sound of his loud, cruel voice loosed chills scurrying up and down his spine, but Zatch never admitted to being afraid. Although most of the visits were short and uneventful, every minute in that stinky hot "royal palace" seemed like a year.

From outside, Zatch finally heard the end of the canoe slice loudly into the clay and a few loud footsteps pattering toward the entrance. Zatch could watch what was happening through a small airhole in the dark, cramped boxlike compartment. Then a tall, thin man with aged gray hair, which still bore a few long ribbons of black running through it as remains of his younger years, walked in his stiff, grumpy manner into the chief's home.

"Ah," Chief declared, tossing his hand up in the air and letting it fall back onto his lap. "What a surprise to see ya today. Especially since ya did'a'not tell me ya were coming."

Manasseh stretched on his tiptoes and sighed. The deep creases on his face told Zatch that something must be bothering him. "Well," he replied awkwardly in his deep voice. "I apologize, Chief. I'll try to notify ya next time. Life gets busy." He always promised that.

"How are ya?"

"Quite well, thank ya," Chief replied with dignity.

"So," Keoko began, obviously eager to get this unexpected meeting over with, "what under tha sun have ya come here fo?"

"I would like ya permission to do something," he declared.

"Ah?" Chief inquired.

"I would like to have five more caves in tha Fire Hills converted into underground shelters fo tha people to hide in during a battle."

"Why under tha sun do ya want that?" Chief asked curiously, a hint of irritation in his voice. "Ya have twelve already prepared. Est tha whole land to be made into a shelter?"

"Indeed, but if tha Tumitatakens ..."

"I know, I know. I'spose ... I'spose."

"Make tha wise decision, High Chief. Scarcely a new moon goes by without me hearing of another sad tale of tha grief and bloodshed caused by that dastardly destructive tribe. How frustrating. Zey hate us and want our land and our lives ... fo no apparent reason."

"El Shaddai save us," Chief whispered. "But I do wish that tha people would'a'not act so hopeless. Do'a'not zey know who est fighting on their side?"

Manasseh smiled to himself as if he were listening to some old man's fantasies. Chief's old mouth was set in a determined line. "Look," Manasseh explained gently, as if he were dealing with a sweet old grandfather, "if what ya say est true, than tha shelters will be used to store maize. Either way, it will be useful. So may I furnish them?"

"Well ..." Chief stroked his chin thoughtfully and glanced at Keoko, who nodded slightly in approval. "I'spose ya may build three."

"Thank ya. But only three?" Manasseh asked.

"Well, all right. Ya may build four. But only four."

"Thank ya, Chief," Manasseh replied politely, rising slowly to leave.

"Y'elcome. But remember, appoint a time when ya next wish to visit."

"All right," Manasseh agreed. "But there est one more thing I would like to speak to ya about."

"Oh?"

"That est tha provisions," Manasseh whispered. "Fo our escape from Orenea. Ya know of what I am speaking."

Chief was annoyed. He detested the idea of removing himself and everyone from this land. "Well, what under tha sun do ya want?" He sighed.

Manasseh smiled and glanced both ways warily as if to make sure no one else was listening. "I think we finally have enough," he declared joyfully.

"Good," Chief muttered. "We'll have enough fo when spring comes around."

"Come now, Chief," Manasseh urged. "This est a happy thing. We'll be prepared to sneak out in tha spring … and why under tha sun wait, anyhow? Why not now?"

"Well," Chief explained, "first off, i'test cold and difficult to find shelter in tha distant mountains in winter. And also because only narrow cliff trails lead out of Orenea—and zey are too icy in tha winter. Besides, that plan could never work. I'test too unrealistic. Do ya really think that we can move thousands of people out of this land without being found out or some traitor giving us away?"

Manasseh leaned in dramatically. "Something *must* be done. Our enemies continue to attack us. Zey have almost one in three of us killed or in slavery."

One in three!

Chief nodded sadly. "I understand that, but I also understand that many more will die if zey catch a large group of us trying to leave. I'test'a'not worth tha risk. Surely ya must see that. There are many among our own tribe who would be willing to spill information under pressure or fo a reward. Ya will remember tha incident at Ten Flower."

"And by tha way," Keoko pointed out, "why under tha sun would ya want to build shelters if we are just going to leave in tha spring anyhow?"

Manasseh stopped short and wrinkled his eyebrows as if this was something he hadn't considered before. Keoko turned away and sighed in disgust.

"And zey only have so many men," Chief continued. "Of course tha Tumitatakens are better prepared and trained, but our tribes are almost tha same size, right? Did'a'not we just add a few more men to our defense tha previous moon?"

Manasseh looked down at his lap solemnly. "But we can'a'not beat *two* armies."

"What under tha sun do ya mean?"

"Well," Manasseh wavered awkwardly, "I have word that tha Tumitatakens have gotten—or are about to get—tha Karuk tribe involved in this conflict on their side."

"What?" Chief gasped. "Why under tha sun have I not heard of this thing before now? Are ya certain?"

"I am afraid so. I'test only a matter of time."

"El Shaddai save us. We do'a'not stand a chance."

Zatch's heart seemed to stop in his chest, and it felt as if there was a lump the size of a tree round in his throat. *As if it waes'a'not precarious enough before. We could all be overtaken any day now.* For such a long time, Zatch's mind had been constantly riddled with the fear that the Tumitatakens would finally win the war, and he suddenly realized, with a sick feeling in his stomach, that his fears might be about to become a reality.

"Well, all right, then," Chief sighed. "And remember: send word when ya are prospecting on coming next time around."

"I will," Manasseh replied as he strode toward the exit. "Goodbye." Keoko and Chief both waved.

Once Manasseh was safely on the opposite shore, the children started to emerge from the walls. Zatch tumbled out onto the dirt floor. Oh, how refreshing it felt to stretch his limbs.

"Come Number Four," Chief called. Zatch stepped forward obediently.

After Keoko had finished touching his face with stripes of black paint in between the purple ones, he carefully put ribbons of yellow paint in Zatch's short black hair to disguise his identity further.

"Chief," Twii inquired nervously, "will tha Karuk nation really come and fight against us with tha Tumitatakens?"

"Likely so," Keoko interjected pessimistically as he worked on Zatch's face, "very likely so."

"El-Shaddai est watching over us," Chief assured with a sigh, although it was clear he was truly worried. "Ya should'a'not worry about a naught." That was what Chief always said when he knew there was trouble on the horizon.

"But …," Zatch insisted.

"Do'a'not ask. Just … do'a'not ask. I have no answers fo ya," Chief said, calmly handing the boy a distinguished pair of footwear.

Zatch carefully fitted the colorful beaded moccasins on his bare feet. Keoko cautiously pinned a train of brilliant shiny feathers to the back of his reluctant apprentice's head. Chief dusted off Zatch's dusty animal skin clothes. Then, the most relevant part of all, Chief placed a shiny golden medallion, which bore the royal emblem of Orenea on it, around Zatch's neck. Zatch beamed with pride because it was a noble honor and a sign of royalty to wear the sign of the Orenean chief around one's neck. Rarely did someone other than royalty have the privilege to feel the weight of that special disk of pure Orenean gold resting against one's chest. It meant that the protection of the chief and his warriors was at his side and that the authority to do important jobs like deliver messages from chief to chief and announce breaking news to the villages had been placed in his hands. It would surely keep him safe in the dangerous, violent Tumitataken village.

But as soon as they had finished a short prayer for protection and he had plopped down in the small canoe to leave, the anxiety quickly began to creep back upon him. "Please go slow," he pleaded with Keoko, who was diligently rowing the plain tiny wooden canoe.

"No," he declared presumptuously. "Tha sooner ya start, tha sooner ya shall have it over with. That est … if ya even make it there. I do hope ya do'a'not get lynched in that horrid village."

Zatch cringed. Keoko wasn't helping comfort his fluttering anxiety. It was a three-and-a-half-hour walk.

"It will be over with," Zatch whispered reassuringly to himself. "Ya will see. Ya have done this before."

Once he was finally on the dry ground, Zatch began to wander through the thick evergreen woods. Because of his embarrassing attire, he hoped he wouldn't stumble upon a hunter or a woman washing clothes in one of the creeks or rivers. People had mocked him before when he was in this silly-looking uniform. But they normally stopped quickly when they noticed his messenger face paint and gold medallion. As he strode briskly along, the medallion bounced against his chest and shined radiantly in the sunshine. A distant crow proudly bellowed his obnoxious squawks in the distance, and a tiny busy pale green hummingbird buzzed through the trees. The sweet calming effect of the peaceful forest almost seemed to swallow up his anxiety … almost.

After about an hour of brisk hiking down the mountain, the trees began to thin and more golden oaks and bright yellow maples began to appear. Soon he reached what the people called tha Sun's Ray Forest. Sunny patches of sunshine polka-dotted the soft light green grass that spiked up from the moist squishy brown earth, freckled by dazzling orange poppies and sunny yellow dandelions. Sprawling valley oaks stretched up toward a jewel of a blue sky. Large smooth gray rocks sprouted up from the ground.

When Zatch turned his head to the left, he could view the broad shimmering lake by which the "newcomers" were camped. It was named Honiton, which translated into "mighty waters." It was a huge deep blue masterpiece of creation. Normally there would be a few canoes from many distant tribes arriving to trade and fish. However, because of the new mysterious arrivals, who still were too mysterious to be called friends yet, the people were prohibited to go by it for a few moons at least or until things could be properly sorted out.

Many a time Zatch and Pona-Pow had frolicked playfully in the Honiton's cool refreshing waters in the hot summer or fished with large reed nets in it. Normally in the rainy season (winter), with all the abundant snow and rain, the mighty lake swelled and transformed this beautiful, lush forest into a deep, dirty dark swamp until it slowly drained away again in late spring. This was why the ground beneath Zatch's coarse leather moccasins was a little mushy and soft, like walking on many freshly skinned hides stacked up in a pile.

Soon Zatch began to grow slightly hungry for lunch. He seated himself on a mossy boulder and pulled out of his leather pouch a small brown raw potato—a common meal or snack in his tribe. He sunk his teeth into the firm yet moist flesh of the potato and gazed thoughtfully out over the clear blue waters of the Honiton. On the distant shore, he could glimpse a small valley of green grass flanked by two colossal mountains which towered authoritatively on either side over the place where the boy sat. Even beyond that, he could glimpse lumps of orange, which were the lovely Fire Hills.

After Zatch had finished the potato, he continued to hike slowly through the lush forest. The sun was now at its highest. Gradually, the Sun's Ray Forest began to dissolve again into the rugged pine forest of the mountain as he continued along, and Zatch found himself hiking up a gentle slope on the mountain opposite the one on which the chief dwelt. His anxiety began to flood back upon him as the trees began to thin and he passed the first Tumitataken house. He was nearing the Tumitatakens village. The hut-like house was roughly constructed of earthy orange clay mixed with straw. The flat roof was thoroughly thatched with reeds and twigs. A rickety tan ladder built of wood and bone leaned awkwardly against the side of its rough, bumpy wall.

Outside, an elderly woman was diligently scrubbing a heap of old clothes. Tumitatakens, unlike their neighbors, dressed scantily. The men slipped colorful dyed loincloths around their waists, and the women strapped long tubes of leathery deerskin around their chests and beneath their armpits, extending down to mid-calf. She glanced up solemnly at the Orenean wearing the golden wheel emblem but didn't speak. The Tumitatakens living on the outskirts or in separate small villages were not as intimidating because they were not so sore and bitter toward the Oreneans as those living near Mittowan's "palace," and a few even sympathized with them.

As he continued, Zatch passed more and more Tumitataken dwellings. Most of the residences ignored him or muttered. Others waved at him gingerly. The pine trees began to thin even more— then there was the village itself. It was much more massive than any Orenean village was. Over 150 people dwelt within. There were many larger dwellings scattered in one large clearing. The tyrant chief, Mittowan, had tried his best to model it after the distant legendary Aztec tribe.

The village buzzed excitedly with activity. A large cart hauled by a noisy bison rumbled between the crude houses, knocking over a few brightly adorned clay jars and reed baskets, which were painted in bright vivid colors or plastered in shining, glistening gold. People were chatting and laughing loudly, and boys laughed boisterously as they chased small wooden balls. *Why under tha sun est it that zey get to have fun all day while I must work?* Zatch thought sourly.

In the center, toward the back of the village, was the largest structure of all, the great serpent's home itself. Mittowan had gone out of his way to make sure his dwelling was the largest of all. Even so, it wasn't very pleasing to the eye. Zatch drew in a deep breath. Now it was most imperative that he let show his special medallion. He quickly dusted his clothes, straightened his bothersome headpiece, and held his scroll out in sight so the people would know he was a message bearer. As he strolled between the homes taking his time, many curious people stared at him. Others spat on the dusty ground in disgust at an Orenean. Some children, whose parents had loaded them with terrifying false myths about the Orenean tribe, fled fearfully into the safety of their crude-looking homes.

When Zatch turned his head, a sickening sight met his eyes. In a neat line on the dusty ground sat a pitiful row of ragged dirty Orenean people. In front of them strolled clusters of Tumitatakens, who carefully examined the merchandise. There were even a few men from distant tribes here to trade. Zatch's stomach twisted.

The Orenean chief had rigged it so that many Orenean raid victims were rescued from falling into the hungry open jaws of the horrible Tumitataken slave trade, but not all could be prevented. The slaves were dusty, ragged, and thin and hung their weary heads in shame. Their callused hands were tied firmly behind their scarred backs. Many had their masters' symbols branded on their foreheads or backs. A tall young Tumitataken man stopped in front of a young boy, who glanced solemnly back up at him with huge owllike brown eyes that had long since been robbed of all their pride and esteem. His hair, which had apparently not been cut in a long time, hung in a matted braid behind him.

"How much for this one?" he asked the slave manager.

"Oh, about … let's say … a half a buffalo skin. Maybe a buck's skin if you can make a good bargain."

Zatch felt like he would be sick. After all, considering the circumstances, that boy might have just as easily been him.

"So little?" the man asked. "That is a good deal."

"As good a deal as you are likely to find anywhere. And this one is experienced as a worker—see all the different symbols branded on the forehead? Was captured over twelve seasons ago so it isn't the raw product." The slave master tilted his head suggestively toward Zatch. This made Zatch even angrier. He clenched his fists furiously, knowing that the man was suggesting that *he* was an example of the "raw product." But Zatch knew better than to react because that would sink him into deep trouble. He quickly hurried away from the horrifying scene.

He hated witnessing slaves being bought or sold. They would often live in tiny crumbling huts near where they labored from before sunrise until after sunset. They often didn't have barely any food, water, and clothes. It gnawed at Zatch in the night to know that he was relaxing sleepily in a large warm and sturdy home with warm, dry clothes and food in his belly while there were at least two other Orenean boys his age who lay shivering in crumbling leaky huts as their hollow stomachs growled painfully at them, hoping that they would not make a mistake tomorrow at work so they would not get beaten … again. Some had lived many years this way. Yet there was little an eleven-year-old boy could do to help that he was not already doing.

Then, before long, Zatch glanced up and realized he was standing before the great serpent's palace itself. It was extremely tall but styled like the other dwellings scattered about. On each side towered intricately carved totem poles whose foreboding gold-plastered faces seemed to shout "Go away, Orenean—we do not want you here!" A long straight tunnellike passageway slithered out from the front of the ugly structure, and on each side of the doorless entrance stood two smaller totem poles. In front, a warrior stood alertly guarding his chief's home. He, like most other Tumitataken men, wore only a stiff painted loincloth, and a large royal feather headdress was set upon his head.

"Stop!" he commanded sternly. He inspected Zatch thoroughly. "You are Orenean, I see. What do you want? And it had better be something important. I don't have time to waste on foreign children."

"I'm here as a messenger," Zatch declared, shakily presenting his shiny medallion, "from tha chief of Orenea fo tha Tumitataken chief."

"Well," he spat, "you certainly sound Orenean."

Upon examining him again, the warrior reluctantly stepped aside. Zatch quickly entered the foreboding dark tunnel. It reeked even more than the village outside and was lighted by eerie, hot smoky torches. The thick fetid smoke stung his throat and created tears in his rich brown eyes. The cracked dirt floor was carpeted by a sparse mixture of straw and wood chips, which crunched beneath his tight and uncomfortable beaded moccasins, making it sound like someone was creeping along behind him. Old cracked yellow human skulls flanked the torches. Their empty dark eye sockets seemed to pounce out at Zatch, who tried effortfully not to glance up at them. He could hear voices echoing at the end of the tunnel, one of which he recognized to be the booming, arrogant voice of Mittowan himself. *Was he in a bad mood?* Butterflies fluttered nervously inside Zatch's stomach as the foreboding voices grew closer and closer. Then, finally, he reached a small sturdy bone ladder, which was plastered with pure gold and slanted upward into the elevated palace floor itself. Quietly and carefully, Zatch began to ascend the ladder. Above, the great serpent was trying to appease one of his many wives.

"No," a hefty high-pitched voice argued, "I still want my face inscribed into the front of your magnificent palace. Now, do you care about me or not?"

"Of course I do, my little buttercup," he soothed, "but let's be reasonable ..."

"I have had enough of reasonable. I want this now. I'm your wife. Do you not love me?" she insisted childishly. Her actions made the boy blush with embarrassment. Then, noticing someone climbing the ladder, the Tumitataken chief gazed with a stony evil stare at Zatch. It was the type of petrifying wicked stare that makes one feel as if the starer's eyes are penetrating right through you. As he had been taught, Zatch always made sure to keep his head lowered respectfully.

"What is this?" Mittowan demanded. "An *Orenean* child? Oh, I see by your medallion that you came from that old Chief Palkente—if he can be called *chief* at all. Well, state your business. It better be good and important enough to be worth my time."

"I have come, oh, Great Chief," Zatch sputtered nervously, "to deliver a message fo ya from tha chief of Oreneans: Palkente."

"Come here," the Tumitataken chief ordered. Zatch sighed and boldly paced up to the chief. He was a stalky man with broad shoulders, sturdy muscular limbs, and thick black eyebrows that always seemed to be furrowed in anger. Mittowan's two glistening pure white front teeth were sanded to points like fangs. His long silky hair was tucked beneath his lengthy, colorful feather headdress. He was naked except for a plain brown loincloth and a large ugly curved knife with a dull blue handle strapped around his sturdy red waist.

The woman, who was certainly the fattest woman Zatch had ever met, sat cross-legged on a small mat near the corner. It seemed that if she had been a few inches taller, she would have been round! Her matted hair was covered in wilted dandelions. *Now I know who not to marry*, Zatch thought.

The Tumitataken chief pointed his finger commandingly to the floor in front of Zatch. Zatch knew well from past experience what the man's routine was. He obediently knelt down on the dusty dirt floor on his hands and knees, letting his head fall limply between his arms. He was bowing respectfully to a chief. *He does'a'not deserve respect of any kind*, Zatch thought angrily. *He is the meanest, most disgusting ...* Before he could finish his thought, the chief ordered him to rise again.

"Well," Mittowan demanded, "what does the old man want?"

"I'spose he wants ya to sign an agreement," Zatch croaked fearfully. "Do ya want me to read it?"

"It's in my language right? Because if it is in one of those savage Orenean tongues, I don't want to bother," the great serpent growled.

Zatch understood what he meant. Of the three languages Oreneans spoke, Honitonax was the only one the Tumitataken chief had bothered to learn to speak. The Orenean languages were Honitonax, Benegelan, and Shonto.

Zatch squatted awkwardly down on the dry clay dirt floor. As he did, one of the small blue wooden beads popped off one of his moccasins and bounced onto the ground. Zatch retrieved it quickly and dropped it into his leather pouch. Twii or Veenatch would probably sew it back on later. He carefully popped the sticky sap seals off the large parchment scroll and unrolled it onto the ground. The young chief stomped his bare foot on the ground impatiently. The scroll, which was penned in the colorful large Honitonax characters, was about two feet tall and three feet long. Zatch cleared his throat and began to read it clearly and loudly. Unlike the English alphabet, which uses only black and white and reads from the top of the page down, Honitonax uses many colors and figures and reads from the bottom of the parchment up. It also reads from left to right, like Hebrew.

The document itself was a lengthy and a boring example of

grown-upish fancy talk. But, shortened (and it really should have been shortened, in Zatch's opinion), it basically was a request to swear (in the name of El Shaddai, of course) not to bother, disturb, worry, or hurt in any way the new small group of people who had settled on Lake Honiton's shore. *Wow,* Zatch thought, *tha Orenean chief must really think that friendship with those people est a good investment. Zey seem like some people that Chief would want to help. And this document est extreme! A vow as sacred as written here would be worse than death fo tha signer to break.*

Zatch stared patiently up at the large red man, who was pacing slowly and unsurely, drumming his huge thick fingers along his smooth red chin. Zatch stood because he expected the tyrant to turn down the suggestion immediately and send him out. Mittowan suddenly halted in front of the young messenger.

"In the name of El Shaddai, eh? Or should I say in *tha* name of El Shaddai?" he sneered, mockingly faking an Orenean accent. Zatch's lowered face flushed bright red with anger. "I sure wish that old geezer wouldn't make me swear in the name of a silly mythical being. In fact, I wouldn't be surprised if he himself thinks he is El Shaddai."

Zatch clenched his fist so tightly that his fingernails dug deeply into his palms. *How dare this miserable tyrant speak of El Shaddai like that,* Zatch fumed. *And of Chief too! That est absurd. He would'a'not ever dream of thinking he est El Shaddai. He knows that as well as I do. I wish I could give him a good smack to tha face.*

Although he had endured the Tumitataken chief's outrageous remarks before, Zatch still couldn't help but grit his teeth in anger every time. He sighed as the man began to boast again.

"Well," the great serpent bragged arrogantly, "if he is indeed El Shaddai, he is not doing a very good job. He can't even defend his own people against my nation. And you would think that someone as strong and mighty as you claim El Shaddai is that he could at least defend his own people against one tribe. Of course, he would have our all-powerful spirits and gods to deal with. Why, your old chief is so old that he cannot even take care of himself. He can't even walk!"

By now, Zatch could hardly restrain himself from screaming "Oh, shut up!" However, he remembered what the Orenean chief had taught him about respect for leaders, even if that leader happened to be Mittowan. Even Chief himself treated Mittowan respectfully, even as the Tumitataken chief shamelessly spat insults in his face. He also remembered what he had learned from the Holy Scriptures about how El Shaddai would conquer all his enemies eventually.

"El Shaddai will punish tha great serpent," Zatch whispered reassuringly to himself. "And all his warriors ... zey will get what zey deserve."

"What did you say?" Mittowan demanded.

"Oh, um ... Oh?" Zatch stammered. "What under tha sun do ya mean?"

"You know very well what I mean," Mittowan bellowed impatiently. "You whispered something, and I want to know what it was!"

Oh no, what a dreadful situation this was. Lying was out of the question because Oreneans were typically taught never to lie. But if he told the truth ... Suddenly, without warning, Mittowan gruffly seized Zatch by the collar and bent down and yanked him up to his full height, where the tyrant and the messenger were eye-to-eye.

"Now listen, you!" Mittowan growled angrily through his teeth. "I know what you said, and now *I* have something to say." He was shaking Zatch so hard that his small headpiece slipped off the back of his head. "The nation of the Tumitatakens will never end. Not now and not ever. We will live, rule, and be sovereign in this city even longer than the Aztecs. Forever! And no El Shaddai will ever conquer us. He is an old myth devised by the Oreneans and will fall with them! Do you hear!"

Zatch forced a gulp down his throat and nodded gingerly.

"Good then," Mittowan concluded. Then he swung his fist down at Zatch, stopping about a quarter inch from his nose. Helplessly Zatch winced and tumbled backward to the ground, and it took a couple of moments for him to realize that he had not really been slugged. Mittowan placed his hands on his hips and glanced at his wife. It was obvious that he had done it partially to impress her. She giggled and clapped her chubby hands together. Zatch, whose face was still pale, scrambled quickly back to his feet. He felt like his ears would shoot smoke.

"About that document …," Mittowan mused. Then he turned his large head to a wretched young slave who was standing readily in the corner. "Servant," he ordered, "go get me something to write with." The slave quickly obeyed. Soon she walked back into the room carrying a set of writing equipment.

Zatch paused. Was he actually going to sign it? He watched in surprise as Mittowan knelt down and signed his name in Honitonax figures neatly in the corner across from where the chief had signed. Rarely did he pay much attention to Chief's documents, especially when he was in a mood like this.

"You may go now," Mittowan ordered stiffly.

"Thank you." Zatch gathered his things and the headdress that had fallen off his head. He walked quickly back across the room and climbed shakily down the ladder. *Ya should have known better,* Zatch scolded himself silently as he wandered back through the tunnel. *Never whisper like that again.* Zatch straightened his messed and twisted shirt as he exited the tunnel and gulped in some fresh air. Although he was somewhat shaken, Zatch resolved that he wouldn't mention this ordeal to anyone, especially not the part about almost getting punched. He didn't want the grown-ups to worry.

In fact, none of the agentes ever told others about things like this—not even to Chief or each other. It would only make Chief feel guiltier about sending them. Sometimes Zatch caught him asking El Shaddai if he should send the agentes home. Knowing that it was even more dangerous to send a boy to deliver a message than he had thought might make him reconsider the idea of having the children involved. Why was it that Zatch didn't want to be sent home? Sometimes he hated this job. It was hard work. Yet somehow Zatch dreaded being idle. Sitting around worrying helplessly, like most Oreneans were, was unbearably tense and monotonous. It felt more effective to be out getting his hands dirty for the cause. Of course, there was always praying—but after praying his whole life, Zatch was beginning to grow weary of letting out seemingly useless prayers. Of course, Chief had never given up praying. But still, it felt much better doing something more tangible. *I hope that Chief dose'a'not ask how it went,* he thought.

"Number Five," Chief called. Mik stood up and walked away from the training grounds where he and Twii, his older sister, had been practicing more hiding techniques with Cedar and Pona-Pow. After Mik had plopped into the small canoe, and he rode in it quickly to the chief's dwelling, where the chief handed him a large parchment and another medallion.

"Go put this on Tha Know in Ore-Cita. Then, on ya way back, get some quimpanitas from there … Oh, and may as well gather some Manzanita berries fo dinner as well."

"Yes, Chief," Mik agreed, "I will do it." With that, he started off, humming cheerfully. "Tha Know Board" was a large board in Ore-Cita, and it held much of the latest news, mostly in symbols or pictures so that all could understand well. It was called that because if you examined it, you would "know" what was going on. One needed to be wearing the chief's medallion to put something on Tha Know, unless he had permission to announce news by the elders of a particular village. It took an hour-and-a-half trek along old deer trails and a couple of buffalo cart rides to reach Ore-Cita.

It was two rows of small hut-like structures, which were constructed of orange hard clay, logs, and sticks, with thatched roofs. Each of them was the place where the lower chiefs lived and worked out deals with other tribes when they traveled to purchase things to take home with them or to discuss battle plans in times of war. The two rows, which faced one another, had a long stretch of clear dirt running between them, where buffalo carts could bump along.

There were few people in the great trading post. Mik didn't quite understand why. He only knew from the stories the people from his village had relayed to him (especially his grandparents) that before the Tumitatakens had become a threat, the village had been much livelier. Other tribes had not been afraid to trade goods, and the other Oreneans were not afraid to come here. He had heard that before the others had become so morbidly timid and nervous, they used to smile as they went about their business. Now, because of the fear that they might get caught in a Tumitataken attack, not many journeyed here anymore for fear of being trapped in Orenea when the tension finally exploded. Only the bravest of traders would daringly venture in, and even then, they would quickly slip back out of Orenea as quickly as possible.

Although Mik scarcely noticed it now that he had been to the village many times, a sense of tense fear hung frighteningly over Ore-Cita like a fog. It was as if it were cursed. Mik had just decided it was a part of all trading post villages.

The huts were flanked by quaint patches of orange poppies. At the spot where the one set of rows forked into two stood a great rock platform atop which sat a sizeable round gong. Behind the gong platform was a large log cabin, which was used as a church or a meeting house in which the lower chiefs met. Out of this building sprouted two more long rows of huts which split away from one another like a sort of V shape. The rest of the Orenean people lived in tiny huts or cabins in little villages scattered all over Orenea, with clever names like Antler Point, Chipmunk's Burrow, Must We Continue?, and The Golden Heart, which was where Mik lived.

Tha Know was posted up near the great gong. It was a rickety old board posted lazily on a pair of stakes. A buffalo cart rumbled by, kicking up a cloud of unwelcome dust in Mik's small face. As he reached up to stick the parchment with sap on the splintery board beside many other earlier notices, he noticed people glancing over at him suspiciously. Mik disliked people looking at him. After he had finished, he stepped back slowly to admire it. It was written in Benegalan, so Mik could not read it. Although he could fluently speak the language, Mik could only read a very little Honitonax, but not Benegalan or Shonto. Many could not read at all.

"Ya have proper permission to put that up, do ya, lad?" an elderly voice croaked. Mik spun around to face a withered old man who was sitting quietly in the shadow of the tall gong platform. He was an elder from a nearby church who made his living carving in exchange for food and furs from outgoing traders. He would sit happily in this shadow every week on the third and fourth day after Sabbath and carve. His carvings that he traded were of very high quality. The man's leathery old fingers, which looked like well-dried raisins, moved almost automatically with his knife to the wood as he asked Mik the question. Mik nodded shyly. The elderly man smiled warmly and nodded.

As Mik slowly wandered away, he noticed a cluster of barefoot boys about his age huddled around a constellation of stones and poking at them playfully with sticks. He recognized them to be a group of youngsters from a village near his.

Oh no, Mik thought. *There zey are. I do'a'not know them very well. I hope zey do'a'not see me. Oh no, too late—one of them est coming.* Sure enough, a small boy marched up to him, followed by the others. Mik guessed that he was likely a few years younger than he was.

"Hello," the boy greeted cheerily. "Ya name est Mik, right?"

"Um … yes. Hello," Mik responded shyly.

"I remember ya from tha orchard," the boy remarked.

"Yes," Mik said awkwardly, "ya too."

"We are here to get some more grapes fo our fa's juice," the boy chimed proudly.

"Yes," Mik agreed, "that sounds like fun." *Maybe talking with boys I do'a'not know est'a'not so bad after all.*

"But ya were'a'not in tha orchard there yesterday," another young boy asserted. "Were ya here to get some grapes fo *ya* fa's juice?"

Mik blushed. "No."

"Then where were ya? Say, ya were'a'not there a lot of times. Are ya in some sort of trouble?" The boys were not trying to be naughty or be bullies; they were just curious and making Mik very uncomfortable.

"Um … no, no," he insisted.

"Then where under tha sun were ya?"

"Um …" For his own safety, Mik knew he couldn't reveal where he had really resided during the times when he was absent. "Um … I … was staying with some friends," he stammered quietly.

"What?"

"I said I was staying with some friends," he replied a little louder.

The boys stared suspiciously at Mik's blushed face, searching to figure out whether what he was saying was true. Mik blushed even more and stared awkwardly at the ground.

"Are ya telling tha truth?" another boy asked. "Because my ma said i'test very bad to lie."

"Um … yes."

Now all the boys suspected that Mik carried some sort of secret, and they were all eagerly searching their minds for a guess. Poor Mik could not have been more uncomfortable.

"Say," another chimed in, "Why under tha sun are ya wearing such a fine gold medallion?"

Mik shrugged his shoulders.

"Wait," the oldest boy exclaimed. "That est tha symbol of Orenea! Just like tha one on tha place where zey have church here." He pointed excitedly to the top of the large cabin where the great symbol of Orenea sat proudly. "Only people from tha chief's family and really important people get to wear those. Are ya tha chief's great-nephew or something of that nature? I never knew that!"

"Actually … I mean … Oh, that est nice." Mik didn't dare argue with them. Then they would just ask more questions.

"Ya sure do'a'not talk much," the younger boy observed.

Mik blushed again with embarrassment. "Do'a'not tell … about me, I mean," Mik said quietly.

"Of course," the oldest boy promised. "We never break our promises ... especially when we promise a prince. Prince Mik! Wow! I never knew that! That est probably where he waes all this time ... with tha chief. He probably sits by tha fire all day and plays and eats roast duck every night. A prince! Near our humble village! Wow! I never knew that!"

"No ... I mean, uh, never mind."

Mik sighed with relief as the boys finally wandered away. He could have chuckled. The daunting training of an agente was scarcely sitting around and making merry all day. *Well,* Mik thought with relief, *another close call.*

CHAPTER VII

"WELL," MR. WINSLOW ASSESSED IN a meeting, "now that we have made new oars, we can explore the land across the lake. Perhaps we shall meet a friendly hunting band." His eyes gleamed with excitement. "Oh, I just can't wait to tell them about the good news of Jesus!"

Charlie rolled his eyes.

"Yes, indeed," Mr. Wilson agreed. "We must organize another expedition … and soon. You don't expect us to stay in this tent forever, do you? Especially with winter on our thresholds …!"

Peter grinned with excitement. Father had promised that Peter could join the men this time, and he was not about to let the opportunity slip past him. Right now he longed to be outside with the other children in the fresh air, for the tepee was hot, stuffy, and somewhat dark, with only a small stream of sunbeams leaking in through the entrance. But Peter could not afford to miss this discussion. He would now be able to inform Andrew about what was going on and be the first of the two to know it.

"What he says is good," Shamaro declared. "But we do not approach them directly. We wait for them to come to us. I do not expect them to act hostile to us, though. They give us gifts and seem peaceful."

"Yes, it is as we mentioned before," Mr. Snows asserted. "But may I ... bear the task of guarding the boat this time instead of going along with the rest of you?" Everyone chuckled softly.

"Sure thing," Mr. Winslow complied. "So let us start to plan on this trip. I was thinking we could explore the shore directly opposite us. We could fan out in groups of two and—"

"We will certainly need to bring a lot of our furs to give the Indians if we meet them," Mr. Thomas interrupted. They had been saving the furs from the animals that they had killed, even though there was little way to tan them.

"Yes, indeed," Father declared. "We shall ask the women to gather a few herbs for us to eat." There had not been much game in the area recently, and Mr. Snows had suggested that they not use up the few arrows they had with too much use, so they had all been living off wild herbs and nuts for a few days now. Peter was sick of them.

Mrs. Wilson's baby, whom she was nursing in the corner opposite Peter, gurgled happily.

"So," Peter inquired curiously, "what are we going to do once we meet the Indians?"

"We?" Mr. Wilson asked. "Who permitted you to come along?"

"My father did," Peter replied promptly. "He said I could come this time ... If you don't wish for me to explore with the rest of you, then I can keep guard with Mr. Snows. And if the group of hunters *does* turn out to be hostile, they will probably be less likely to attack if there are more of us."

There was an awkward silence. Mr. Wilson chuckled in the way grown-ups do when they think your idea is silly for your age. Peter moaned with frustration. Grown-ups were always underestimating him.

Mr. Thomas spoke up. "Then they will be more likely to attack us because they will think we are so weak that we will resort to bringing young children."

"Is Andrew coming?" Peter asked.

"Well ... yes ... but ..."

"Not to be argumentative," Peter pointed out, "but he *is* my age."

Another awkward silence followed. Peter shook his head disappointedly. There appeared to be little chance that he would wind up being able to join this time.

"Be reasonable," Mr. Wilson urged, as if the boy weren't even there. "The child is practically an invalid." Peter wanted to slap him.

"I *did* promise him he could join us," Father whispered.

"Well …" Mr. Winslow sighed. "I suppose you may come along, Peter, if you will behave yourself."

Peter perked up again. "Truly?" he asked excitedly.

"Yes, truly," warned Father, "but I must tell you that it is not going to be easy as you might think. It is going to be difficult."

"Oh, I know," Peter assured him happily. "I know it will be difficult but thank you very much." Peter could scarcely contain his excitement. He couldn't wait to inform Andrew. Back at Plymouth, only a precious few of the most skilled grown men were selected to participate in endeavors like this, which were only organized about once every few months. And most of them were not nearly as exciting as this one. Peter shivered excitedly as he listened to the men as they began to plan their routes carefully. Just then, Charlotte wandered into the tent carrying one of the damaged corncob dolls.

"I want to go too," she announced in her loud childish voice, which always made her sound like her nose was stuffed up. Her father, Mr. Thomas, smiled fondly at her.

"No, dearest," he replied softly, "you are too young. And besides, you can stay and help the ladies like a big girl."

"But I *am* old enough," she protested, puffing out her little chest proudly. "I'm five and a little older too." They all chuckled.

"I'm afraid that isn't quite old enough," Mr. Thomas explained. "Now you go back out and help the ladies."

But Charlotte seemed determined to get her way. "But Peter and Andrew are going," she protested.

"But you will not. So go back out and let the men talk," Mr.

Thomas urged gently. Charlotte marched disappointedly outside to sulk and brood about not being let on the exploring party.

Outside, the women were drying berries to collect for the winter. Today there had been generously gifted them a fine set of small reed baskets, a few with lids. In these, they would try to preserve as much food as possible for the long months ahead.

On her way out, Charlotte muttered something about how she *would* somehow join that exploring trip.

"What!" Keoko exclaimed. "What under tha sun were ya thinking! I told ya that ya must'a'not go near tha ... new people, or whatever zey are called, any longer. We now know that zey are not hostile."

Cedar hung his head in shame. "I'm sorry, Keoko," he apologized sheepishly. "I did'a'not remember that ya had told me that. But I promise that I will never do it again. I waes delivering a message to tha village of acorns, like Chief said, and ... and I waes curious."

"Yes, well," Keoko growled irritably, "just listen closely next time. I have a good mind to give ya a good whoppin' and send ya home."

"Now, now," Chief consoled. "Do'a'not be so hard on him. There est never a reason fo ya to explode like that. I'm sure he did'a'not intend to disobey ya." Keoko paced hotly about the small room.

"Well, all right," he admitted reluctantly. "I ... I waes wrong to burst out like that."

Cedar nodded forgivingly. This was not the first time he had endured one of Keoko's angry outbursts, although they were few. There were a few minutes of awkward silence. Veenatch was carefully mending Zatch's moccasin. Twii was disposing of the scraps from their lunch, which had been enjoyed about an hour ago. Zatch was instructing Mik on how to block a corner angle kick. And Pona-Pow was out gathering nuts for dinner.

The fire crackled idly in the fire pit in the center of the room.

An endless slender column of grayish smoke drifted gracefully out through the large smoke hole in the roof. The warm sun, which had traveled to a little over mid sky, managed to force a few of its cheery rays into the dark smoke-filled room through the hole in the roof.

Keoko cleared his throat. "So," he inquired curiously, "what under tha sun *did* ya hear at tha tepee?"

"Oh," Cedar mumbled thoughtfully. "Nothing of note ... Wait! I do remember something interesting. Zey said zey were going to explore tha other side of tha Honitan. I'spose that tha land zey will be looking at est tha Sun's Ray Forest. But I can'a'not swear on that."

Chief suddenly seemed unusually enthusiastic. "What else did zey say about this trip?" he interrogated eagerly.

"Oh, I think zey are traveling by boat. And zey are also leaving tomorrow at dawn. Zey will also bring food. Tha tall hair faced one seemed excited about that. Why under tha sun do ya want to know?" Cedar asked.

"Keoko," Chief commanded, ignoring Cedar's question, "go out and blow tha whistle to summon tha others."

"Wait," Cedar interjected. "What? What under tha sun are ya doing?"

Chief's old brown eyes flashed excitedly. "I have an idea. Ya will see in a second. Now go get tha beaver water clothes."

"Ya mean tha ones we swim in?"

"Yes, and hurry ..."

"Wake up, you sleepyhead," Mother whispered. She gently shook a sleepy Peter by the shoulders. Peter drowsily opened his eyes, yawned, and stretched.

"This early?" he complained grumpily.

"Yes," Mother replied. "Now get up and get ready. You didn't expect to wake up at noon to go, did you?"

Peter sighed drowsily and slowly stood up. Most of the other people were already milling about outside the tent, preparing for the big day. Peter, now out of habit, strapped on his valuable sword. He would not wish to forget it … not today. Mother quickly handed him a meager handful of nuts.

"Breakfast," she declared.

Peter stretched again and shuffled outside, the nuts enclosed in his right hand. The sun had not yet reached the pale gray horizon, and the blank sky was still ashen gray, but people were already scurrying around hastily. Mr. Winslow and Mr. Kenelm were instructing Father, Cakechiwa, and Shamaro, who were loading the necessary goods—furs, bows and arrows, food, and the like—into the worn wooden boat. Mr. Wilson, Mr. Thomas, and Mr. Snows were chattering excitedly about the trip, and the women were fussing in a woman-like way over a turkey that must have been caught in the traps earlier this morning. *Good,* Peter thought, licking his lips, *we will have warm food to eat tonight.* An excited chill crawled over him, and he did not regret waking up early.

Andrew bounded joyfully up to Peter. "Hello, Peter," he greeted him.

"Hello, Andrew," Peter replied. "Oh, I just can't believe we are really going to participate in a real exploration trip!"

Andrew beamed. "Yes, we missed you last time."

"So," Peter inquired, "do you know anything new?"

"No," Andrew reported, "not yet at least." He turned his freckled face and stared up into the quickly lighting sky thoughtfully. Peter noticed that the cold crisp morning air had made it so that his warm breath appeared like puffs of smoke.

Peter wandered away, crunching on his small hard nuts. Andrew followed, remarking wishfully about how he missed the food back at Plymouth. The sun was just poking above the horizon when Mr. Kenelm announced that it was time to leave. Just as Peter was about to start walking back toward the shore, Elisabeth walked up to him and lovingly threw her little arms around his thin body. Peter smiled and gently returned her goodbye hug.

"You and Father are not going to get hurt, are you?" she asked worryingly in her quiet voice. Tears sprang up in her small blue eyes.

Peter smiled. "That is not in my plan. Don't you worry," he replied gently. "I tell you what I have a mind to do. When I come back, I will bring you some leaves and flowers from over there for you to look at." He smiled reassuringly. She rubbed her eyes and nodded.

"Be good, all right?" Peter requested.

"I will," she promised.

"And have a lot of fun playing with your sister and Charlotte."

"Yes," Elisabeth replied. "Where is Charlotte?"

Peter's eyes searched the camp. "I don't know," he replied, "but I'm sure she's around here somewhere. She is likely still sleeping."

"Peter," Father called. "Come along. We are going to leave."

"Oh, yes, sir!" Peter shouted.

Once everyone was gathered in the boat, a prayer was offered and the boat was slowly launched into the calm lake. Peter glanced over at the new oars. They were most likely the ugliest man-made wooden creations he had ever seen. They looked like giant, bumpy, lopsided wooden fish with extra-long tails, for the only knife they had carried with them was old, dull, and not intended for use in carving. The radiant sunrise had spread across the sky, splattering the sparse clouds with glowing orange, pink, and yellow. The water, which reflected this marvelous scene, was calm and cool, with a little disturbance here and there, when an unseen fish touched its surface from beneath.

The sun was just beginning to paint color on the silhouettes of the two flanking mountains and the armies of trees. The boat itself still reeked miserably from the miserable days before it had landed here. It made Peter's stomach wrench to remember. Andrew was quietly sitting directly across from Peter.

"I like it when we go on exploration trips like this," he commented dreamily, "because it makes me feel like … almost like we are … um … not just struggling to survive and stranded but are really making a life for ourselves."

"Yes," Peter agreed.

Andrew stared sadly off into the distance toward the direction of Plymouth—east. Peter knew that Andrew missed home terribly because that was where his old aunt lived. Peter wasn't familiar with any of his extended family. He only knew that somewhere, on a remote farm near Scrooby, England, he had a grandmother and grandfather, along with two uncles and three aunts on his father's side, who knew nothing of him. When his father had boldly fled his country because of his beliefs, he had literally "put his hand to the plow and not looked back." Mother had no family. Even so, Peter longed to hear the bustling of busy feet, to gaze upon a great ship being unloaded, and to smell the stench of grazing livestock. He wondered what would become of his family's tiny, cozy cabin that Father had labored to build on their first year in the New World. It seemed years ago since they had last seen home. In fact, sometimes Peter wondered if it had ever existed in the first place—or had those places and people been all a great dream? But every time these thoughts entered his mind, he would always remember something to convince him that he was mistaken: the clothes he was wearing that he remembered receiving for the first time (although they had been much finer then); his sister's little dolls (how they had possibly managed to survive the river journey, he didn't know); and, of course, his sword. All of that seemed so far off now. He imagined the friends of those who had been on board weeping because they supposed their companions had perished in the raging waters. He imagined Pastor Brewster preaching a memorial service for them all. It made him gloomy to imagine. Peter wondered if some of the cruel boys who had teased him would feel remorseful now that he was dead. *No*, Peter thought, *I must not think about this. Not now at least. Not today.*

For the rest of the time, Peter and Andrew discussed more pleasant things, and by the time the rowboat finally struck the farthest shore, over an hour later, Peter was in merry spirits. Soon they had organized groups of two and trekked off, taking great care not to become lost. The land on this far shore was gorgeous. The lush light green grass, the sun's yellow rays determinedly penetrating the branches of the healthy forest, ancient valley oaks, and the colorful, vibrant scattered wildflowers combined to create a peaceful and charming atmosphere. Peter smiled contentedly and perched on the edge of the boat next to Mr. Snows, who was scanning the forest alertly for any sign of danger. The battered rowboat tilted to one side wearily, a large pile of furs sitting on the far end of it. Most of the time all was still and quiet, dotted with bits of casual conversation, most of it centered on Indians.

Sometimes Peter could not get over the eerie feeling that someone was watching him, as if he and Mr. Snows were not the only ones present, but he automatically dismissed it as only a ridiculous notion. Peter could not help but wonder why the men had decided to bring so much fur to trade. Was it possible that they even caught that many animals since arriving? Perhaps the women had insisted. Peter was startled when he noticed the pile of equipment in the boat shift suddenly.

"Mr. Snows!" Peter exclaimed. "Look! It moved!"

"What moved?"

"Our pile of things! I could have sworn that it moved!"

They watched in surprise as a small coif-covered head slowly emerged. Soon they could fully view a small freckled face.

"Charlotte!" Mr. Snows exclaimed with shock. The young girl laughed nervously.

"Why ...? How did you get here? You were supposed to stay home!" Peter shouted disappointedly. He couldn't believe that she had the nerve to stow away.

"You and Andrew were coming," she protested, "so I wanted to come too."

"Well," Mr. Snows muttered reluctantly, "you can sit watch ... I suppose. There is nothing else for you to do."

Charlotte smiled. "Hooray!" she cheered excitedly.

Afterward, Charlotte received a detailed lecture from Mr. Snows about how terrible it is when children disobeyed their parents. (He was skilled at this because he had been a detention master back in

Plymouth.) Peter could not fathom how a five-year-old had been able to hide like that and stay still for so long—all without getting caught! He gazed back at the disheveled lump of furs, which had been greatly reduced in size now that the girl had crawled out.

When the others returned for lunch, they were annoyed to find Charlotte there, especially Andrew.

"You will be punished for this, young lady," Mr. Thomas, her father, warned.

"I'm hungry," Andrew announced, patting his stomach. "When do we eat?"

Peter smiled. *Good ole Andrew.*

"Right now, if Mr. Winslow approves," Father replied. Peter wasn't very hungry, and besides, the small mound of wilted herbs that he had been given was quite unappetizing anyway. But he courteously swallowed a few small bites for good measure. How he longed to eat a warm piece of that turkey tonight.

"Are you going to eat that?" Andrew asked greedily.

"No," Peter replied, generously pressing the remainder of his meager lunch into Andrew's hand.

"Thank you. I had to share my lunch with my little sister," Andrew explained with a trace of resentment in his voice. "How I wish she hadn't come."

"Me too," Peter agreed.

"How did she sneak in, anyway?"

"I don't know," Peter said with a sigh. "She was hiding beneath the pile of goods. But how she managed to hide in there is a mystery to me."

"That girl will do anything to get her own way. She'll probably slow down the whole expedition," Andrew complained.

"Maybe, but perhaps it is not quite as bad as we think."

The men briefly considered returning to the other side of the lake to drop off Charlotte and let the women know she was all right. But Charlotte claimed that she had told of her secret plan to Rebeccah and Elisabeth, and considering how Rebeccah enjoyed chattering, everybody would certainly be quickly informed about her whereabouts. And besides, it would waste the rest of the day to row all the way there and back.

"Do we have to go out again?" Charlie complained defiantly. "I hate it so, and my legs are tired."

Father, who had been Charlie's unfortunate partner as it came to groups of two, stared at the ground and rolled his eyes in exasperation.

The others took pity on him and had Charlie replaced with

someone else as his partner. A few other pairs were switched, so it did not appear to have been aimed directly at him.

As the rest of the day slowly wore on, it did not differ much from the first half, other than that Charlotte's mouth seemed unable to stop chattering and singing obnoxiously. She, of course, was staying near the boat with Peter and Mr. Snows as the men continued to wander through the nearby woods, searching for friendly Indians and taking mental notes. Slowly the sun sank below the distant snowcapped mountains and the sky grew dark. Shimmering silver stars appeared in the dark navy sky. Night had fallen. The men slowly reassembled and hastily prepared for the trip home. Peter climbed wearily into the boat and waited for everyone to be ready. He couldn't wait to arrive home and fill his stomach with some hearty dinner.

The pale ghostly moon, which reflected on the cold deep black water, glowed in a pure heavenly white. The mountains and trees were dark mysterious silhouettes against the enormous autumn night sky.

Mist-like clouds shifted restlessly across the great cosmic star tapestry. Pillars of smoke rose mysteriously out from the mountainsides, where the natives, whoever they were, dwelt. The fire, where the women were lovingly preparing their dinner, was like a tiny orange firefly on the distant shore. Everyone, even Charlotte, seemed to be too weary for conversation, so they rowed silently. The children all sat quietly near the back of the boat. The gentle rocking of the boat on the water was beginning to make Peter sleepy.

Cedar stuck his painted face above the dark surface of the water and silently gulped in the fresh and clear crisp air. His eyes searched the broad lake until they rediscovered the quiet small vessel paddling near the middle of Lake Honiton. Just then, Veenatch popped her head above the dark surface. Because it was so dark and the agentes were all wearing the smooth black beaver skin caps, it was difficult to discern who it was. A few yards behind him, another head popped up, presumably belonging to Mik or Pona-Pow. Early that morning, a few Orenean warriors had secretly swam to the spot where the boat's passengers would explore as sort of a protection against any opposing Tumitatakens from a distance. Keoko, who was somewhere in the water with them now, had charged them to "help them in any way possible." Now he and the agentes were silently stalking the boat to ensure that they made it home safely, without Tumitataken interference.

Keoko, who was a very strong man, could hold his breath for much longer than any of the agentes could. He was almost constantly nagging the children not to stay long above the surface of the water. (He also made sure they didn't stay under for too long.)

Cedar was thankful for the warm waterproof clothes. Without them, Cedar couldn't imagine how bitterly cold he would be in the frigid water. With one last long quiet sip of air, he sunk silently back beneath the surface.

Peter leaned his head sleepily against the side of the boat. His eyelids grew heavy. Charlie, who was growing quite bored, crept up stealthily behind Peter.

"Boo!" he shouted suddenly. Peter jumped in fright. Charlie snickered cruelly.

"Stop!" Peter retorted firmly. "Don't annoy me. Or I'll inform Mr. Winslow."

"Oh I am soooo scared," Charlie sneered sarcastically. "Little String Bean needs some help. Oh no!" he rattled with laughter. Peter sighed sadly and leaned his head against the side of the boat, away from Charlie, and closed his eyes. Charlie's foul words and cruel laughter rang repetitively in Peter's head. Suddenly, Charlie crept up behind Peter again and gave him a hard shove in the back.

"Stop!" Peter commanded angrily, "leave me alone! Must a man pay silver and diamonds to get a moment of sleep around these parts?" Charlie snickered again cheesily.

"Don't provoke him," Mr. Kenelm demanded defensively. Mr. Snows shot a rebuking glance at Charlie, who smirked nervously and shrank back.

I wish that he wouldn't loom over me like that, Charlie brooded. *But perhaps there is something else I can do to amuse myself.* Charlie's eyes rolled around searchingly at the other people around him. *Oh, say, look at that.* A crooked smirk formed on his dry lips. *It's Charlotte. Just sitting there, right at the rear of the boat.* Cautiously, Charlie crept up behind her and tried to snatch her little coif off her head. Charlotte, who only noticed he was there at the last minute, lunged backward forcefully to avoid him. Peter was trying to catch a few minutes' worth of zzz's and didn't realize what was happening until an ear-piercing scream and loud splash met his ears. Peter bolted upright alertly and glanced around. Andrew shrieked in panic. A pair of flailing arms disappeared beneath the surface.

"Charlotte!"

"What's going on back there?" one of the men shouted.

"Charlie threw Charlotte in the water!" Andrew wailed.

"I did not!" Charlie retorted, "I only startled her—that's all."

"Everyone in after her!"

Suddenly, chaos exploded. It all happened so quickly. Mr. Thomas was the first to plunge bravely into the cold, dark water, and Charlie, who seemed truly stunned by all the unexpected drama, was the last to slip awkwardly off the side. Suddenly, Peter was alone. Because he didn't know how to swim, Peter helplessly stayed put by himself. He expected them to surface quickly, carrying the sputtering little girl within moments, but as the seconds trickled away, his heart began to thump rapidly with worry. Where could she have sunk? Why was she not found? Was it too late?

There was chaos rapidly growing under the dark surface. Because it was so dark, it was next to impossible to see. The water was so frigid that some of the men almost considered giving up immediately. There were so many people frantically searching in one small area that a few of them mistakenly took one of the others for Charlotte. Finally, after about a minute, Mr. Kenelm secured his large hand around a small foot, which, unbeknownst to him, belonged to Pona-Pow, who quickly scrambled out of his grip. Every once in a while, one of them would surface for air, and this would cause an unwelcome spray of water to splash Peter's cold face and make a great deal of splashing. He was still stunned by all that had so unexpectedly occurred and still did not have all the details of what exactly Charlie had done. The idle rowboat drifted a little to the right.

Peter stared anxiously at the shimmering white reflection of the moon. He wished with all his heart right now that he could leap off the side of the boat and drag Charlotte to the surface. For Andrew's sake at least ... He couldn't imagine how panicked he would feel if it was one of *his* sisters; and it just as well might have been, for Charlotte and Rebeccah seemed to always be at one another's sides. He probably wouldn't be able to bear it if ... But what could he possibly do? Pray. Yes, that was what he should do. That would be the rescuers most effective resource. Peter pressed his cold white hands together and shut his blue eyes. He began his prayer with the old traditional words.

"Our Father, who art in Heaven ...," Peter mumbled. His mouth seemed dry as a desert, but once he began, words spilled off his tongue and he began to feel slightly less worried and afraid. Five minutes ... fifteen minutes ... thirty minutes ... No Charlotte. Every man silently knew that their rescue dive had turned into just a hunt for the body. A cold lump appeared in Peter's throat. Poor Andrew. Poor Mr. Thomas. Especially since a few years ago, they had already walked Mrs. Thomas to the shore of the Crystal Sea. Occasionally, Peter spotted Andrew's bluish face break the surface. How dreadfully cold and pale he looked in the moonlight. His eyes seemed so desperate and despairing. It made Peter's stomach twist. Finally, an exhausted blue Mr. Snows rolled back into the boat, shivering uncontrollably.

"Well?" Peter asked sadly.

"I ... It's useless ...," Mr. Snows mumbled hopelessly through his chattering teeth. "I ... It's ... a ... n-natural ... b-burial." Then he curled up tightly in a miserable ball beneath one of the benches and continued to shiver. Peter wished he had a blanket or towel to give him. One by one, the other shivering men climbed shakily back in, the last two being Father and Andrew.

"I ... Just a l-little more," Andrew begged. "J-ust one more try, p-please."

Mr. Thomas, who was staring at the floor, shook his head gravely. The oarsmen shakily reached for the oars and slowly began to paddle to shore. Peter noticed Father, who was huddled up in a miserable ball, shivering. Peter hated to watch him like this, so he crawled up behind him and gently tapped his numb shoulder.

"Wh-what is it, s-son?" Father stammered.

"May I sit by you?" Peter offered. "To keep you warm, sir?"

"Y-yes," Father whispered gratefully. "Th-thank you." His huge arms coiled around Peter, drawing him close against Father's cold dripping body to keep him warm. Peter was glad to be of some service. An icy breeze grazed the lake, sending a new round of shivers on everyone.

Andrew huddled near his father, staring silently into the dark water that had so suddenly swallowed his small five-year-old sister. Mr. Thomas's hand rested tenderly on his son's shivering shoulder.

And Charlie? He was huddled by himself near the edge of the crowded vessel, looking quite stunned and not Charlie-like. He had obviously not intended for his frivolous prank to go this far.

"A-are you all right, lad?" Mr. Snows inquired compassionately.

"Oh, y-yeah, fine," Charlie stammered, flustered. "Must be the cold." But Peter could discern that it wasn't really the cold. Was Charlie finally feeling a twinge of remorse?

The ride home seemed to last forever. The poor oarsmen, whose strong arms were still clumsy and numb from the cold, couldn't seem to tug at the oars correctly. Finally, the boat limped to the shore where the tent was located. Father, who was grateful for Peter's source of warmth, reluctantly released his grip on Peter and apologized for the fact that he had also gotten him damp. The men all stumbled awkwardly out of the boat and staggered numbly toward the tent. Rachel Cox ran joyfully out to meet them.

"Hello," she greeted gaily. "How did it go? We prepared some supper for …" She stopped dead in her tracks when she noticed that they were soaked and saw the distraught expressions on the men's faces. "What happened? Is there something wrong? Did the boat capsize? And where is Charlotte? We knew she had snuck out with you, but we—"

"Rachel," Mr. Winslow interrupted grimly, "Charlotte is dead. She drowned on the way back."

Rachel's face turned pale in horror. "Oh my," she gasped. "Oh my—that would explain why you all are so wet. Well … are …? You all should get close to the fire." She glanced suspiciously at her brother. "You didn't have anything to do with this, did you, Charlie?"

"I'm afraid he does," Mr. Winslow mumbled. Charlie hung his head shamefully. The men all quickly followed Rachel to the small fire, where they huddled eagerly. The women slowly passed out the plates of tender meat and listened to their sobering tale. Peter was hungry but didn't feel like eating. He forced a few tasteless bites down his dry throat for the women's sake. Mrs. Cox stared speechlessly at her son, who flushed sheepishly. No one wanted to break the silence.

"Peter," a small voice whispered behind him.

"Oh," Peter replied wearily, "hello, Elisabeth. Are you all right?"

She nodded quietly. Peter handed his small sister a handful of slightly wilted leaves and flowers that he had quickly gathered in the Sun's Ray Forest before they returned home.

"I didn't forget," Peter mumbled. Elisabeth nodded quietly.

"Thank you."

Everyone's worn clothes were almost completely dry about an hour later. Andrew stared solemnly at his untouched plate of roast turkey. The terrible reality that his sister was dead was finally beginning to sink in.

"What time is it?" Mrs. Wilson asked Father, who always carried his trusted pocket watch.

"A little past ten," Father replied sleepily. Mrs. Wilson nodded in thanks and cradled her sleeping babe.

Peter gazed sleepily up at the sparkling stars. He often wondered what stars really were and how high one would have to go to touch them. Suddenly, Andrew stood up and quickly walked away along the rocky beach. Soon his silhouette had almost blended in with the darkness around him.

"Where is Andrew going?" Mr. Winslow asked quietly.

"Well ... I don't know," Mr. Thomas mumbled. "I-I best go get him."

Poor Mr. Thomas. He looked so sorrowful and exhausted.

"No, sir," Peter volunteered. "I will go and get him. You may stay here and rest."

"Well, really, I ought to ... Well, I suppose it would do no harm. You may go and fetch him. Thank you very much. I'm ... tired ..."

Peter rose stiffly to his feet and walked away quickly into the blackness. He needed to keep a quick pace to catch up with his friend and was continually stumbling over loose rocks in the darkness. Finally, he managed to catch up with Andrew, whose face was turned out toward the lake. Peter grabbed hold of Andrew's sleeve to help keep up the pace. Andrew didn't acknowledge Peter's presence.

"Do you want me to go away?" Peter asked. Andrew shook his head slightly, still keeping his face turned out toward the lake.

"Are you all right?"

Andrew didn't respond. The two walked in silence for a few minutes. Then Andrew slowly turned his freckled face toward Peter, and Peter realized that tears were trickling silently out of his hazel eyes. Andrew could no longer contain his sobs. That must have been why he wouldn't show his face. Peter watched gingerly.

"Let's go home," he suggested quietly. Andrew nodded through his sobs.

Just before Peter was about to turn around, a sharp orange glow caught the corner of his eye. "What's that?" he asked curiously.

"What?" Andrew sniffed.

"Over there. It looks like a fire on the shore. Should we investigate?"

"N-no," Andrew declared shakily. "They might be dangerous."

"But if they *are* dangerous," Peter pointed out quietly, starting to get a little excited, "then we *really* must find out and warn everyone else." Andrew loudly choked back another sob. "And," Peter continued, "Remember when that little Indian boy back home used to teach us how to walk quietly in the brush?"

"Th-they'll see us," Andrew whispered.

"Not if we go into that clump of trees over there."

Andrew, who decided that a diversion from his thoughts and grief might actually be a welcome thing, followed Peter quietly. They both tiptoed into the clump of trees, Andrew whimpering pitifully. Peter turned around and pressed his finger to his lips in an attempt to quiet him down.

Moving silently through the brush, the two boys cautiously approached the small glowing blaze.

"Looks like no one's here," Peter declared quietly.

"That's odd," Andrew muttered, his voice shaky,

Peter noticed a rather suspicious lump or bundle right next to the small campfire. Suddenly, the lump sat upright. Peter's heart nearly stopped until he recognized the familiar form of a little girl's face in the moonlight.

"Charlotte? Is that you?" Andrew exclaimed, rushing up to his sister and nearly falling on top of her. Relief washed over Peter's mind.

"Oh, Andrew!" Charlotte exclaimed excitedly, obviously eager to speak. "Angels saved me. They were here! I saw them!" A huge smile spread across her freckled face. "I was sinking down in the cold water, and I was quite frightened. But then they took me up in the water and took me back to the shore!"

Peter sat excitedly down by the dying fire to warm his hands before they went to inform the others. She continued to rattle on.

"When I said I was cold, they made a fire for me!" She pointed excitedly to the tiny flickering fire. "Then they went home back off into the woods and I stayed here."

Peter was intrigued. Someone or something had obviously saved her.

"What did they look like?" Peter inquired.

"Funny thing," Charlotte continued, "is that I always thought angels wore white clothes, but these ones wore black. They wore black clothes all over. They were rather small too. They were very kind, though."

Andrew and Peter glanced questioningly at one another. It didn't exactly make sense. Were angels really guarding their camp?

CHAPTER VIII

The following is another entry from Charlie's journal:

Saturday, October 23, 1624

For once, I don't quite know what to say. The events that have recently taken place are too difficult to put into words. Something happened yesterday that thoroughly shocked and startled me. I think it shall haunt me forever. (Not that I can't handle it, of course.) I know you don't hear me writing often about my feelings, much less my conscience (which I didn't even know existed till last night). I can't bear to write about the horrible thing I have done, but I can say that I do believe that I almost murdered young Charlotte. How dreadful it would have been for me if I had.

I don't exactly know what happened when I was searching for her in the water, but I do know that it was something. It got me thinking about all the nasty things I have done. All the people I have hurt. I have never thought like this before. Not even after I got us stranded. And yes, I do firmly now admit that it was my doing. Sometimes I think that these new thoughts are just a passing phase that will soon leave me alone. Maybe if I start acting better for now, then this phase will eventually fade away. But what if it isn't just a phase? They always said that I would someday do something that would near scare the knickers off me—and that I would be less "troublesome" after that. Now I know what they meant.

Mr. Winslow fumbled searchingly through a small disorganized mound of gifts the Indians had given them. They had certainly been generous, and their useful gifts had made the lives of the stranded cluster of settlers much easier. Among the numerous gifts were many sturdy plain baskets of varied sizes, a handsome clay jar, which was adorned with many different-colored shapes and lines, a few bows and arrows, a large elaborate woven mat, and some raisins. They had used a small portion of the tepee, which the Indians had also gifted them, to store the few items in their possession. In another corner were stacked a few other jars and baskets (also gifts), full to the brim with dried berries and nuts for the winter. Even the younger girls were now laboring tirelessly with almost everyone else to cram as much preservable food into the baskets and jars as possible before the weather turned contrary.

Earlier that day, he had been feeling a little sick and so had stayed inside to get some rest, but he was now feeling better and had decided to gather some more acorns for a while and get some fresh air. He sighed with concern. They didn't even have enough space in the baskets to cram enough food to stretch even one week for them all. Mr. Winslow decided that they would probably need to trust in God to supply them with sustenance when the snow began to fall. He stretched and walked out into the bright sunshine.

Yesterday's rainstorm had delayed the work, and now everyone was scrambling to catch up. Women sat in a cluster chatting merrily by a large flat gray rock, where they were placing berries to dry. Others were diligently collecting nuts or more berries in the nearby forest or gathering the already dried berries and loading them into baskets. The rest of the men and boys, except for Shamaro, were out deer hunting.

"Hello," Rebeccah greeted cheerfully, waving to Mr. Winslow. He smiled and waved back. He was glad to observe everyone working so diligently and happily. Just as Mr. Winslow was about to wander into the forest to collect berries, he noticed Shamaro's stalky pillar-like silhouette standing silently by the large lake and gazing solemnly over its deep blue waters, his long braided black hair stirring slightly in the gentle breeze. Shamaro's hands limply gripped the handle on his large reed basket. Mr. Winslow debated in his mind whether to investigate and finally concluded that it might be wise to check on him. He slowly made his way over to Shamaro. Shamaro's rich dark eyes gazing sadly out over the peaceful, gorgeous waters. His dry lips were set in a solemn line.

"Are you well?" Mr. Winslow inquired with concern. Shamaro's lips pressed tighter together, and he nodded lightly. Mr. Winslow could guess what was on his mind.

"Are you thinking about home?"

"Yes," Shamaro replied gravely in his deep, heavy voice. "My people, my village, and"—he paused for a moment— "my family."

"Oh." Mr. Winslow sighed softly. "Do you have a wife?"

"Yes," Shamaro replied quickly, "and a baby daughter, but now ..." He sighed heavily and bit his lip. "I am afraid I will never see them again. I miss them very much. They think we are dead."

Mr. Winslow nodded understandingly.

"It makes my heart sad," Shamaro continued gravely, "not to see my little daughter grow up and to never be there to give her away in marriage."

"I am sorry," Mr. Winslow apologized solemnly. "I feel it is my responsibility for this whole issue. All I wanted was for us to have a little sun and fellowship. But then ..."

"No, no," Shamaro insisted, "it is not your fault that the waters carried us away. Even if it were ... I do not know if I could be angry at you. After all, you are the one who told us of the Jesus way. We, our entire tribe, are very grateful for that. If it were not for you, we would all still be perishing in our sin. I am sure that there will be much grief among us for you."

"Oh, no, no," Mr. Winslow corrected humbly. "It was God who really saved you. You all should be grateful to Him."

"Of course," Shamaro replied. "But if you had not come and told us, then we would still not know." Mr. Winslow smiled half-heartedly.

"Say," Shamaro inquired, "do you have a family at your home village?"

"Do you mean Plymouth? Why, yes, I do. I have a wife, whose name is Susanna. I also have two sons named Resolved and Peregrine. I miss them very much."

"Why did your family not come with us?" Shamaro asked.

"Little Peregrine had a runny nose. Susanna felt obligated to keep the two younger children at home while Kenelm and I saw to the picnic. After all, we had already invited everyone. I also invited my two brothers, John and Gilbert. They had various reasons for not attending. I miss them as well," Mr. Winslow explained. Whenever he glimpsed the married couples with their children, it made him miss his own family even more painfully.

"Say," Mr. Winslow inquired, "what about Cakechiwa? Does he have a family at home?"

"What ... him? No. Not one of his own yet. He is only, as you white men say it, fifteen years old. But I do believe he has a mother and father."

"He's only fifteen?"

"Yes," Shamaro replied. "He is mature. I think he almost enjoys the adventure of being stranded and having to fend for himself."

"He *is* mature for his years," Mr. Winslow commented. "It is sad to think that he may never marry among his people."

"It is all that Charlie boy's fault," Shamaro grumbled with a hint of bitterness in his voice.

Mr. Winslow sighed. "Perhaps," he counseled, "but we should not be angry toward him. I think he has learned his lesson well and is not likely to do anything like that again ... at least not in the near future."

"Perhaps you are right," Shamaro agreed, turning around and marching into the dense forest with his basket. "I am rapidly getting over it."

Cedar shoved a huge savory piece of salmon into his mouth.

"Goodness, Cedar," Zatch teased good-naturedly with a cheesy smile, "how many fish waes it that ya ate so far?"

"This est my fourth one," Cedar replied, swallowing the last morsel. "Very good."

"Wow," Zatch joked, "better be careful or ya will clear tha whole river of fish."

"Ha-ha," Cedar mumbled sarcastically, "and I see that *ya* have cleared … three and a half and rapidly progressing toward four. Not much less than me, I say."

"Well, i'test just good. That est all."

"Thanks be to Chief," Pona-Pow declared. "He cooked it."

It had been last night when the agentes and Keoko had rescued Charlotte from the lake, and now a heavy rain pattered outside from the dark sky.

"I'test starting to get dark earlier," Twii remarked. "I like it that way."

They were all sitting cross-legged around the small fire where the fish had been roasted, munching on the savory fish off flat wooden slabs.

"Well," Keoko announced, "we all must go to bed early tonight because I'spose we must go fishing again early in tha morning. We need to catch more of them to preserve fo tha winter before tha fishing season est over. Or else we will be surviving on pine needles forever."

"Really?" Cedar asked excitedly. He enjoyed fishing much more than training.

Keoko nodded in affirmation. "Just be careful not to fall in. Many drown from falling out of tha canoe."

Cedar grinned excitedly and shifted his weight. A sweep of wind sprayed the rain violently onto the roof in vast torrents. A loud, bright clap of lightning lit up the little hut, momentarily causing Mik and Pona-Pow to jump a little.

"I'test really raining severely out there," Veenatch commented.

"Tha crops need it," Chief pointed out wearily. He sighed. "Oh my ... I'm getting sleepy. Perhaps I ... will go to sleep soon."

Cedar pitied old Chief. He stared absentmindedly into the hot orange blaze. Chief was so old that his withered legs could no longer hold him up, although it was evident that he desired to stand again and ...

Suddenly, a soaked, shivering Tumitataken man, whose hair and red and yellow facial paint were ruined by the rain, stumbled into the small cabin.

"Ruex!" Keoko exclaimed, "Come closer to tha fire. I'test raging rain out there. Hopefully ya will'a'not die of cold."

"Th-thank you," Ruex panted. Cedar knew Ruex a little. Just before the agentes had been hired, Chief and Keoko had been missing a crucial link to the agente plan. How would they be informed when the Tumitataken chief would be planning his attacks? Then Ruex, who was one of the lesser chiefs of the Tumitataken tribe, showed up. Because he was sympathetic to the Orenean plight, Ruex had agreed to risk much to inform the Oreneans when the Tumitataken warriors were planning to assemble, although he could not be there himself. Chief was very grateful to him for this. After all, not only was he risking his highly regarded chief's position, but also providing information about secret battle plans to the Oreneans would be considered high treason—a crime punishable by death. There would most likely be a little unplanned excitement tonight. There always was when Ruex showed up. Keoko draped a warm fur blanket around their guest's shivering body.

"Est there a reason why ya have come to us, Ruex?" Chief asked anxiously.

"Yes, Great Chief Palkente," Ruex replied respectfully.

"Just call me Chief," the old man corrected.

"Oh, yes," Ruex replied hurriedly. "There is a meeting being planned among the Tumitataken warriors. I believe it is quite secret. I cannot be certain that it is relevant to us, but ... I will not take any chances."

"Good. There est no room in this operation fo people who take chances," Chief declared.

"When under tha sun est this meeting?" Keoko demanded hurriedly.

"Tonight. I think there is just enough time for you to hurry there before the meeting starts."

Cedar knew what to do even before he was instructed. He and the other boys hurried frantically to Keoko's cabin. That was where they stored their black suits. He waited impatiently in Keoko's dark, still dwelling for Mik to finish slipping on his tight black suit. The agentes, who had been strictly trained to dress in less than a minute, took turns in the cramped, private corner, veiled only by a bear hide hanging from the ceiling.

As soon as Mik was dressed, Cedar dashed behind the bear hide to scramble hastily into his black suit. Cedar tugged up on the tall and tight boot-like moccasins, which extended up just past his knees. He would need to remember to ask the chief for some better-fitting moccasins. Next Cedar slipped on a pair of loose pants that extended down a little past the knee. This would aid him in running faster. Then he quickly fitted on the headpiece and face mask. This was like a tight coarse black bag over his head with a gap over the eyes and forehead. Next came the close-fitting black shirt and gloves. Then Cedar burst out of the closet and darted feverishly back to Chief's house, fighting through heavy torrents of rain. Most of the girls were already in their uniforms. Cedar tilted back his head and squinted his eyes shut so Keoko could smudge the uncovered part of his face with slimy waterproof green and brown paint. Twii rushed in uniform out of the veiled corner.

"Are ya all here?' Chief asked.

"No," Veenatch replied. "Number Four est'a'not here yet." (As previously mentioned, the agentes answered by their numbers instead of names when in uniform.)

Soon Zatch stumbled hurryingly in.

"Are ya all here now?" Chief repeated.

"Yes," they all replied. The agentes all knelt around their chief.

"Oh, come now," Ruex sighed, "be reasonable. You don't have nearly enough time to pray. That meeting will start very soon. You need to let them go now!"

"We allowed them a few minutes to dress," Chief reasoned. "Praying est much more important." After a short, hurried prayer, Keoko rushed them outside and hurriedly rowed them to shore. It was pouring so hard that a puddle of water formed on the floor of the canoe. The dark lake was alive with the large falling drops of water, and huge dark clouds veiled the moon and stars, causing pitch-black darkness. Cedar jumped out onto the soggy pine needles as the canoe hit land again.

"Hurry," Keoko reminded them, "and be careful. May El Shaddai protect ya."

Cedar nodded and dashed off into the woods with the other agentes. Although it was dark, Mighty Cedar and all of the other agentes were already trained to know their way in the darkness. Huge drops of water rolled off the pine needles, and a few landed on Cedar's head. Suddenly, Cedar ran head-on into a post. *I must have reached tha horse hut,* he thought as he carefully but quickly felt his way to the entrance.

The horses made little excited noises as the children swung the leather flap open. A sudden clap of lightning from the outside momentarily illuminated the familiar gentle faces of the beasts. Chief's messenger pigeons cooed from the perch not far above. The floor was littered with bird and horse droppings and dried grass. In the darkness, a horse eagerly nudged Cedar's hand, hoping for a treat. Quickly Cedar hopped onto its bare back and waited for someone else to join him. Because there were only three horses, there had to be two people for each one, and soon Zatch hopped on back with him. Number Three and Six had mounted one of the others, as had Number Five and Two. One by one, each horse exited awkwardly back out into the rain. (Orenean horses have never been of the best quality.)

Now came the easy part—the horses knew the way completely on their own. They sped down the mountain—sometimes galloping, sometimes slowing to a canter for a distance to conserve the horses' energy. The unceasing rain continued to pour down profusely out of the dark sky. Occasionally a slimy wet pine branch would smack him in the face or the horse would stumble as it cautiously waded through a stream, many of which had been nonexistent before the storm had started. The ones that had originally been there had swelled to at least twice their size from all the rainfall.

Finally, a while later, Cedar realized from the flat topography of the land that they were in the Sun's Ray Forest. The contentious rain was starting to transform the squishy soil on the forest's floor into sticky, slimy, slippery mud mixed with dirt-caked blades of grass. Suddenly, another clap of lightning lit up the image of the immense Mt. Moggog—the mountain opposite the one on which the Orenean chief lived. Somehow he had to get this exhausted horse up part of the mountainside … and fast.

"Ya think we are too late?" Zatch shouted above all of the noise.

"I hope not," Cedar replied. He shivered in the cold.

Quickening the horses pace a little, they then set off to conquer the mountainside … or at least the foot of it. The journey upward proved difficult because the rain had made the leaves and pine needles on the slope dreadfully slick and contrary.

The rain was not about to subside one bit as far as Cedar could tell, but he hoped it would. Finally, an exhausted lot of soaked agentes and their horses staggered into the other discreet stable near the outskirts of the great Tumitataken village. Smoke drifted up above the trees from the many scattered dwellings, where cozy fires warmed sleeping Tumitataken families. It made Cedar wish, once again, that he was at home sleeping. On foot, they raced as fast as they could to the edge of the village, hiding silently behind trees.

"Over there …," panted Pona-Pow. She extended her finger toward the royal "palace." Frightening guards stood solemnly alert for any sign of movement near the entrance. Twii-Wa placed her gloved finger to her lips and silently motioned for the rest of the numbers to follow. They crept silently up around the back, where there grew much tall brush against the back wall. They wormed their way as quietly as possible into its sharp wet branches.

"Do ya think zey have begun yet, Number One?" Twii whispered to Cedar over the patter of the thick rain.

"I … I do'a'not know, Number Three," he replied quietly.

"Who under tha sun will go and see?"

"Um … I'spose I shall."

Cedar eased out of the brush and quietly fingered the dark wall for the ladder. Finally, his fingers found a small wooden step jutting out of the side of the wall. He planted his numb, cold foot on it and determinedly forced his sore, wobbly legs to carry him up the slick, steep ladder. Finally, he reached the top step and felt quietly along the wall again. He slid his gloved fingers into a notch and tugged at it gruffly, almost losing his footing. A section of the clay wall fell off easily into his hands with a small amount of noise. Cedar held his breath for a tense second, hoping desperately that nobody had heard him. In front of him, inside that hole, was a secret crawl space, one that even the great serpent chief didn't know about. It was a small dark space beneath the platform, where Mittowan would be addressing his band of trusted warriors. No noises came from the outer room.

Cedar crawled noiselessly into the small dark space and peeked out a small air hole, which allowed a few rays of golden firelight to leak into the secret crawl space, to investigate what was going on in the room. Surprised, Cedar discovered that they had, just as planned, arrived early. The only one in the large, empty room was one of the chief's many small daughters, innocently chasing a colorful clay and gold ball across the dusty dirt floor. Cedar smiled and bit his lower lip.

Zatch poked his head curiously into the opening. "What under tha sun est going on, Number One? Ya are almost as slow as Chief," he said in as soft a voice as he could.

"That est'a'not nice. Chief can'a'not help being slow. But I think we are early. There est'a'not anyone in there except fo a little child," Cedar reported excitedly. Zatch crept back down the ladder to inform the others that it was safe to sneak in.

Although the inside air was stuffy and a little putrid, Cedar was grateful for the rest and warmth from the small fire in the middle of the room. He squirmed in the meager space. Cedar was only ten, but he was so large for his age that he was the tallest agente. Because of this, his number was "One." Veenatch, who was second tallest, was Number Two; Twii, the third tallest, was Three; and so on. Soon all six agentes had wedged themselves silently in, the smallest near the front, just as they had been taught. The agentes were trained not to speak or jostle against the walls, as this might give them away, although the walls were padded with bundles of dried weeds to buff any small noise. Cedar was breathing as quietly as possible when a tall, burly warrior marched into the large room. His body, which was clothed only by a small loincloth, was streaked solid with vivid blue and black paint that had been slightly damaged by the rain. He leaned his long stone-headed seven-foot spear against the clay wall. The child scampered away in fear.

"I'm early. Story of my life, I suppose," he mumbled, tossing his long feather-braided lock of shiny black hair. The rest of the warriors, which were all attired much like the first, trickled in small clusters into the large room, all wet from the rain. The agentes were more silent than ever.

Then the drums began to pound wildly as the great serpent himself pranced arrogantly into the assembly. He was just as unsavory-looking as ever. Like his warriors, he was streaked with black and blue paint except for his face, which was solid bright yellow. Behind him he dragged a long brown deerskin train—an extension of his headdress. Branching out from his huge colorful feather headdress were two long extra-sharp deer antlers with many pure white branches and points, which were adorned with tacky strings of homely beads that swayed as he moved. As he walked up to the front, the others dropped reverently on their hands and knees, letting their heads hang between their burly arms. Cedar held his breath as the man strode closer and closer, finally stepping onto the platform directly on top of the agentes. Twii carefully slid a tiny scrap of wood out of her small dress pouch so she could take notes. The warriors slowly rose to their feet.

"Warriors of the great and wonderful Tumitataken tribe," Mittowan boomed. "As always, we are here to destroy the Oreneans and put an end to their evil ways. Am I not correct, men?"

In response, they all let out deep warlike howls and shook their spears boisterously in the air.

We never did anything to them, Cedar thought angrily.

"And so," Mittowan continued, "I, your strong, great, mighty, spirit-guided, superior, humble chief, have summoned you tonight to make another surprise attack on one of their small villages."

Cedar paid close attention.

"Why small villages?" a warrior shouted with frustration. "Why can't we just pick off one of their trading posts like Pina, which is only a few miles from here? When we attack small villages, we just are—"

"*Silence!*" Mittowan bellowed angrily. The agentes could tell that Mittowan was in an irritable mood. "Just do what I say! And I say that we *will* dispose of one of the smaller villages. The larger ones are in the power of the spirits, and I cannot afford to anger them at such a crucial time. I have my eye on a village at the top of the mountain Nogogg, the one which is called Chickapookanogganawan. It is the highest village in Orenea. It is not the largest Orenean dwelling place, but I heard that there are many hardy villagers there that will fetch very good labor value here. They are also located remotely, so perhaps they will be less prepared for attack. I gathered this information from a divine source." (He had actually heard it from a wife of his).

"When do we attack, Great Chief?" the leader of the warriors asked with a smirk.

"Tonight," Mittowan declared.

Tonight!

Twii motioned for the agentes to slip back out into the dark. Veenatch was the first to crawl out. As he slipped back into the hammering rain, Cedar could hear the chief still booming out orders, instructing as to which warriors would go. The agentes knew exactly where to head now. Cedar didn't have the way well memorized in this part of the Mogogg Mountain, and he struggled with finding his way uphill in the rain and dark. The cold wind mercilessly hurled torrents of rain in Cedar's eyes, but he ran wholeheartedly, with a newfound sense of urgency.

Finally, he nearly collapsed in the tiny dingy village of Pina! It's dark muddy huts reminded Cedar of a smaller version of Ore-Cita, without a gong in layout. Just behind the last building, the agentes stumbled wearily up to a cave.

"Asa! Asa!" Pona-Pow shouted frantically into its small dark opening between gasps. Almost immediately, a tall and handsome sturdy man with a torch peeked his head out.

"Ya must remember not to shout my name like that. That could get me in terrible trouble."

"Oh," Pona-Pow whispered between heaving breaths, "I'm sorry."

"We ... just came from tha Tumitataken chief's meeting with his warriors," Twii exclaimed exhaustedly. "Zey are planning to attack a village on top of Nogogg Mountain! I'test Chickapookanogganawan ... I think."

"When under tha sun will zey do this?" Asa demanded.

"Tonight."

"Tonight!"

"Yes. We must hustle."

"Yes, indeed. Ya boys go get tha horses. Ya girls come and help me get things ready. Tha other Orenean warriors are at tha Orenean border. So it looks like I will need ya six. I, my wife, and any others of us we could spare."

The Orenean warriors were an extensive secret cluster of Oreneans who helped free captives, evacuate villages, and gallantly fight off small bands of hostile Tumitataken warriors. Asa, who was an Orenean war chief, was the leader of the warriors. He and his wife lived in hiding in this cave, where the warriors met because they were wanted by the Tumitatakens. Any Tumitataken had absolute permission to shoot and kill any Orenean warrior on-site without consequence. Right now only one warrior other than Asa was present in the cave. Cedar sprinted with all the strength he could muster up to a crude run-down stable where the horses lived.

In Orenea, horses were so rare that many youths Cedar's age had rarely laid eyes on one. Cedar staggered into the small stable, which was so dilapidated that it was difficult to shake off the sensation that it would suddenly crash down on one's head. In the small stalls stood fourteen lovely horses, which neighed happily when the boys entered. At the other dark end of the stable were tied three large cooing pigeons that were used to deliver messages from one place to another. The rain continued to clatter on the roof.

"How many do we need?" Cedar asked hurriedly.

"Four … No! … Um … five," Zatch replied feverishly. They frantically untied the five finest horses, and Cedar and Zatch each mounted one. It felt wonderful to sit down again.

"Here are tha horses," Zatch called as they quickly cantered back up to Asa, whose wife immediately flung a large roll of furry things over the soft wet back of a golden stallion.

"Are ya sure that ya need us?" Cedar asked, "We have never gone to help in an evacuation previously. We do'a'not know what to do."

"We *need* ya this time around," Asa replied, feverishly strapping on his bow. "My wife and I, along with this lone young warrior here, simply can'a'not do this alone. We need more people."

115

"But consider," the woman pointed out, "zey are but children."

"And I am sure there are also children in tha village we are serving who need rescuing," Asa declared. "If our noble chief would consider these young ones old enough and honorable enough to serve our people, than I'spose zey will do. Besides, zey *must* do; we have no other option." The other warrior, who could not have been more than seven or eight years older than Cedar, stared doubtfully down at his new young coworkers.

"What under tha sun est that fo?" Mik whispered shyly to Zatch, pointing to the bundle of goods Asa's wife was loading onto the horse.

Asa's wife overheard and quickly replied, "I'test snow coats and other warm things … along with some weapons and a map."

"Snow coats and other warm things?" Pona-Pow asked curiously.

"Because tha village where we are going est very high up on tha mountain. I'spose it could be snowing there."

"Snowing!" Twii exclaimed. "This early? Autumn est'a'not even over yet!"

"Yes, I'm afraid that will delay us. But we can be grateful that we do'a'not need to travel there in tha winter. Zey sometimes get fifteen feet of snow!"

"Fifteen feet," Cedar marveled breathlessly with a long whistle.

"All right, people, come here!" Asa summoned. He carefully unrolled a large parchment map. It was a crude Indian map of all of Orenea, which had many blue and yellow dots. The yellow dots represented Orenean villages, and the blue represented Tumitataken ones.

"We are here," Asa explained, pointing near a particularly large yellow dot on the side of Mogogg Mountain, which represented Pina.

"Chickapookanogganawan est here." He slid his finger over to a smaller yellow dot on the top of Mount Nogogg. I'test tha highest village in Orenea, and est on tha very summit of that higher mountain. I'spose it will take us hours to reach it, but we should make it there before sunrise. We must hurry if we will reach it before tha

Tumitatakens do—if we leave immediately. We have brought warm clothes in case we end up needing them. But before we leave, we must pray to El Shaddai. We will need His help fo sure."

Asa bowed his head reverently and quickly spilled the words out of his mouth. "All right," he announced breathlessly after the rushed prayer, "everybody mount. Number Two, ya ride with my wife. Number Three, ya ride with ya brother, Number Five. Number Four, ya ride with ya sister, Number Six. Number One, ya ride with me. Oh, and young warrior, ya ride with ... um ... yaself and tha goods."

Everyone feverishly jumped onto the bareback horses and galloped off into the wet, dark woods. Cedar sighed with excitement. He was riding behind, the one who was considered one of the bravest men in Orenea. Normally the agentes' job ended when they delivered the message to Asa. But tonight things would be different ... a lot different. Cedar wondered if Chief and Keoko would grow concerned when they took so long to return.

Asa, along with his wife and the warrior, were clad in all black like the agentes, except for the fact that they didn't wear gloves or headpieces. Instead, their faces were adorned in a few stripes of black on the cheek, and a shiny golden headband, which bore Orenea's insignia, was fastened tightly around their heads. The horse that Mighty Cedar and Asa were riding was a majestic black stallion named Midnight. It was the fastest, strongest, loyalist one of all. Cedar wondered what the other young people in his village would think if they knew what kinds of adventures he was having. Frigid rain rushed onto Cedar's face as the stallion gracefully leaped a creek, which had been a small, humble trickle before the storm had transformed it into a raging rush of rapids. Lightning flashed in the sky.

Because of all the mud caused by the relentless rain, the horses couldn't gallop as fast as their potential. Often the horses were slowed to a gallop or even a walk to conserve their precious energy. Despite the constant nagging pounding of the rain, the steady bumpy gallop of the horses, and the occasional clap of the lightning, Cedar was steadily becoming drowsy. Wearily Cedar leaned his head against Asa's back and somehow managed to doze off. He continued on a steady cycle of dozing off for a few minutes and shifting into consciousness for a few minutes for what seemed like quite a long while.

When he finally shook himself to full wakefulness, Cedar noticed that although there had been few lower on the mountain, there were almost no oaks anymore; numerous pines had replaced them. The horses had to wade a few narrow frigid rivers from time to time, and the steep, slick uphill path was difficult on the horses. Sometimes in the light of the lightning, he glimpsed the golden horse that his friend Zatch and his sister were galloping on behind him. He was grateful for the privilege of using the rare animals. He was awakened (apparently he had fallen asleep again) much later by something wet and icy plopping onto his cold stinging nose and realized that what was pouring out of the dark clouds was no longer rain but sleet. As they continued to advance uphill, the sleet further transformed into swirls of icy pure white snow ... an abundance of snow. Cedar shivered uncomfortably as the frigid wind swirled the thick armies of white snowflakes around him and into his watering eyes. It was still pitch dark.

"I-I-I- c-c-cold out here," Veenatch called from behind them.

Cedar was startled to hear a voice from the man in front of him who had remained so silent all these hours.

"Ya are right!" Asa shouted back. "Let us stop here fo a moment."

He hopped agilely off the horse and into the newly sticking snow as the other horses reeled to a stop behind him. Asa tossed each traveler a warm fur coat and insulated moccasins. Cedar, who wasn't going to bother dismounting to save time, gratefully pulled off his tall boot-like black moccasins and slipped on the new ones. Oh, how refreshingly warm they were! After Cedar had finished sliding into his bulky jacket, Asa remounted the tired black stallion but didn't begin to move immediately.

"Listen, everyone!" he shouted behind him over the howling wind. "We are in tha midst of a classic autumn mountain blizzard. Thankfully this est'a'not half as dangerous as a winter blizzard. Tha snow est growing to be deep. Be careful. If ya go alone into tha blizzard and get lost, ya do'a'not come out."

Then, with a shout and a clip of the reins, the hardy horse began to canter reluctantly on. In a flash of lightning, Cedar glimpsed ahead of him a few wisps of smoke rising in the midst of the swirling thick snowflakes.

"Est that it?" Cedar asked hopefully. Asa glanced over doubtfully at the cluster of cozy huts.

"No, that est'a'not it!" he shouted loudly enough for everyone to hear. He cocked his head toward a large sign that read Fawn's Nose Village.

Cedar sighed in frustration. *Will this dreadful journey ever end?* Lightning flashed again. How strange snow looked in the light of the lightning! Ahead of him, Cedar's numb ears caught the unmistakable roar of a raging river.

"Est that directly ahead of us?" Cedar asked worryingly.

"I'm afraid i'test actually," Asa replied. Suddenly, Cedar found that they had come before a wide surging icy river. It gushed violently and foamed profusely, adding to the dark chaos. The sound was almost deafening. A huge log raced along uncontrollably in the racing, rushing, romping rapids of the river and was violently dashed to a hundred pieces on a large rock. This all intimidated Cedar greatly. How was it possible to cross?

"We can'a'not allow tha horses to carry us through," the warrior declared wearily. "It would be too much fo them."

"We are'a'not going to have to swim that, are we?" Twii wailed.

"Oh, no. No. Do'a'not worry about that," Asa replied. "Tha current est way too strong, and tha water est too cold anyway. Ya would die the second ya hit tha water."

"Then how are we going to cross?" she cried despairingly.

"Do ya see that bridge over there?" Asa pointed with a shivering finger. Again lightning flashed.

"Tha one that looks like i'test about to fall apart?" Zatch asked.

"Yes," Asa declared. "Onward!"

"Are ya sure this est safe?" Cedar inquired nervously. "Tha water … It …"

"Roars?" Asa guessed.

"Uh … yes, I'spose."

Asa nodded. "There est a reason why zey call this tha Dragon River."

"Dragon River? Est that because i'test so loud?"

"Partially," Asa explained. "It only gets like this part of tha year."

He leaned in and said as quietly as could be heard, "Have ya ever read tha books of Job in tha holy scroll?"

"Yes," Cedar replied. "Part of it."

"Well, legend says a leviathan once lived in this river."

"Leviathan?" Cedar asked.

Asa nodded. "T'twaes a dragon that could shoot flames from its mouth, so zey say."

"Est that true?" Cedar asked skeptically. "Waes there really a leviathan in these waters?"

Asa straightened his back. "Probably not," he replied, "I'spose we should be going on now." He clicked the reins confidently. The antsy horse whined and inched back nervously. "It's all right, Midnight," he coaxed.

Cedar thought the talk about the leviathan was fascinating, but he still did not have an answer to the question about the bridge being safe.

It took a lot of doing to convince the beasts to move over to the bridge. Upon closer examination, Cedar realized that the river was really in a sort of gorge. But the rapids were so wild and profuse that the gorge was almost filled to the top with violent bursts of white foam. Somehow they managed to coax the horses to step onto the frail old vine bridge. The bridge, which was barely wide enough for a buffalo cart to cross, swayed a little in the strong wind. The snow rushed down. Lightning flashed. The river roared. The bridge swayed.

Praying that the bridge would not snap, Cedar clung to Asa's thick winter shirt as the horses inched gingerly along on the unstable surface. More than once, the wind swayed the bridge precariously, but Asa, who seemed almost magical with horses, somehow managed to keep them from getting spooked or panicked long enough to get them across. It seemed like hours before they finally stepped back onto solid ground again on the other side of the river. Cedar was pleasantly surprised by the unexpected strength hidden in these aged vine bridges.

Asa sighed shakily. "Are ya all right, Number One?" he asked shakily. Cedar could only nod as he gulped down the lump in his throat. "Come to think of it," Asa commented thoughtfully, "we probably should'a'not have brought tha horses across and simply walked, but what est done est done." With that, they continued along a trail together. The exhausted horses trudged along wearily. Lightning flashed once more. Suddenly, welcoming wisps of smoke caught Cedar's eye.

"Look ahead! Est that Chickapookanogganawan?" Twii asked hopefully.

"Yes!" Asa exclaimed excitedly, "I'test! We are here!"

Before them was a sign that read Chickapookanogganawan.

Asa immediately began to spit out orders above the roar of the wind.

"Number Five and Number Two, ya tie up tha horses. Number Six and Number Three, ya alert tha villagers. Number Four, ya go find a decent buffalo cart. Number One, ya have strength; sound tha gong."

Because they had been sitting on horseback for the past hours, it took Cedar a few moments to regain his balance. The icy wet snow started to seep through his thick winter moccasins. His eyes scanned the barely visible dark shapes of the village. He jogged effortfully through the deepening snow toward the huge gong, which sat in the center of the cluster of small dwellings. Hurriedly Cedar's numb fingers dug through the snow and found a long wooden stick with a hard ball on the end. He was so cold that he didn't think his fingers and toes could stand one more minute. Numbly he lifted the stick above his head and swung it at the gong powerfully. Again and again and again he beat the old gong, creating deafening noises that echoed over the barren snow-covered rocks. At the sound of the wild beating of the loud gong, frightened people scurried fearfully out of their small, humble homes and out into the blizzard as Twii raced from hut to hut, banging urgently on the sturdy walls and shouting at the top of her lungs.

Near the middle of the humble cluster of homes, there was a large

Know Board blanketed in crude pictures of current happenings in the surrounding area, posted up on sticks atop a wide platform, which was only slightly visible through the swirling snow. Cedar rubbed his stinging runny nose. Tears from the cold grew in his eyes. Cedar quickly brushed them away before they could run down his face or freeze, causing his cheeks to be even *more* numb. Shivering, Asa stepped in front of the small, terrified huddle of villagers. His voice was loud but rushed.

"Dear Oreneans, tha Tumitatakens will attack at any moment. Please stay calm and load any things ya wish to bring with ya into tha buffalo cart that ... will pull up right here any moment. Try to go faster than ya can. We must leave im-m-mediately."

The people immediately sprang into action, darting in and out of the houses, carrying various personal items. Cedar was dreadfully tempted to dash into one of the houses to warm his numb hands by a hot fire just for a moment, but he wisely decided to stay out. Asa's caring wife was skillfully helping to comfort a few whimpering children, and the warrior was carrying a stunned withered old woman into the large cart, which Zatch had driven over. A pair of grumpy shaggy buffalo grunted unhappily and shook out their thick fur coats. The pile of things inside quickly grew larger. Everyone had accumulated into the cart until there were almost layers of people.

"Let me drive, Number Four," Asa offered.

"Oh, no. Asa ... I mean, Chief. I can. I know how."

"Get off Number Four," Asa ordered. "I will drive this time. Ya do'a'not have quite as much experience."

Veenatch mentally counted the villagers. "Zey are all here!" she shouted confidently.

"Are ya sure?"

"Yes."

"Then let's go!"

Then, with one clip of the reins, the grunting, lowing buffalo lumbered reluctantly off into the snowy forest. The huge round wooden wheels groaned loudly. Cedar situated himself on top of the large pile of stuff and peered over the edge of the cart. Oh, how frigid it was! All twelve villagers sat behind him, worried expressions twisting their cold faces. They had probably heard rumors of the seemingly distant tension below them, never expecting that it would find their high secluded hamlet. How terrified they must feel now. They had probably also heard of the Orenean warriors dressed in black who rode in on those strange creatures called horses, never expecting them to arrive here. Some of the other agentes galloped ahead on horseback with Asa, while two of the girls made sure that everyone was secure in the large rumbling cart. A small baby screamed loudly when catching sight of the monstrous rushing rapids of the river.

They could not see at all in front of them, but somehow Asa found the bridge again and managed to coax the bison to carefully step onto it. Warily the bison inched onward. Cedar thought he felt a vine snap. The journey back across the bridge was even more distressing than the first crossing. Cedar could sense every pound of the heavy cart weighing down on the thin layer of woven vines, which was the only thing separating them from the surging water below. The water was so close to the bottom of the bridge that sometimes Cedar could feel the spray on his already dismally numb face. It was easy to imagine a leviathan feeling at home down there.

The buffalo continued to advance forward slowly. The bridge often swayed slightly in the strong wind. Little children whimpered and cried fearfully. Gingerly Cedar peeked over the edge of the cart. He couldn't see anything, only hear the loud, intimidating noise of powerfully rushing water. Asa's words kept playing over and over again in his mind ... *"Ya would die tha second ya hit tha water."* What if he fell? Snow had quickly begun to accumulate on Cedar's head, but Cedar was afraid that if he even moved his hand back to brush it off, he would either shift too much weight in the cart or lose his balance and tumble off the side. His eyes stung. The wind howled. The river gushed. Was it just his imagination or did Cedar glimpse a fiery orange glow down in the gorge? Inch by precarious inch, the cart slowly progressed forward. Cedar was nearly convinced that the bridge had expanded in length since they had last crossed. Shouldn't they have made it to the other side by now? It seemed hours since they had first started the cross. And what about the Tumitatakens ... and the danger of freezing to death?

Finally, with a blunt bump, the wheels of the cart safely found land again. Relief and thankfulness washed over him as they continued to rumble on through the snow to the nearby village of Fawn's Nose.

Even after they had crossed the bridge, the going downhill was much more difficult than the struggling uphill. Needless to say, Cedar was very relieved when they finally reached the village. The residents hospitably took the desperate people of Chickapookanogganawan into their warm homes.

"Ya poor, poor souls," fussed the woman who had helped them get dry clothes and had started to heat up some water for them to soak their hands in. "Ya are half frozen too. I'test a very fortunate thing that ya were'a'not out there longer. No telling what could have become of ya all." The agentes would need to stay the short remainder of the night.

Cedar was relieved to finally sit down by a hot fire, where he and the other unmarried boys would sleep. Zatch huddled close to the fire. Icy air rushed in from beneath the canvas entrance, but by the cozy fire, one could scarcely notice. It had only snowed near the very summit of Mount Nogogg, and the rest of the land had received a heavy shower of cool rain. Cedar wrapped the blanket tightly around his shoulders as his limbs slowly thawed.

"That waes probably tha hardest mission of all," Cedar mumbled sleepily.

"No doubt," Zatch replied softly, his heavy eyelids half-closed. "I'm glad we were'a'not too late. I'spose all that waes well worth it. Chief will be proud sick of us." He stared dreamily into the fire. "I wish we had gotten to look at tha land from up here in tha daylight. I heard ya can see all Orenea from tha top."

"Maybe tomorrow morning," Mighty Cedar replied. "Good night, Zatch ... I mean, Number Four."

Cedar had almost forgotten that they were still in uniform. Wearily Zatch lay down his head and dozed off. His deep sleeping breaths reminded Cedar of how tired he was. The water for soaking their hands in was still warming up, but while the thought of soaking his numb fingers was tempting, Cedar was too tired to care. But before he pulled off his soaked coat and moccasins to fall asleep, one of the small refugees who was about five years old spoke up. His dark eyes twinkled and gleamed in the fire's soft glow.

"When I grow bigger," he whispered with a small grin, "I want to be a hero just like ya are."

Cedar smiled weakly. "By tha time ya grow bigger, we will hopefully not be needed."

"Look at that red-and-black bird," Peter asserted, pointing to a bird clinging to the bark near the top of a tree. The early morning sunlight shined brilliantly through the branches, which were still wet from the previous night's rainstorm. "It looks like a woodpecker."

Elisabeth turned and stared, intrigued at the rather large red-crested bird, which was pecking vivaciously at the rough grayish bark with its long hard beak. "Why is it hitting its head on the tree?" Elisabeth asked with concern. "Will it be hurt?"

"It's actually not hitting hit its head," Peter explained. "It's pecking with its beak—like chickens back home do."

Peter and Elisabeth would normally be helping the adults find food, but Mother had graciously allowed them to take a short walk together because she knew that they enjoyed it very much and it could only do them good. Otherwise, Peter would still be hunting with the men or setting the endless berries to dry. Peter dreaded the tedious chore of setting the berries to dry. He had been even more dismayed when he and Andrew had been assigned to labor alongside Charlie. But one thing that puzzled Peter was that the expected bucketloads of teasing and ridicule that normally followed the troublemaker around were never delivered. Charlie had simply kept to himself and his basket of blackberries. Curiously, Peter had arranged his berries in a pattern on the rock where the berries were drying. Surely Charlie would notice and cruelly criticize him for being childish. But Charlie had simply glanced at the berries and then at Peter and continued his work. What was more was that he had only griped once about the day's chores! Come to think of it, Charlie had not teased Peter in a few days, which, at least as Peter suspected, was Charlie's favorite activity. What had changed?

Elisabeth quietly crept closer to the tree's trunk as not to frighten the creature. A sweet small smile appeared on her face as she continued to watch it. Peter couldn't help but grin too because, unlike Rebeccah, Elisabeth was shy and rarely smiled.

The sky was a deep light blue ocean with occasional white puffy cloud ships journeying slowly across its endless expanse. A wisp of wind gently stirred the towering trees, and the bird fluttered away. busily.

"Come now, Elisabeth," Peter announced. "Let's go back home."

"Why?" she asked, looking disappointed. "Are your legs sore?"

"No," Peter replied. "I just think that we must get back because our walk is almost spent. We must work."

After a few minutes of silence, Elisabeth spoke again shyly. "Why did you say we were going home?" she asked.

"Huh?"

"But the tent isn't home. Our home is back at Plymouth."

Peter stared sadly at the ground and nodded solemnly. He didn't miss many of the other children back home. Most of them either made fun of him or stayed away because they felt sorry for Peter. Even so, this land could never truly be his home, even if the kind Indians offered him and his family a successful, happy life among them. Peter had expected to raise his children in a home that he had built himself if he was ever strong enough to lift those huge, heavy wooden beams. He desired to sit them on his lap and proudly tell them the history of the great settlement in which they lived and which he had helped found. He might buy his wife some nice things from a ship from England or enjoyable toys for his children. Peter had wondered why God would allow a godly group of faithful people to build a large successful settlement but not allow them to enjoy it. It was the home Peter and his family had suffered and paid so much blood, sweat, and tears to help found, and it seemed cruel to be snatched from it now.

"Will we ever go home?" Elisabeth whined.

"We'll see," Peter mumbled doubtfully, "but we should still be grateful that God spared our lives. If the odds had prevailed, we would all be dead. As it is, He has allowed our lives to continue. And I am glad that *you* are alive. There was a time in that boat where I was sure that you or Rebeccah must have been knocked over the side at some point because of the waves and sharp turns. I was quite relieved to find you both alive and well."

Elisabeth stared sweetly into Peter's eyes. "Because you love me?"

"Yes, I suppose," Peter replied, taking up her small hand and squeezing it affectionately. "Now come along. I don't fancy getting scolded by Mr. Snows again."

It was the following morning before the agentes were finally able to leave the mountain peak village of Chickapookanoganawan and return to Chief's isolated home. The deep snow was only beginning to melt as the weary grunting horses stumbled their way down the steep, slick slope. Veenatch retold the tale of what had happened in her mind because she wanted to remember it precisely for when they returned to the chief. After the tense evacuation, which took place just in time, the Tumitatakens had crept up on the tiny village only to discover it was deserted. The unprepared, underdressed warriors had almost given up the climb when the snow began to fall a little way down, and they were almost relieved that they didn't need to do any dirty work and could turn away from the bitter cold, but they did take the liberty of burning down the small meeting/church house, if not only to keep from freezing to death.

"Well, well," Asa declared when they encountered the frozen body of a Tumitataken warrior on the bridge. "Though zey be many and we be few, we win out because we come prepared." He patted his thick fur coat. "Had zey brought warm things to put on and planned things out, zey probably would have beaten us to Chickapookinogganawan and this poor soul here would likely be living still. Always remember, tha greatest mistake any war chief can make in a battle est to over-recruit and under-plan." The young warrior, who was riding in front, nodded in agreement.

No one else spoke as they carefully guided the horses down the slope. It took more than four hours full before they finally trooped wearily back to Pina.

The village was not busy, so the agentes were able to sneak unnoticed into the small cave behind the far hut. The rest of the warriors who had returned earlier that morning, were relieved that their faithful leader, his wife, and the other warriors had returned and were unharmed.

"We returned and found out ya were gone," the oldest one explained. "We were worried something had happened to ya. We are glad to see ya are all right."

They all enjoyed a hardy lunch of chewy raisins, tender venison, and cool water in the dark, cozy cave and listened intently to the stories of the other warriors about their recent adventure, also telling their own. Veenatch enjoyed listening to their tale of the warriors' successful assault on an outgoing foreign trading party that had been attempting to smuggle five slaves out of Orenea. There was a sign at Orenea's entrance that proudly warned military action if anyone attempted to smuggle captured Oreneans out of Orenea.

That was exactly what the Black Warriors had done to a rebellious trading party who had willfully defied the order. Veenatch was pleased when the agentes continued to quickly trek home alone on foot after lunch. It felt refreshing to stretch her cramped legs after riding on a horse so long. Veenatch hoped that Chief and Keoko would not be worried about their whereabouts. She knew well how panicky Keoko could be when he was worried. Finally, the tired party reached the familiar old pond with the two adjoining islands right in the center. Although it had only been a day, it seemed to Veenatch as if it had been a long while since they had laid eyes on the place, that, a majority of the time, the agentes called home. After Cedar, blasted the gold-plastered whistle loudly, Keoko jumped energetically into their small canoe and rowed it skillfully to the mainland. Veenatch knew what Keoko would say next. Sure enough …

"Goodness' sakes!" Keoko exclaimed with relief. "We were worried crazy about ya. We thought tha Tumitatakens had skinned ya alive! I hope ya are ashamed—truly ashamed!"

He will think differently of our adventure when we tell him what we really did, Veenatch thought with a smile. Once the agentes had settled comfortably back into the chief's cozy cabin and changed out of their tight, damp, and itchy uniforms, which had long since begun to sag and twist uncomfortably, they crowded around Chief to relay the tale. Chief smiled proudly after they had all finished telling him the tale.

"Well done," he declared approvingly.

"Sometimes I do'a'not know how under tha sun ya do these things. Keoko has indeed trained ya well." Keoko nodded respectfully. "But I must admit," Chief continued, "I waes growing worried about ya when ya still had'a'not returned when tha sun rose this morning."

"I'm sorry, Chief," Twii replied sincerely.

"It took us a while to get back," Veenatch declared.

"Say," Chief remarked thoughtfully, "when under tha sun waes tha last time ya had a vacation to return to ya families?"

Veenatch's face lit up at the mention of going back to her village, The Golden Heart. She loved returning home. It provided the much-needed opportunity to be, and be around, normal people. Zatch, who normally kept track of these things, wrinkled his forehead thoughtfully.

"I do'a'not remember," he replied sheepishly.

"Well then, I'spose i'test about time," Chief declared.

"Really?" Twii squealed excitedly. "We get to go home?"

Chief smiled broadly. "Yes, ya may—but fo only a couple of days. We can'a'not spare ya fo long. Now, now ... stop jumping around and squealing like savages. Ya must rest up and then leave. Tomorrow est tha Sabbath, but I'spose it will only take ya an hour or two to get there."

"Unless it rains," Keoko added.

Darkness had settled over Orenea. Clouds shifted restlessly over the hazy white moon as a lone owl hooted eerily in the distance. Extravagantly painted warriors stood silently in the large meeting room in Mittowan's palace-like hut. Torches flickered cheerlessly in the corners of the place, making their smooth painted bodies glisten. A few of the lesser chiefs, or magicians, of the Tumitatakens slumped solemnly and motionless on a large dull woven mat near the wall. Because of the fearful silence that hung in the stinky, stuffy, stagnant air, no one dared speak. Not all of the higher chiefs were present, and everyone felt as if something dreadful was about to happen. Suddenly, the drummers began to pound their drums wildly. The Tumitataken chief Mittowan himself was marching arrogantly into the thick congregation of warriors. They bowed reverently as his large red bare feet pranced past them, making smooth prints in the loose dust; his stern, angry face was gazing superiorly on the others in the hut, an evil look in his intimidating brown eyes. Mittowan's longest, most elegant headdress dragged on the ground behind him. Once he had reached the front, he stomped up on the platform and raised his large hand authoritatively. Immediately the hollow drumming silenced and the warriors arose shakily.

"Warriors of the Tumitatakens," he began, "you might be curious as to why I have summoned you back this early after our last ...

advancement. But I have already devised another major plan. This time I would like a quarter of all of the warriors to be involved in this attack."

"A quarter of them, Great Chief?" a lesser chief asked timidly. "We normally only commission less than a sixth. Those tiny villages fall as easily as a stick leaning against a tree."

"Yes, indeed they do," the Great Serpent replied, "but I really want to make sure that this one does fall for sure. And don't tell anyone about this, you hear? I have a feeling one of you is leaking information. The Oreneans seem to have eyes and ears everywhere. Either that or they have made alliances with the spirits of the rivers and trees. They obviously are trying to spare the villages. It makes me so frustrated."

"But, Chief Mittowan," one of the magicians pointed out, "the Oreneans can't have made messengers of the spirits of the rivers and the trees. You know very well that the Oreneans refuse to worship or appease any supernatural thing other than their one El Shaddai."

"I suppose so," Mittowan agreed angrily, "and that is why we must hate them. But they are getting their information from somewhere, and I have my suspicions about who is at the source. That is why I have not informed Angry Stick, Sitting Vulture, Reux, and some of the other lower chiefs about this meeting, and I expect you to keep it secret also. But now to the reason why you were summoned here … I have another plan for an attack. We will now wipe out that annoying little white man's settlement by Lake Honiton. It will be very easy to take down. If the residents are strong, healthy, and fit to work, you may take them back with you to labor. The rest you may kill. We will be advancing tomorrow night just before sunset. Burn the tepee and take those you will keep alive. Make sure not one escapes."

CHAPTER IX

Peter sat down heavily beneath a tall pine tree. Hunger pangs rolled up and down his body. He was pleased that another long and difficult day of hard work was over and it was finally time to eat the evening meal. The heavy burnt scent of campfire smoke drifted into Peter's nose, and with it was the delicious savory smell of roasting turkey. The men were clustered together, lively discussing the things that men like to talk about, and the women were clustered together around the smoky glowing cooking fire and lively chattering about the things that women like to chatter about.

Today the mysterious Indians had left for them a large winding of coarse thread and a brittle bone needle, which the women were thrilled about because it meant they could finally repair the numerous rips and tears in the clothing. They were still clueless about who was sending the gifts so secretly, and they were anxious to find out. Yesterday morning Mr. Kenelm and Mr. Wilson had woken up in the wee hours of the morning to try to find their generous giver, but no one came. Mr. Snows had risen in the night *this* morning as well, but he carelessly dozed off, and by the time he roused again, the Indians had gone already. Andrew wandered up to Peter and plopped comfortably down beside him.

"I'm hungry," he announced.

"You're always hungry," Peter joked playfully with a smile. The younger girls, who were clustered behind the colorful tepee, were playing contentedly with their battered dolls, and Charlie was sitting, unusually silent, with the men.

Andrew leaned forward. "Do you know why Charlie is acting so … well … strange?" Andrew asked in a low voice.

"I was wondering the same thing myself," Peter replied softly "But I hope it lasts. I could get used to living without his teasing and bothering us."

Just then Rachel approached them carrying two plates of steaming meat. "Would you two gentlemen like some supper?" she asked playfully with a warm smile.

"Yes, please, ma'am," the boys replied, eagerly accepting the battered wooden plates.

"We will be asking the blessing soon and then you may eat," she explained before walking briskly away.

Peter sighed as the warm, savory aroma of the hot meat floated into his nostrils. The smell made his stomach growl impatiently. Finally, after a prayer that seemed to last much too long, Peter and Andrew began to heartily devour the tender turkey. Soon, although he had only consumed scarcely more than half the plate, Peter pushed the plate away from him. He leaned leisurely against the tree and patted his stomach.

"Are you going to eat that?" Andrew asked greedily.

Peter smiled. "You may have it, Andrew."

"Thanks," Andrew replied, eagerly seizing the plate.

Peter stared wearily out over the lake's blue waters, which were reflecting the beautiful glowing sunset. He sighed wearily.

"I heard that Mr. Kenelm will be telling one of his world-famous stories at the fire tonight," Andrew informed him excitedly.

"Really?" Peter replied enthusiastically. Andrew grinned and nodded. "That will be fun. I'll look forward to it."

Rachel walked up again. "Would any of you boys like a little more?"

Andrew sat upright quickly. "There's more?" he asked.

For goodness' sakes, Peter wondered, *how can that boy fit so much food in his stomach?* Just then, Peter thought he heard an unusual noise in the woods, but when he turned around, he didn't notice anything unusual.

The distant darkening horizon was robed in a glowing sunset as the two boys relaxed and enjoyed the few hours before it was time to sleep again. The small weakening fire crackled cozily.

"Let's play Nine Men's Morris," Andrew suggested.

"Good idea."

Andrew arranged their pieces on the "board" that Peter carved out of the dirt, and they began to play. The sun set a little lower in the sky, and some of the grown-ups began to prepare to go to bed.

Peter rolled one of his small round gray stones, which acted as playing pieces, across the clay board and grinned victoriously. Andrew sighed and raised his hands in surrender.

"How do you always win? You are starting to not be fun to play with anymore!"

Peter shrugged. "Lots of practice I suppose. I just enjoy playing it a great deal."

"Me too," Andrew agreed. "So did most boys back home. I know it isn't a game for girls, but I did try to teach it to Charlotte. It didn't work out too well. I suppose she is just too young to under—"

Suddenly the terrible bloodthirsty shrieks of the angry Tumitataken warriors rang out from all around the place. The tepee burst into flames. Surprised and afraid, Andrew jumped back and Peter fearfully let out a loud cry. Savage warriors coated in a bright layer of blue and stripes of black leaped agilely into the clearing, shrieking violently and raising their bows, long spears, tomahawks, and stone daggers. An arrow missed Peter by only a few inches. On the other side, a host of more warriors leaped out, some dressed in black and wearing black face paint with dark green or brown stripes.

"Run, Peter, run!" Andrew shouted frantically.

But Peter's legs were frozen to the ground, and, except for his eyes, which were darting around in a panic, he was motionless as a stone. His heart pounded wildly in his chest.

"Run, Peter, *run!*" Andrew repeated.

Finally, Peter leaped to his feet and bolted for the woods with all his heart and soul and all that his thin and clumsy short legs could offer. Chaos had fallen over everyone, and they were all racing frantically in different directions, knowing it was useless to fight. Arrows shot all around Peter aimlessly. Blindly he reached over and jerked his sword out of its sheath. He didn't know why he did that—it just seemed like the right thing to do at such a time. Then, after he had finally almost set foot in the dark forest, Peter felt the butt of a tomahawk ram bluntly into his ribs from behind. The sword flew out of his hand and struck the ground with a loud clamor, and Peter tumbled face-first to the rocky ground. The blow nearly knocked the wind clear out of him, but for only a second or two. When he revived, he could feel himself being roughly dragged off the ground and securely tucked under the burly painted arm of a Tumitataken warrior like a bundle of sticks. Peter's heart was pounding as rapidly as the flapping of a hummingbird's wings. Panic flooded all over him. His back throbbed where he had been struck.

If I scream, Peter decided, *maybe someone will hear me and come help me.* So Peter began to scream and wail wildly at the top of his lungs.

"Help, somebody! Please … anybody!" He struggled desperately like a wild animal in a trap, but with every squirm, the Tumitatakens' firm lock seemed to tighten.

"Help, please!"

"Quiet, you little fire-headed devil," the young warrior snapped gruffly in a tongue that Peter couldn't understand. "I'm taking you to the war chief."

The Tumitataken war chief, who was a little lower than the great serpent himself, was not much of a better man than Mittowan and was much favored by him. The young warrior bowed and smiled proudly.

"I have taken one of them," he declared proudly, displaying his squirming, screaming prisoner. The war chief's colorful light headdress shimmered in the last of the fading sunset's glow. The tall man took one quick glance at Peter. "Well," the warrior said impatiently, "should I tie it up to bring home?"

"No," the war chief grunted. "Too scrawny. Probably wouldn't last a single moon at labor. You should have known that and taken care of it on the spot. Take it away. You know what to do. Kill it."

"What's the use of capturing them if I can't earn profit from it," he muttered grumblingly.

"I said to do away with it!" the war chief shouted impatiently. "You younger warriors have yet to learn that a weak laborer is no laborer at all. So do us all a favor and get rid of it."

"But ... But he is just a young child."

"Do not think of them as children. Think of them as merely ... failed business transactions. Now go and waste no more time."

The warrior sighed and walked away obediently. Peter couldn't understand the words of what the war chief had commanded, but from the tone of his voice, he did understand part of what it had meant. He began to struggle and scream even more desperately.

"Oh God!" he pleaded helplessly. "Have mercy on me, please! *Please!*"

Time seemed to slide before his eyes very slowly. The warrior carelessly threw Peter to the ground and pinned Peter's arms to the ground with his knees. Peter watched the warrior slide a stone dagger out of his belt and raise it above him. The warrior paused for a moment, his fingers curled around the knife precariously, for although he had been trained to do away with victims, he was quite inexperienced. Although the prisoner that he had caught might be the enemy and was supposedly not fully human, it still had arms and legs, eyes and a mouth, and breathing lungs and a beating heart. And it yelled and screamed, just like Tumitataken boys did. Peter let out one last loud and final shriek, waiting for the Indian to plunge the jagged blade into his chest. But instead, the extended hand was yanked away swiftly by another hand. It was Father. Father easily pinned the warrior's hand with the dagger to the ground with his large foot and tried to pry the other arm of the warrior off his son. The next few moments were a jumbled blur. Peter caught a glimpse of a smudge of Father's brown beard, a hint of the darkening sky, and a glance at the burning tepee. The next thing he knew, he was lying safely in the thick brush and Father was gently shaking him.

"Peter, Peter! Are you all right son?" Peter's body stopped squirming, and he relaxed and found himself staring into his father's concerned face.

"I ... then ... are ... he ...," Peter's words spilled out of his mouth in a jumbled mess. His heart pounded in his ears, and his heavy rapid breathing had not yet calmed.

"All is well. You are all right," Father soothed softly.

As the reality that he had almost died snuck into him, Peter realized that he was trembling slightly. For a moment, he thought he might cry, but he didn't—real men never cried. Zealous battle cries and the loud ping of arrow strings echoed from the nearby shore into his ears. How quickly everything had happened.

"Th-thank you, Father," Peter mumbled shakily. He truly was very grateful. Father, who was trembling a little himself, nodded solemnly.

"Are you all right, Peter?"

"Y-yes. My back hurts a little, but not much ..."

Without a word, Father immediately rolled Peter gently onto his stomach to examine his son's large purple bruise where the tomahawk had collided with his back. "Oh my, that's a beauty," he muttered thoughtfully. "Does it hurt a lot?"

"Yes, sir ... for a bruise at least." Father nodded and thoroughly examined Peter's back again.

"All right, Peter," he announced, "I'm going to push a little on your side. Tell me if you feel any pain." Gently Father applied a little pressure to each of Peter's small well-defined ribs.

"What are you doing?" Peter asked curiously.

"I'm checking to see if any of your ribs are broken," Father explained.

"Broken?" Peter exclaimed, a little startled. "It doesn't hurt that terribly. I don't think any of my ribs could be broken."

"Neither do I," Father replied. "I'm just making sure."

Suddenly, there was an angry shout from outside the small, cramped cove of brush. One of the long curved stone swords thrashed blindly into the brush inches from the back of Father's head. The Tumitataken, who obviously hadn't noticed the two defenseless white men hiding within, loudly called something else out toward the lake. Neither dared move. They both waited in suspense, still as statues. They hadn't yet been discovered because the man was gazing away, but all the warrior had to do was turn his head ... Peter's heart was pounding so loudly in his ears that Peter almost imagined that the brutal attacker could hear it. Then, after the few longest seconds of Peter's life, the brightly painted warrior finally darted agilely off into the deep, dark, dangerous woods.

"Thanks be to God," Father whispered gratefully. "He is surely protecting us."

Peter nodded sincerely in agreement. It was difficult to believe the contrary, although he was still shaking fearfully.

Father glanced around searchingly. "Well," he declared softly, "we surely can't stay here."

"Then where will we go?" Peter asked, slowly sitting up.

Father pointed out through the bushes to a tiny wooded island in the middle of the deep blue lake, which was growing black as the last remnant of the sun slowly disappeared below the distant peaks, burying the chaos in darkness.

"Do you see? We will be safe there," Father explained. "You don't know how to swim yet do you?"

Peter shook his head silently.

"Then get on my back."

"But will I be too heavy?"

"No. I have swum with heavier loads before. Now quickly! Who knows when another Indian will come and find us!"

Peter crawled carefully onto his father's large back. Father steadily rose to his feet and crept stealthily to the edge of the dark woods toward the lake. Because the fighting was so far away up the shore from Father's clever hiding spot, Peter couldn't make out any of it except for a few confusing silhouettes leaping, shouting, and fighting in front of the large glowing orange fire, which was all that was left of the tent. Putrid smoke floated into his nostrils. Peter's stomach tied itself in sickening knots. He and his father had survived the siege, but what about Mother, Rebeccah, Elisabeth, Andrew and all the other close friends? The gothic yellow moon glowed solemnly behind a sheer gown of clouds as it surfaced slowly above the distant peaks. After he had glanced around quickly to assure that he wasn't being watched, Father gingerly scurried across the rocky clay shore and ducked behind a large gray boulder.

"Are you ready son?" he whispered. Peter nodded and filled his lungs and cheeks with cool air. Father waded hip deep into the water and hastily took one more glance around him. Peter took one last look at the horrific scene. Something wasn't right. There seemed to be a lot of fighting! It was not unexpected for a battle, but how were a few inexperienced men and women able to fight the vast multitude of warriors? And fighting with what? Father slid down into the dark water.

The water was so cold that Peter's body was stunned for a moment or two. Father surfaced to take a glance at the destination and to take a quick gulp of air and then dove skillfully back down into the deep dark water. Peter coiled his skinny arms and legs tighter around his father as the freezing water quickly drenched him and his clothes. Father continued to swim heartily far beneath the water, and Peter's lungs started to burn uncomfortably from lack of oxygen.

Finally, Father began to swim upward and broke the surface of the water. Peter gasped, sputtered, and choked desperately for air. A cool breeze grazed the surface of the vast lake, causing Peter to shudder miserably. The tiny island, which was still a hopelessly long distance away, was a large black speck in the faint moonlight.

Father sucked in a mouthful of air and dove under again. It seemed like an agonizing eternity before he finally rolled wearily onto the rocky pine needle–carpeted shore of the island. Peter wound his arms tightly around his numb, shivering body and tucked his knees under his chin. His teeth chattered uncontrollably.

"P-Peter," Father sputtered between chattering teeth. "Are y-you all right?"

Peter coughed and sputtered in reply. Father rolled on top him gently to block the cool wind, which seemed much, much colder when rushing against a soaked cold body. He squeezed his shivering son tightly, trying to share the little precious warmth left in between them. The clouds had quickly shifted over the moon, and the only light left was a glowing orange speck on the distant lakeshore, which was the flickering fire that had devoured their tent. Peter imagined wishfully where he would be if the warriors had not attacked. He would be dry and secure and curled up asleep peacefully with his warm blanket and pillow and his family all huddled up around him. All would be normal and peaceful. Why did those cruel warriors have to spoil everything? Why, indeed! Had they not previously left generous gifts? How cruel to allow the settlers to grow comfortable and to act friendly toward them only to stab them suddenly in the back as soon as they turned around!

Because of how flat and broad the lake was and the way noises bounced off the landscape, they could still clearly hear the loud, hideous war noises echoing across the shore clearly. But after a long while, the sounds gradually died away until all was silent … too silent. The orange speck flickered a little lower.

Father bickered with himself unsurely in his mind whether or not to swim back. If they stayed, the Indians might discover them and cleverly surround the lake to starve them off the island. Or even worse, what if some of the others lay wounded and in need of help?

And the thought of huddling close to that fire was tempting, although it would involve getting drenched again on the way.

Father glanced over at Peter as he slowly eased himself up. Both of them were still shivering miserably. "P-Peter," Father whispered gently, shaking his son. "G-get up. We are g-going b-back to the shore."

Peter groaned loudly.

"N-no, no," He shuddered, pleading. "Not back in the cold water again. P-please …"

"We m-must, son. Now g-get up."

"No … It's just t-too cold."

Father sighed shakily. "Th-there is a f-fire," Father explained. "Y-you can get warm …"

Peter groaned and reluctantly crawled onto Father's broad back, hooking his arms and legs securely once more around his father's sides. Father uttered a quiet prayer before plunging again into the dark water, and the previous process repeated itself. This time the water seemed even colder than before. A cool night breeze scaled the shoreline as exhausted, cold, and drenched Father finally rolled onto the shore. Because the moon was still hidden by clouds, everything that wasn't near the hot orange blaze was smothered in pitch blackness. With his painfully numb hands, he gently pried Peter's shivering arms off him. Everything was silent and still. The large fire gave off a little crackle cheerlessly from atop a large gray mound of powdered ash—their tepee. Peter coiled his thin arms tightly around his scrawny body and tucked his knees against his chest, shivering uncontrollably. His teeth chattered loudly.

Father, who was much too cold to think of anything except getting warm, quickly scooped up his son and headed for the fire, being careful not to accidently step on any hot coals. Gently he placed Peter near the ashes by the fire and held out his numb hands to savor the refreshing warmth.

Although he was still shivering, Peter relaxed a little and waited for himself to thaw and dry. Oh, how wonderful the warmth felt!

Father rung out his soaked shirt and let it dry by the fire, and Peter slowly sat up and did the same. Peter's pale white skin was coated in tiny goose bumps. Nearby, in the woods, a lone owl hooted eerily. Did those same woods hide armed Indians waiting alertly to pounce? Or did they contain a tiny group of raged, frightened refugees who were hiding from them? Peter nourished a burning hope in his heart that at least a few of them had survived. He didn't dare consider otherwise. Peter leaned forward to hold his shivering hands near the warm flames. About a half hour passed, and Peter's soaked clothes were beginning to dry slowly.

"I feel achy," Peter complained.

"That's good, son," his father explained. "That means you are starting to thaw and get warmer."

He slid out his heavy metal pocket watch. "Ten o'clock sharp," he declared.

Peter ran his fingers through his short curly red hair. He prayed a sincere prayer of thanks that he was alive and all right. The fire shot out another spark, which stung Peter in the hand mildly. When he glanced up, Peter noticed that Father was staring solemnly into the fire. Peter could tell what was on his mind.

"Father," Peter asked hesitantly, "where is Mother … and the twins?" The words clogged Peter's throat almost as if they didn't want to be spoken. Father stared down at his lap sadly, as if that was the dreaded question he knew was bound to be asked.

"Peter, I … don't know," he confessed solemnly.

"But what do you *think*?" Peter urged. Father bit his lip thoughtfully, "Please," Peter begged, although he didn't know if he wanted to hear the reply. "I must know. You can tell me. I'm eleven years old now." He straightened his back erectly.

Father gave in. "All right, son. I-I'm not sure, but unless God worked a miracle, there is little chance that any of them … survived."

"No!" Peter snapped almost automatically, his eyes wide. He turned his face away shakily toward the blackness. He didn't wish for his father to realize that he was scared. But Father seemed to

143

somehow see through him and placed his hand gently on Peter's scrawny shoulder. Peter shuddered and shakily rubbed his arms with his hands, trying to fight back tears.

"I know. I'm afraid too. God forgive me. I am afraid. We must pray Peter. Pray as hard as you can. God will be with us." Peter nodded shakily. "Peter, there is still hope," Father quickly added. "I said unless God works a miracle. And that is quite possible."

"Miracle?" Peter inquired curiously, trying to change the subject. "Do you mean like Charlotte's angels? Do you think they were here?" Father cocked his large head in thought for a moment.

"I don't know about Charlotte's angels," he pondered. "That is very bizarre."

Peter yawned wearily and nodded. "Why wouldn't they be real?" he asked softly. "Don't you believe in angels?"

"Yes, son," his father speculated. "Of course I believe in angels. But dressed in black? And Charlotte is so little. She could have been mistaken or made it up easily."

"But how else could she have made it to shore? I assume she didn't know how to swim. Especially not that far," Peter said thoughtfully.

Father chuckled half-heartedly. "No, she could not," he agreed. "I didn't say it wasn't possible ... but there are other possibilities. Perhaps Indians rescued her."

"Indians?" Peter asked with surprise. "The same ones that attacked us?"

"That is another thing that baffles me," Father mumbled absentmindedly. "I don't understand why they would act friendly toward us first, then ... Perhaps we did something to anger them accidently."

"It *is* fun to think of angels ...," Peter mumbled sleepily with a yawn.

Father glanced over at his son, whose eyes were half-closed and his weary head hanging in fatigue.

"Go to sleep, Peter," Father urged. "You have been through much in the past hours. Your body needs rest."

"Won't you sleep also?" Peter asked courteously.

"With your mother and sisters missing …? I don't think I could," he mumbled.

Peter curled up by the flame, and his father tenderly placed his hand on Peter's slight chest to pray a blessing over him, like he did almost every night. When Father concluded the prayer, he discovered that the tender, familiar drone of his deep voice had quickly lulled Peter into a weary, deep, troubled sleep. *He must have really needed it,* he thought with a sigh.

He noticed that a large fragment of the burnt tepee had not burned completely. Carefully he felt underneath to make sure it was not too hot. Gently he pulled it up over his son, like a blanket, until he was completely covered and warm. While Peter slept heavily by the fire, Father slowly wandered around the camp to search for any of the others who might be hiding around the clearing. He found Mr. Winslow's beaten, battered hat on the clay ground. *This doesn't necessarily mean anything bad,* he thought nervously. *It could have easily blown off.* There were also many deserted war weapons strewn around in a disorderly manner.

Father also discovered Peter's sword, which lay on the ground near the edge of the woods—just as it had been left. In addition, he found Peter and Andrew's game of Nine Men's Morris untouched, just as it was. Father picked up Peter's sword and tucked it under his arm.

Eventually, Father returned to the fire, which had grown smaller. Peter stirred restlessly in his sleep from beneath the parched scrap of tent as his father wearily seated himself and started to brush off Mr. Winslow's hat. Suddenly, Peter bolted upright, his eyes wide. He was panting in panic, his heart racing wildly. A large salty drop of sweat rolled slowly down his neck.

"Peter!" his father exclaimed. "Are you all right?"

"Father?"

"It is I, son."

Unable to speak, Peter nodded and slowly lowered himself back down.

"Was it a nightmare?" Father asked softly.

"Y-yes, sir," Peter croaked hoarsely. He didn't remember anything about the terrible dream, but he did know that it was certainly the most terrible nightmare he had ever experienced. Father slid Peter into his large arms and squeezed him tightly. The boy closed his eyes and bit his lower lip.

"What if they're gone?" he blurted out.

"We mustn't think like that," Father scolded. "There is still hope. Pray, Peter. Keep praying."

Peter nodded in agreement and silently prayed again. "Please help our friends and family," he begged desperately. After his prayer was finished, Peter realized that he felt a little better. He glanced peacefully at his father. "Do you think—?"

"Wait ... Shhh," his father interrupted softly, cocking his head attentively.

"What?" Peter asked.

"Did you hear something?"

"No, where?"

"Over there, up the shore ... Oh, listen! There it is again."

"I still don't hear anything," Peter declared. Then the little noise echoed again, and this time Peter heard it. It was a faint cry or call. Because it was so distant and barely noticeable, Peter could not make out what the obviously human voice was trying to say.

Father argued unsurely with himself in his mind as to whether to check and see whose voice it was. What if the voice was a clever trap by the Indians to lure any remaining refugees? But why so far away from the original campsite? Were some of the others being held hostage up the shore? Finally, he decided to quietly investigate.

"Stay here Peter," he instructed. "I'm going to see what that is. If any Indians return, run for your life."

"Please let me come," Peter begged. "I want to come with you."

Father stared down into Peter's pleading blue eyes. What if

he didn't return? Father was sure that Peter, whose knowledge of surviving in the wild was very limited, wouldn't last long in a forest full of hostile Indians and the long cold winter marching steadily closer every week. And he didn't like the thought of leaving Peter alone. But still, it was a very dangerous endeavor for even one person … let alone two.

"Please, please," Peter continued pleading. "I promise I will be quiet. Please let me come."

Father sighed. "Are you ready for a long walk?" he asked hesitantly. Peter nodded eagerly. Slowly Father rose and stretched. "All right then," he announced, extending a hand to help his son to his feet. "Let's go … Oh, and you might want to put your shirt back on. They are drying around the back of the fire. And might as well bring mine too while you are at it."

Peter smiled gratefully. "Thank you, sir." He scrambled around the back of the dying blaze to retrieve the still slightly damp shirts.

"Are you going to be all right?" Father asked.

"Yes, sir," Peter replied readily as he slid quickly into his torn gray shirt. Father put his shirt on, and he and Peter began their long walk.

Because of the thick clouds concealing the moon, they had to stumble blindly along the shore in complete darkness. The fire grew farther and farther away, until it was just a faint orange speck in the distance. Peter held Father's hand loosely just so they wouldn't lose each other. It was so dark that Peter, who was closest to the water, sometimes accidently wandered in and soaked his worn moccasins. Exhausted, he stumbled along, tripping clumsily over rocks and dragging his sore feet. Sometimes the ground on the shore was freckled with contrary stones, and other times it was soft and sandy clay, which was smooth as crisp paper. Each labored step seemed like torture after a while. His legs burned horribly. After a while, noticing his son's heavy breathing, his father insisted that they rest a little. Peter sat down heavily on the ground and almost fell asleep before they set off again.

"Peter, you can't go on," his father declared. Peter didn't reply but knew that was likely true. But Peter *had* been the one who had begged to join his father, and he felt the urge to prove himself.

Father stared pityingly at his boy struggling back to his feet and scooped him up securely in his strong arms.

Almost as soon as he had found a secure grip on Peter, he was sound asleep again. They had come too far for Father to return Peter to the fire. *I'll wake him before we get there*, his father resolved.

The soft calls continued, getting closer and closer as they made their way slowly up the shore. The closer they drew, the surer he was that the voice was not that of a hostile warrior, but he dared not start getting his hopes up yet. Father quickened his pace. Soon he could sense that the noises were very close, and he gently woke Peter and placed him on his feet. After another minute or so, they could recognize the calls as being their own names. Peter grinned excitedly and, despite his weary legs, forced himself to walk a little quicker. Soon they could barely make out a black silhouette. The figure gasped in fear at the sight of another figure emerging out of the thick darkness.

"Don't worry, Martha," Father called. "It is I."

"John!" Mother shouted, rushing forward and nearly collapsing into her husband's arms. "Oh, I was worried sick about you! I called and cried out for you, and they all said I was crazy, but I knew you would hear me. You were *not* dead. I knew it. Oh, I'm so glad you are all right!" Tears flowed from her eyes.

Then, delirious and sobbing, little Rebeccah stumbled up to Father, who gently cradled her against his broad chest. Peter was almost overwhelmed with relief. Then Mother, who had not yet noticed Peter, gasped at the sight of her son. She threw her arms around his small body and, weeping with joy and relief, half smothered Peter in kisses.

"Peter, y-you're alive! You're alive! When we heard Andrew t-tell us he saw you fall, we found your sword on the ground. I ... I ... thought that it was too late for you," she sobbed.

"Don't cry, Mother," Peter comforted. "I'm all right. Thanks to

God, I'm all right." Peter wisely decided not to reveal to his mother the incident with the warrior and the tomahawk … yet. As for Andrew watching him fall, he had probably caught a glimpse of Peter tumbling to the ground after he had been rammed with the tomahawk.

Mother guided Peter and Father cautiously to where the others were diligently building a stick shelter in the nearby forest.

"Who goes there?" a familiar voice called alertly out of the darkness.

"It's John Washingsworth. And Peter is with me," Father called. Mr. Snows stepped out into view and embraced his friend.

"Is Elisabeth with you?" he asked softly.

"No," Father replied. "Isn't she here?"

"No, she isn't," Mr. Snows explained. "She is the only one still missing, now that you two have returned."

Worry welled up inside Peter all over again. He glanced worryingly into the woods, not daring to believe the worst.

"Is she … lost?" he asked nervously.

"I don't know," Mr. Snows mumbled sadly.

"Are the rest of you all right?" Father asked kindly.

"Yes, it's a miracle," Mr. Snows explained excitedly. "All of us are completely all right for the most part. Even with all those warriors, God must have been protecting us. The only injury we have is a bad gash on Mr. Wilson's hand. Poor fellow."

A crowd had congregated around the two. They were especially pleased with Peter's return because they had concluded that he was as good as dead. Father gave Mr. Winslow back his hat, which he had brought with him from the original campsite.

Suddenly, Andrew dashed out of the crowd and threw his arms around Peter joyfully, nearly picking him up off the ground. "Peter, you're alive and all right! Oh, I'm so glad you are all right," he gasped.

"Thought you had finally gotten rid of me, didn't you?" Peter joked.

"Oh, thank goodness you are all right." Andrew sighed, ignoring Peter's joke.

The dark clouds still curtained the moon, and a drop of rain splashed onto Peter's nose.

"Everybody inside the shelter," Shamaro instructed. "There's a storm coming."

The rain grew harder every second as all the people wedged themselves tightly into the small, crude, dry shelter, which some of the survivors had hastily thrown together. The rain was even more severe than it had been on the night of the Chicapookinogganawan siege. Storms this size only struck Orenea once every other year or so, but when they did wander in, they struck with full fury. The raindrops seemed as if they were the size of cockroaches, and light blue lightning cracked the sky loudly, threatening to strike the trees, which bowed and swayed violently in the strong, forceful wind. There was so little room inside the shelter that everyone had to almost wedge themselves together to fit everyone inside. Breathing room was scarce. Rebeccah, who was terribly afraid of lightning, clung to Father tightly and screamed fearfully each time lightning struck.

"Do not fear, my little butterfly," he comforted softly. "It is simply God's mighty hand at work." Indeed, it almost seemed as if God was delivering an angry message to those who had attacked his precious children.

Elisabeth hadn't liked lightning any more than Rebeccah. It was terrible to imagine her lost, drenched, alone, and frightened. Peter's head nodded sleepily, and he felt as if his eyelids weighed a hundred pounds. He silently laid his head on the pine needle–carpeted ground behind his mother and closed his eyes. But all he could think about as he drifted off to sleep was Elisabeth, lost in the woods.

Now I will finally tell you about what *really* happened during the attack. Apparently, as the Tumitatakens had begun their march to the lake, some of the Orenean warriors who had been working out in the forest at the time discovered them. Not wanting to be seen, they followed the army through the bushes and managed to overhear some of them talking about where they were headed. Quickly the Oreneans rushed back to their cave, passing through villages to get recruits along the way, for they knew that they alone would not be enough to defeat this much larger clan.

Dashing from village to village, they valiantly sounded the gongs and called for all the able men to come quickly to fight for their new friends. In a minute's notice, the bold men deserted their work; snatched bows, knives, and fishing spears; kissed their wives goodbye; and with a quick "Say a prayer fo me" dashed toward the direction of the lake, where they would meet the other warriors. Once they reached the massive lake, they quickly discovered that the Tumitatakens had just begun the attack only moments ago. The strong, trained warriors in Asa's army lifted up their war weapons, and the bold yet inexperienced Orenean recruits raised their hunting bows and fishing spears and boldly leaped into the battlefield.

Although the Tumitataken warriors were strong and well trained, the Oreneans had a helpful advantage in that they outnumbered the Tumitatakens five to one, with more volunteers arriving by the minute. But the most vital advantage they could ever have was that the great and powerful El Shaddai was also fighting for them. As more trained Orenean warriors joined the battle, the cowardly Tumitatakens, realizing they were now severely outnumbered, fled fearfully, although they had only lost a few of their warriors. Asa commanded the Oreneans to pursue the Tumitatakens until they were far away and no longer a threat. So with great shouting and commotion, they victoriously chased the Tumitatakens halfway around the lake, through the Sun's Ray Forest and all the way around the base of Mount Mogogg.

Some of the Orenean warriors returned to the spot where the battle had first taken place and where the small group of people they had defended had dwelt. But the site was deserted and silent. The spot where the tent had been was now a roaring fire, and the weapons of war were still strewn randomly on the rocky ground. Had they been secretly captured or killed? Concerned, the volunteer warriors diligently searched the dark woods directly surrounding the place to find the small group, but they could not. Although this victory had added life to the candle of hope in the hearts of the Oreneans, Chief knew that the Tumitatakens could still easily crush the Oreneans with all their warriors and recruits. But this battle proved conclusively which side had the most spirit and bravery.

Peter yawned drowsily and cracked open one eye. Dull gray light leaked in from the entrance of the crude shelter that had been hastily constructed with prickly branches and sticks. Muscles still slightly sore from yesterday, he sat up groggily. The shelter was partially empty, except for Peter and the other soundly slumbering children, as well as Mr. Wilson, who was slumped in the corner.

"Good morning," the man greeted quietly, taking care not to awaken the other young ones, who had generously been allowed to sleep longer.

"Yes," Peter replied. "Good morning to you." It was then Peter noticed that Mr. Wilson's left hand was wrapped thickly in ugly soiled makeshift bandages that had probably been torn from his wife's apron.

"Oh," Peter mumbled. "Are you all right, sir?"

"What? Oh, this? Yes, I'm well. I was apparently a target for a weapon from the Indians."

"Does it hurt?" Peter asked thoughtfully.

"Yes, some. But at least it is just one hand. I wanted to help set up the tent, but my wife wouldn't let me. You know how women are."

"What tent?" Peter asked curiously.

"Oh, yes. You don't know, do you? Well, all I can say is I woke up this morning and there they were—two new cone-shaped tents. Just like the previous one, along with a few baskets and other odds and ends. I must say, I am so confused. Why do they hurt us and then shower us with gifts? It doesn't make sense." He shrugged his shoulders casually.

Rebeccah stirred restlessly and awoke. She immediately began to whimper and cry deliriously. Poor Rebeccah. She had probably suffered nightmares last night. Peter crawled quietly over to her and placed his pale slight hand gently on her heaving shoulder. Rebeccah shifted her head into her brother's lap and clung to him helplessly.

"Elisabeth," she sobbed. "I want Elisabeth. Where is she?"

Peter wrapped his arms tightly around his sister's body and squeezed her as hard as he could. *No, Elisabeth isn't lost for good. She can't be. She is coming back. She must.* Even if it wasn't true, Peter resolved to believe it.

Rebeccah sniffed, and another small tear rolled down her blushed cheek. "I want to see Mother," she whimpered.

Although he was eleven years old, Peter could barely lift his delirious five-year-old sister off the ground very high, as they were almost the same size. Therefore, embarrassed, he quit trying. Noticing his dilemma, Mr. Wilson crawled over (the roof wasn't high enough for him to stand), scooped up the little girl with his one good hand, and carried her outside.

"Thank you," Peter said politely. Peter leaned his head against the makeshift wall and stretched broadly. As he rose to leave, he accidently put his foot down on Rachel's hand.

"Stop it, Charlie," she murmured automatically in her sleep.

Outside, the sun was hidden behind gray clouds and the ground was damp from the storm last night and littered in pine needles and small sticks, which had been violently torn from the trees by the strong wind. Men and women were milling quietly about their business with worried expressions plastered to their faces. If anyone decided to say anything, it was done quickly and in low tones, almost like the way people would behave if they were gathered in a bedroom where someone was sleeping. A tense mist of worry and fear lingered in the air. The men were just finishing setting up the two tepees, one significantly larger than the other, and organizing search parties for Elisabeth, while the women were carefully inspecting the new tepees.

A V-shaped flock of geese honked talkatively far above the deep blue waters of the lake. The search parties were being formed on the fly, as if they didn't really expect to find anyone and were reluctantly doing this out of support for the family—and Peter didn't like that. Peter felt two large warm hands on his shoulders. He spun around and realized it was Father, who gathered him close in a hug.

"I'm going now, Peter," he explained solemnly. "You and Mr. Thomas are staying here to protect the ladies."

"May I please come with you?" Peter begged.

"No, you will be needed here."

Trying to read his father's thoughts, Peter stared quietly up into his great wise eyes. "I'll pray for you all," Peter promised faithfully.

"Thank you, son," Father replied with a small smile. "Charlie is coming, so we'll need it."

Peter smiled half-heartedly. Father placed his hands firmly on Peter's shoulders again and bent down on one knee so that they could be at eye level.

"Take care of your mother and sister for me. I love you dearly."

Peter nodded solemnly.

"John," Mr. Winslow called, beckoning him toward the woods with the others. "It is time to go now."

Father stood up and strode quickly over to the other men.

"Goodbye, Father!" Peter shouted. Father turned and waved before marching off silently into the woods. Peter watched them until the misty gray forest completely swallowed them up. Once they were gone, Peter turned away and stared at the ground. He thought about when his father had charged him to care for Mother and Rebeccah. Mixed emotions were bunched inside him about that. On one hand, it made him worried because it was almost as if he had been telling Peter this as if he thought he might never return. Peter prayed ever so hopefully that this would not happen. He knew how perilous searching the woods would be now that the Indians had violently turned against them.

However, on the other hand, it made Peter feel more grown up. Father had been treating Peter like a young man recently instead of a little child, as most people considered him. It made Peter feel proud. Father would not dare entrust his wife and daughter to anyone unless he trusted that person fully.

Just then, Peter noticed that Mother was sitting on an old rotting log facing the lake. She was clutching Rebeccah. Peter walked slowly over to her and seated himself by her side. He watched timidly as she wept quietly, her shoulders rising and falling heavily with each sob. Now was his chance to be a man and take care of them as Father had instructed. Father had always tenderly comforted Mother when she was sad or grieved. *Let's see, how did he do it?* Peter straightened his back up as tall as it would stretch and placed his thin arm around her shoulder, gently drawing her close to him. Then he reached over and grasped her hand tightly. Noticing what Peter was doing, Mother flashed a smile through her tears and placed her head down on Peter's shoulder. Peter screwed his eyes shut and prayed as hard as he could that his father and the other men would return—carrying Elisabeth too. And Peter could tell from the way she squeezed his hand that Mother was praying also.

CHAPTER X

THE NEXT FEW DAYS WERE terribly difficult for Peter. Every night the men staggered home wearily, looking more discouraged than ever. Every time Peter asked hopefully if they had found any sign of her. And each time they replied no, an ever so tiny bit of hope drained out of his heart. Sometimes he stood at the edge of the forest (he was not allowed to stray into it) and called her name loudly, hoping for a reply, but the only response was the empty, hollow echo. Because they received a splatter or two of rain, the children sometimes had to stay inside the smaller tepee, which was also used to store food and the gifts from the natives, both of which were increasing in number.

One morning Peter and Andrew sat quietly outside, solemnly playing Nine Men's Morris on the ground. There was not much work for the children to do since the men had started leaving to search in the mornings. Peter was lying on his stomach, his feet crossed up and his chin resting in his hand. He sighed drearily.

"Your move, Andrew," he mumbled sadly.

"But I just had my move," Andrew pointed out.

"Oh," Peter replied, slowly making his turn.

Andrew stared sadly into Peter's gloomy eyes. Peter hadn't been acting nearly himself lately. There was silence for a minute or so. The large low-hanging clouds loomed over the camp and cast shade gently on certain parts of it. It was strange the way some of them were fleecy white and others were dark gray yet they all mingled together.

"Do you think it's going to rain?" Peter asked, glancing up thoughtfully at the sky.

"It wouldn't surprise me," Andrew replied. "It has been raining a lot lately."

Peter nodded gloomily and moved one of his pebble pieces.

"Um … Peter," Andrew corrected. "It's actually my turn. You just went already."

"Oh," Peter replied. "Sorry. I'm … Sorry. I've been really … distracted lately. Elisabeth has been missing, and that is all I can think about. I'm … worried about what might have happened to her."

"I couldn't imagine how I would feel if Charlotte were missing for a week. I have to admit that I miss your sister a little bit too. You must be going mad," Andrew said sympathetically.

"Yes," Peter mumbled.

Andrew inspected the game board. "Say," he pointed out with a cheesy smirk, "you must really be going out of your mind."

"Why?"

"Because I just won!"

Peter smiled half-heartedly at Andrew's joke, and Andrew grinned too.

Peter's smile dissolved again, and he sighed nervously. He could almost sense in the air that something terrible was about to occur. Solemnly, Peter began to reset the game board. Just then, the search party of men emerged slowly from the woods. *Why were they home so early? Could it be …?* Peter jumped to his feet excitedly. The men filed solemnly into the tent, their heads bowed gravely. Something was amiss. But even so, a shot of hope tingled through Peter's heart. He hurried nervously toward the tent on wobbly legs. Father slowly exited from the tepee and met Peter halfway.

"What happened? Did you find her?" Peter asked hopefully, although he knew by the expression on Father's face that this could not be the case. Peter had never beheld such a dreadful expression before. Father grasped Peter's hand limply and stared sorrowfully at the ground.

"Peter," he explained, "your sister … is not coming back. She is with Jesus now. We … have decided to give up the search."

"What?" Peter croaked softly, his bottom lip trembling. He wanted to say something else, but a boulder-sized lump had formed in his throat and all he could do was let out a squeaky, raspy whine.

Father paused and then replied, "I said … Elisabeth is dead."

Peter gasped and staggered back painfully. It felt as if someone had suddenly run his chest through with a sword. Grief, pain, and shock flowed over him profusely like a flood ready to drown him. Peter leaned forward painfully as if he had just been shot in the stomach.

"No," he choked out, his eyes clogged with tears. "No. Not her, not my Elisabeth. It can't be her."

Father sighed shakily. Peter spun around wildly and allowed his clumsy, scrawny legs to race wildly into the woods. Not knowing or caring where he was heading, he stumbled and tripped clumsily over sticks and rocks, his eyes blurred thickly with tears. A low-growing vine suddenly caught Peter's foot, and he tumbled headfirst to the ground beneath an ancient pine. It took a moment or two to realize that the heavy yet quiet sobs that drummed in his ears were his own. Each weeping sob required so much effort and energy that it made his whole body ache. He did not know how many long hours he spent beneath that great tree draining his tears, but it seemed like one hundred. Then he felt a warm hand placed gently on his sweaty back. It was too small to be Father's yet too large to be Rebeccah's. Painfully Peter turned his head. Through blurry, tearful eyes, he could just barely make out the shape of his loyal friend Andrew. He didn't care that Andrew had witnessed him cry. He didn't care who saw him now.

"Hello, Peter," he mumbled sadly. "Are you all right? I'm very, very sorry about Eli … I mean, your sister."

Peter, whose eyes were still gushing tears, could not reply.

"I was sent out here to come bring you home," Andrew explained.

But Peter felt as if his sobbing had sucked every crumb of energy out of him. Peter opened his mouth to speak, but it was a minute or so before he could convince words to come out. "I-I can't."

Andrew gently pulled Peter to his feet, locking his arm around his friend, and started to half carry, half drag him through the thick woods. The next few minutes were a swirling blur. The next thing Peter could recognize was that he was in the huge warm arms of his father and being carried away slowly into the woods. Father sat down slowly beneath a huge tree and leaned against it, cradling his grieving son in his lap. Peter tried to bury himself in his father's huge chest. Giant tears rolled out of the corners of Father's eyes, streamed down his large cheeks, and dripped down on Peter's red head like rain. Father used part of his shirt to dry Peter's flushed face. Then he began quietly reciting the Psalms that always comforted him when he was troubled.

"He is our rock and our fortress, our stronghold in times of trouble ..."

These *were* times of trouble.

"Even though I walk through the valley of the shadow of death, I will fear ... I will fear ..." Suddenly, Father broke into sobs and squeezed Peter tightly.

"Oh, Peter, how terribly I miss her."

"Coonechinan! Coonechinan!" the leading man in the procession crowed authoritatively. "Make way! Make way!"

The curious people in the crowded, messy, smelly Tumitataken village dutifully cleared a wide path for the large committee of Orenean chiefs who partly ruled the country, along with High Chief Palkente and the second chief, Keoko.

Raised atop the approximately fifteen chiefs on a stretcher-like mat erectly sat Chief Palkente of Orenea himself. His long gray hair was braided hastily down his spiny straight back, and his useless sticklike old legs were crossed beneath him.

"Boo! Boo!" rudely shouted one of the half-naked Tumitatakens near the back of the thick crowd of spectators.

But Chief was much too furious to even pay the man a glance. Even the men diligently bearing his stretcher noticed that the normally talkative, friendly chief was much too cross to speak or smile. In fact, they had never witnessed this elderly chief so angry since the first aggressive raid by the Tumitatakens. Not that they could blame him for being so irate. After all, Mittowan had promised—swore signing his name "in the name of the almighty El Shaddai" on a parchment— not to do something and he had broken that promise. He had struck the tent dwellers in a raid. How dare he! In Orenea, there could be scarcely a greater more shocking offense. That was almost as if he had deliberately lied to El Shaddai. And not only that, but in front of all of his tribe and the Oreneans! How dare he!

Chief clenched his wrinkled, bony fists so tightly that his yellow fingernails dug into his palms. The solemn parade suddenly halted in front of the Tumitataken chief's large "palace." The guards, noticing the shining golden medallions bearing the Oreneans government emblem hanging around their necks, stepped aside stiffly without a word. Quickly the men marched through the dark, narrow tunnel, and Chief was lowered a little so that he would not scrape his head against the low ceiling. The hall was completely silent except for the foreboding crackling of the bright torches and the soft *crunch, crunch, crunch* of their beaded moccasins on the straw-scattered ground. At the end of the long hall, they discovered Mittowan sitting cross-legged on the floor alone. He glanced up at the approaching guests and seemed surprised to find not a messenger but Chief himself visiting the palace. The tall, muscular man gracefully rose to his feet and paced up to the men arrogantly. The Oreneans lowered Chief slowly and gently placed him cross-legged on the dusty ground.

"Finally gathered up your courage to come visit me, old man?" Mittowan taunted.

Angrily Chief shook his old fist up at him. "Why under tha sun did ya do it?" he demanded.

"Do what?"

"Oh, ya know right well what I mean," Chief snapped. "Ya signed in the name of El Shaddai. In tha name of El Shaddai! Ya signed a sacred vow and then deliberately did directly tha opposite! Why did ya do it? Do'a'not ya know in whose name ya signed?"

Mittowan stared blankly at the Orenian chief. "I still don't know what you are talking about," he insisted cluelessly.

"Well, allow me to refresh ya memory," Chief stated matter-of-factly. "A boy messenger of mine came through here a couple of moons or so ago and brought this document, which ya signed. See, there est ya signature, in tha upper left corner." Chief shoved a parchment scroll at him. "See fo yaself."

Mittowan quickly snatched the parchment, unrolled it, and carefully inspected it for a few moments. He nodded thoughtfully. "Yes, I recognize it," he declared, untidily rolling it back together and tossing it back at Chief carelessly.

"Well?" Chief demanded. "What under tha sun do ya have to say fo yaself?"

Mittowan shrugged casually. "What is there to say?" He paused. "Say, if you ask me, I would say the reason you are getting so upset about this is not that I broke your sacred little promise but because you love those lake dwellers particularly for some reason. Why is that? Ha! It is like the fetus standing up for the ant. You obviously must favor them a great deal to bring all your wimpy government officials with you. Except for one. Where is your tiny second chief? Let's see … Why is Keoko not here? Where is that sourpuss twerp?"

"Of course he est'a'not here. Ya beat him and banished him from ya palace on the penalty of death a long time ago. Remember?" Chief pointed out.

"Yes, I suppose I remember," Mittowan mumbled.

"And as to combat ya original accusation, no, no we do'a'not favor tha lake people more than any of my own villages," Chief declared solemnly. "It really grieves us every time ya raid our villages and murder tha innocent people or sell them fo only a measly fur or two. Ya obviously do'a'not appreciate tha value of people in tha long run. And zey are as important as ya are. In the loving eyes of El Shaddai, we are all worth tha same."

Mittowan laughed heartily. "Ha, all worth the same, eh," he taunted proudly. "That sounds so much like something I would expect a sweet old man like you to say. All equal. The smallest child to the, um, greatest chief?"

"And speaking of children," Chief inquired. "I have it that ya warriors did something to a little white foreign child who lived by tha lake. Est this true?"

Mittowan suddenly seemed mysteriously hesitant to reply. "Well, uh … How should I know," he stammered. "I was not there."

Chief wisely decided to leave that be for now. After all, their great serpent's warriors often did as they pleased without warning their chief.

"So why are you making such a fuss over some people you scarcely know?"

Chief, who was growing weary of this useless discussion, threw his thin old hands in the air impatiently. "How many times do I need to tell ya," he exclaimed with exasperation, "that est'a'not why I'm here. I'm here because ya broke ya promise—"

"In the name of El Shaddai. I am bored with your constant mention of childish myths. El Shaddai, El Shaddai, El Shaddai … Why must you be so obsessed with such an ignorant fantasy?" Mittowan cried impatiently.

"No," Chief retorted angrily. "He est real, more real even than ya are!"

"Oh, he is, eh?" the Tumitataken chief challenged confidently. "Then prove it."

Chief simply stared back up at his opponent, smirking coolly. "Well, if tha spirits and ghosts ya people worship are so real," he said calmly, "then prove it."

"Well, there was ... Uh ...," Mittowan stammered desperately.

"Oh ... just forget it ... Supernatural things in general cannot be proven anyhow. Besides, even if your Jesus path is the truth, I would choose not to believe or follow it. There are far too many impossible limits and commands."

"How under tha sun do ya know that?" Chief argued. "Ya have never even given faith a chance."

"I don't need to," Mittowan insisted spitefully, his aggravated tone dripping with sass and disgust. "I can watch your people worship and pray constantly to an invisible God and clearly see that your religion is trapping you in a prison."

"Trapping us in a prison eh?" Chief argued sensibly. "Well, let's take a look at what ya believe. Let's see ... In tha morning, ya must offer a sacrifice of two madrone tree branches to tha spirit of good health, and tha time of ya sacrifice est announced by tha rising of tha sun. Then, in midmorning, at tha sound of tha morning gong, ya must burn three dozen pine needles—no more, no less—and sprinkle tha ashes on tha bank of a creek fo tha gods and spirits of tha sky, trees, and earth. Then, before tha afternoon gong, ya must sacrifice a bird to tha spirits of tha rocks and tha clay. Then, as tha sun sets, ya must burn part of a deer's skull—this est only to be done every other day—and who knows what else to tha goddess of good crops, tha spirits of tha forest, and tha spirits of tha wildflowers. Then light holy fires after tha stars appear to appease tha ghosts of ya ancestors. And if ya do'a'not observe all of these ceremonies perfectly, ya will supposedly have their wrath upon ya and constant bad luck until tha next new moon. Est'a'not this true?"

Mittowan sighed and caressed his forehead stressfully.

"Mittowan," Chief explained passionately. "El Shaddai loves ya. He wants to forgive ya and set ya free from all ya spirit worship and wrongs. If only ya will let him."

Mittowan stared thoughtfully into space as if trying attentively to make a decision. Chief's heart pounded in his chest as he waited silently for an answer. Suddenly, the sinister scowl returned to the

Tumitataken chief's face and he stomped his large bare foot on the dirt floor stubbornly.

"No!" he declared. "I will not. I hate El Shaddai and his Jesus followers. He is the most outrageous ... ridiculous myth I have ever heard. I swore years ago to do all I could to destroy them all, to the very last one. I can now make good on that oath. So you Oreneans can just kiss your miserable lives goodbye and wait for my pounce."

Chief, who was now more irate than when he had entered, shook his tightly clenched fist up at his enemy. "Oh, I ... Ya had better be glad I can'a'not stand," he fumed furiously, "because if I could, I'spose I would stand up and punch ya in tha nose."

Mittowan glanced fearlessly back at the frail old man and did something that was a cross between a grunt and a chuckle. "A lot *that* would hurt," he mumbled sarcastically.

The lower chiefs gently hoisted their steaming chief back onto his seat.

"Oh, and by tha way," Chief added as they turned to leave. "If ya religion really waes true, than ya spirits and ghosts are very angry at ya right now."

"What? Why?" Mittowan demanded.

"Because tha afternoon gong just sounded twenty minutes ago."

Two weeks slowly crept past. Peter, who was ill for most of this time, spent most of his time miserably lying in the tiny storage tepee for privacy, listening to the rain tap-tap-tap steadily on the leather roof. Because Peter was trapped with much idle time, he could only sleep and pray mostly. But he quickly discovered that prayer soothed his grief, at least a little. The other people were very kind to the Washingsworths, and Peter was often cared for by some of the other women who took turns sitting by him. Rebeccah also preferred to play quietly with her brother in the storeroom. Sometimes when he was alone, Peter would turn his head drowsily and expect to find

Elisabeth sitting faithfully next to him, just like always. Instead, there would only be the side of the tent to greet him. Mr. Winslow kindly decided to wait until Peter was well enough before they would hold a makeshift service to remember the girl, although they had no body to bury.

So when the sun shined brightly and Peter finally left the tiny cramped tent, they decided that today was the perfect day to hold her service. In a tiny, beautiful, quiet maple grove in the woods on a still, peaceful Sabbath afternoon, the ragged eighteen remaining refugees gathered solemnly to wave goodbye to Elisabeth Washingsworth. Peter tried in vain to keep the tears stuffed back inside. It didn't seem to help. He just turned his face away whenever he felt a sob coming, and therefore he spent most of the service with his head turned toward the maple tree behind him. His poor mother wept the hardest.

The two Indian oarsmen stood sternly at the far end of the gathering, Shamaro whispering translations periodically to Cakechiwa. The Cox family stood beside them, Mr. Snows nearby, and Charlie, who was still acting strangely wholesome and quiet, made no trouble. Behind them were the Wilsons, little baby Paul cooing quietly, and the Thomas family beside the Washingsworths, Mr. Thomas's callused, wrinkled hand on Father's large shoulder. And on the other side, Mr. Kenelm stood gravely, his head bowed sadly.

Mr. Winslow solemnly recited the familiar droll funeral service in front of the rickety homemade cross. At the foot of it was a smooth and flat heavy stone with words crudely etched into it. Peter could not read the words, but he knew that it spelled the name Elisabeth Washingsworth. There. It was official. She was not coming back. Peter would not see her again—this side of eternity at least—which seemed so distant that it didn't comfort him much. At least whenever Peter wished to remember her, this empty makeshift grave would be still waiting for him to visit. This quiet, peaceful little grove seemed so ... so her. It was almost as if the yellow-crested maples silently whispered her name. It reflected Elisabeth's tender, kind personality. So peaceful and quiet—happy yet without a smile. This was evident in every detail, from the majestic towering maples gently swaying in the soft breeze to the rocky murmuring creek, which trickled below a small drop-off by the gravesite.

After Mr. Winslow finished, the little party solemnly sang Elisabeth's favorite hymn, which was a calm, sweet tune based on the 128th psalm. "Blessed are all who fear the Lord, who walk in His ways ..." Elisabeth had always been quietly humming that song childishly and out of tune, which used to annoy Peter after he had heard it for the twentieth time. But now what he wouldn't give to hear her singing that again. Tears poured profusely out of his eyes like the gurgling stream nearby as the familiar melody droned on. Sobbing uncontrollably, his mother clung to his father helplessly for support, although he was trembling too.

"May the Lord bless ye from Zion all the days of thy life ..." The old tune was about to end. Just as the last low note was sung, Mother fainted into Father's arms. With a grunt, Father gently scooped her up into his strong arms and carried her away. The people wandered off one by one after that, but before they left, they each somberly placed a small wildflower on the gravestone. The men left first, then the women. Finally, only Peter and Rebeccah remained in the still grove. A restless blue jay called out cheerfully from the trees nearby. Peter sighed and slowly rose from where he was sitting to catch a clearer glimpse of the dark blue little bird, which cocked its tiny crested head inquisitively and stared at him with large black eyes.

Peter couldn't help but stare. Elisabeth would have been thrilled by the little bird. Eventually, with a cheerful chatter, the blue jay fluttered away out of sight. It was then that Peter turned around and noticed Rebeccah weeping quietly in front of the crude stick cross, which had been made lovingly out of two think pine sticks bound securely together by a scrawny vine. Peter knelt down sadly behind Rebeccah. He gently placed his thin, trembling arm around her little chest, drawing her near, and placed his head affectionately on top of her blonde one.

"Shhh, shhh," Peter whispered comfortingly. A cool breeze brushed against Peter's pale sorrow twisted face like soft, cool, gentle feathers. Rebeccah bellowed out a loud painful sob, and Peter squeezed her as hard as possible. He pursed his lips together tightly and squinted his eyes shut to try to keep from crying again, but some tears escaped anyway. Before he knew it, Peter was sobbing just as hard as Rebeccah was. Rebeccah clung tightly to her brother's arm and leaned heavily against him.

Peter glanced through tear-blurred eyes at the golden beams of cheery light trickling in from between the bright yellow autumn leaves. Such beauty and happiness in the air seemed almost obscene at such grievous times as these. Emotions raged like ocean waves in Peter's burdened soul. Grief, despair, worry … homesickness. It was only now that he realized how homesick he really was. However, he did not long merely for that little cabin or to see his family's friends again. He desired for things to go back to the way they were in old times. Father's hearty laugh, the smell of Mother's bread baking, Rebeccah's bothersome chattering … Elisabeth's quiet humming. He missed hearing Mr. Kenelm's stories with the other children around that great fire and quiet nights when all the members of his family were together. Feeling safe, happy, and quiet, without worries or fears looming all around him. Now he could only view such occasions through a window into a room he would never gain entrance to again—home, like a once-prosperous beggar observing a feast enviously from a window facing the street.

Now there seemed to be only one option left for Peter: moving onward. Perhaps they would somehow be able to start fresh, make a new home. Peter knew he should be excited about this possibility, but somehow he knew it could never be the same, so still he gazed longingly back through the window.

Peter kicked up the thick pine needles on the ground in front of him as he meandered through the woods. Another week had slowly crept by—a long week. He was still recovering from the loss and found himself depressed often, but Peter preferred not to let anyone notice this and threw himself diligently into his chores and duties more than ever. Sometimes he would be getting berries, wild herbs, or nuts in the forest and would think he saw a flash of Elisabeth's puffy curly blonde hair, then quickly turn his head in that direction and realize that it was only an autumn leaf swirling to the ground. Or he'd think he heard her quiet sweet humming and then realize with disappointment that it was just a bird call or a babbling creek.

A few days ago, there had appeared by the flap of the tent a few small fishing nets, which were used to catch many large fish. Oh joy! What a delicious, welcome change it was from reluctantly eating the same meat and wild berries for every meal, although by some sort of miracle, the ladies were to make even venison for the fifteenth time in a fortnight taste relatively decent.

Peter felt sorry for Mr. Wilson because his painful hand injury wasn't healing well. It seemed to be swiftly growing more infected every day, to the point that he couldn't do anything with his hand.

Now Peter was taking a much-needed break and was seeking Andrew to see if he wanted to catch lizards and frogs on the smooth rocks with him. They hadn't played together recently.

"Andrew, Andrew, where are you?" he called loudly. Peter wandered into the small grove where his sister's grave was. "Andrew, are you here?" It was then that he noticed his father sitting solemnly in front of the cross, gazing silently upon it, his chapped lips moving slightly in prayer. Glancing up, he noticed Peter.

"Oh," Peter mumbled politely, "I'm sorry, sir; I didn't mean to disturb you. I was only—"

"Oh, no, no," Father interrupted quickly. "It is all right; no need to apologize. Come sit down. I was hoping you would come here."

The lizards can wait. Peter seated himself next to Father on the soft mossy ground, which was covered thickly in the moist dead leaves. The next few minutes were spent in silence. Peter watched a fuzzy caterpillar inch slowly up a rough tree trunk.

"I like to come here," Father commented. "It is a very good place to think and pray."

"What do you pray about?" Peter asked.

"I'm glad you asked," Father replied. "I pray for help."

"Help?" Peter inquired curiously.

"Yes, son, I need help ... to forgive. I need to forgive those who killed Elisabeth."

Peter glanced up at his father in surprise. Had he been back home at Plymouth, that would have sounded like the expected classic answer to every question about dealing with hurtful people ... But this was different. Peter couldn't imagine even trying to forgive those Indians.

"Why would you do that?" he asked, more bitterly than he intended for it to come out.

Father sighed thoughtfully. "Because it's the right thing to do," he replied.

"But how can you do it? I couldn't do it even if I tried. I'm just so ... so angry at them," Peter said.

"I understand, son. I—God forgive me—am angry too. I can't forgive them on my own. That's why I am praying."

Peter sighed thoughtfully. "I don't know," he mumbled. He stared at the ground unsurely, hugging his knees. It was almost as if he sometimes didn't even want to forgive. As he lay down to sleep at night, Peter would sometimes wish he could draw his sword and brutally pay back every one of that tribe for what they had done.

"I'll not force anything upon you Peter," he said, "but if you ever want to pray with me, you are welcome."

Peter nodded agreeably. "All right, Father. I will sometime."

Father stood up and stretched his arms casually. "I must go help gather some firewood now," he announced, patting Peter on the back heartily.

"Might I please stay here a while?" Peter begged.

"Yes, you may stay. But be careful, as I shall need you back by later this afternoon. We could use an extra person to help catch fish for tonight's supper," Father instructed.

"Yes, sir," Peter promised.

Father turned away and strode erectly back toward the lake. Peter, who was glad to be alone, was just about to start praying as Father had told him when the one person whom Peter had least wished to see suddenly emerged from behind the ancient maple. It was Charlie. Peter inched back fearfully, sighed nervously, and braced himself for Charlie's next battering comment. Although he *had* been acting less cruel lately, Peter was sure he would not be able to resist an opportunity like this. After all, for the first time in a while, they were all alone.

"Go away!" Peter snapped. "I don't need your insults now. Can't you see that I'm not to be disturbed?"

Charlie sighed shakily. "I … I'm not going to bother you. I promise. Just … give me only a few minutes. Then I'll … I'll leave. I promise. Just hear me out."

Peter stared suspiciously at Charlie, who somehow didn't seem so aggressive and mean as he normally did when he approached; he even seemed a little timid. But Peter would not let his guard go slack just because Charlie had been more docile lately.

"Really?" Peter demanded skeptically. "Is this a trick?"

"No," Charlie promised. "I swear it's no trick."

Peter was confused. Why was Charlie acting so … civil? He would have expected that this good behavior spell would have worn out by now. "Go on," Peter coaxed cautiously. Charlie sat down gingerly on the ground a few feet away.

"I … Well … What I'm trying to say is …," Charlie stammered awkwardly. He took a deep, shaky breath. "Peter," he admitted, words cramming timidly out of his mouth as if he were trying to get it over with as quickly as possible. "I'm so sorry for all that I've done to you. I am … very ashamed of it, so … I know that I certainly don't deserve it, but would you please somehow forgive me?"

Peter was shocked. Never had he dared hope for this moment ever to come. He stared speechlessly at his foremost enemy and nemesis, who now appeared to be surrendering. "This is a joke, is it not?"

"No. No joke. I've been talking to Mr. Winslow, and … I've decided to make many major changes in my life." Charlie continued. "I know I've done many terrible things to you, and I know that I wouldn't forgive me if I were you. But please do. I heard you and your father speaking and thought that now would be a good time to beg you for amends. You are fortunate to have a man like him. I promise that I will never hurt you again."

Peter sighed thoughtfully. Compared to the challenge of forgiving those who had murdered Elisabeth, this task of forgiving a few bruises, cuts, and mocks was much easier. Charlie waited hopefully for Peter's reply.

"Y-yes," Peter decided hesitantly.

Charlie grinned with relief. "Thank you, Peter!" Charlie replied bashfully

The joyous expression on Charlie's smooth tan face and the genuine tone of his voice were enough to wash away completely every speck of doubt about the apology. Then Peter did something he hadn't been able to do since Elisabeth had died: he smiled—a large, real happy smile. Oh, how wonderful it felt to be happy again, just for a little while. It was more refreshing than being bathed in cold water on the most scorching day of summer. Was Charlie a Christian? Peter didn't know about that, but at least he didn't need to be afraid anymore. Satisfied, Charlie nodded, stood up and began marching off into the woods.

"Oh, and by the way," he mentioned before leaving, "don't tell anyone about this. I'm apologizing to everyone separately. I don't want everyone to know."

"All right," Peter promised. He quietly watched Charlie disappear into the woods. Still wearing his smile proudly, Peter jumped excitedly to his feet and skipped off merrily onto the forest trail to find Andrew to catch lizards and frogs.

"Come on Twii!" Veenatch called impatiently. "Ya are so slow!"

"Well, why under tha sun am I always tha one stuck carrying tha heavy food basket?" Twii complained.

"Just hurry up," Veenatch said. "Do ya want to waste away tha last day of our break? Tomorrow we're back to work."

"All right, all right. I'm coming," Twii called from behind. "Say, where under tha sun are we going anyhow?"

'I do'a'not know. Let's just find tha perfect picnic place."

"I sure do hope i'test'a'not too far away. I'm tired," Twii declared.

"Yes … indeed," Veenatch mumbled absentmindedly, observing the small clearing they had just wandered into.

"Please tell me this est tha spot," Twii begged impatiently.

Veenatch shook her head disapprovingly. "No."

"Oh, why not?" Twii moaned, "I do'a'not see why it can'a'not do. And look, it even has grass that est'a'not all dry and poky."

"See," Veenatch explained, cocking her head at the moist light green moss. "I'test too wet. We would soak our clothes. My mother would'a'not like that very much."

Twii groaned and glanced back into the shady forest. "Why under tha sun can'a'not we just find a dry place among tha trees and eat there?"

"Maybe …" Veenatch muttered absentmindedly, trying to think of a place to go.

"Perhaps we could just eat in tha woods and then find ya perfect place to eat lunch and do whatever we want fo tha rest of tha day," Twii suggested. "After all, we do have breakfast, lunch, and dinner in tha basket. We have a lot of time before sunset."

"True," Veenatch agreed.

The newly risen sun cast its warm orangish glow on the tall

limbed up giant trees. The speckled horse that Twii's Father had kindly let them borrow grunted loudly, its breath like steam in the cool clear morning air.

"We could go over to Eagle Feather and see Water Star," Veenatch suggested.

"No," Twii objected. "Her brother Black Sparrow is a real bully."

For a moment, there was silence.

"Say, Veenatch. I just had a wonderful idea," Twii exclaimed, grinning broadly, her eyes bright and excited.

"What?" Veenatch asked eagerly.

"We could eat on tha Fire Hills."

"Tha Fire Hills?"

"Yes," Twii continued, grinning. "Just think. Rolling hills covered in orange poppies. We could weave them into our hair and bring them home fo pressing, and we do'a'not need to go far into them."

Veenatch listened and said thoughtfully, "I do'a'not know. I'test too far away. Besides, tha bright colors make my head hurt, and my brother says tha flower's smell causes people to ... um ... see things that are'a'not really there."

"Oh, not with ya brother again," Twii cut off, "ya are a coward if ya think that est really true. A flower? A pretty, sweet, innocent flower? Really? I am certain he waes joking—our warriors often do."

"I'spose he probably waes," Veenatch decided, looking a little less worried. "And tha colors have'a'not given me a headache in a long time, come to think of it. I'spose we might give it a shot. If ya really wanted to."

"Then i'test a plan," Twii declared enthusiastically.

Veenatch dug her fingers deeply into Twii's upper arm (as she was like to do) and started running at top speed, roughly dragging Twii behind her, who almost spilled the food.

"Gentle, gentle!" Twii wailed pleadingly, although she was giggling uncontrollably at the same time. Veenatch released her friend to allow her to climb onto the horse. As the horse trotted quickly through the forest with Twii sitting in front, they snacked casually on their breakfast, although the trotting of the horse made it difficult to eat. Gradually, as they trotted speedily down the wooded mountain, the ground grew flatter, the trees thinned out a little, and there became fewer towering evergreens and more sprawling oaks. Bright orange poppies dotted the ground above the thick carpet of dead pine needles. The sun had risen a little higher in the sky, sending its magical golden rays through the tree branches. Soon they were traveling through the colorful Fire Hills. Twii grinned. The lazy rolling hills were carpeted solidly with vibrant orange poppies, which were packed together so tightly that there was scarcely a single patch of bare ground not covered in orange flowers for miles. If you gazed at it correctly, the hills really did appear to be ablaze.

The horses slowed to a stop. "Mmmm." Twii sighed, deeply inhaling a fresh noseful of floral-scented air. "Tha Fire Hills are so beautiful. I enjoy visiting."

"Yes, I'spose so," Veenatch agreed. "I could spend tha course of my life on tha Fire Hills."

"I do'a'not know about that," Twii-Wa asserted, "but zey are nice to visit."

Twii paused thoughtfully. "Are'a'not we near tha place where Keoko grew up?"

"I believe so," Veenatch replied, "him and all nine of his younger brothers and sisters."

"He est tha oldest of ten?" Twii asked, a cheesy smile spreading across her face. "I wonder what he waes like as a child."

Both of the girls chuckled at the thought. How could such a pessimist like Keoko come from such a cheery place as this?

For the most part, the hills were not very large or steep. Between some of the hills wound little rocky creek beds, which often dried out in the summer, only to be revived again when the rains came. There were very few trees, but every quarter mile or so, there was a hill with a tree standing proudly on top. The trees were giant, wise old valley oaks whose branches, over time, began to get so heavy that the tips of the branches touched the ground so that you could go in the sort of "cove" formed by the branches and feel like you were in a kind of house. In fact, the people who lived on the hills lived in "tree places," which were houses that were built out of the living trees by plastering the spaces between the branches of the oak trees with a mixture of thick clay and dried flowers. A ravine of plain old trees could be turned into a village!

Twii and Veenatch passed many of these "tree villages," both Tumitataken and Orenean, but didn't enter any.

Time passed quickly. Veenatch, who had insisted on driving the horse for a while, suddenly cried, "Whoa, Whoa!" With a sputter, the specked animal obediently slowed to a halt.

"What under tha sun est wrong?" Twii asked worryingly.

Veenatch scanned the hills. There was not a single village in sight. "Do ya know where under tha sun we are?" Veenatch asked nervously.

"Well … no, not exactly," Twii replied calmly. "But do'a'not worry; we are'a'not lost. We can always find our way back to tha mountains." She pointed back across the Fire Hills to the hovering twin mountains, which were visible from any part of Orenea, making it difficult to get lost on the Fire Hills.

"Oh," Veenatch replied with a touch of relief in her voice. "But should'a'not we stay in eyeshot of a village?"

"No need," Twii assured her. "I'test'a'not as if we would be in any sort of danger … And besides, out here no one can hear us. Zey will probably think girls like us are either too young to be out here by ourselves or too old to be away from our work to be making merry like this."

Finally, the girls decided to find a "decent" picnic site. Twii-Wa suggested that they dine on the side of an extraordinarily large hill, which loomed above the rest like a gentle giant. Eagerly they tied the horse securely with vine to a little tree at the base and scampered up a little ways. The delicious lunch consisted of crisp, sweet quimpanitas, tender, juicy meat, and plump black Orenean grapes. And oh, what grapes! After the meal, the girls played gaily for a while. They raucously rolled down the hillside and collected many flowers to bring home to press.

"All right," Twii-Wa announced, "let's go back home. It would be very embarrassing if anyone waes to come and see us. After all, i'test normally a workday."

"Yes," Veenatch agreed, stopping to catch her breath. "It might take a while to ride home."

"But," Twii suggested with a smile, "let's roll down tha hill one more time."

"And we will see who can make it to tha top first," Veenatch added playfully.

"No fair! Ya are so much faster than me, and I am more tired than ya are." But no sooner had Twii said this than she was off on a head start up the tall hill. Veenatch gave a little shriek and started racing up the hill as fast as her long legs would bear her, the two girls' messy long pigtail braids bouncing and flopping wildly behind them in the cool, refreshing breeze.

Wearily Twii slowed to a halt at the top to gaze out over the breathtaking view. From the rounded summit of the hill, one could look out over almost every acre in the beautiful land. There were the notorious flower-blanketed hills, stretching all around up to the distant purple snowcapped mountain range, which appeared to be about an hour and a half's gallop away. If you searched carefully, you might catch a glimpse of the bright glimmer of the great winding river, which flowed into the large Lake Honiton, peeking out from between the still, lazy hills. Then there was a visible portion of the lake itself, bluer even than the endless expanse of sky, between the enormous twin mountains, which jutted out far above the hills like intimidating green monsters, with a slight dusting of white snow near the high summits casting their great motherly shadows over the belittled hills.

"Veenatch," Twii called, "come see."

Veenatch skipped up to the top of the hill and glanced out over the land. "Est that all ya wanted to show me?" Veenatch asked disappointedly.

"How under tha sun can ya expect more?" Twii exclaimed. "I am showing ya tha whole land."

Veenatch paused. "This est boring. Let's go back down," she insisted.

Twii, who was the kind of person who could be giddy and excited one moment but calm and solemn the next, continued to gaze absently into space. "Can'a'not we stay longer?" she pleaded dreamily.

"No," Veenatch replied firmly. "Remember, we promised my ma that we would be home before sunset."

"Oh, very well," Twii agreed reluctantly.

"Let's race," Veenatch suggested, "down tha other side of the hill."

"No," Twii disagreed. "Ya always win when I do'a'not have a head start. Maybe we could just run."

"Oh come now, I am as tired as ya are. We shall race down tha other side to … um … that bush over there. Ready?"

"Well, I'spose so."

As they began to run, Veenatch halted suddenly and grabbed Twii-Wa's sleeve. "Wait."

"What under tha sun est it now?" Twii sighed.

"Look over there." Veenatch pointed curiously to a small ravine.

"What about it?" Twii inquired. "I'test just a clump of trees."

"Look," Veenatch persisted, pointing again. This time Twii noticed what Veenatch was talking about. A plank of wood was secured firmly to an old gray post, which was so old and weathered that it leaned to one side in front of the clump of trees. Suddenly, Twii realized with surprise and a hint of fright that it was more than just a ravine behind that sign. It was a village—an extinct, silent village.

"Oh," she mumbled warily. "Let's get out of here."

"No," Veenatch protested, "let's take a closer look."

"Why?" Twii protested. "What if there est a starving mountain lion or a crazy witch doctor in there?"

"There are'a'not any mountain lions this low," Veenatch pointed out.

"What about crazed witches ... or coyotes? That looks like tha perfect den fo them."

"Come. Stop being such a humbug," Veenatch coaxed shakily.

Twii took a deep breath. "Oh, all right," she agreed, "but if I go insane, i'test ya fault."

Cautiously the two girls approached the empty huts. Twii gripped Veenatch's arm fearfully as the girls silently approached the eerie place, their rough bare feet noiselessly creeping along the soft ground, as if the village were sleeping and they were both afraid to awaken it. It actually seemed as if the old village was not sleeping but dead. The empty tree huts, with their crumbling clay walls, the large fire pit, and even the trees housing the huts, although their leaves still maintained a dull green color, seemed to contain a dead spirit. Each empty house seemed to be mourning its lack of inhabitants. A mouse scurried busily out of one of the vacant dwellings. The two girls halted just outside the village.

Twii whined, "Please tell me ghosts do'a'not exist," she fretted, almost startled by the sound of her own voice.

Veenatch sighed in exasperation. "Ghosts do'a'not exist," she recited. "Look who est tha coward now."

Once they approached the sign, Twii squinted and leaned in attentively to read the faded barely visible characters. "Village of Harmony," she read slowly.

"Do ya suppose tha Tumitatakens attacked this place?" Veenatch asked.

"No," Twii replied, "if tha Tumitatakens were here, zey would have burned everything. This place has been rotting fo many moons."

"I'spose so," Veenatch agreed. "Well, come on, let's go in that village."

"We're going in?" Twii asked, sounding alarmed.

"Yes, we are."

"Oh, all right. But if I faint from some terrible fright, I'test all ya fault. And we will'a'not stay long in any case."

"Agreed."

Warily Twii and Veenatch, hand in hand, walked quietly into the presence of the rickety huts. The flowers had regrown over the ground, which had once been dusty and firm from being trodden underfoot. The homes' aged walls were crumbling and caving in. The spooky faded totem poles appeared as if they were about to topple over. This community was just like any other except that there were no people and had not been for a long time. In the center of the scattered tree dwelling, there was a large overgrown fire pit. Twii stared dreamily at it. If she could imagine just hard enough, Twii could see a cheery flame inside, a warm orange blaze exhaling fragrant smoke on a warm dark summer's night. And if she imagined just a little more, there were people too, happy people, gathered in a circle, their bellies full from dinner and their cares buried far away for now. There might be young mothers nursing their babies, laughing and chatting gaily. Or old people playing their wooden pipes or teaching the children ancient chants and know-how. Twii then blinked, and all the merry people quickly vanished and all was desolate and solemn again.

"Twii, come over here," Veenatch called from another part of the village.

A bit startled by the sound of her friend's voice, Twii quickly hurried over to her. "What under tha sun est it?"

"Look. Do ya know what under tha sun these things are?"

There, in front of them, were two tall once brightly painted stone pillars, one tilting wearily to one side.

"Shrines?" Twii speculated. "Then this waes a pagan Tumitataken village."

Veenatch and Twii stood silently for a few moments, trying to figure what to make of it. Twii stared thoughtfully at the leaning yet proud old pillars, which represented the pagan practices of this long-dissolved village. They were so frail and old that one of the girls probably could have pushed them over without much hardship.

"Do'a'not these eerie old huts make ya shiver?" Veenatch whispered.

"Yes," Twii replied quietly. "Zey look haunted. How old do ya suppose zey are?"

"I do'a'not know. Maybe fifty full moons or more."

"Really?" Twii replied. "But how under tha sun could these old walls still be standing? Wouldn't zey be collapsed by now?"

"These clay walls are built to last, I'spose," Veenatch responded confidently. "I hear tell that zey can survive fo a far longer time."

"Zey still scare me."

Twii gazed uncertainly at the frail old structures. Quickly Veenatch spun around and grabbed Twii's arm.

"Let's go inside one!" she suggested excitedly.

"What!" Twii exclaimed. "No, of course not! I'm afraid of empty houses."

"I understand. An empty house once attacked me when I waes five springs old, and I still have'a'not recovered from tha memory of it." Veenatch replied wittily.

"Ha-ha," Twii mumbled dryly. "Honestly, I do'a'not feel comfortable going in there."

"Pleeeeeaaaase," Veenatch pleaded. "This est one of those adventures ya are always hoping fo."

"Are ya mad?" Twii protested. "There could be a skeleton or a dead body in there!"

"Maybe," Veenatch replied thoughtfully, "or maybe not."

"Perhaps," Twii suggested, "ya could go in and I could stay out here and wait … if ya ever come out."

But when Twii stared into Veenatch's disappointed eyes, she realized that Veenatch would probably be sheepish to enter alone. (And she couldn't blame her!) *And besides,* she reasoned, *what under tha sun could happen?*

"Oh, very well," she relented reluctantly. She quickly added, "But if I see a skeleton in there and go hysterically mad, i'test all ya fault."

"Deal," Veenatch agreed confidently.

Step by silent step, hand in hand, the two agentes nervously approached the nearest hut. They both halted nervously before warily ducking inside. The old spooky room, which, like most of the others, was built in an oak tree, with the rough mossy brown trunk in the middle and the crumbly clay branches and walls in a circle around it, forming a dome at the top. The place was falling apart, and it made one feel concerned that it might collapse around them.

"I'test empty," Veenatch whispered. And indeed it was. Lacy cobwebs graced the walls and ceiling. The floor was carpeted in weeds.

"All right," Twii insisted nervously, "let's leave now. There est nothing to see."

Suddenly she glanced over at the far wall and gasped in horror. There, hanging on the wall in a neat row, were about five or so human skulls, each intricately painted in a design, although the paint was faded. For a moment, Twii and Veenatch just stood frozen, staring. They would not have been so startled if it had not been for the spooky surroundings. After all, they had glimpsed the skulls in the Tumitataken chief's palace many times before. But because they were spooked, Twii and Veenatch wasted no time in scrambling out of the village.

"See, see," Twii exclaimed shakily, once they were safely outside the place. "There were skeletons in there. What under tha sun did I say? Now I will go mad."

"There were no skeletons," Veenatch pointed out, "only skulls."

"I wonder where zey came from," Twii mused uneasily. "Curious people who wander into abandoned homes? Maybe that est where tha crazy witch lady lives! Now she knows we are here!"

"Ya saw tha spider webs," Veenatch argued. "No one has been in there fo years."

"Then where? How? Why? Ya know that normal Tumitatakens do'a'not just have skulls in their homes—and certainly not Oreneans. Only tha Timitataken chief does that ... unless zey were'a'not Tumitatakens."

"What under tha sun are ya talking about? There are no other tribes in tha area ... or at least there have'a'not been fo generations."

"Do'a'not ya listen to tha stories around tha fire?" Twii explained excitedly. "It might have been a Honitonax village!"

"Ya mean tha tribe that waes here before us Oreneans?" Veenatch asked.

"Perhaps."

Veenatch paused thoughtfully. "That makes sense. I heard zey kept tha skulls of their dead loved ones ... as a way to remember them."

"How sweet," Twii crooned sarcastically.

"I'test utterly disgusting," Veenatch remarked in a low voice. "Why could'a'not zey just ... Wait. What under tha sun est that?" Veenatch pointed curiously toward a majestic old oak at the base of another hill.

"Oh no, not something *else* ..." Then Twii understood what Veenatch was pointing at. Beneath the tree, which swayed peacefully in the cool breeze, was a large rocky dark black circle in the side of the hill. Then she realized it was not merely a black circle but a hole in the earth.

"A cave!" Twii exclaimed excitedly. "We found a deserted village *and* a cave in one trip. Oh, how tha boys and Pona-Pow will be jealous once zey find out we were having all those adventures without them. Now we must leave ... *Please.*" Twii turned away and looked back at Veenatch over her shoulder, hoping that she would follow, but Veenatch swiftly grabbed the back of her clothes to keep her from leaving. Twii groaned loudly.

"What now?"

"Let's go look," Veenatch insisted.

"Please no. Do we *have* to?" Twii protested indignantly. "I'm not going into that dark and probably unsafe cave! And come to think of it, I will'a'not let ya go in either. Think of what your ma would say! There may be some kind of crazed beast inside there."

"I do'a'not want to go *in* it. I just wanted to peek my head inside," Veenatch assured. "Then we can leave."

"Promise ya will'a'not make me go in there?"

"Promise."

"Then we will leave?"

"Of course," Veenatch promised.

"Hmmm ... all right. But this had better not take long and do'a'not blame me if a savage wild animal attacks ya as soon as ya pop ya head inside. I've heard stories about—oh, never mind," Twii muttered.

They crept slowly up to the mouth of the dark mysterious hole, half expecting to be attacked by some wild animal like Twii-Wa had said. Warily, Veenatch leaned inside. All was dark and quiet.

"I have an idea," Twii suggested. "Ya know how tha warrior men are always searching fo underground hideouts? Why do'a'not we give them our cave?"

"Great idea," Veenatch agreed enthusiastically. "Or fo tha hidden villages that Menessah wants to build. It would save Chief a lot of trouble."

Twii, who was still badly spooked by the abandoned village and the dark cave, nearly jumped clear out of her skin when she noticed something dark lying in the grass.

But it was only a harmless old rotting plank of wood. She squinted hard to read the faded Honitonax writing on the sign. Slowly Twii began to make out the faded words: "Here in the earth lies the dwelling of Chief Hillowatha."

"This waes a palace of chiefs?" Veenatch asked. "Chief will certainly want to know about this. Maybe we can explore it with Keoko."

"Perhaps," Twii said. "There est'a'not a very good chance that we will get to go with the men inside, though. Ya know how tha chief feels about girls participating in such things. But in tha meantime, we must get home soon, so we need to get back to our horse. But we'll come back fo sure. And remember, do'a'not tell any Tumitatakens. Not even Ruex. If zey do eventually use it as a place to hide our warriors, tha Tumitatakens must'a'not know."

"Of course not," Veenatch replied assuringly. "Ya may surely have my word on that."

CHAPTER XI

YELLOW MORNING LIGHT STREAMED INTO the dark tepee. Peter rolled sleepily onto his back and stretched luxuriously. *I must have slept poorly last night*, Peter thought drowsily. *Why am I so tired?*

Many of the others were still snoozing silently (except for Charlie, who was snoring loudly).

Just as Peter almost dozed off again, he heard Mother whisper, "Peter, Peter, are you awake?"

Peter stirred. "A little," he moaned.

"Well, get up," she replied gently, "you must finish your morning chores before ten o'clock."

"May I please rest a little longer?" Peter begged. "The firewood can wait."

"No, but if you are diligent at your work, then you may sleep a little more this afternoon," Mother offered.

"Yes ma'am," he agreed, reluctantly sitting up. It was a much warmer morning than usual outside. The pale gray sky was broad and clear. The early risers, as usual, were already bustling about busily, having already finished breakfast, which had probably consisted of nuts, berries, or leftovers from last night's supper, as it was every morning. There was very little diversity in Peter's diet nowadays.

As he wandered around searching for something to do, Peter noticed Father walking swiftly toward him.

"Oh. Finally. There you are," Father said hurriedly. "We're eating fish again tonight, and we'll need to catch some more. I think you and Andrew should take the rowboat out and catch a few. Get as many as possible."

A wide grin quickly spread out over Peter's excited face. "Me and Andrew. Go fishing?" he exclaimed. "On the rowboat? Alone? Today? Oh, Father! Thank you so much!"

Father smiled. "I thought you would like that job. So pack a lunch and ... Oh, by the way, have you eaten yet?"

Peter shook his head. "No, sir, I'm not hungry."

"Are you sure?"

"Yes."

"Well, I suppose it figures," Father mumbled. "You're so skinny ... Well, anyhow, what was I saying? Oh, yes—as soon as Andrew wakes up and gets ready, you may leave."

"Oh, so we're leaving tomorrow?" Peter teased.

"Ha-ha. Very funny."

"I don't think you need to worry about us not catching enough fish, Father," Peter declared with a smile, "because our names are Peter and Andrew—the fishermen from the Bible. That ought to bring us in a fair boatload."

Father chuckled. "Run along, son, and help collect firewood before you leave. Oh, and be careful."

"Yes, sir."

Peter felt sore all over, as if he had slept with his whole body in a wrong position. After he had quickly collected an armload of dry twigs, he noticed Rebeccah, who was sitting calmly on the ground, humming tunelessly. With her soft little hands, Rebeccah carefully gathered the reddish clay dust on the ground into a tiny hill, around which she had already formed a few other small hills.

"What are you doing?" Peter inquired curiously.

"Making hills," she replied simply, without glancing up from her work.

"What for?" Peter questioned.

"For the ants," she replied, "so they don't have to make them." Rebeccah carefully poked a hole right on top with her tiny finger and proudly surveyed her work before starting another. Peter decided not to inform her that her makeshift "ant hills" were useless. After all, she was just trying to be kind to the tiny creatures.

"Don't you have something you should be doing right now?" Peter asked.

"Actually," Rebeccah replied courteously, focusing on forming her next hill, "I've been waiting for you."

"Why?"

"Because I want you to come pick blackberries with me."

Peter sighed in frustration. From the tone of her voice, he knew that she was determined. Telling Rebeccah that he didn't want to come pick berries would not stop her from asking him to come. He hated it when his sister selfishly made her own unchangeable mental plans without asking Peter first and then expected him to accept them happily. Rebeccah had done this often.

"I can't," Peter replied firmly. "I have to go fishing today, and I must begin getting things ready."

Rebeccah's face quickly turned with disappointment. Pleeeaaasse?" she begged insistently. "I want you to come with me."

"But I can't. Andrew and I *must* start getting ready."

"You could come pick berries with me first and *then* go fish."

"But I …" Peter stammered. Rebeccah had cornered him. If Peter tried to excuse himself simply because he "didn't want to," Rebeccah would retort that he was being selfish. And after all, what could he say to that? He *would* be behaving selfishly. And if Peter attempted to ask his parents for help, they would probably err on Rebeccah's side.

"Well … all right," he relented crossly, "but not for more than three minutes."

"Five?"

It was useless arguing with the stubborn girl.

"Oh, very well. Five minutes, but no more."

After Peter had trudged back to his parents to inform them where he was going (Mother was very paranoid about things like that these days), he reluctantly headed back to Rebeccah, who was carrying a small basket in which to collect the berries.

"Let's go," she announced happily. Followed by her reluctant brother, Rebeccah marched off cheerily into the thick woods.

"Can't we walk any faster?" Peter complained. "Andrew is probably waiting for me."

Just then, they reached the large tall clump of wild blackberry bushes, whose sprawling, tangled, thorny branches were dotted with ripe black, juicy fruit. (In Orenea, the blackberry season stretches all the way into the autumn). Reluctantly Peter began plucking the sweet, soft berries, being careful not to scratch himself or rip his clothes on the sharp thorns.

"I'm going to get enough to make a pie," Rebeccah explained proudly.

Peter was about to explain that it was impossible to make a pie because there was no flour or sugar for the crust, but he was interrupted by an odd noise. It sounded like heavy footsteps in the pine needles and brush behind him. Alertly Peter spun around to scan the forest for the intruder. There it was. The most enormous mountain lion Peter had ever heard of was just a few yards away. It cocked its furry head and stared curiously at the two with large and inquisitive black eyes. Peter had never beheld a mountain lion before, but he knew that it could definitely rip open him and his sister. Peter jumped. Rebeccah froze. The beast stepped forward.

For a moment, Peter was frozen in terror, like a moment in a nightmare. Then, in his panic, Peter shrieked, "Run!"

Instantly the two raced frantically from the large beast. Rebeccah bolted quickly through the woods, and Peter sped along on his scrawny legs, not far behind her. Of course, one should never flee a wildcat (Peter did not know this), but thankfully it was still full from its last meal and didn't even bother chasing Peter and Rebeccah—but the children kept running anyhow.

As they ran deeper and deeper into the unknown forest, Peter began to lose speed quickly. He was growing exhausted. *Very* exhausted. His legs ached terribly and his lungs were sore from trying to breathe in enough air. Peter's too-large clothes were so sweaty that they clung to his flushed skin. He had never run this long before, and his frail body apparently didn't like it one bit. But frightened by the mighty image of the mountain lion, Peter forced himself to keep on as he prayed silently in his head that the beast would not overcome them.

Then, just as Peter believed he couldn't go on one more jogging step, he spotted something. Water? Yes, a cool gently flowing creek. Peter slowed on his last few wobbly steps and buckled to his knees before the cool, refreshing water. Thirstily, Peter crouched over the creek and started gulping the delicious water down his dry throat, scooping it up in his hands and pouring it gently down his face and hair, which were now about the same color. Oh, how refreshing that felt!

Peter glanced over at his sister, who seemed a bit shaky but not half as exhausted as her gasping, sputtering brother. She scanned the unfamiliar sea of trees looking as if she were about to burst into sobs. As Peter let his eyes roll lazily around the strange forest, he saw that the mountain lion was nowhere to be seen, but the sickening reality that they were lost started to sink in. Lost. Lost in mountain lion–infested and Indian-inhabited woods. But Peter was much too fatigued to care about anything at the moment.

With effort, he sat up and leaned wearily against the mossy trunk of a towering old pine, still trying to catch his breath. The tiny rocky creek that Peter had been drinking out of gurgled peacefully, unaware of the distress of the lost children on its moist banks. The stream formed a sort of miniature waterfall, which poured into a clear small pool like a natural basin (which was the spot from which Peter had drunk), before busily trickling on again like any creek.

The land on the opposite side of the stream steeply sloped uphill.

When Peter gazed uphill through half-closed, glazed-over blue eyes, he noticed a sunny green flat spot up high on the side. *Maybe,* he thought drowsily, *if I can climb up there, we can see far away. Maybe even find our way home!* It might be his only hope of getting himself and his sister back to the lakeshore.

Soft crying noises were coming from the place where Rebeccah sat hugging her knees in a pitiful little ball. Weakly Peter leaned over and placed his hand on her little shoulder.

"It's all right," he whispered softly between breaths. "We'll be all right. I'm just a little tired. Don't cry. I promise all is well." Peter had confidence in what he had just promised. They couldn't be more than a fifteen-minute walk from home, yet how far away it seemed in these huge, mysterious forests. Peter was confident that if he didn't find his way home through climbing the slope, Father or the other men would certainly find them.

"Let's go," Peter announced.

"Where?"

"Up there." He was too tired to explain.

Peter stirred painfully and tried to get up but each of his limbs seemed to weigh a hundred pounds. Once he finally made it to his feet, Peter felt as if he was going to be sick. His chest and legs hurt a lot. He could feel each heartbeat all over his body. It was clear that there was something much more wrong with him than being merely out of breath.

Peter stumbled effortfully across the stream, soaking his moccasins, but he didn't care. It actually felt refreshing. Peter paused and stared up at that enormous slope looming over him like an intimidating giant. *Lord, please take me up,* he prayed silently. *Just let me last.*

This hill reminded Peter of the hill that the first search party had described but *that* slope had been on the other side of the lake. The climb was extremely difficult for Peter. Each torturous step took more effort, strength, and will than his worn-out body had left.

Had someone weighted his shoes? Sometimes he needed to lean on Rebeccah for support.

By the time they had almost reached their destination, it became apparent that something *was* radically wrong. Peter's face had quickly changed from bright red to snow pale. There was a painful dizziness and throbbing in his head and Peter was so soaked from his own sweat that one might have assumed that he had just been swimming in the lake. Each heartbeat Peter could feel all over. But he was determined to press on to the top. He had come this far, hadn't he?

Peter's hand slid up to wipe the sweat off his brow. It was then he realized he was very hot—hot as Mother's cooking fire. *Please let me last until the top,* he prayed again. Then, after what seemed like an eternity, they were there. The sunny flat spot, which was probably some sort of hunting ground, was blanketed in tall swaying grass. Hopefully, Peter gazed out wearily down the hill to try to catch a glimpse of something familiar. But though his eyes scanned the woods thoroughly, there was not a familiar trail in sight. Peter had wasted all that was in him into a worthless mission. He let out a loud half moan; half wail and threw himself onto the ground with his last crumb of strength. Inevitably, Peter's sleepy eyes shut, and he instantly floated into a deep, still slumber.

Rebeccah, who still had no clue why they had climbed up here in the first place, softly tiptoed up to where Peter lay asleep and gently prodded him with her foot. But he would not wake up. *It's just as well,* she thought calmly, not suspecting that her brother was ill. So Rebeccah simply sat a few yards away from him and waited for him to awaken.

Five … ten … fifteen … thirty minutes inched by, and still Peter didn't rouse. Rebeccah started growing frightfully bored, and, of course, everyone knows that a bored, unsupervised five-year-old is like an accident waiting to happen. First she picked flowers, but there were almost none. Then she tried to have a nap time with her brother, but she wasn't tired. After that, she wandered aimlessly around the clearing. Suddenly, Rebeccah noticed something in a shaded corner that she hadn't spotted before. It was an intricately curved brightly painted totem pole. It was like the one Father had described to her when he had returned from the first exploration trip, except a bit smaller. The wide eyes and wild faces frightened Rebeccah, but only a little. In fact, she appreciated the presence of its exquisite colorful figures, which somehow eased her sense of loneliness.

As the bored little girl wandered around the small clearing, humming tunelessly to fill the silence, she happened upon a lush tree that was dotted in clusters of small round orange/red berries. Realizing how hungry she was, Rebeccah eagerly plucked and ate about half a dozen of them. Of course, she shouldn't have done this because she didn't know if they were poisonous or not—but luckily they weren't harmful.

As Rebeccah was chewing on the last berry, a large pale yellow butterfly with black stripes fluttered gaily into the clear. She loved butterflies, especially since Father often fondly called her his "little butterfly." The butterfly happily settled on the tree where the berries grew, batting its gorgeous wings playfully. Rebeccah decided she would catch it. Yes, she would. And when Father would find her, she would give it to him as a present. This seemed like a perfectly easy and delightful plan in Rebeccah's little five-year-old mind.

However, capturing the determined creature was not as easy as Rebeccah had assumed it would be. Just as the butterfly glided low enough for her little arms; it would flap up high in the air again. Finally it fluttered out the other side of the clearing, but the stubborn girl was not about to give up. The other side of the clear, which was almost steeper than the one she had just climbed with her brother, had a dusty old deer trail winding up it. At the bottom of the hill was a large old mossy gray boulder. As she scampered playfully up the slope after the butterfly, Rebeccah carelessly stepped on a loose rock. The next thing she knew, she was tumbling uncontrollably down head over heels, along with a miniature avalanche of dirt and small rocks down, toward that large boulder. Crash! Her head was knocked firmly against the hard stone. Limply Rebeccah rolled to the ground.

Peter stirred painfully and moaned. Every part of his small body ached frightfully, and his breaths came in labored heaves. A sick, weak sensation blanketed him thickly like a fog, and a searing pain throbbed in his head. It was as if every bone inside him was shattered. His legs and chest burned the worst.

"Ooooh … Father, Mother, I don't feel …," he mumbled in a raspy voice before remembering that he was still in the woods. Peter, who had not yet bothered to open his eyes, reluctantly cracked open one eye. It was as if he were peering through blurry glasses. Slowly his sight began to form, and Peter let his eyes roll lazily around the sunny clearing. Where was his little sister?

"Rebeccah, Rebeccah," he called weakly.

Oh, what Peter wouldn't give for a nice long sip of water! Although he had had water only less than an hour earlier, he felt as if he hadn't had anything to drink in days.

"Rebeccah!" he called again.

Groggily Peter rolled onto his stomach and weakly propped himself up. Never had he had so much difficulty in doing so. He felt as if someone had strapped a six-hundred-pound burden onto him. Pain shot profusely through his body every time he moved. Slowly he tried to sit up. Dark, fuzzy purple spots appeared before his eyes.

"Where are you?" he called wearily. Peter was almost too ill to be worried—almost. He ran out of energy to sit up and collapsed shakily back down, softly crying out in pain as he hit the ground. Another large, sticky glob of sweat dripped off his face. One thing was certain: Peter needed help … and quickly! And the only way he could get it was to find Rebeccah.

Using his aching arms, he weakly dragged himself aimlessly around in the tall grass like a dying lizard, stopping every foot or so to catch his breath and call for Rebeccah. It was so painful that everything quickly fogged black before his eyes and he couldn't see anything. Suddenly, Peter collided with something large, cold, hard, and mossy, which he assumed to be a boulder or rock. Peter reached up blindly and put his hand down in something warm, wet, and sticky. Although he couldn't see much of anything, he could distinguish the bright red color on his hand through the foggy darkness.

Blood? Peter wondered. *Where in the world did that come from? I know it didn't come from me. But who else …? Oh no!*

"Rebeccah! *Rebeccah!*" he cried in a panic. Forcing himself to sit up against the rock, Peter glanced down and could just make out the limp, motionless shape of a little girl beside the large rock, with more of the thick, sticky red fluid on her head. Panicingly, Peter shook her shoulders and shouted her name desperately. The thought of losing her too was more than he could bear. But at least she was still warm.

"No! Help! Please help!" he shrieked half deliriously, although not a soul was within the vicinity to hear. Not knowing what else to do, Peter somehow stood up and started half stumbling and half running blindly back into the woods, hoping that somehow he might just make it home. It hurt so excruciatingly to move that tears were streaming down his cheeks. Running, running, running along the side of the slope, away from that horrible sight. The terrible blackness still fogged his eyes so he couldn't watch where he was headed, which caused him to collide blindly into trees and tear his sweat-soaked clothes on sharp, prickly tree branches. The difficulty, effort, and pain of just moving made the previous hike uphill look like a badly stubbed toe. But Peter didn't care. He didn't want to lose Rebeccah.

"So … Cedar," Zatch inquired playfully as they hiked through the forest together, "where under tha sun shall we shoot fo deer today? No man, woman, or child can tell a perfect hunting ground better than ya can."

Cedar chuckled, "I do'a'not know about that."

"Admit it," Zatch teased. Cedar brushed him away playfully. "But really," he continued seriously, "ya should pick a site. Perhaps that one with a creek by that village ... i'test a very good one. Or maybe tha Conkanicashawn family site. Tha last time I went it was crowded with fat deer." (In Orenea, it is custom to name public hunting grounds after a certain family patriarch. The "family hunting site" was often a small grassy clearing marked by the families' signature totem pole.)

Cedar stared thoughtfully into space for a moment or so as they wandered along. "Or we could just go to tha Choksaw family ground."

"Choksaw? Why under tha sun do ya want to go there?" Zatch questioned. "Everyone knows tha deer never gather there anymore."

Zatch was right. Besides, it would take the whole day to walk there. Although there seemed to be no reason to hunt at Choksaw, Cedar still felt a mysterious burning urge to travel there.

"We should still go," he declared unsurely.

"Why?" Zatch persisted, "I'test awful close to tha lake. What if tha white men find us?"

Cedar sighed and racked his brain for a decent answer. "I ... I do'a'not know," he admitted. I do'a'not know how to explain it, but ... I have a very strong ... hunter's intuition, I'spose ya can call it, that tells me that Choksaw est tha place we should hunt at."

A smile spread across Zatch's dirty face. "Do ya suppose that El Shaddai est tha one telling ya?" he asked half jokingly.

Cedar paused. "Do ya really think so?" he asked, taking Zatch seriously.

"I waes'a'not serious," Zatch replied. "But ya are a better hunter than I, and Chief said to let ya choose tha spot. So no matter how mad ya are, Chocksaw i'test. Besides, maybe tha deer *do* gather there now."

"I'spose i'test worth a chance."

So together the two boys trooped quickly through the calm, peaceful forest. Along the way to Choksaw, they began talking excitedly about what might be awaiting them at the hunting grounds. In fact, they grew so intent on getting their hopes up and adjusting their bows that they forgot to watch where they were walking, relying on their un-faulty subconscious to guide them. Suddenly, Zatch halted nervously. When he glanced around at the endless trees, it all seemed strangely vague and unfamiliar. It was as if they had suddenly begun walking down a completely different path. A disoriented expression spread across Cedar's face.

"What under tha sun happened?" he asked, confused.

"I ... do'a'not know," Zatch declared, looking just as baffled. We could'a'not have turned off our path. We were walking straight tha whole time." Indeed everything around them was strangely vague and unfamiliar. After a few more uncertain steps, Zatch discovered a partially hidden sign strapped loosely to a tree. It read in Honitonax, "Nazereth Village east of here."

"What's this?" Zatch asked nervously. Cedar stared thoughtfully at the old piece of wood as if he recognized it.

"This village est only a short walk or so from Choksaw!" he announced.

"Huh?"

"I am certain. Keoko took me there from Choksaw, and it only took a short walk."

"But that est impossible! We have only been walking fo less than a third of the way there and it takes half tha day to go this far!"

Cedar shrugged nervously. "Something weird est going on."

Zatch, who was trying to think of a logical explanation for the strange occurrence, shrugged his shoulders and concluded, "Maybe i'test something in tha air."

"Maybe."

"Could we have been sleepwalking somehow? Or maybe there are two villages called Nazareth," he suggested quietly.

"No," Cedar declared surely, "I recognize tha area."

"Are ya sure?"

"I think so."

Zatch shuddered shakily. "I must admit, I'm quite spooked."

"Do ya suppose that El Shaddai did this too?" Cedar asked hesitantly, as if the words were clogged in his throat.

Zatch replied unsurely. "Either that or we are just going mad!"

"Both of us?" Cedar said. He stared wide-eyed at the sign.

"Good point. Let's just keep going and see what happens."

After walking for a while longer, Zatch and Mighty Cedar finally stumbled upon the long abandoned hunting site. The wind toyed restlessly with the tall, thick grass and weeds which carpeted the small meadow-like clearing.

"Well, Zatch," Cedar declared, "do ya see anything?"

"No," he replied, "not a thing."

Cedar stared disappointedly at the empty, grassy clearing. "Do ya suppose we made a mistake after all? Nothing est here."

"Well what under tha sun did ya expect, fattened bucks to come running to greet us?" Zatch said, putting an arrow in his bow. "Now come and help me over here. We do'a'not have all day."

The tall weeds and shrubs provided many excellent hiding spots for the two as they silently crouched down to wait. Zatch noiselessly set down in the tall grass the large woven sack he had been carrying and carefully slid out a large bow and a thick bundle of arrows. Cedar had already loaded and drawn his bow, his sack lying on the ground next to his coworker. Zatch's eyes scanned his surroundings for any signs of life. Then, by a large boulder, his eyes caught sight of something bright blue partially hidden by the tall grass. He put down the bow and nudged Cedar lightly.

"What under tha sun est that over by yonder rock?" he whispered in a soft voice.

"What?"

"That blue thing over there on tha ground."

"What blue thing?"

"By tha boulder, just to tha left."

Cedar squinted, then his eyes widened excitedly. "Oh, now I see something. A sleeping animal, maybe?"

Silently the two moved slowly through the brush and weeds along the edge of the small meadow to try to find a place where they could more clearly view the mysterious object. Suddenly, Zatch grabbed his friend's arm.

"Stop, Cedar! That est a person!" he cried softly.

Cedar stopped and gazed at the object intently, "Are ya sure?"

"Yes ... Well, it looks like a person from here."

"What under tha sun are we going to do?" Cedar asked quietly. Gingerly Zatch shrugged his shoulder. "That person might be hurt."

"Or sleeping."

"What under tha sun est that red thing on it?"

Warily Zatch inched closer on his hands and knees like a curious raccoon and craned his neck to get a better view. "Blood," he concluded, "I'test blood." Cedar's eyes got as wide as the eyes of a spooked horse.

"How bad est it? Est he dead?"

"I do'a'not know. Well ... I'spose tha only thing left to do est to go over and see." They both cautiously crept closer to the motionless lump. Suddenly, Cedar, whose eyes were still open wide and alert, halted a yard or so away.

"I'test one of those white people!" he exclaimed excitedly. "Did'a'not tha chief order us not to make contact with them until his time?"

"He said not to make contact with them unless i'test necessary," Zatch reminded him. "This est very necessary."

"I'spose, but what if he awakens and tries to attack us?"

"It looks like only a little child."

"Oh," Cedar replied with relief. "Est it a boy or a girl?"

"Hmmmm ... I'd say i'test a girl, but who can tell? Zey wear such exotic clothing."

"Est ... est she hurt badly?" Mighty Cedar asked hesitantly.

"Yes," Zatch replied urgently. "If we do'a'not help her soon, this girl could bleed to death!"

"Oh, then we'll be sure to help," Cedar declared softly. "Besides, Chief will likely praise us fo helping her since tha white men might be more interested in befriending our tribe if we assist one of their children."

"Yes, well, anyhow, she est cut on tha forehead."

Cedar cocked his head back thoughtfully for a moment. "I have an idea!" he whispered excitedly. (For some reason they still felt the urge to speak in hushed tones.) Quickly he began to tear off the hems of his rough deerskin trousers. "Here, use this as a bandage."

Zatch accepted it. "Ooooh …" he moaned, rubbing his forehead. "I do'a'not feel so good. Perhaps I shall move her out a ways—away from this puddle." Carefully he dragged her by her legs away from the small bewildering scarlet puddle on the grass.

Cedar, who was starting to feel a bit ill himself, looked away briefly. "How under tha sun do ya suppose this happened?" he wondered. "Do ya think Tumitatakens did it?"

"Who knows?" Zatch replied as he somberly got back to work. "Most of them are either devoted to tha 'hate-all-Oreneans-and foreigners'-business or are against it. If she collided with a hostile one, zey would have certainly killed or captured her. Most friendly or moderate Tumitatakens would'a'not lay a finger on her. This whole affair est just getting more and more odd."

"How under tha sun can I help?" Cedar inquired.

Zatch shook his head, discouraged. "I can'a'not stop tha bleeding. We may lose her … i'test too bad Veenatch est'a'not with us. She always carries wound dressing oil in her game sack. That would save her life," Cedar nodded solemnly.

"By tha way," Zatch continued, "I'll need another bandage."

"I shall get ya one," Cedar promised. "Just wait while I go back over there to get my skinning knife out of my sack to cut off tha hem of my clothes. I'test very difficult to tear." He jumped up and quickly jogged back over to the sacks, which had been back over on the other side of the clearing. Hurriedly Cedar opened one sack and rummaged through it. Then, looking confused, he opened the other, rolled it over, and then glanced at his own sack again thoughtfully.

"What under tha sun est taking ya so long?" Zatch called, "Hurry up! I can'a'not do this task all by myself."

"What? I must have picked up tha wrong hunting sack ... This must be Veenatch's."

"Veenatch's! Does it have tha medicine?"

Cedar dove his hand eagerly inside the inner pouch, his fingers fumbling with excitement. "Um ... yes! Yes, it does!" he replied excitedly. Quickly he scurried back carrying the small, painted clay jar and the skinning knife.

"What an odd and fortunate coincidence." Cedar mumbled again as he used his skinning knife to carefully cut a decent bandage out of his coarse clothing. "I do'a'not usually take up tha wrong sack."

"Please, Cedar," Zatch requested wearily. "Will ya please help me apply pressure? I need some more help."

Cedar nodded and gingerly took over what his friend was doing.

"And ... and," he requested again awkwardly, "may we please pray as well?"

Cedar scarcely glanced up from his work when he said, "Sure thing. Heaven knows I already am."

Peter felt as if he had been walking aimlessly for an eternity. Although by now his dwindling strength had nearly run dry, he kept stumbling around blindly among the trees. The pain was so excruciating that tears crowded out of his glazed-over eyes and ran profusely down his pale cheeks, along with drops of sweat. Wearily Peter leaned against a rough tree trunk to allow his exhausted, fever-stricken body to rest a little. *I mustn't rest for long,* he decided. *Then I'll keep going, which reminds me ... where was I going, anyhow? I must've been delirious.*

His clouded, misty vision revealed that he was somewhere out in the middle of the great forest. Where was he? Where had he left Rebeccah? *Why, oh why, did I leave her?* he wondered remorsefully.

Now she could get eaten by animals or captured by Indians! Her life might depend on my being there!

Off in the distance gushed the tantalizing sound of the creek, which flowed below him down the hill. It was water. Fresh cool water! Oh, how Peter's throat burned with thirst! But he knew that if he tried to make his way down the steep slope, he wouldn't be able to make it back up. Step after labored step, Peter diligently forced himself to go on, striving desperately for some unlikely hope that he could somehow find his way back to the meadow.

Peter's feet and legs were throbbing terribly, pleading for him to give up and rest. But Peter knew that if he stopped and lay down for but a moment, he would probably not be able to get going again. Because of his sickly dizziness, the land before him seemed to pitch and heel unevenly like the deck of a ship. Ever since the long and tedious voyage across the Atlantic, Peter could sometimes still feel the ship's slow teetering and tottering in his fever. As he slowly continued to press on, he noticed that his aching head seemed to have a strange light sensation, which continued to worsen. It grew so unbearable that it became clear that Peter would soon pass out before he could even reach where he was trying to go.

Discouraged, Peter leaned heavily against a tree to rest. Then, as the darkness slowly cleared from his eyes, Peter could just glimpse a grassy clear spot just a yard or so away. The clearing! He had made it! Slowly, Peter's blurry vision cleared enough for him to notice that Rebeccah had vanished from where she had been lying by the boulder. Suddenly, he noticed something that made his blood freeze in his veins and the hair on the back of his neck stick up on end. Indians! Two of them! They were hunched over a small lump of something in the tall grass. Peter realized with sudden horror that the lump was his little sister.

They are killing her, he thought, panicking. *They are murdering her just as they did to Elisabeth.* All of the sudden Peter no longer felt faint—his pain vanished. The weariness fled from him. All he could feel was panic and dread. The thought of losing the other twin made his heart nearly jump out of his chest. Panicingly, Peter remembered all of the agony and grief that he had suffered when he had learned that Father had given up on trying to find his sister, and he gritted his teeth, firmly deciding that he could not bear that again.

Almost without thinking, Peter hastily jerked out his bronze sword and rushed out boldly into the clearing. Zatch and Cedar, who had been tending little Rebeccah's wounds, jumped with surprise. Zatch dropped the skinning knife. Cedar jumped to his feet. Zatch followed. Both parties stood frozen for a moment. Peter held out his long sword about a yard from Zatch's stomach, his blue eyes throwing sparks, his heart pounding loudly.

"Don't touch her!" he snapped as authoritatively as possible. "Or neither of you will see the end of it!"

"What under tha sun are ya talking about?" Cedar demanded, trying to sound important.

"I'm not going to let you take her too!"

"Ya have lost ya mind!" Zatch stammered, still getting over the surprise.

Peter suddenly realized that he had probably just made the dumbest mistake of his life. Although they looked to be about his age, Peter knew these two could easily overtake him because, of course, they were each twice his size. *That's it*, Peter thought. *I've just committed suicide … maybe … but I'm still the one holding the sword.* And hold it he did indeed.

Hesitantly Peter glanced down at the little motionless form, which must be Rebeccah. She was so pale from loss of blood that Peter could scarcely recognize her.

"Tell me, what have you done to her?" he demanded, still keeping up his sword. The words left behind a painful lump in his throat. "Have … have … have you … killed her?"

"What? No! Of course not!" Cedar explained defensively. "Ya have got it all completely wrong!"

Peter could scarcely understand these strange people because of their odd thick accents. He couldn't remember ever hearing ones like this before. They sounded somewhat like half Italian, half Irish, and freckled with bits of British, German, and Hungarian. It was very odd to listen to. Suddenly, it occurred to Peter that these natives should not be speaking English at all! They were hundreds of miles away from any British settlement. But for now Peter decided to focus on what he was doing rather than ask questions.

"We were *helping* her," Zatch explained, looking at Peter as if he were very dumb indeed.

"Yes," Cedar added. "Without us, she could've died. See fo yaself. We only bandaged tha head!"

Peter glanced down and noticed that they had indeed only bandaged her wound. Peter abruptly realized the situation that he had gotten himself into.

"This whole affair est just getting more and more odd," Zatch muttered to himself in Honitonax.

Awkwardly Peter lowered his sword and chuckled nervously. "Um … Well … thank you, thank you very much, dear friends. And I'm sorry," he apologized awkwardly. "You see, I … Well, I … thought that you were hurting her. At least, that's what it looked like from over there. No offense, of course."

"Quite a remarkable change of attitude," Zatch replied. "First ya threaten to kill us, then ya dub us 'dear friends.' Tha sort of fellow to rapidly change opinions, are ya?"

"Apology accepted," Cedar replied, ignoring Zatch's snarky comment.

Peter had to admit that he was very relieved and embarrassed. Cedar, who was still shaking a bit from having been held at sword point, was most disturbed by Peter. After all, why was this drenched young white boy, who couldn't be more than six or seven years old (and was obviously a few arrows short of a quiver), carrying that huge knife (or whatever that was) and running lose in the woods?

"Who under tha sun are ya?" he demanded. "How old are ya? Where under tha sun are ya ma and fa?"

"My what?"

"Ma and fa. Ya parents."

Peter realized that the boy had obviously underestimated his age. "I'm eleven years old," he declared, drawing himself to his full height. The two stared blankly at him as if he were still deranged.

"Fat chance," Zatch remarked skeptically.

"It's true," Peter insisted. "If you were to ask my mother, or almost anyone back at home, they would agree with me."

"Oh," Cedar said, not wishing to begin an argument.

It suddenly occurred to Peter that these two kind young Indians might be his ticket home.

"Thank you again for helping my sister," he said gratefully.

"Y'ekom," Cedar and Zatch replied.

"But I need another favor."

"Oh?"

"You see, the only reason that Rebeccah and I are out here is because we are lost. If you don't mind ... I mean, if it isn't too much trouble, would you please lead us home?"

Cedar stared intently at Peter's face as if trying to read whether it was a trap. "Um ... very well," he agreed, warily glancing at Zatch. "As long as ya do'a'not pull out that ... that thing again."

Peter chuckled, sliding his sword back into its sheath. "Don't worry. I promise."

As if the sound of his sword sliding back in was a trigger, all the exhaustion, fever, and pain, which had been temporarily hidden by his reflexes, flooded suddenly back into him.

"Oh, I ... Ohhhhh ...," Peter moaned, staggering back a few steps painfully. His face turned white as snow.

"Are ya all right?" Cedar asked.

"The lake," Peter mumbled weakly as his eyes started to go black. "Take us back to the tent, please."

The two Oreneans watched as Peter toppled limply to the mossy ground.

It was the next afternoon before Peter finally opened his eyes again. All he could see was a foggy mass of blurry, fuzzy shapes and colors. Strange yet familiar voices boomed and echoed loudly all around him. Their words seemed so distant and smudged together that Peter couldn't make out what they were discussing. He moaned softly. The burning soreness was so terrible that it seemed as if every square inch of his body was ablaze so that he wasn't able to move at all. It felt as if every bone in his body was shattered; he was saturated in sweat. Peter noticed that one of the fuzzy large objects slowly moved closer to him and gently pressed something to his mouth. Soon cool, sweet water touched his parched lips. As he let the refreshing liquid trickle down his dry throat, his vision started to unfog and his hearing began to clear a little. With relief, Peter realized that he ws back safely in the tent, and he recognized the woman who was kindly giving him water to be Mrs. Wilson. Mrs. Cox watched worriedly behind her.

"There, there now, Peter," Mrs. Wilson soothed gently, setting down the wooden cup. "Your mother and father will come soon. They are just outside working. But they have been taking very good care of you."

Peter opened his mouth to express his appreciation for the water, but no words came out.

"Don't try to speak now," Mrs. Wilson continued softly. "You're very ill. Now you must rest."

Mrs. Wilson, who was probably about eighteen or nineteen years old, brushed aside some of her frizzy strawberry-blonde hair that stuck out from beneath her worn white coif. She looked weary and disheveled.

Mrs. Cox, a short, sturdy woman, had dark brown hair like both of her children, which she liked to keep tied up in a bun. She gently pressed the back of her hand against Peter's sweaty pale forehead.

"How is he?" Mrs. Wilson whispered solemnly.

"Still burning up," she replied. Then Mrs. Cox turned to Peter and gently asked, "How are you? Do you feel any pain?"

He gathered up his meager strength to answer, "Y-yes," he uttered weakly. That was nearly the greatest understatement of Peter's life. It took everything he had left in him just to speak.

"Where does it hurt?"

"Uh … yes." He stammered. The two ladies exchanged glances and sighed pityingly. Suddenly, a troubling thought burst upon his mind. What had become of poor little Rebeccah? Urgently Peter opened his mouth weakly in an attempt to speak, but it was the second or third attempt before he could finally roll the heavy, raspy words off his dry tongue. "Where's Rebeccah?"

"What did he say?" Mrs. Wilson asked Mrs. Cox.

"I believe the boy wants to know about his sister," Mrs. Cox replied, and then she turned to Peter.

"Lad, I am pleased to say that all is well with the little girl. After about a fortnight of rest, she is expected to survive just fine—thanks to the gracious ones who tended her wound, whoever they may be. But dear me, what a gash for such a small, gentle creature. It is sheer providence she did not contract hospital fever."

Peter wanted to say something but didn't know what. His mind was groggy and hazy, like looking through a fogged-up window. He just laid there, his mouth ajar.

"Do you need any more water?" Mrs. Wilson asked holding up the tempting cup out of which Peter had already drunk about half of its contents. Peter tried to nod, but that caused the room to spin. Mrs. Wilson somehow understood.

Gently Mrs. Cox propped up Peter's aching head as Mrs. Wilson slowly poured the water into Peter's mouth. But as he drank it, he swallowed some of the water wrong. This sent a host of violent coughs racking up and down his aching body, causing an electrifying wave of fresh pain to wash over him. Peter let out a soft cry and gnashed his teeth in agony. It hurt to move. It hurt to cough. It hurt to breathe. Mrs. Cox sighed with pity.

"You poor boy," she mumbled sadly. "You poor, poor child."

Peter was almost too ill to be embarrassed by the fact that she had called him a "poor poor child." Soon Peter's head began to swim once more. His heavy eyelids closed, and Peter sank deeper and deeper into the black ocean of feverish sleep.

"Oh, cursed be me for leaving them in the first place!" Mother snapped at herself bitterly. "My word! I sit and sit by him, awaiting the moment he opens his eyes, but I leave for but a moment and that is when Peter decides to wake up. My poor son!"

"Don't take too much blame upon yourself, Martha," her husband soothed calmly. "How could you have known?"

Mother sighed. "Yes," she admitted. "I suppose so. But even so, I greatly wished to be there for him once he opened his eyes."

John nodded solemnly. "As did I. But I say we both benefited from the good air."

Mother stared impatiently at the water, which was being heated slowly in an animal's skin stretched out above the fire. The water needed to be heated a little at a time until it was very warm. This took a while because the skin was stretched rather high over the fire so that it wouldn't get burnt. Mrs. Cox, who had left Peter with Mrs. Wilson, strolled over to Martha and John. Mother eagerly rushed over to her.

"How are they?"

Mrs. Cox sighed. "Both fast asleep now."

Father gazed out thoughtfully over the deep blue rippling waters of the lake.

"Say," he remarked, pointing to a low-flying pigeon, "That little bird sure is flying low. I say, it might pass right over us."

Sure enough, the pigeon glided closer and closer … lower and lower … Then Mrs. Cox gasped in terror, for the bird was flying directly at her! Gracefully the pigeon glided to a halt just about two feet in front of her on the moist ground. Mrs. Cox, who was terrified of almost all living creatures great and small, leaped back and began screaming hysterically, the bird just gazing at her inquisitively, not moving a muscle.

"*Heeelllp!*" she shrieked. "It's attacking! Help! *Help!*"

Mr. and Mrs. Washingsworth stared at her as if to say, *It's only a bird, for goodness' sake.*

People began to flood out of the tents like bees from a hive to discover what the matter was. Mr. Snows was the first to reach Mrs. Cox, who was still screaming hysterically. He feverishly drew back his bow and aimed carefully at the pigeon.

"No, stop!" Mr. Kenelm cried, quickly grabbing his friend's bow and jerking it down toward the ground. "Look, it's tame."

Everyone crowded excitedly around the little gray pigeon and the screaming woman. Mr. Wilson mumbled to himself, "She is loud enough to wake the dead."

The pigeon, which seemed perfectly comfortable around humans, actually seemed to enjoy all the attention. Mrs. Washingsworth gently guided away Mrs. Cox and gently tried to comfort her to the best of her ability. Slowly Mr. Winslow got down on his knees to study the small bird. It stared at him with its tiny black eyes and cocked its tiny head as if it expected him to do something.

"Well, aren't you a pretty little thing?" he said softly. Everyone else just stared at it silently, as if they didn't wish to frighten it away. Then the gray little pigeon stuck up one of its thin tiny legs, which looked too brittle to hold up the rest of its body, out toward Mr. Winslow.

"Maybe it wants to shake hands," Andrew joked. Everyone chuckled. "Suddenly, Mr. Winslow noticed that there was a fat little gold tube attached securely to the back of the little leg. Mr. Kenelm noticed it too. Gently he picked up the little creature while his brother tried to pry open the lid of the tube with his thumbnail. He succeeded and pulled out a tightly rolled-up tiny piece of parchment. He carefully unrolled it.

"It's in English!" he exclaimed in surprise. Because of the tiny lettering and poor spelling, the message was somewhat difficult to read. This is the gist of what the note said:

Helo,

I am cheef Palkente of tha Oreneans. I want too meet with ya leedar. This est'a'not a trap. Iff ya want too know wat is hapening among wee red men, I wil meet ya near tha rige over tha lake. Com today or tomorrow wen tha sun est at mid to low sky.

"Well, I'll be," Mr. Washingsworth remarked. "What do you make of that?"

"It still might be a fake," Mr. Kenelm reminded.

"Yes," Mr. Winslow agreed thoughtfully, "But what if it's not? It would be very useful information to know what on earth is going on in those woods with the natives."

"But what if it *is* a trap?" Mr. Thomas pointed out. "Is it worth the risk?" The question hung in the air unanswered.

Mr. Winslow paused. "I'll go," he decided firmly. Cakechiwa stepped forward and declared something in his language.

"He said he'll go with you," Shamaro interpreted, "and so will I."

"I will too," Mr. Kenelm offered. One by one, each man courageously stepped forward and offered to go.

"Thank you very much, friends," he replied gratefully, "but I don't want to bring a crowd with me. I will accept my brother's offer, though."

"When do we go?" he inquired.

"In about an hour if we want to be on time."

The cool autumn breeze fidgeted playfully with Mr. Winslow's long, curly hair, which spilled out from beneath his battered old hat. His hands also fidgeted restlessly at his sides.

"Are you sure we made the right decision?" Mr. Kenelm asked nervously.

"No," his brother replied uneasily, "I don't know what to think."

"I just hope that we don't wind up like Elisabeth Washingsworth."

"Don't mention such things, Kenelm."

The weather was quite calm. Fluffy white clouds were scattered across the deep blue expanse of sky above the thick evergreen's branches. The pine needles crunched softly beneath their worn, tattered shoes. The chipper song of a lone songbird resounded throughout the forest.

"How much farther do you suppose we are from the cliff over the lake where this chief shall meet us?" Mr. Winslow asked.

"Um, we should be getting close," replied Mr. Kenelm, "if we are headed to the correct cliff."

"How could we be wrong? There's only one cliff over this lake that we know of."

So the two men continued to trek uphill. Suddenly, they stumbled upon a rocky clearing in the deep green pines and cedars. At the edge of the space was a rocky vertical drop-off, which descended about three hundred feet or more. Oh, the view! From here, one could gaze out over to the opposite mountain. The countless lush trees almost looked like scales on the skin of a giant dragon. Mr. Winslow almost wanted to walk to the edge to look down on the lake, but he dared not do that. What if the enemy warriors were hiding around here? They would be able to pounce on him suddenly and fling him over the side.

"Suppose this is the place?" Mr. Kenelm asked.

"Yes, i'test," replied an unfamiliar voice from behind. Startled, Mr. Kenelm and Mr. Winslow spun around alertly to face a petite pencil stub of a man with long shiny black pigtail braids, which were so long that he could sit on them if he wanted to. A rather large gold medallion studded with crystals and bearing a strange wheel-like symbol hung loosely around his neck, and intricately beaded moccasins were on his feet. He did not smile, but he did not seem cross either.

"Hello, I am glad to see ya have arrived safely. I am tha second chief of tha Oreneans, Keoko. I shall guide ya to tha highest chief

Palkente so ya do'a'not get lost, as ya white men are likely to do. Now follow me. We do'a'not have all day."

Keoko turned around and motioned briskly for the two to follow him.

Before proceeding, Mr. Kenelm leaned in and softly whispered to Mr. Winslow. "So," he asked, "what do you make of him?"

"Keoko?"

"Yes, of course."

"I don't know … yet. He seems to speak English relatively well, behind the bizarre accent, that is."

"What do you propose we do?"

Mr. Winslow glanced behind him at their guide and shrugged uneasily. "Well … go on, I suppose. He seems like a calm enough fellow, and besides, it is two to one."

"Oh, all right—maybe. But stay on your toes. He looks like the kind who would play a nasty trick. And who knows, he might have brought a friend or two around here somewhere."

"You're right. Try to play it smart."

Keoko, who had been patiently waiting (and ten to one listening in on their conversation), motioned to the two to follow him again. He crossed his thick, muscular arms across his broad chest and started marching off into the great woodland.

Suspiciously the two men followed their guide back into the trees. On, on, and on they quietly hiked up the mountain. Keoko's mood remained unchanging.

"So," remarked Mr. Winslow, trying to break the ice, "it is a very pleasant day, is it not?"

Keoko glanced solemnly up at the sky and wrinkled his nose. "Perhaps for now, but even tha sunniest days can produce great storms."

"Um … Oh, I suppose so," Mr. Winslow stammered awkwardly. There was a long pause.

"How is it that you know English?" Mr. Kenelm inquired.

"English? What under tha sun est English?" Keoko asked.

"You don't know?" Mr. Kenelm replied. "It is the language we are speaking now."

"I do'a'not know that word. My people call this language Benegalan."

"How do you know it?"

"The chief will tell ya."

"Why is it that the chief did not come to us himself?"

"Because he est'a'not able to walk anymore," Keoko replied matter-of-factly.

"What caused him to be unable to walk?" Mr. Winslow asked in a low voice.

"Old age," Keoko explained. "He fell and damaged his hip many seasons ago. Ever since then, he can'a'not stand nor walk. And never will again."

"That's too bad," Mr. Winslow said sympathetically.

"Yes, i'test," he replied sadly. "But he does'a'not complain. El Shaddai bless his heart."

The two continued walking quickly on in silence, broken only by the snapping of a twig beneath their feet or some pessimistic mutter from Keoko.

"I must admit," Mr. Kenelm whispered, "that I'm starting to get more comfortable around this sour Keoko fellow."

"As am I," Mr. Winslow replied softly. "He might be a wet blanket, but something about him tells me that he means no harm."

Then, all of a sudden, they came upon a large pond of water with two large islands stationed peacefully in the middle. On these islands were two quaint, rough cabin-like dwellings sitting innocently on their islands, casting their eye-pleasing reflections on the clear water. Yellow autumn leaves, which had fallen from a nearby maple, drifted lazily in the cool water, like little stray sailboats casting their shadows on the small silver fish. Cattails grew in the water on the opposite edge of the pond.

Keoko drew out his whistle and let out one long ear-piercing blast toward the middle of the pond. Instantly, out of the house on the right island jumped two boys, both wearing the large medallions. They skillfully shoved a small canoe into the water and quickly paddled it across to the three men.

"Thank ya, Number Four and Number Five," Keoko said politely as they all climbed in. The canoe was rather crowded as it made its way back across, and Keoko muttered something about capsizing.

Finally, the bottom of the canoe sliced into the shore of the island. Mr. Winslow's worn muddy boots made a loud thump as they hit the moist, sandy soil. Zatch (Number Four) and Mik (Number Five) politely drew back the embroidered deerskin flap of a door. Mr. Kenelm peeked in cautiously before entering. The dusty dirt floor was carpeted in bare footprint impressions. Number Four and Number Five scurried to the other side of the room, where a neat row of other children, each wearing medallions, were standing with their backs to the wall, leaving behind a trail in the dust of moccasined footprints. A withering fire crackled weakly in the fire pit. On the other wall hung a huge tapestry with the same wheel-like emblem as what was on the children's and Keoko's medallions. In front of that tapestry, on a little wooden stool, hunched a withered-up old man. He too wore a medallion. The chief slowly glanced up through wrinkled old eyes and squinted in the dim light.

"Ah," he croaked energetically with a warm smile, "welcome, welcome. Thank ya very much fo meeting me."

"It is our pleasure, Great Chief." The two visitors bowed deeply.

"Oh, no, no. Let's have none of that," Chief Palkente insisted, motioning them back up. "And ya may call me chief. All of my friends do."

"Thank you, sir—uh, Chief," Mr. Kenelm replied.

Chief then turned to the children, who were sitting in a neat row from tallest to smallest from the left. "Children, please introduce yaselves." The tallest one slowly stood up and introduced himself as "Number One." The second one then stood up and introduced herself as "Number Two"—and so on, in an orderly fashion which had obviously been rehearsed more than once. Mr. Winslow and Mr. Kenelm found it rather odd that these young people introduced themselves only as numbers.

Keoko quickly retrieved two more wooden stools from his dwelling place for the visitors to sit on, placing them across from the chief.

"I will start off this conversation with a question," the chief announced.

"Oh?" Mr. Winslow inquired.

"Have ya ever heard of tha Fur Christos Gelflown group?"

"No," Mr. Winslow replied.

"No, I ... Wait. Yes, actually," Mr. Kenelm said thoughtfully. "Were they the ones who fled from Germany and disappeared at sea?"

"Tha very ones," the chief confirmed with a nod. "But do ya know what under tha sun happened to them?"

"No."

"Then I shall tell ya."

"Wait," Mr. Winslow interrupted. "What does that have to do with anything? And how do you even know about them anyhow?"

"Listen and learn, my friend," the chief replied with a sly smile. "Listen and learn."

CHAPTER XII

Pona-Pow smiled as the chief began his story. She had heard it countless times around the fire at night, but the chief was such an engaging storyteller that she didn't mind a bit hearing it again. There was something almost magical about the tone of his voice and the way he spoke that drew one into the story. She wondered what the two white men would think about it and how they would react.

The chief began this story as he always did: "Many seasons ago, across tha great waters, in a land far away, there was a faithful group of people from many tribes who loved and feared El Shaddai. Tha other people of tha land hated them fo it …"

Pona-Pow knew well what it meant to be hated, for faith's sake. All Oreneans did nowadays.

"Wait a moment," Mr. Winslow interrupted. "You know who El Shaddai is?"

"Yes. I do very well," the chief replied with a bright smile.

"The same El Shaddai who spoke the Heavens and Earth into existence?"

"Yes."

"The same El Shaddai who sent his son Jesus to Earth to die?"

"Tha very one."

Mr. Kenelm seemed confused. "Who is El Shaddai?" he whispered to Mr. Winslow.

"It is the Hebrew name for God Almighty. The name is mentioned several times in the Bible," he replied.

Mr. Kenelm turned to the chief. "You follow Christ?"

"I and most of us Oreneans do, yes."

"Then why did you attack us? You murdered one of our young chil—"

"Keep listening and ya will discover who attacked ya and why. I think it would be easier that way."

"Continue."

"As I was saying," the chief continued, "some people hated these faithful people, who had started to call themselves Fur Christos Gelflowns, which means in tha language of tha country that zey had been living in 'Fo Christ Fled.' So zey decided to flee their country into four giant canoes and cross tha great waters to settle safely away from those who hated them. Their leader waes a humble, great man named John Paul Pell. There are a few stories as to tha events that proceeded tha long journey across tha great waters, but to save time, I will bypass them."

"Anyhow, as zey traveled across tha water, a great wind from tha north blew them off course, and instead of traveling west, as zey had begun their great journey, tha wind blew tha canoes south. Mighty winds blew from all directions, and tha water became very angry as to make them think, by its great tossing of their canoes, that it would crush tha canoes and slay them all."

"Fo many moons, zey did'a'not see land. Finally, tha four great canoes drew near to land. Tha land there waes dominated by a very large tribe called tha Aztecs. Many people had come great distances to trade with tha great tribe, and many traders were present. Thankfully, tha traders took pity on tha boat people. Zey fed them and housed them fo a little while. Then zey started wondering what to do with these strange people. So half-jokingly, zey set them and all tha animals, clothes, and belongings up for trade as a bulk—just to see what would happen. To their surprise, someone did buy them—a large tribe that lived miles to tha northeast, tha Honitonax."

"Zey loaded all of tha people, things, and livestock from tha ships into huge boxes with wheels pulled by bison and traveled many miles north, past tha Aztecs, past tha Pueblos, and up into tha mountains—into tha Honitonax homeland, tha land we now call Orenea. Pastor John Paul Pell, who couldn't pronounce tha real name fo this land, observed that there waes much gold found here so he used tha word ore, meaning gold, and called tha land Orenea …"

Chief then explained how, over time, the land began to be known as Orenea and the Honitonax tribe became known as the Orenean tribe. The two peoples married together and had families. The Tumitatakens, who were also living on the same land, would not accept the white people's new religion or mixed culture. But they still accepted their neighbors tolerably well—until now.

"Most of us Oreneans are tha descendants of either tha Fur Christos Gelflowns, tha Honitonax tribe, or both! Tha white man brought us many new inventions, animals, seeds, and even languages. Tha newer European alphabet est a lot easier to read than tha old Honitonax. Many Oreneans follow Christ, or at least zey say zey do. That est why tha Tumitatakens harbor such dreadful animosity toward us."

Chief explained sadly, "We are like glimmers of light in this dark land. El Shaddai's word tells us that the world will always hate tha light. So we can'a'not say we were'a'not warned. As I have said, tha Tumitatakens have tha power to succeed in getting rid of us, especially if zey ally with tha Karuks. Tha last thing zey wanted waes more light to show up to assist us. That is why zey attacked ya."

"So it is the Tumitatakens who are hostile and not you Oreneans?" Mr. Winslow clarified.

"Precisely," the chief declared. "Mind ya, we tried to stop them. Made that Mittowan promise not to attack … but he did. Then we got wind that some of them were headed to tha lake to snuff ya out. So men from all over fought them off to keep ya safe."

"How can we ever thank you?" Mr. Kenelm gratefully stammered in surprise. "You saved our lives."

"What? Oh! Do'a'not thank me," the chief replied humbly. "I'twaes tha brave people who left in a moment's notice. I did'a'not even find out until after it had almost all blown over."

"Who was it that was leaving those wonderful gifts?" Mr. Kenelm inquired again. "We certainly have benefited greatly from them. I assume it was not that Tumi ... Tumita—um, other tribe that you spoke so ill of."

"No, I'twaes'a'not," the chief replied with a chuckle. "Ya are indebted to Chief Respinowow. He est tha trading chief of Orenea and lives in tha village of Santinowa, near tha great Lake Honiton. He est tha one who generously bestowed those useful items upon ya. Tha reason there are'a'not many villages near tha lake est because tha soil est hard as a rock and very unsuitable fo growing crops. Back in my day, there used to be a few villages in that area, but now only hunters and fishermen go around tha great lake's waters. Also, I hope ya do'a'not think that every man, woman, and child among tha Tumitatakens est a blood-drinking villain. I suppose many of them are quite moral folk ... or at least a few are."

Mr. Kenelm leaned in and lowered his voice gravely. "One of our children was killed by that tribe, you know."

"Yes, I know." The chief sighed somberly. He seemed genuinely grieved about the loss. "I hear many stories like that from my people."

Mr. Winslow, who wished to change the subject, sat up straighter and gestured toward the agentes. "So, Sir Chief, are those your grandchildren?"

Number Three snickered quietly.

"No," Chief replied with a chuckle. "I have never been married. Zey are some children from tha village where I grew up—Tha Golden Heart. I lived in that village until I became chief." he smiled and stared absently into space as if recalling earlier days. "I remember," he recalled, "living in that village as a ten-summers-old boy. My family and I went to Ore-Cita fo a day. John Paul Pell—he waes chief at tha time—happened to be passing through on his horse that day. I waved shyly at him, and he waved back and smiled at me. He was then probably about tha age I am now. Yes, he waes my hero. I'twaes he who translated parts of El Shaddai's scriptures into our language and served as our best chief fo so many years."

Mr. Winslow glanced back at the children. He could recognize the difference in skin color, suggesting that there may have been some European influence involved (especially in Mighty Cedar, Mik, and Twii-Wa). Then the three men launched deeply into a boring conversation about grown-up things for about an hour.

After they had finally finished a conversation about Orenean politics, Mr. Kenelm regretfully announced that it was growing late and that they would need to leave. Chief, who was just as sorry to see them go, generously declared that he had a few gifts to send home with them. Number One and Number Five each carried over a small bag full of fruit. Pona-Pow opened her mouth to tell the white men how they had rescued the little girl the night she fell out of the boat (as she had been hoping to get a chance to do before they departed), but Zatch quickly reached over and pinched her on the arm to keep her quiet, which annoyed Pona-Pow exceedingly.

"Zey are tha best grapes and quimpanitas in tha land," the chief declared as Number One handed a sack of fruit to Mr. Kenelm.

Mr. Kenelm briefly glanced into the bag with the quimpanitas in it and chuckled softly. "Look, Edward," he exclaimed, "remember we had these at home in England too! Except there we called them apples!"

For the next few days, Peter remained ill. He continued lying down, although there was no blanket or pillow for him. It was one of the most painful illnesses of Peter's life, although he spent most of his time lazily drifting in and out of consciousness. Worried, his parents prayed for him and diligently did all they could to care for him. Mother faithfully stayed with her son during the day, while Father kept night watch, which was even worse than caring for him by day because these were his most painful, feverish hours. In fact, he was in so much pain that he couldn't move an inch. He legs burned and swelled the most. Sometimes when he was awake, Peter would deeply desire water yet be unable to request it. Other times, the fever would cause him to feel so hot that it was as if he were roasting over a cooking fire; then, a moment later, he would feel so cold that it was as if he were lying in a casket of ice. Either way, he would always be gushing sweat. Peter felt as if he would crack under the weight of all the pain burning inside his muscles. Rebeccah, who was rapidly getting well, chattered on endlessly into the space from where she lay near him, like many little girls do, but for once Peter was pleased to hear it.

The day after the day he first awoke was filled with the most agony for poor Peter. However, Peter awoke on the next morning feeling a little better. The fever was down, the pain was a tad less, and his unconscious spells were shorter and fewer. The day after that brought even more improvement. And the day after that, he was even able to swallow a little food. The two sick children were always kept safely in the supply tepee for privacy and so they wouldn't get stepped on.

On the day after that, the Orenean chief generously invited his new friends to attend an Orenean church, and some of the grown-ups decided to accept his invitation. Somewhere along the way, the Fur Christos Gelflown's miscalculated exactly what day it was and accidently placed their Sabbath on an English Thursday! It took a while for Keoko, along with some of the lower chiefs, to locate a church that held services in English (known to Oreneans as Benegalan), but they eventually found one in a tiny village on Mt. Mogogg. The service was much different from a Puritan service. For one, the congregation sat on the floor, with the children sitting in the rafters. The chant-like hymns were mostly in another language—and there were many of them.

The three Orenean languages (Honitonax, Shonto, and Benegalan) were all throughout Orenea, but Honitonax, which was the indigenous tongue, was most popular. Shonto (Italian) and Benegalan (English), however, had an easier writing system. All three tongues were used in the hymns, but the service was in Benegalan because most of their villagers were descended from the British or Irish. Even so, the thick Orenean accents were difficult to make out.

But the men enjoyed the service (from what they could understand). Chief then invited everyone to come to a large feast held in their honor the following evening. Peter was sorry that he was still too weak to attend. The lavish meal was served at sundown the following day.

Drip-drop, drip-drop, drip-drop … The raindrops flicked steadily at the tepee's slanted roof. Andrew slumped lazily in a corner, idly twiddling his thumbs. There was nothing to do—nothing. Because of the pouring rain, almost everyone had crowded back inside the small tents, except of course for the Washingsworth family, who were occupying the supply tent, and Mr. Snows, who was checking the animal traps with Mr. Wilson. Andrew, who had not yet been allowed to visit his friend, wondered how Peter was getting along out there in the "other tent." *It must get awful lonesome out there*, he speculated. Then, Mr. Thomas, who had previously been chatting with the grown-ups, wiggled out of the crowd and plopped down comfortably beside his son.

"Say," he asked, "what are you doing?"

"Being bored," Andrew replied dully.

"Would'st you mind if I be bored as well?"

"Yes, so long as you do not do it too loudly."

His father chuckled, showing off his many wrinkles. Mr. Thomas was short, with balding hair and bits of gray streaking the hair he did have. He wore a tiny pair of spectacles on the tip of his large rounded nose. One of the lenses had cracked.

"Say," he remarked, "that sure was some feast last night. I'm still full."

Andrew nodded thoughtfully. "Aye." There was a pause.

"Uh … Andrew," Mr. Thomas asked, "is there something on your mind?"

"Yes," Andrew admitted solemnly.

"What is it, if I may ask?"

"Well," Andrew replied thoughtfully, "I was just thinking how much of a disappointment it would be if I had been too sick to go last night."

"Yes, it would have been," Mr. Thomas agreed, "but you weren't."

"But Peter was."

"Oh. Well, that's very kind of you to think of him, Andrew."

"I want to visit him."

"I'm sure that could be arranged. In fact, you could probably go now if you wanted to."

"But … I'm a little nervous. Do you think he will be rolling around on the floor and screaming deliriously?"

Mr. Thomas chuckled. "No, I suppose not. But still, be gentle with him. He might not be up to visitors. Don't stay too long."

"I won't, Father," Andrew promised. He stiffly found his footing and worked his way through the thick bulk of people. It was raining quite hard. Great drops of rain poured profusely out of the ash-colored clouds. Andrew bolted quickly across to the supply tent, covering his head with his hands in a meager attempt to keep dry. Once there, Andrew hurriedly thrust his head inside the flap. It was somewhat dark inside the small tepee. With what light there was, Andrew could make out Peter's small form lying motionlessly on the hard ground, his head turned away. There didn't seem to be anyone else in the tepee. Andrew ducked inside to get out of the soaking rain, unsure of whether Peter was awake or not.

Peter turned his head toward Andrew as he entered. A wide smile broke across his pale face. "Oh, hello," he greeted warmly. "It is good to see you. It's been a while."

Andrew found himself automatically smiling back. "You as well. How do you feel?"

"Better," Peter replied, effortfully sitting up. "My back and legs still hurt, but as you can see, I can now sit up."

"That is good … Do you want me to leave?"

"Oh, no. Please stay if you wish," Peter replied. "It gets so lonely in here. Though I don't know why you would want to stay in this place. It's quite dull."

"Not more boring than where everyone else is. Where are your mother and father?"

"Father is working on the traps. I believe Mother is bathing Rebeccah. She was starting to smell foul."

"Oh."

"Say," Peter apologized, "I'm sorry you missed our fishing trip."

"Huh?"

"Our fishing trip—remember, we were about to go fishing the day when I fell ill."

"Oh, yes! Well, it's all right. It's not as if you *wanted* to grow ill."

Peter chuckled. "No, I definitely did not."

Andrew searched his mind for decent things to converse about. "How do you feel now?"

"Much better than yesterday," Peter replied. "Mother fed me a good breakfast this morning. My legs still burn, though, and I have an elevated temperature, but it's all right now. I'm getting well."

"Did you think you would die?"

"I don't know. I suppose not."

"How is Rebeccah?"

"She is well," Peter replied. "Still has a tender scar on her head, though."

Andrew paused and stared out into space thoughtfully. "Peter," he inquired, "how did Rebeccah get injured?"

Peter straightened his back a little. "Well," he began, "that's a long story. But to answer your question ..." He coughed loudly.

"It's all right, Peter. You don't have to speak," Andrew offered politely.

"No," Peter insisted, "I just caught a tickle in my throat. I'm not *that* ill. But as I was saying, I don't know how she acquired the wounds. I was asleep at the time."

"But what do you remember happening just before you fell asleep? My father heard the story from you when you told it to the men yesterday, but he was terribly vague when he relayed the story to me. Do you remember any Indians giving you the knife or the pouch?" Andrew questioned.

"What knife and pouch?"

"You don't know?"

"No," Peter replied thoughtfully.

"Well, you were found with them beside you. Perhaps the Indians gave them to you as gifts. I think that your father was waiting to give them to you when you recovered."

"They were found beside me in the meadow?"

"No," Andrew explained, looking surprised that Peter did not already know these things. "They didn't find these things in a meadow. You and your sister had them beside you."

"But I fell unconscious in a small clearing. That I remember," Peter said, puzzled.

"But you were not found in a meadow. Mr. Kenelm found you beneath some brush, side by side with your hurt sister. They found you only a few yards away from the lake."

Realization flooded Peter's eyes. "So those Indian children *did* honor my request."

"What?"

"Just before I collapsed, I asked the Indians to bring us back home."

"What Indians?"

"I can see that I'll have to tell you the whole story."

In detail, Peter relayed to Andrew the whole tale of his adventure.

"Wow," Andrew remarked after the story was complete. "That is quite extraordinary. Who do you suppose those children were?"

"I don't know. But I suppose we shall never meet them."

There was a pause.

"So do you want to hear about the feast last night?"

Peter's blue eyes widened. "Yes! Don't leave out a thing. Did you see Indians? What were they like?"

Andrew smiled and began the story. "There were many people there. Most of them were grown men. I think they were all lower chiefs or something of that sort. The highest chief is very old. I think he said he was almost ninety-five!"

"Did you get to meet him?" Peter asked excitedly.

"Yes, actually," Andrew explained. "His name is Thomas Palkente. But everyone just calls him Chief."

"Did you sit near him while you ate?"

"No, I had to sit with the rest of the children."

"Were there many children there?"

"No, only us and about six Orenean children."

"Do you know what their names are?" Peter inquired curiously. "Are they really odd and difficult to pronounce?"

"Odd, yes," Andrew explained. "Difficult to pronounce, no."

"Oh?"

"Their names are Number One, Two, Three, Four, Five, and Six. Strange, eh?"

"Are they siblings?"

"No."

"That *is* odd. They didn't seem like ... slaves, did they?"

"Nay, they acted perfectly comfortable around Chief and the other chiefs."

"How old were they?"

"As a guess, I'd have to say mostly about our age. Some a little younger."

The rain outside increased in intensity.

"What kinds of food did you eat?"

"Many things. Let's see … There was duck, turkey, goose, squirrel, and—oh, yes—rabbit. They also had lots of fruit. We also had a soup of stewed apples."

Peter chuckled. "All that at one feast?"

"Yes. And I must say, after eating venison, blackberries, and nuts for so long, food like that has never tasted better. Wanna know how much I ate? Three apples, two large servings of grapes, three helpings of—"

"I understand," Peter interrupted.

"Well, anyhow, I suppose the Oreneans are very kind people—even though I can't always understand what they are saying. I think me and Number One are friends now. He's ten."

"That's right fine," Peter replied. "Did anything else interesting happen last night?"

A huge cheesy grin spread across Andrew's face. "Yes, actually."

"What happened?" Peter asked eagerly. "This didn't involve Charlie, did it?"

"It actually did."

"Oh no. What happened?"

"It really wasn't anything cruel. Just a childish joke. You see, when we were asked to introduce ourselves, Charlie introduced himself as 'Your Majesty.'" Andrew chuckled.

"Huh?" Peter asked.

"Yes. That way, people would call him that. 'Come to the table, Your Majesty,' 'Want to play, Your Majesty?', 'Wish for some more food, Your Majesty?'"

Peter snickered. "And they actually called him that?"

Andrew nodded, effortfully trying not to laugh.

"Why? Didn't they realize …?"

"No," Andrew explained, "I really don't think they know what the word 'majesty' means. So to the natives, it's just another strange white man's name."

"Oh no."

225

"But that's not the best part … Number Six accidently mispronounced it and called him 'Your Maggotsy' by mistake." At this, the two boys started howling uncontrollably with laughter. "And then," Andrew continued, between peals of laughter, "they all figured that *that* must be the right way to say it. So they all called him that." This sent a new round of boisterous laughs over Peter and Andrew.

"Your Maggotsy. Ohhhh … that's rich."

Suddenly, Peter stopped laughing and patted Andrew urgently on the arm. Both boys froze, red in the face, for there standing in the entrance flap was a fuming "Your Maggotsy" himself.

"Why … you … you … *you two little beasts!*" he shouted angrily, storming furiously back out into the rain.

Once he was gone, Peter snickered softly. "Well, you know what they say," he whispered happily. "Laughter *is* the best medicine."

A few more dull days passed slowly. Each day was an improvement for Peter. One morning Peter opened his eyes and rolled over sleepily on the ground. He dozed again for a moment or so and then roused himself once more. All he could hear was the sound of Father's deep heavy sleep breathing from the other side of the tent. Peter sat up slowly and let his sleepy eyes roll around the room. Among all the bows and baskets of food for the winter, Rebeccah was curled up asleep on the ground, surrounded by Mother and Father. Peter stood up and stretched stiffly. It was then when Peter's stomach growled and he realized how hungry he was.

Quietly Peter tiptoed past his parents and pulled back the tent flap. Immediately, a blast of frosty air brushed against him. But Peter stepped out anyway and gratefully treated his lungs to a few deep breaths of fresh air. Briskly Peter walked up the rocky clay shoreline, rubbing his arms to keep them warm. He could see his own breath.

The sun hadn't yet risen, and no one had roused. The sky was an ashen gray color. Out over the great blue lake, a large brown eagle with a white head swooped down and skillfully caught up a squirming shiny silver fish out of the water. *How remarkable*, Peter thought. *Andrew will likely enjoy hearing about it.* He knelt down at the water's edge and scooped up the cold water with his hands, and splashed it on his dirty face. Then he took up another handful and poured it into his mouth. Oh, how refreshing it felt to wash that stale sickly taste out of his mouth! The frigid water caused his hands and face to sting in the cool air. But Peter simply put his hands into fists and blew on them gently.

He wandered happily off into the woods to get something to eat. The blackberry bushes, which were not very far into the forest, were just about out of blackberries, but the ones there were large, sweet, and ripe. Peter popped a dozen or so into his mouth. Then, satisfied, he decided to take a short walk. The horizon was just starting to grow a pale pink color, and an orchestra of birds chirped joyfully above his head as he strolled slowly along. Peter sleepily slumped down beneath a fatherly old oak tree, which had shed most of its leaves already. He yawned and leaned against its huge mossy trunk. *I must not stay here long*, he decided, *for I feel like I might fall asleep.*

But he must have fallen asleep anyhow, for the next thing he knew, the sun had begun to peek timidly over the horizon and commission its warm, cheery yellow rays through the tree branches. *What a pleasant sunrise*, Peter thought drowsily while observing the brilliant hue of yellow and orange. Then, suddenly, a disturbing thought occurred to him. What if his parents were awake and didn't know where he was? They would get awfully worried, especially Mother, and he would get punished.

Peter frantically scrambled to his feet and stumbled off on the old deer trails. As he jogged along the familiar path toward home, Peter hoped and prayed that nobody had already started searching for him. Peter crashed through the tree branches and found himself on the lakeshore again. His fears were confirmed. The men were already organizing search parties for him. Quietly Peter walked up behind the circle of men.

"Looking for me?"

Startled, they spun around and were clearly surprised to find Peter standing there before them. Peter smiled nervously. Mother, who had been standing nearby, raced up to her son and planted her hands firmly on her son's thin shoulders. By the half-angry, half-relieved expression on her face, Peter could tell that he was in for a great deal of trouble.

"Peter Edward Washingsworth, where have you been?" she cried, tears quickly springing up in her eyes. "I worried myself half to death about you!"

Peter gazed down at his shoes shamefully. Mother had a way of making just the right facial expressions to make one very sorry for anything. Sometimes Peter thought she did it on purpose.

"I'm sorry, Mother. I didn't try to do any harm. Honest! I just went for a walk, and ... I should have managed my time better."

"No, no," Mother said, wiping the tears out of her eyes with her sleeve. "I'm sorry. I shouldn't have become angry with you in that way. I'm just glad you are all right. But look at your clothes! They are quite twisted, and the seat of your knickers is covered in pine needles."

Father walked up to Peter, put his hands on his hips, and looked his boy over thoroughly. "Well, son," he observed with a smile, "I'm glad to see you up and about again."

"Yes, sir," Peter replied happily. "Me too."

"How do you feel?"

"Very well."

"That is wonderful ... and you are all right? No pain?"

Peter nodded.

"All right," Father announced. "Now we can get back to preparing the furs we have caught to present to the natives for tomorrow ..."

"Why are you packing the furs?" Peter asked. "Are we going to see the Oreneans again tomorrow?"

"No, we are going with the Oreneans to search for a place for us to live, and then after that, they will serve us supper."

"Can I please go?" he begged. "I'll be good, I promise."

"That's *may* I please go," interjected Mother, who was listening in on their conversation. Peter sighed and quickly corrected himself.

Father stared intently at Peter. "Are you sure you are well?"

"Absolutely, sir."

Father stroked his beard thoughtfully.

"Please let me go with you, Father," Peter continued as innocently as possible. "I won't cause trouble—I promise."

"Oh, I didn't think you would," Father quickly assured him.

"Then I may come?"

"It really won't be very exciting," he warned. "And perhaps you should stay here another day. You know you were gravely ill?"

"I feel well now," Peter insisted. "Perhaps we shall see if I am still well tomorrow, which I am certain I will be."

"Well … I suppose one day wouldn't hurt you any."

Peter beamed excitedly. "Oh, thank you! What time do we leave?"

"At dawn."

Peter smiled eagerly and rushed back toward the supply tepee to get his sword strapped on for the day.

"Oh, and Peter," Father called, "please try not to disappear again."

The next day was rather intriguing for Peter. It was interesting to meet new people and observe the new tribe. And it was a great opportunity for Peter to meet new Orenean friends for the first time. Vaguely Peter thought he recognized Number One and Number Four, but eventually he dismissed the thought. The meal that evening was excellent, and Peter wolfed down almost everything on his plate. Overall, the journey was unsuccessful, however. So the next day Peter woke up bright and early to meet the Oreneans and their horses yet again. He popped five small hard nuts in his mouth for breakfast. The morning was cool yet sunny. A small crowd had gathered to wait for the Oreneans. Finally, Peter heard the familiar sound of horses cantering through the underbrush.

Keoko, who was heading the rest of the Orenean men, was seated on a fine mahogany-colored horse. He appeared even shorter up there.

"Good morning," Mr. Winslow called cheerily.

"I do'a'not see anything different about it," he muttered. "Are ya ready?"

"Yes," everyone replied.

"All right. Get on a horse, two apiece. We are headed to tha Fire Hills. But first I want to show ya a place in tha Sun's Ray Forest. Of course, tha Sun's Ray Forest est flooded now, but this part est on tha edge and est'a'not flooded—yet."

Peter glanced briefly around at the others. Mr. Wilson was now able to join the others because the herbal treatment, which the Oreneans had sent to him for his infected hand, had amazingly healed it well enough so that he could come along. Most of the women also desired to help—except Mother and Mrs. Wilson. They stayed back with Rebeccah, Charlotte, and Paul, Mrs. Wilson's baby son. Peter noticed other people climbing onto horses and found an empty spot behind Zatch. Peter tried determinedly to climb up on the bareback of the horse, but he kept slipping. Noticing his difficulty, Zatch grabbed Peter firmly by the hand and pulled him up easily. Thankfully, no one saw that he had needed assistance, which would have been quite humiliating since most of the others could easily climb onto their horses.

"Thank you, Number Four," Peter said quietly.

"Y'elcome," Zatch replied.

Peter, who was having a hard time staying on the slick back of the horse, clung discreetly to the back of Number Four's shirt. The tan horse snorted impatiently.

"So," Peter inquired curiously, "why are you always with your chief? Are you related to him?"

"No."

"Then why?"

"We help him ... Actually I am'a'not allowed to say exactly what we do. But I'm here. Numbers Two, One, Three, and Six are here. We will help with tha horses and lunch. Number Five est staying back with Chief. He needs tha help when Keoko est'a'not there."

Then Zatch whispered something quietly in the horse's ear. The horse suddenly started walking, causing Peter to lurch backward and nearly tumble off.

"Hold on!" Zatch warned.

Andrew and Charlie, who were both riding a white horse together, rode past Zatch and Peter.

"Hello, Andrew. Hello, Your Maggotsy," Zatch said as they passed him. Charlie blushed bright pink as Peter and Andrew tried to swallow laughter.

Why under tha sun, Zatch wondered, *do people think i'test so amusing whenever I speak to him?*

"When did you first start being the chief's helper?" Peter questioned.

"Many moons ago," Zatch answered. "Keoko est my uncle, so I had a better chance of getting chosen."

"Did you want to get chosen?"

"I really did'a'not care. I waes young at tha time. My sister, Number Six, got recruited later."

"Did the others get chosen too?"

"Yes, we are all from tha same village, chief's home village, Tha Golden Heart, so he knows our parents."

"Do you get to see your parents sometimes?"

"Of course—every full moon or so."

"How old are you?"

"Eleven winters."

"Me too! I'm eleven winters. It's true. Ask any of us."

"All right ... Number Five est eight autumns, Number Two est eleven springs, Number One est ten summers, Number Six est eight summers, and ... well, Number Three gets a little confusing. She waes born just as winter waes turning into spring, so I'spose ya could say she est eleven winter/springs old. I'test complicated, but then again, I'spose all girls are complicated. Especially her."

Peter nodded in agreement. "I suppose so."

Clip-clop, clip-clop. The horses continued to canter calmly through the peaceful forest, occasionally stopping to drink from a small stream along the way. The trip was boring and speckled with brief snippets of conversation. Finally, the large party of people arrived at the place in the Sun's Ray Forest. It was a calm, secluded, peaceful spot. The young oaks were somewhat spaced out compared to the thick mountain woodlands, yet it was still somewhat shady here. The pale green grass grew a little past Peter's ankles, and since it was at the edge of the Fire Hills, orange poppies polka-dotted the moist ground. A gentle restless breeze blew soothingly through Peter's curly red hair.

"What under tha sun do ya think?" Keoko asked agilely sliding off his horse. "It does flood sometimes—every ten winters or so."

Most of the men had climbed off their horses and inspected the land. Peter jumped off too and helped Number Four tie the animal to a tree.

"This is a very beautiful place," Mrs. Cox marveled admiringly.

"Yes," Rachel agreed. "I think I could be content to spend the rest of my life here."

"As could I," Mr. Wilson added. "It's perfect."

"But we would need to do some clearing," another person reminded them. "We don't have time for that before winter."

"That's right," Mr. Winslow agreed. "And there is less game in this area, I'll wager. I think we ..."

Suddenly, out of seemingly nowhere, appeared about fifteen Tumitataken braves. Everyone froze. They were surrounded. There was no way out. Peter recognized the shiny blue painted faces of the hateful warriors. His heart pounded so loudly that he almost fancied the enemy could hear it. Rachel gasped fearfully and clung to her mother.

Then out pranced the chief of them all—Mittowan himself. He crossed his arms across his chest and walked proudly up to Keoko, smirking menacingly. Keoko, who tended to never let it show when he was afraid, stood his ground bravely.

"So, little man, I'll get right to the topic," the Tumitataken chief sneered in his own language. "How would your old chief like to get rid of me once and for all, eh?"

"What under tha sun does that mean?" Keoko demanded. "I'm sure he would jump at tha opportunity, but I'm sure there est a great many things ya are'a'not telling us."

"For once, you are actually right," the great serpent replied, pausing thoughtfully in front of Keoko. "There are."

"What under tha sun est this catch?"

"I'll tell you, Keoko. I'll tell all of you—if you interpret to them."

"Agreed."

Mittowan slowly backed up a few steps and began addressing everyone as if in a speech, pausing every few sentences to allow them to be interpreted.

"Dear, dear, people," he began sarcastically, "I have now decided that I have grown weary of all of this tension that has been haunting me for the past twelve autumns."

Haunting him, eh? Keoko thought as he reluctantly interpreted the words into English.

Mittowan continued. "So I have come to a decision. We will end this discord. There will be a contest tomorrow when the sun is at its highest." Out of his loincloth, he drew a sharp, long swordlike knife. "A fight ... Or as you white men call it, a duel. Since I will choose one of you white men here to be my opponent, I think it is fitting to fight in the way you are accustomed to. When I win, you will all be at my mercy. I will eliminate every Orenean in this land and make the very name of your terrible tribe an obscenity. Then everyone will know forever how decisively powerful I am. They will know—dare I say the name—that El Shaddai could not help them."

"What if we win that duel?" Keoko asked.

"You won't."

"Maybe not. But i'test'a'not a level contest if there are'a'not stakes on both sides."

"Very well, very well. The stake on your side will be my people leaving Orenea, never to return or bother you again. Now are you satisfied? Are the stakes even enough for your tastes?"

"Will ya release all of our people ya have as slaves in captivity?"

"Oh, very well. It will not make any difference anyhow. I have been practicing with knives every day since I could first walk."

Mittowan chuckled cruelly and rubbed his large hands together.

"But what under tha sun happened to that alliance that ya were so excited by with tha Karuk people?" Keoko asked. "I thought they wanted to help ya with ya in war against us. Why under tha son have ya not waited fo them to arrive first?"

"They decided not to ally with us," Mittowan replied matter-of-factly, as if it did not matter a bit to him. "No great loss to me. I do not need their help anyhow. Now for the interesting part—choosing my opponent."

"May we select our own warriors?"

"No, of course not."

"Wait!" Keoko shouted. "What under tha sun happens if we do'a'not accept ya challenge?"

"You must if you are smart," Mittowan replied simply. "Because if you do not, I will just annihilate you all right away. I just thought I would be kind and give you a chance."

Keoko drew back and considered his options. "Yes," he decided reluctantly. "As if we have much choice."

"You give your word?"

"Yes, and ya give ya word?"

Mittowan smirked and nodded. "Yes, I do."

"I'll need ya to swear an oath."

"I will."

Solemnly Keoko faced Mittowan, and they both took the oath.

"What are you doing?" Mr. Wilson cried. "None of us can fight at all!"

"I have no choice."

"But shouldn't you talk to Chief Palkente first?"

"I know him well enough to know what he would decide. Besides, if I wait, Mittowan might change his mind and take tha liberty to kill us all. We know he has tha power to do so."

As the great serpent proudly strutted about the possibilities for opponents, he examined each one up and down with his evil brown eyes and a stony, cruel gaze, which would make one cringe in fear at the sight of it. Everyone stood silently frozen, hoping desperately not to be selected. The suspense was so thick that you could slice it with a knife. Mittowan's large bare feet moved slowly and silently along the ground, gradually making their way in Peter's direction. Suddenly, the Tumitataken chief locked eyes with Andrew. Andrew fearfully stared back, his eyes the size of saucers.

Peter watched in horror as the Tumitataken chief took a few striding steps toward him. Andrew looked as if he was going to be sick. Mr. Thomas watched helplessly as Mittowan dug his fingers into Andrew's spiky blond hair and gruffly yanked his head back so he could gaze directly into his eyes. Andrew looked terrified and panicked, as if he was about to scream. Peter couldn't blame him. After all, staring into that intimidating face from a distance was foreboding enough. That cruel smirk of Mittowan's was almost too terrible to be true. Peter was sure that he must practice it at home.

Finally, the Tumitataken chief released Andrew and turned toward Charlie. Andrew quietly let out a deep breath and relaxed. Mittowan, who was now examining a frightened Charlie, scratched his head thoughtfully as if trying hard to decide if this was his opponent. *He is the biggest coward I have ever seen!* Peter thought angrily. *Not only is he not letting the Oreneans choose their own warriors, but he is only considering inexperienced people half his age!* Then a dreadful thought suddenly occurred to him—what if Mittowan noticed his sword and decided that since he already had a weapon, he would make the perfect candidate? He had shown that he was cowardly enough to choose someone Peter's age.

Slowly Peter shifted his hand over the hilt of his sword as if to partially hide it. Then Peter's worst nightmare came true. The Tumitataken chief had sensed a bit of movement in the still, dismal tension when Peter had moved his arm, and now he was looking looking straight at him! It was the most horrible, terrifying, almost demonic gaze you could imagine. Peter suddenly felt sick. An evil smile spread across Mittowan's ugly face, and he started to walk menacingly toward the boy. Peter wanted to bolt, but his feet were frozen to the spot. His knees felt weak and wobbly. The great serpent paced slowly in front of him, tapping his large ugly cleft chin steadily with his finger and continuing to thoroughly inspect him. Peter prayed silently with all his heart that he wouldn't notice the bronze sword, which he was still trying to partially conceal behind his hand. But too late. Mittowan walked up to Peter's side and lightly touched the hilt of his sword. Although it was in its sheath, it was obvious he could tell that it was a sword. Mittowan's evil grin widened. Peter's heart raced at the speed of a thousand galloping horses.

"What's your name boy?" Mittowan demanded in his own language. Keoko interpreted.

"P-P-Peter."

"Peter, eh?"

Hearing his own name coming out of Mittowan's mouth made Peter feel almost angry for a moment. He did not know why.

"That sounds like a white man's name," he declared mockingly, pointing at Peter's very fair skin. "And see, he is a really white man." He chuckled at his own joke. No one else thought it was amusing.

"So," he asked Father, "how old is that red worm of yours?"

"He wants to know how old Peter est," Keoko whispered.

"I'm not telling him that!" Father shot back.

"If I were ya," Keoko advised, "I would tell him. He has quite a temper. No telling what terrible things might happen."

"If I must … He is eleven years old."

When Mittowan was told, he chuckled loudly. "Eleven!" Mittowan jeered. "Oh … that's the greatest joke I ever heard. That squirt! Eleven! I do not believe it!"

He turned to the Tumitataken warriors, who were still surrounding the place. "This scrawny one will do nicely. Go back home straight away and prepare a place to hold him until tomorrow. I'll escort him there myself."

Peter fought to process what had just happened. Now he *really* felt sick! Mittowan grabbed Peter tightly by the wrist and gruffly led him away. The feeling of Mittowan's fingers curled around Peter's skinny wrist made him feel as if he might panic. Peter stumbled awkwardly along behind, trying to keep up with Mittowan's broad strides. He glanced back over his shoulder desperately.

"Help!" he cried hoarsely.

Father had had enough. "Stop!" he ordered firmly, angrily rushing a few steps forward. "I won't let you take my son!"

As if understanding what he had said, Mittowan spun Peter around to face his father, jerked out his large knife, and pressed it threateningly against Peter's neck. "One more step forward and he dies!"

Peter didn't dare breath. His muscles tensed. Father froze. Peter could feel the sharp stone blade pressing menacingly into his throat, like a ravenous lion crouching on top of him. Peter felt dizzy. No sooner had Keoko interpreted than Father helplessly stepped back in surrender. Much to Peter's relief, the knife was lowered from his throat.

"Good," Mittowan declared calmly. "Now we can go."

"Wait!" Keoko called, "Mittowan …"

"That's Great Chief to you," the Tumitataken chief chided.

"Yes, whatever ya wish, but anyhow, I think it would be more appropriate if we were tha ones to take him to our village fo tha night. After all, does'a'not tha tribe normally each present its own warrior. If ya were to take him away, it would look like a kidnapping. And tha chiefs of tha other tribes would think ya are cruel and unjust." *As if zey do'a'not think that already,* Keoko thought resentfully.

"You take him, huh?" Mittowan questioned suspiciously. "This sounds an awful lot like one of your hideous schemes to hide him away, you cowards, because you are too scared to allow him to face me tomorrow."

"No," Keoko replied, "i'test'a'not. We will take him to our village and bring him here tomorrow. I swear."

"I still don't trust you."

"What if *we* took him to ya village?"

"And you promise not to play any tricks?"

"Yes, I do."

"And you'll keep your word?"

"Of course."

"Ha! Well, you Oreneans only have one thing close to coming to good, and that is that you always keep your word. But if you don't"— he cocked his head at Andrew—"I have a backup. Now all of you get out of my sight. I want to see the skinny one in my village within an hour. And, Keoko, I'll see you tomorrow, in your blood."

Peter couldn't believe what was happening. He pinched himself skeptically to find out if he was dreaming or not. The ring of warriors around them began to disintegrate, and Keoko and Father walked quickly up to Peter.

"Are you all right, son?" Father asked.

"Yes, sir," Peter replied, more bravely than he felt.

"Don't worry, all right, Peter?"

"I would," Keoko said gravely.

Father ignored him. "Just remember David and Goliath—and pray."

One of the blue-painted warriors gruffly shoved Father away. Keoko turned to Peter and declared, "Ya do'a'not need to worry about what zey will do to ya while ya are there. Tha worst zey would do to ya est a good beating."

"Will they be likely to do that?" Peter asked nervously.

"Oh, certainly. But I do'a'not think zey will torture ya or kill ya. At least I do'a'not *think* zey will." Keoko's speech was not very comforting.

"W-will I really be fighting him tomorrow?" he asked quietly.

"Yes," Keoko explained. "Tomorrow—at midmorning. That est'a'not very far away. Ya see that other Orenean man over there?

He will take ya to tha village. I would go myself, but if I do, zey will kill me. And by tha way, fencing est an art, est it not? Do ya have much experience with it? Because if ya did, ya might have a chance at winning, if a small one. Mittowan *has* been practicing fo a long time, but he only knows how to stab and slice with his large knife, no formal art."

"I have scarcely taken my sword out of its sheath in the year that I have had it, sir," Peter replied.

"I suspected so," Keoko said gravely. "Goodbye to that idea."

Peter, who was still trying to process what had just taken place, was led by the other man to a horse and gently lifted up onto its back as if he were a little child. The man glanced sadly at Peter, then at Mittowan, who was gleefully leading his warrior back home to plan the victory celebration. Peter knew what the man was thinking. If Peter was killed tomorrow, which he certainly would be without help, it would mean himself, his family, and his tribe would all be slaughtered within a week. Peter glanced back over his shoulder at *his* people. It would mean their lives too. Numbly they watched Peter being slowly led away into the forest. Peter memorized every detail about them in his memory because he might not ever lay eyes on them again. The thought chilled him.

"Ya pray, boy?" the Orenean man asked somberly. "Because if not, now would be a good time to start."

Butterflies fluttered nervously inside Peter's stomach as he laid eyes upon the place where he was to be kept. It was an outdoor prison in reality, although the great serpent preferred to call it a campsite. It was a large dreary, shady, bare spot of ground on the edge of a dark ravine, surrounded by a large ring of Tumitataken warriors with tall spears and mighty bows. The air was polluted with a foul, rotten stench from the Tumitataken village, which sat only about a quarter mile away. The "campsite" introduced itself as being very lonesome and uninviting. And to make matters worse, who should be waiting for him but Mittowan himself.

"Good morning, Peter," he spat out sarcastically in his native language—as if Peter's name were a curse—as Peter slid off the horse. Then he strode over to the boy and placed his large hands roughly on Peter's skinny shoulders, looking him over and smiling giddily as if celebrating in his mind how easy this would be tomorrow. Then Mittowan began to speak to Peter, and by the intimidating tone in his voice, Peter didn't even want to understand what he was communicating in his own tongue.

"I hope you enjoy this place, for this is the last place you will see before I kill you. I could crush your puny ribs now if I wanted to. I'll be sure to cut your dead body up into smaller pieces so that vultures will have an easier time eating you ..." He also described a few other things that I shouldn't mention here.

After he had apparently grown weary of terrorizing Peter, Mittowan suddenly scooped him up in his strong arms and carelessly tossed him into the circle of warriors like a log. Peter biffed hard onto the firm clay ground. Mittowan chuckled as Peter groaned and gently rubbed his throbbing backside before walking calmly away. Peter slowly rolled onto his back and stared blankly up into the broad cloud-scattered sky. A confusing mix of emotions swirled through his head.

"Why me, Lord?" Peter muttered, "I'm the last man for the job." He sat up and hugged his knees. The only two other things in the clearing were a young lonesome oak tree and an old fire pit, which appeared to have not been used in at least a fortnight. A couple of birds frolicked playfully high above his head. It was already painfully lonesome here. The Indian guards, who were all standing perfectly still, stared expressionlessly into space like statues. They were not painted blue, but they did carry weapons to make sure Peter did not escape. The ground was freckled with hard stone like clumps of clay.

For a while Peter just sat still, straining to process his situation. He remembered what Father had said about David and Goliath. (How long ago it seemed since he had last seen Father!) While that was an encouraging story, there were many significant differences between Peter and David. For one thing, David faced Goliath voluntarily—something Peter would never dream of doing. He couldn't even fathom having two-thirds as much faith as David. The other difference was that David's weapon was one that he actually knew how to use. Peter, who had only inherited the bronze sword about a year ago, rarely removed it from its sheath. It looked ridiculously large on Peter and extended nearly to the ground when strapped on, and the wide belt covered about half of his belly.

He slowly stood up, unsure of what to do next. Carefully he pulled out the sword and examined it. Although it was hundreds of years old, the bronze still gleamed shamelessly in the sunlight. Proudly it displayed its many scratches, which had been well earned during medieval battles. On the hilt, right beneath the blade, was the Washingsworth family coat of arms. Peter studied the faded colors and shapes carefully. Some of the designs and creatures had faded beyond recognition, but he could distinguish lots of the color red. Peter knew that in a coat of arms, the color red meant bravery in battle. Right now Peter didn't feel any bravery. In fact, he was afraid half to death. He actually didn't even know what he was afraid of. Was it failure? What about letting down the Oreneans? Was he afraid for his parents? Was it Mittowan? Or was he just afraid of pain? He knew that it wasn't death that he was afraid of, for he was a Christian and had never feared what would become of him after he was taken away. It appeared as if the possibility that he might die had not yet fully sunken into him yet—it seemed he ought to be more grieved and upset.

Peter slid the sword back into its sheath and carefully unstrapped the worn-out leather belt, setting the sword beside him so he could kneel more easily. Then he began to pray the way he had been taught to do ever since he was old enough to say the Lord's Prayer. The hours crawled by slowly. Peter soon grew tired of repeating the old prayer over and over and even tried practicing with his sword but soon gave up because he didn't know what he was doing.

Peter was grateful for the tree, which provided some shade so his fair skin would not burn in the sun. The guards, who remained still, became almost invisible to Peter, although they did sometimes grow bored and gave in to whispering to one another occasionally. Peter also grew increasingly bored. He amused himself by arranging rocks into neat little rows and patterns on the ground.

His thoughts drifted toward his family. He imagined what Mother would say when she discovered what had become of him and where he was. She had always been so paranoid about her children, and

Peter's stomach twisted within him when he thought of her worrying about him so much. He wished so very badly to visit his parents, but in his heart, he almost hoped that neither of them (especially Mother) would be there to watch him be brutally butchered. The thought of dying depressed him—he certainly didn't want to die. It made him even sadder to think of his family grieving over him, the second of the three surviving children to be cruelly snatched away—that is, if Peter's family hid away from the Tumitatakens long enough to have a chance to grieve.

Peter wondered what Andrew, who was like a twin brother to him, would think about his friend dying. Still, although he was beginning to feel more depressed, his mind was unable to *fully* swallow the wretched reality that he might be the next stop on the death angel's constant grievous journey from one doomed life to the next. Peter's faith waned as he pleaded hopelessly with God to cancel the fight or to somehow cause him to beat Mittowan, which he knew full well that he could not possibly accomplish alone. Yet the commandment "Thou shalt not kill" echoed repeatedly through his mind like something being shouted into a cave. Obviously, there must be exceptions in battle. After all, hadn't God commanded the Israelites to go to war with the Canaanites and handed them the victory?

The hours continued to roll by at a painstakingly slow pace. In the meantime, Peter was doomed to remain suffering from loneliness and suspense. It was about five o'clock and the sun began to sink quickly below the darkening trees. All Peter had consumed that day was about a bite of nuts and a small gulp of water for breakfast, and now hunger and thirst made his head dizzy, his throat crack, and his empty stomach churn dismally.

As darkness quickly set in, the air grew cold and Peter's fingers numbed. Just as Peter was about to stand up to try to find something to build a fire in the fire pit, an Indian suddenly passed through the ring of Tumitataken guards and quickly approached him carrying a small bundle of sticks. Remembering Keoko's not-so encouraging speech about beatings, Peter nervously scooted back. Noticing the fright in Peter's wide blue eyes, the man slowly set down the bundle of sticks.

"Don't worry, boy," he assured gently in hesitant English. "I will not hurt you."

The man was dressed in a feather headdress and loincloth much like the great serpent, and Peter guessed that he must be a lesser chief, but he didn't have that cruel, evil hint in his brown eyes. In fact, Peter thought he had a glimmer of refreshing kindness in them.

"You must be Peter. Hello. I am Ruex, lesser chief of the Tumitatakens. Well, actually, I'm just a chief, but he makes us call ourselves lesser chiefs. He told me about the contest he devised. I'm just here to light your fire."

"By 'he,' you mean Mittowan?" Peter clarified.

Ruex gritted his teeth bitterly. "Yes. Him," he muttered. By the hateful way he mumbled 'him' and the obvious way Ruex avoided uttering Mittowan's name, as if it were a cuss word, Peter assumed that Mittowan's arrogance and cowardice were as unpopular with Ruex as they were with Peter. He squatted down by the fire pit and diligently started to form a tiny tepee of little twigs and pine needles, which was an efficient way to prepare a place for a tiny flame to grow.

"Thank you," Peter declared slowly.

"For what—this? Oh, you are welcome. It is nothing. I tried to convince him to keep you in a more comfortable place instead of this prison. He only let me come see you so I could start this lire … I mean fire. Pardon me. I'm just beginning to get … understanding at your language."

Peter nodded understandingly. Many Wompinowog Indians back home were just learning English, and Peter had even tried learning some of their language, but he only knew a few scattered words and phrases.

Having completed his little wooden cone, Ruex surrounded it with small mounds of pine needles and twigs. Skillfully he rubbed two twigs together until one of them caught fire and then stuck it inside the little tepee. Ruex added the remaining sticks as the flame eagerly swelled and came to life. Once satisfied, he stood up to leave.

"Oh, and Peter, your mother and father have been trying to come and see you all day, but he wouldn't let them come and made them to leave. I decided you ought to know."

"Yes," Peter replied gratefully. "Thank you very much." As Ruex turned to leave, Peter gingerly called after him.

"Uh ... excuse me, but might I please have some water ... and maybe a bite or two, please?"

"I'm sorry, but that is another thing that man won't let you have," Ruex replied pityingly. "I would honestly bring you food and drink from my own home if I could."

Peter sighed disappointedly and slumped over by the fire.

"Oh, and ... boy," Ruex called awkwardly before leaving, "I've never said this to anyone before, but ... may El Shaddai bless you."

"Thank you," Peter replied. "To you too."

Ruex's silent tall figure melted into the blackness as he walked away, and again Peter was left alone. The night was pitch dark except for the places affected by the cheerless orange light of the lively flames. The sky was congested with clouds, concealing the stars. Peter curled up in a little ball with his feet facing the heat. His stomach growled up at him dismally. For about the tenth time, Peter brooded angrily about how unjustly Mittowan had handled the situation. The Oreneans had reluctantly entered into this unfair agreement in the first place. Then, after he had forced them to accept his proposal, he had robbed the Oreneans of their choice of their own warrior by selecting the easiest contestant in sight. And after all of that, insisting on holding him near his camp and treating him like a prisoner ... And was it a coincidence that the guards snorted or grunted every time he started to drift off to sleep? Why, Mittowan was probably at this moment bragging and feasting gluttonously over his future victory.

He'll probably go down in history as the greatest coward that ever lived. Nothing but a childish bully, I say, Peter thought spitefully, before quickly reminding himself that he shouldn't think of others like that.

So to pass the time, he recited the old Bible passages that Father had taught him. Hearing those familiar poetry-like lines caused a wave of loneliness to wash over him. Father, who didn't know how to read, had memorized those old familiar pages of scripture. Peter had fond memories of listening to his father recite those precious words to him at night as he drifted off to sleep. If none of this cruel foolishness had ever happened, Peter would probably be peacefully lying in the tepee nestled closely beside his sister and parents to ward off the cold. He hadn't yet realized how much he had favored those warm hours together until they were gone.

For a long while, Peter tossed and turned uncomfortably. Suddenly, a terrible thought struck him like a lightning bolt. He was about to die. It was true that the idea had been wandering around vaguely in Peter's dazed mind all day, but it had not really hit him as reality yet. It had now. His heart pounded in his chest. *Tomorrow it will beat no more.* His breaths came in frightened gasps. *These breaths are some of my last.* His wide eyes stared at the moon. *I had better look closely; this is the last time I'll ever see it.* For a moment, he fancied that he could feel every bone, muscle, and organ in his body—parts that would soon be ripped out of place. Nausea briefly washed over Peter. A deep sense of panic engulfed him thickly like a black veil, and he bolted up to run as hard as he could away from this terrible place, but he had nowhere to go. Slowly his legs eased him back down to the ground, and his panic gave way to deep sorrow and loneliness. He wept in a way that only those condemned to death know how. Finally, after what seemed like many hours, he began to calm down. It was then that Peter wiped his eyes and made himself a promise.

When it comes time that I should go to fight, I will not run like a coward or cry like a little girl. I will stand bravely and fight to the best of my ability to the very end, not only for my sake, but also for the whole of the Orenean tribe and my family. And if God wills that I should perish in the fight, I will go honorably like a man. No one will ever say that Peter Washingsworth died crying for mercy or without doing all he could to defend his people.

With this resolution, Peter lay himself back down in his former position by the fire.

One by one, the guards surrounding him switched off with fresh men and ended their shifts. Then finally, around two o'clock, Peter was carried away into a restless nightmare-haunted doze.

Peter grunted softly and rolled onto his back. Today was the fateful day. Reluctantly Peter opened his groggy eyes. The cheerless sky was gray and overcast—a sign of how he was feeling inside. His stomach growled once more.

"Hello there," a chipper young voice greeted him.

Peter jumped in surprise and quickly sat up. About a yard away from him sat a girl about his age, whom he recognized to be Number Three (Twii). She smiled pleasantly and pulled a small sack from behind her.

"How long have you been here?" Peter questioned with surprise as she rummaged diligently through the sack.

"Only an hour or so," she replied. "Are ya hungry?" Twii didn't even glance up for an answer, but Peter nodded anyway. Out of the sack, she drew a wooden slab that served as a plate, which had been covered in an animal's skin to protect its contents from spilling out, and a cup, which was also covered. Hurryingly, She removed the coverings and presented Peter with a cup of cool water and a plate of delicious food, which on the way had gotten all mixed and jumbled together on the slablike plate.

"Thank you," Peter declared. He leaned over his food and tried to say the "Thank you for the food" prayer as quickly as possible, although the smell of fresh food combined with his hunger made it nearly impossible to wait until the end of the prayer. The first thing he grabbed was the cup. Thirstily, Peter chugged down the sweet much-needed water. Oh, how deliciously refreshing the sweet water felt washing down his dry thirsty throat. He was so nervous about what would happen in the fight that he almost didn't feel like eating, but his hunger won out in the end. Off the plate like slab disappeared first the turkey, then the maize, then—best of all—the plump, juicy black Orenean grapes and the sweet crisp quimpanita slices. As Peter cleared his plate with his fingers, Twii stared dreamily into the gray cloudy sky. (In Orenea, it is impolite to stare at someone while the person is eating). After he had finished, Peter pushed the plate aside and thanked Twii again.

"That sure was fast. Ya really must have been hungry," Twii remarked.

"Oh … uh … sorry."

"No need to apologize. Ya were going to eat anyway so may as well do it at extremely high speeds." She collected the empty plate and cup and dropped them back inside the bag. "I'm quite sorry I couldn't come to ya yesterday. Tha chief sent me then too, but only now waes I allowed in. Are ya all right? Ya are'a'not hurt, are ya?"

"No. Thank you."

Peter stared searchingly into Twii's cheerful hazel-colored eyes. Nothing seemed wrong. But that was exactly what confused him. Why was she so … so … not gloomy and terrified? Didn't she know what was about to happen?

"Uh, Number Three, are you well?" he inquired.

She stared back at him blankly. "Yes, why under tha sun do ya ask? There est'a'not anything wrong that I know of."

"That is my point. Why are you so … calm? How can you be calm now?"

"Why under tha sun not?"

"Because … because of the fight between me and that Tumitataken chief fellow. You have only but to glance at me to see that it is impossible for me to beat him. And you know what that means for you and your family right? And … and I'm not happy, because … because I'm going to die." Those words made his throat ache and tears threaten to squeeze out of his eyes, but Peter did not allow himself to weep in the presence of a girl.

Twii stared intently into this gloomy face as if trying to decide whether or not to speak. "Est that really what ya think?" she asked softly. Peter nodded solemnly. "That est'a'not what chief believes."

"What does that mean?"

Ya may choose to think that Mittowan will kill ya today. But we Oreneans have reason to believe otherwise."

"Truly?" Peter asked excitedly. "The fight was cancelled?"

"No."

"Then why do the Oreneans not expect me to die?"

"Because, as Chief put it, ya have tha most powerful weapon in tha world on ya side that Mittowan has never had. That weapon est El Shaddai—Chief's words, not mine."

"But how can you know that He will really help me. We can't know."

Twii paused thoughtfully. "Ya are right. We can'a'not know, but I think that ya victory est very likely. All of Orenea has been praying fo ya since we heard tha news. Zey are faithful people who have been praying faithfully fo forty-eight seasons. Only recently has El Shaddai seemed to hear our plea. Why under tha sun would he abandon us now?" Twii had obviously had a long conversation with the chief.

Surprised and deeply touched by the notion that so many had been diligently praying for him, Peter gazed down speechlessly into his lap. "People were praying? For me?"

"Oh, yes," Number Three replied. "Even now, most Oreneans are gathered in Ore-Cita to pray together. I think ya are El Shaddai's tool. Imagine what will happen when ya win! All of tha other tribes will catch wind of it and know how powerful He est. El Shaddai could really collect tha glory on this one!"

Peter gazed thoughtfully into the dying embers of the fire. "Your tribe's faith does you credit," Peter declared wishfully. "I wish I had faith like that. I must admit, I'm scared to death."

"I'm afraid too," Twii replied sadly. "I envy Chief's faith. But ya know what zey say; ya only need faith as big as a mustard seed. I actually do'a'not even know what a mustard seed est. But I am'a'not too worried."

"Do you know how many people will be there to watch me?" Peter asked curiously, changing the subject.

"Yes, actually. Only twenty-one should be allowed to watch. Tha chiefs do'a'not want to draw up a powwow-sized gathering. Ten Oreneans and ten Tumitatakens. And also Mr. Winslow will be there to represent ya white folk too. And there will also be a few messengers there to carry tha word out to tha villages." She beamed and proudly pointed to herself. "I will be one of them."

"I'm glad that my mother will not be there," Peter commented. "She cannot stand to watch violence. Especially when it is against a loved one … You know how mothers are."

"Yes, I know," Twii replied. "Well, anyhow, I had better get going now. Tha chief told me not to stay too long. So I have already stayed long enough." She leaned in and whispered, "These guards are starting to glare at me." Peter was very sorry to watch Number Three pack up the empty dishes and leave. She had been a welcome relief from the loneliness. "Goodbye!" she called before gingerly slipping past the foreboding guards. "I'twaes nice speaking to ya!"

"You too," Peter replied, "Thank you!"

Again Peter was without company, which was not quite as dull now that he had lots of food for his stomach and food for thought to sort out. Never in his life had Peter met anyone like these Oreneans. How could anyone compare an inexperienced young boy like himself to a strong well-practiced man twice his age and, from the way Number Three had described it, still be certain that the smaller could defeat the latter? It didn't make much sense. Peter, who was still quite skeptical about the possibility of his being able to conquer the Tumitatakens most-celebrated champion, began to consider trying out some Orenean faith for once. A burst of confidence and relief leaked all over Peter, from the top of his head to the soles of his feet. *Finally, a little hope.* Then, just as Peter had started to pray eagerly in request for some of Chief's faith, a rough-looking Tumitataken walked sternly into the clearing to collect Peter and "escort" him over to where the dual was to be held. Peter's heart froze.

"Ready to die?" the man spat out pitilessly.

"Yes, if I must," Peter replied more bravely than he felt, for he remembered the resolution that he had made the previous night.

"Well, it don't matter none." the Tumitataken taunted, obviously trying to go out of his way to intimidate and frighten Peter. "'Cause you will either way. And I'll sure enjoy watching you do it. You'll be facing a man who's lived his whole life by the sword."

"He who lives by the sword dies by the sword," Peter recited wittily, although he didn't know if he even wanted to kill Mittowan.

"Well, we'll see about that. Anyhow, make haste and strap on that sword of yours child," the man growled, pointing at the bronze sword, which was still lying patiently on the ground where Peter had left it yesterday. Carefully Peter pulled the fragile worn leather belt through the rusty brass buckle. He could feel the man's wretched eyes staring impatiently into the back of his head from behind. His fingers fumbled nervously over the straps.

"I *said* make haste!" the Tumitataken snapped angrily, slapping Peter harshly across the side of his face.

"Yes sir," Peter replied hastily finishing up with the strap. Painfully, the Tumitataken man grabbed Peter tightly by the shoulder and yanked him to his feet.

"Now follow me. And don't try anything stupid or you will be caught and dead before you can say a single word."

Obediently Peter walked on wobbly legs along behind the Tumitataken man like a slave humbly following his master. Gruffly he was shoved onto the back of an under-broken horse behind his escort, and they rode off into the dark forest. Peter, who was having difficulty staying on the back of the jittery horse, wondered what he would find once he arrived to wherever he was being taken. His face still stung from where he had been slapped.

The sky remained gray and overcast when Peter arrived later at the place where the fight was to be held, which was not far from the

Tumitataken village. It was a clear spot in the forest, where a long rope of vines had been stretched tautly around four trees to form a large square in which the fighting would be conducted. Around the outside of the square milled most of the twenty-one delegates from the two tribes. Over on the left, Peter recognized the chief, Keoko, and Mr. Winslow. It was refreshing to glimpse the friendly face of a person from home.

"Hello, Peter," Mr. Winslow called, hurrying up to him.

"Hello, Mr. Winslow," Peter called back. "What's going on?"

"Mittowan will arrive here any minute now. He proposed that it would be more 'dramatic' for him to show up at the last minute. Now, when you go out there, do not strike till you hear the whistle blow," Mr. Winslow explained. "So now we shall pray over you and get ready." The chief was having a discussion with a lower chief, Manasseh, who was—shall we say—annoyed with children of all ages.

"Why under tha sun did ya have to bring ya agentes?" he complained angrily. "Are ya trying to turn this place into a playhouse? This est'a'not a place fo children."

"No," Chief assured calmly. "Zey will only stay until the fight est over. And knowing tha agentes, zey will'a'not cause trouble or mischief."

Manasseh, who had already been exasperated at Chief's bringing the young agentes, nearly lost it when he noticed Peter. "And who under tha sun, may I ask, est that?"

"That," Chief explained, "est our fighting man."

Manasseh looked like his head was about to explode. "Him," he whispered in horror. "When ya said small and somewhat young, I ... had no idea."

Ruex, who seemed to be undecided as to which side he was on, marched quietly up to Chief. "Palkente," he informed, "the Tumitataken chief has sent your warrior this." He held out a curved stone plate with some straps on it.

"What under tha sun est it?" Keoko asked.

"I'test an arm block," Chief explained. "So if someone swings at ya, ya can put ya arm up and block it." He demonstrated by quickly swinging his arm up in front of his face.

"Looks too big," Keoko commented.

Ruex motioned Peter forward to try to strap the heavy arm block onto his skinny arm, but try as he might, Ruex couldn't make it fit.

"I'm sorry," he declared. "You will need to go without it."

Then the Tumitatakens began to beat their drums wildly. Out of the woods proudly strutted Mittowan himself, like a proud rooster, carrying his sharpest, longest stone knife with a blue handle. Peter again felt as if he was going to be sick. He could feel his heart beating in his stomach. Even worse was the thought that his heart might soon *stop* beating—for good.

"Come here, Peter," Mr. Winslow called.

Peter obediently stood in front of him as Mr. Winslow gently placed his hand on Peter's head. All of the other Oreneans crowded around him and placed their hands on him too. Then the others closed their eyes and Chief prayed earnestly over Peter. The prayer was rather as Peter would have expected it would be—a prayer for strength, courage, and victory for Peter. "And, dear El Shaddai," he continued, "please fill him with ya Holy Spirit. Show ya glory through this boy."

"Come on out here!" Mittowan shouted. "Let us just get this act done quickly."

Bravely Peter marched up to the edge of the square and ducked inside. The fight that would determine the future of Orenea was about to begin.

CHAPTER XIII

PETER QUICKLY DREW OUT HIS sword, which made an authoritative *shing* sound as it slid out of its battered sheath. Mittowan scowled forebodingly as he marched briskly out to the middle of the square. Peter was afraid, but not quite as much as he had expected to be. He had been feeling surprisingly calm ever since Chief had prayed over him. Confidently Peter hurried out to the center to stand across from Mittowan and prepare for battle.

As the great serpent stared searchingly into Peter's wide blue eyes, a hint of fear flashed through his own. What had happened to most of that terror that had been so obvious in Peter just a day before? Why did he seem so confident and bold all of the sudden? What had happened? Did Peter know something that he didn't? Truly, in his heart of hearts, Mittowan had expected his small opponent to flee or faint immediately so even the slightest bit of courage seemed troubling. Suddenly, the powerful Tumitataken chief didn't seem quite so terrifying anymore. The tips of his fingers were trembling. But he didn't lose his nerve for long and quickly regained his confidence. Peter held his sword out in front of him with both hands to be sure he was ready. To the people on the side he looked as tiny as ever, and the sword a few sizes too large. Peter felt his whole body shaking slightly with anticipation.

The air was tense. No one moved. All was still. Suddenly, a crisp loud whistle pierced the silence—the signal. Instantly the Tumitataken chief skillfully swung his great knife down at Peter, aiming for his neck, but Peter quickly saw it coming and clumsily reeled backwards so that the stone blade missed him by barely a half inch and pounded bluntly into the dust. Mittowan attempted to slash at his stomach, but once again he swiftly jerked backwards, nearly falling. It felt to Peter as if someone else were bending and moving his limbs and body for him.

Mittowan jumped a couple of steps back. Peter jumped a couple of steps forward. Confidantly, the Tumitataken chief swung down at his opponent's neck again. Peter plunged desperately downward to escape the blow and found himself on the ground. He leaped up quickly to his feet. Peter, who was utterly disoriented, held his sword out before him and whirled around stupidly for a few seconds. He felt faint and considered for a moment that he might have really been hit. But worst of all, he had no idea where Mittowan was. Mr. Winslow's shouting voice jolted him back to reality.

"Peter, what are you doing?!"

Peter finally turned around to see his opponent towering over him only yards away, about to bring down another blow upon him. Gripping the sword with both hands, one around the hilt and one near the top of the blade, Peter quickly poised with the sword blocking his face and reeled backwards. He squinted his eyes shut as the stone knife clashed with the bronze sword. The knife hadn't struck his body but the impact resonated through him all the same. His knuckles were snow white from clutching the hilt of the sword and were starting to hurt. Sweat crept down this neck. In awe, Mittowan reeled back and stared at Peter, eyes wide, mouth hanging open. Though still early in the contest, it was nothing short of supernatural that Peter had lasted this far along. The people watching were just as amazed as the Tumitataken chief.

"He's doing it!" Pona-Pow squeaked ecstatically. "El Shaddai's actually making him do it!"

"Keep it down," her brother chided softly, his eyes glued to the scene in front of him.

"It's a mistake!" Mittowan shrieked in frustration, realizing that this was not quite as easy as he had expected. "Someone made a mistake!" Then Mittowan lunged panicingly at Peter. Almost automaticly, Peter flung his sword up through the air and slashed across the man's face leaving behind a nasty gash. At this Mittowan became furious in a way that was truly horrific to behold. His eyes shot sparks of hatred. His face wrinkled up. The veins popped out of his neck. At this point he was fueled by only one soul objective, not saving his tribe's livelihood, not gloating rights over his magnificent victory, not exterminating the Oreneans, not even saving his own miserable life, but killing the boy. Passionately, Mittowan drew back his knife for a final attempt to stab Peter through the heart, but as he thrust his weapon toward his opponent, Peter forcefully swung his sword up like a tennis racket to a ball and met the other sword midway with a loud clash. Mittowan's weapon flew out of his hand. Like a flying disk, the knife spun through the air and embedded itself firmly into the bark of a nearby tree with a resounding *whack!* The force of the blow caused Mittowan to tumble clumsily to the grassy ground, and in an instant, Peter was pointing his sword down at Mittowan.

No one dared breathe. Mittowan, who had always been a great coward, stared up in disbelief at the scrawny eleven-year-old whom he had been mocking only twenty-four hours earlier. Peter stared into Mittowan's eyes threateningly and held his sword close against the man's neck. Trembling, Mittowan's eyes darted from side to side as if frantically searching for something to fight with.

"I ... I ... I surrender," he uttered reluctantly.

"He said he surrenders!" Keoko cried joyfully in English. Instantly the entire company of Oreneans came alive with ecstatic screams and shouts as the Oreneans jumped up and down excitedly, not able to contain their joy. A few sobbed. No more tyranny! No more cruelty and hate! No more slavery! No more fear! It was almost too good even to be a dream. The Tumitatakens stood stunned in horror.

For a few moments, Peter just stared down blankly at his sword in disbelief. Then, as if suddenly realizing what had just happened, Peter shoved his bronze sword back inside his sheath and let out the loudest, most joyful whoop of all. He began leaping into the air ecstatically, still shouting, his large grin stretching from ear to ear. Never again would he complain about being short and ill or let anyone's teasing bother him.

"Thank you! Thank you! Thank you!" he shouted joyfully, gazing up to heaven. Peter could scarcely contain all of the abounding joy that was swelling up inside his heart. He thought that his chest might explode! His soul was full of gratitude to God, who he was sure had fought the battle for him. Never had he been so overjoyed in his life! Then a voice arose out of the crowd of Orenean delegates.

"Kill him! Kill the great wretched Tumitataken! Pay him back for his gruesome villainous crimes! Let us be rid of this dirty great serpent!" A few others whooped in agreement.

"Yes, yes, listen to them!" Mittowan cried in his native tongue from the position that he still held on the ground. "I cannot bear to live knowing I have been defeated by a little boy. Take my life, please!"

A translation was shouted from the crowd. Soon at least six Oreneans were screaming for the death of his opponent, who was himself begging pitifully to die.

Peter thought for a moment and then confidently declared to Mittowan, "No, you shall live. I now see that living with this defeat of you and your tribe would be worse for you than dying as a result of it." The Oreneans, who seemed perfectly content with this arrangement, burst out laughing in reply.

Once he finally left the square, the other Oreneans crowded around Peter, everyone speaking at the same time. A short fight it had been, yet it seemed to have lasted hours.

Twii rushed up to her brother Mik, who was almost crying. "Say," she cried. "Look! An even bigger miracle! I'test Keoko! He est smiling. Look!" It was true! There stood Keoko with a wide, bright smile spread across his normally stern, solemn face. Neither of them had ever before beheld Keoko's smile and most likely never would again anytime soon. One had to admit that he looked much more attractive wearing it. Chief sat on his stool nearby, tears streaming down his wrinkled old cheeks.

"At last!" he whispered joyfully. "At last my eyes have beheld tha salvation of my people!"

Ruex slowly approached him. "Well, Chief," he declared solemnly, "my heart is filled with both joy and sadness today. I always have hated Mittowan, but for my tribe's sake, my heart breaks. But I must admit that I learned something today. I have never met anyone quite like you Oreneans. In the past, I never understood why you all adored El Shaddai so much. Now I understand."

Chief just smiled at him through his tears and emotion and nodded his wise old gray head in reply.

The hooves of the horses clippety-clopped loudly on the ground as the agentes cantered joyfully through the forest in the direction of Ore-Cita. Unable to contain their excitement, all six of them sang old praise hymns and chants at the top of their lungs.

"Harevatcha! Harevatcha! O, herrene Adonai. Harevatcha! O, herrene Adonai! Harevatcha! Harevatcha! Lemogashi lo gay vie!"

Then everybody suddenly stopped singing and started uncontrollably laughing. The wonderful sensation that was flooding the six young people's souls because of the victory can be described by no one word in the English language—or an earthly language, for that matter. Their future, which had before been a constant downward spiral swirling ever so much closer to some sort of hellish Armageddon, was now adorned with hope and promise.

So they continued to ride through the trees, proclaiming the joyous news loudly to anyone who might be there to hear it. Finally, the party started nearing the great trading post of Ore-Cita. More and more excitement swelled up inside Zatch. He couldn't wait to inform all of the people who were gathered praying that their prayers had been well worth the effort. The battle had been won! The twelve-year nightmare had ended at last!

Veenatch cried, "Yah, yah!" to bring her horse to a gallop. The other five did the same, and they all sped toward the trading post as quick as lightning bolts. Pona-Pow could glimpse the tops of pillars of meandering smoke poking their white heads curiously above the trees against the gray cloudy sky. Then the agentes rode out into the trading post itself. Never in their lives had any of them beheld so many people at once. There must be at least seven hundred of them! Each person was kneeling down on the dusty ground around the simple buildings and quietly crying out to El Shaddai. Their voices all blended in with the others to form a large mass of sound like many drops of water forming a stream. The Know Board blared the once-frightening news of the duel, which had now become joyous news instead.

"Make way! Make way!" the agentes called, their voices quivering with excitement as they trotted through the masses toward the great gong, which was where the news was to be announced. All who had cared to glance up at them could tell from the color of their face paint that they were the ones to announce the news. Some of the most faith-filled Oreneans glanced up at the messengers expectantly, while other doubting ones gazed at them in dread. Although it was not currently a very large tribe, Mik, Twii, Cedar, Veenatch, Zatch, and Pona-Pow, who were all from the same village, recognized few.

Quickly they tied up their horses at the base of the gong platform and agilely climbed onto it. Cedar firmly grabbed hold of the gong sounder and swung it hard against the gong. The worn old gong loudly sang out its deep rhythmic toll of *bong, bong, bong, bong.* Everyone's eyes were now pointed toward the platform. Mik blushed shyly. As all the nervous people held a collective breathe in suspense, the children waited for the gong tolls to stop echoing so that everyone could hear.

Some Oreneans stood up so that they would be able to hear the announcement clearer.

Finally, after the longest five seconds in the history of time itself, the deep vibrating and echoing came to a stop and Zatch rushed to the edge of the stone platform, shouting in his loudest, most joyful voice, "Tha battle has been won! Orenea est redeemed! Orenea est redeemed!"

What followed cannot be reenacted in any way, shape, or form. Once the wonderful news echoed out over the people, the entire company leaped to their feet and came alive with ecstatic shouts and screams of joy. All their cries combined to sound as one long, loud, and wonderful roar. Some people leaped into the air, screaming, dancing, and singing with joy. Others broke into sobs, and still others just sat stunned on the ground. El Shaddai had finally avenged the blood of the slaves and martyrs and removed the oppression from the land. It was unlike anything Orenea had ever witnessed.

This joyful chaos lasted about an hour. The agentes happily joined in from the platform. Then, out of the forest, as if back from the dead, gushed those who had been enslaved and forced into labor—still coated in dirt, grime, and scars from their former life—to join the glorious mayhem. From the other direction streamed the Orenean warriors who had been fighting for the land for so many years. The tyranny was gone. Orenea was indeed redeemed! The thought would bring a smile and tear to even the most hard-faced Orenean. Most everybody knew someone who had been murdered or died in forced labor. But now that ugly film of fear and sorrow that had hung over Ore-Cita for so long had been banished away forever. The battle had been won! Orenea was redeemed.

After the two-man battle was over and the Oreneans at the duel site had finished loudly rejoicing over their victory, Peter was put inside a cart pulled by buffalo to take him back to the lake to pick up the rest of the white people to bring them to the victory feast hosted by the Orenean chief. The top of the empty cart was covered so that in case Tumitataken thugs showed up looking for Peter, they would mistake it for a funeral cart. Inside the cart with Peter were Mr. Winslow and Asa's wife, whose husband was driving the bison. Because of Peter's foul night's sleep and the fact that he was simply exhausted from shouting and jumping up and down, the boy curled up comfortably in the corner of the large cart and fell into a deep and peaceful doze, despite the ruckus bumping and jostling up and down of the clumsy cart.

Peter was awakened seemingly moments later by Mr. Winslow gently shaking his thin shoulders. "Peter, Peter. We have arrived now. Get up," he whispered. The cart slowed and then abruptly halted. Peter stretched his sore arms and legs and yawned sleepily.

"What time is it?" he mumbled groggily.

"About half past one o'clock, I'd wager," Mr. Winslow replied. "Now come on out. I'm sure everyone wants to see you."

Peter grinned at the thought of how proud all his friends would be of him. He stood up. Mr. Winslow climbed out first so that he could assist Peter in exiting since the cart walls were about two times as high as Peter was and didn't provide any tread for climbing. Once he had made it over the side of the cart, Peter stood on the wheel and leaped off excitedly to the ground. In front of the tent gathering were all Peter's family and friends, who had obviously already found out the results of the duel. Peter's grin swelled as he darted toward them as fast as his legs would carry him.

Excitedly they crowded around him with much rejoicing, like fish in a net, all seeming almost as joyful as the Oreneans were. Peter turned around and noticed Mother standing there, staring speechlessly at him. Her mouth was hanging open, but the edges of it were curled up in a smile. Tears of joy streamed down her flushed cheeks. Able to restrain herself no longer, she bent over and threw her arms tightly around Peter as if she would never let go. Mother squeezed him as tightly as she could and planted about a half a dozen kisses on his cheek. Then, as Peter finally escaped her, he noticed his father standing right behind her, staring down at him, his mouth stretched into a huge grin—the first that Peter had caught father wearing since Elisabeth passed away.

"Hello, Peter," he said fondly.

"Hello, Father."

Slowly Father bent down on one knee so that he could be eye-to-eye with his son. Seeming somewhat unsure of what to say, Father placed his large warm hands on Peter's shoulders and stared into his face as if marveling over the miracle that had just occurred.

"Son," he declared quietly, "ever since you were born, I knew you were very special, as most parents do when a child of theirs is born. But … but I must admit, I never expected anything like this. I just want you to know that I am very proud of you. You, at eleven, are braver than many men full grown. And by the way, congratulations!"

"Thank you, sir," Peter replied humbly. "But really, I didn't do a thing on my own. It was God, or should I say El Shaddai, who did all of the work for me. My job was easy."

Proud of his son's humility, Father smiled even wider and gave Peter a warm hug around the shoulders, squeezing him heartily. Calmly Peter squeezed Father back, closed his eyes, and securely rested in the fact that he was finally safe.

"I want one too!" Rebeccah demanded childishly from behind. Peter, who would have normally been angry at her for interfering, chuckled at her comment. With a smile, Father gathered Rebeccah up in a large bear hug.

"Everyone give ear!" Asa announced cheerfully. Everyone quieted down and turned their heads attentively toward him. "We shall all depart now. Tha Orenean chief has prepared a feast fo ya in a cave near tha outskirts of Orenea to celebrate this occasion. Tha cave est complements of Number Two and Number Three, by tha way. Unfortunately, we can'a'not fully trust tha Tumitatakens to keep their word. Fo ya safety, ya will all be staying tha next few days there in tha cave. So bring all of ya belongings!"

Peter walked back inside the tepee for the last time to help load everything into the wagon. Once everyone and everything was loaded, the wagon again started to rumble along. The space was cramped and crowded, but no one seemed to care very much. They were all still giddy with excitement. Peter settled in a corner next to Father and Mother. It seemed as if everyone wanted to know every single detail about Peter's adventure—from how he felt out on the "battlefield" to what kind of food Number Three brought him. They all listened closely above the loud drolling rumble of the Indian wagon and kept asking more questions, which Peter gladly answered. Rebeccah, who normally took an afternoon nap, curled up sleepily beside Peter and fell asleep with her head on his lap.

The trip took over five hours, although one would have normally been able to get there in three and one half hours. But because the bison were slow and clumsy animals, the trip was lengthened. Peter must have dozed off somewhere along the way, for he was awakened by the sudden halt of the wagon, which bumped him forward lightly. It was quite dark. Gently Peter awoke Rebeccah and stood up to disembark once more. The sky was now dark and free of clouds. The tiny vivid stars glowed white against the velvety dark sky like tiny sparkling white diamonds on a navy satin pin cushion. The moon was a sliver of a crescent, its light just barely revealing the vast rolling Fire Hills, which surrounded the place. The lonely oak trees that hunched atop on some of them looked like mystical mysterious silhouettes of large creatures.

Directly behind the wagon, Peter could just barely make out the remains of what must have been a small village at one time. Golden light streamed calmingly from what appeared to be a hole in the side of one of the hills in front of him. Cheerful noises boomed and echoed from within. One by one, each person ducked inside the large cave. The ceiling was low, but once inside, Peter didn't need to duck. He had never entered a cave before and was fascinated by the long cone-like stalagmites and stalactites that hung from the ceiling and jutted up from the floor. *Splat!* A cool drop of water dripped onto his cheek from above. Noting Peter's puzzled expression, Asa's wife smiled and explained, "Tha cave has kissed ya."

"What?"

"I'test a cave kiss. If ya get kissed by tha cave, ya will have good luck!"

"Do you truly believe that?"

She chuckled. "Of course not! I'test all just good fun."

Peter continued to admire the amazing works of the cave. On the ceiling in various planes were tiny twisted sticks of sparkling crystal protruding from the walls and ceiling and twisting crookedly around one another in all directions, somewhat like how Mother's hair was in the morning. The light that was in the cave seemed to be coming from behind a sort of shallow hill in front of him, so Peter cautiously walked forward in the narrow space toward it. Somehow, the top of the hill seemed wrong. Peter soon discovered why: the curved edge behind which the light was glowing was actually a drop-off instead of a hill. The sharp cliff extended down about twenty-five feet, and below that was a small open fire in a giant space, over which a woman was slowly turning a roasting bird on a spit.

Suddenly, Peter jumped a little in surprise when he noticed a man standing precariously behind her, spear in hand, arm drawn back. Then Peter realized that it was just a statue and relaxed. In fact, there were many statues scattered around the great cathedral-like room below him, casting odd shadows in the cheery firelight. Some of them appeared calm and docile, while others appeared warlike and intimidating. Some were part animal, part human creatures that appeared strange. On the edge of the drop-off were the remnants of what must have been at one time a small stone wall to keep people from tumbling off.

"Peter," Mother called nervously. "Back away from the edge. It worries me when you stand so close."

Peter obediently took a large step backward and followed everyone else down a wide set of stairs that led down the ridge like the steps on the side of ancient Aztec or Mayan temples. They were so steep and the steps so tiny that Peter had to walk almost sideways to get down. Once he made it to the bottom, Peter wound his way around the strange life-sized carvings, their once bright paint partially faded and chipped off.

"These weird statues are spooky!" Peter whispered to Andrew.

"Yes," he explained. "Mr. Asa was just telling me about them. I suppose the people who lived here a few hundred years ago were great chiefs ... or something of that nature. Well, anyhow, they apparently carved statues of their dead chiefs and heroes to honor them. Asa was telling me about why some of them are part animal. See that one over there that looks like a man's head with a bear's body—or that hawk with a man's head and feet? Well, apparently, different animals symbolized different characteristics. Like a bear might symbolize strength, or a mountain lion might symbolize courage, or an eagle might mean wisdom, for example."

"So this was a royal home?"

"Oh, yes. See over there on the ceiling? It looks like someone hammered gold onto the stalagmites—and over on the wall there, above that big rock, you can see someone tried to paint there."

How quickly things change, Peter thought. *Just last night I was lying in a prison and no one gave me anything to eat or drink (how long ago that seems!) and tonight I will be feasting in a palace!* Peter continued to walk toward the end of the great room, where he found the chief, the lower Orenean chiefs, and their families sitting in a large circle on a massive colorful mat on the ground, all of the food arranged in the middle. Andrew licked his lips.

"I'm very sorry we are late," Asa apologized.

After a pleasant prayer by the chief, which took much too long in Peter's perspective, the feasting began. Peter had worked up quite an appetite, and he chowed down two entire helpings of food, which was a lot for Peter but paled in comparison to what Andrew devoured. There were many available food items, many of which Peter had never heard of before, but he could identify most of them. There was fruit, maize, sweet potatoes, meat of many kinds, including roast duck and goose (two of the finest Orenean delicacies), a shredded mixture of crushed squirrel, goose, and deer meat (even finer), and also fried lizard (*very* fine but not very appealing). Peter heard that they had planned to have even *more* types of food but had simply lacked time to prepare it.

The feast was a very jolly one, with lots of laughter and conversation. Instead of sitting with the children, as was normal for him, Peter was seated with the highest chiefs like an honored guest. After dinner, which lasted about two hours, there was lots of happy singing, chatting, and even playful games and contests. After a while, Peter realized that the agentes were nowhere to be seen and hadn't been all night. *How odd,* he thought curiously. *I wonder where they've gone.*

"Can ya believe it?" Veenatch whispered excitedly. "Our very last mission!"

"Yes," Twii replied attentively. "But keep it down. If we make a mistake, this may be the last thing we do as well."

"But Chief said that since the Tumitatakens do not have their thumb on us any longer, we are in less danger than we were before," Pona-Pow pointed out.

"True, but still ..." Cedar reminded her.

Veenatch's stomach fluttered as she skillfully tied her horse up in the secret stable about a mile from the great Tumitataken village. This was indeed the last time that she would be rushing through the forest at night—for this purpose at least. The pale glowing sliver of a moon shown down on Veenatch through the thick tree branches. Cold misty air seeped through Veenatch's think black clothes in an attempt to chill her through. The purpose of this last mission was to listen in on the Tumitataken chief's house to make sure there was no planning of rebellion, but Veenatch wasn't worried. After all, she figured that the Tumitatakens would be so shocked and intimidated by El Shaddai now that they knew that he was real that it would scare them clear off the land. Besides, if El Shaddai could turn up a skilled warrior out of an eleven-year-old, why could he not turn the whole Orenean tribe into warriors?

Creeping silently through the dark, the six of them stealthily made their way along toward the Tumitataken village. As usual, Twii was diligently struggling to keep up with the rest of the pack on her large slow feet. Even from this far away, the sorrowful wails and lamentations of the Tumitatakens echoed through the trees like the voices of lost souls wandering the woods. Finally, all of them reached the village itself. How pitiful it was now! Everyone milled idly outside of their houses, weeping bitterly or uttering many a lamentation and curse. Some were mournfully packing their belongings into large bundles. *That est a good sign,* Veenatch thought with encouragement. *That means zey are actually planning to leave.*

Some buffalo carts were parked in front of the huts, waiting to be loaded up. Noises of a petty riot echoed from the other side of the village. The fact that everyone was outside presented a problem; how would they sneak through the maze of houses and to the Tumitataken palace without being caught? Before, everyone in the village had been sleeping, so making their way there was not an issue. The frustrating question loomed in the air for a while as each of the agentes waited for another to come up with a solution. Finally, one of them (I think it was Number Four) daringly darted out and dodged silently behind one of the nearest huts. One by one, the rest followed. Veenatch's heart pounded hard inside her chest. Cautiously she peeked out behind the side of the house to make sure no one was walking dangerously close. Thankfully, the residents of this dwelling were all inside so there was not much danger here.

Silently, Veenatch counted the agentes to make sure all of them were present. In horror, she realized that one of them was missing! Trembling, she glanced frantically around. In the dim light, Veenatch could just barely distinguish a hint of motion in the shadow behind one of the other huts and realized that Number Three had already darted behind the next hut. The others noticed too and cautiously scurried behind to the same place. This continued until they had finally made it to the bushes behind Mittowan's large home. Then Veenatch was selected to climb first up the ladder that led into the little cranny beneath the platform, which was their hiding place. As quietly as possible, she gently pried open the small trap door. Veenatch stuck her head in. All was silent.

"I'test all right," she whispered loudly enough for those down below to hear. Quietly as a cat, Pona-Pow climbed in first and crouched inside the dark crowded space to await the others. Veenatch curiously pressed her eye to a crack to peek out. All she could detect in the dim torch glow was the shadow stretched out against the wall; it was a man pacing back and forth. The man himself was out of the sight range of the tiny crack, but she could easily watch his shadow pacing back and forth—and from the shape of his feather headdress, Veenatch guessed that he was probably a lesser Tumitataken chief, but not Mittowan. From the steady way he was walking, she supposed that he had likely been pacing like that for hours. By now, all of the others were wedged into the space as well. Everyone had also glued their eyes intently to cracks and peepholes, watching the shadow sorrowfully pace back and forth, muttering angry poetic lamentations to himself.

"Oh, the agonies of life. One day you live in luxury as the war chief of a great tribe, and the next, your tribe must leave your land where you were born and raised, like an unwelcome guest, and find somewhere else to live. And all because of those Oreneans ... Why, oh why, did those Fur Christus Gelflowns have to bring their God to our land? Why, indeed? To destroy us? Their El Shaddai is even more powerful than our great spirit. Now what is one to do? Can we go on worshipping the ghosts and spirits or El Shaddai, who is so much more powerful? I suppose one can't know for sure."

Veenatch was just about to suggest that they should leave because there didn't seem to be many plans for rebelling when another man scurried into the room as well, this time carrying a bundle of rags.

"Oh, great war chief," he reported, "I have news."

"Speak up."

"Great Chief Mittowan has killed himself."

"What!" all of the six agentes whispered to one another.

Veenatch couldn't believe what she was hearing.

"Is this true!" the war chief demanded.

"Yes."

For a moment, Veenatch sat stunned. How could a proud, egotistical man like Mittowan commit suicide? She had assumed that he would be able to build himself back up again after the loss. Veenatch couldn't help but celebrate inside.

The war chief sighed. "Well, I suppose it was bound to happen. He was so depressed after ... Well, you know. I suspected that he would let himself off later. It's too bad. I liked the man."

"Yes, as did I."

Veenatch stared curiously at the bundle that the other man was carrying. It didn't appear to be extremely large, but it was not that small either.

"What under tha sun est that?" Mik asked softly.

"A person!" Pona-Pow exclaimed.

"Really?" Twii asked, squinting attentively at the mysterious object. "Ya really think so? It looks too small."

"A child! An Orenean child!" Pona-Pow insisted.

Veenatch stared intently at the shadow of the bundle and realized that Pona-Pow was right. On the top, she could vaguely make out the shape of a little face, and at one point, the child stirred uncomfortably and groaned.

"What is this?" the war chief asked irritably. "And what is it doing in here?"

"This is one of the great chief's personal slaves."

"And why was it not released with the others?"

"Apparently she was forgotten. She was only found an hour ago. Shall I hand her over to the Oreneans? Our agreement …"

"I know what our agreement was. But let's just kill this one now and no one will know. It would be too much of a bother to return her all the way back to the Oreneans before we leave tomorrow. Looks pretty banged up and half-starved so she shouldn't be worth anything."

"B-but, Chief …," the other man stammered.

"No buts, guard," the war chief demanded firmly. "If you choose to be such a coward, I will do it myself."

The war chief's shadow strode over to the other side of the room to get a spear and started making his way back. Veenatch's heart thumped like a rapidly pounding drum in her chest as she frantically thought of what she should do. In all of her years of training as an agente, the first thing she had learned was to be fearless in everything. In fact, that was the first thing she had been told by Keoko on the first day she had arrived at Chief's home. The only reason she had been taught to be fearless was so that she could save people. So without even thinking, Veenatch gave the wall of the space a forceful kick, which battered the side, creating a hole.

"Wait! Stop!" she cried as she scrambled out of the hiding nook and through the hole she had created. "Do'a'not hurt her!" Once she was out and standing in front of the two men, one of which was carrying a seven-foot spear, Veenatch realized that she had made a dreadful mistake. Blowing her cover was certainly suicide. And besides, she probably wouldn't be able to save the little girl anyhow. She wanted very badly to run and hide now, but bravely Veenatch stood her ground. It was too late to hide anyway. Every bone in her body felt wobbly. Glancing over her shoulder, she realized that four of the rest of the agentes were all boldly standing behind her and Twii was just now slowly crawling out to join them. Veenatch expected the war chief to be furious, but he just stood there, staring motionlessly at her, his jaw hanging in shock. She could not tell whether he was angry or not.

"Magala," he whispered to the other man hoarsely. "It is the spirits of the rivers and the trees."

Wide-eyed they stared down at the six of them as if they were indeed spirits. Veenatch had forgotten that she was wearing her black uniform, which covered everything except her eyeballs. Not many of the Indians in Orenea had seen such exotic attire before. The war chief and his friend probably thought they were spirits! Humbly the two men both knelt down before the agentes and pressed their foreheads to the ground in reverence.

Slowly they both rose to their feet, yet they still respectfully kept their heads lowered.

"See," the war chief whispered excitedly. "I told you the Oreneans have made alliance with the spirits of the rivers and the trees. They even talked like Oreneans when they spoke!"

"Yes," the other replied. "You were right!"

The war chief began elegantly addressing them. "Oh, great almighty spirits, live forever. What is it that you wish? I hope we have pleased you well with our alms and sacrifices."

Lowering her voice and trying to mask her Orenean accent, Veenatch replied shakily, "We want tha … uh … tha girl, oh, Chief."

"You want us to sacrifice her? Oh, of course! We will do it tonight."

"No. Just put her in front of me on the floor."

"You want us to sacrifice her on the floor?"

"No. Uh … we want to have her alive. Just lay her down in front of me—gently."

"Oh, very well. We would do anything you ask of us."

Willingly, the man who was with the war chief gently laid out the child he had been holding, placing her in front of Veenatch on the floor. Her fearful little eyes gazed unsurely into Veenatch's masked face. She didn't look to be any more than five or six years of age. She was so laden with crusted filth, mud, and overall muck that at first Veenatch hesitated before shakily scooping her up into her arms. Weakly the child placed her dirt-smudged hand on her rescuer's shoulder. Shakily, Veenatch turned around and ducked underneath the stage to leave, followed by the rest of them.

For a few minutes, the war chief and the other man stood staring dazedly into space in disbelief.

"That was remarkable!" the war chief's friend declared, wide-eyed. "Now we can tell our children and grandchildren that we, mortal men, have gazed upon the spirits with our own eyes!"

"Yes," the war chief replied dreamily. "And to think they chose us!"

The campfire inside the cave flickered cheerily, throwing strange dark shadows over the walls as Peter wearily prepared himself to go to sleep. The cave was now quiet as everyone curled up cozily under the fur blankets and dozed off. Peter slowly dipped his hands into a basin of warm water and washed the dirt off his face and neck. He had been instrumental in preparing a place for everyone to sleep. The way Oreneans sleep is this: everyone lies on the ground in a circle around the fire, with their feet facing the flame. A large stick is placed on either side of the fire as a divider between the girls' half and the boys' half. Married couples had their own little sections to themselves. They all shared one large fur blanket, which was circular so that it fit all the way around to everyone, with a hole in the middle to sit around the edge of the fire pit in an overall doughnut shape.

On the boys' side, Peter found a spot between Andrew and some other Indian boy. Quickly Peter curled up in the warm blanket by the fire and tried to get settled in. How wonderful this day had been! He didn't want it to end, but it was so warm and cozy beneath the blanket that Peter began to feel drowsy. He scooted closer to Andrew to benefit from some of his body heat.

"I ate too much," Andrew grumbled softly as he began to fall asleep.

Peter considered shooting back a witty reply but simply decided that he was too sleepy. Soon he too began to doze off, but he was roused by a strange sound echoing through the cave. He bolted upright and cocked his head attentively. Sure enough, there it was again. It sounded as if someone was shouting frantically into the cavern. A small commotion started as people awakened and jumped up to check what all the shouting was about. Peter suddenly felt worried. Had the Tumitatakens suddenly decided to attack?

Hurryingly, Peter shook sleeping Andrew by the shoulders. "Wake up, Andrew! Wake up!" he shouted. Andrew grunted and stirred without opening his eyes. "Andrew, listen!"

Groggily he opened his eyes and stared at Peter in confusion. "Wha-what's going on?"

"I actually don't know. But something's going on. Look! Everyone is going outside."

"Is it the Tumitatakens?"

"I sure hope not!"

By now, almost everyone had wandered outside to investigate, so Peter and Andrew stood up to hurry outside too. As quickly as possible, Peter climbed the steps and stepped outside into the cool night air. Peter shivered. It was much chillier out here than it was inside. A few feet away, a large crowd of people had excitedly gathered around something and were all talking at once. Some were carrying torches to ward off the darkness. Out of the crowd walked Charlie from amongst the great cluster of people.

"Hello!" Andrew called eagerly, "What goes on there?"

"Not much," Charlie replied dully, as if he wished that he hadn't bothered to come out. "I suppose someone went out and brought back a slave child who hadn't been released. She's here now. And from the way people are swarming around her, you would think they came back with a treasure chest!"

"Oh."

"Yes. I saw the poppet. Looks pretty mistreated, if you ask me."

Curiously, Peter and Andrew approached the edge of the thick crowd to try to catch a glimpse. "Can you see anything, Andrew?" Peter asked.

"No. Too many people. I can't see a thing!" Andrew declared.

"May your Zacchaeus friend stand on your head?" Peter asked jokingly. "That could help."

"Ha-ha," Andrew replied sarcastically.

"Is my father around?"

"Yes, over there. Do you want him to hold you up?"

"No, I want to see if he will let me stand on *his* head."

"Good luck with that. I'm sure he doesn't want permanent shoe impressions in his skull."

Peter chuckled. Suddenly, he had an idea. Carefully he knelt down and stared through people's legs, shifting slightly to get a better view. Sure enough, Peter could clearly view the face of the child. Her head was turned toward him, but her eyes were closed as if unconscious. The tiny mouth was slightly ajar.

"Whoa, she *is* battered!" remarked Andrew, who had squatted down next to him. Peter squinted and stared at her face attentively. He couldn't get over the feeling that he had somehow met her before, but he didn't remember where. Could it have been at the previous dinner with the Oreneans? No. Was she the one who had saved Rebeccah by patching up her head? No, it was before that.

Suddenly, an idea struck him like a lightning bolt, an idea that he didn't dare believe. Peter leaned in and stared as hard as he possibly could. It was much too wonderful to be true. This must be a dream! Could it be? Wait. No. Was it possible? It couldn't be true! They had never actually found a body, but ... Yes! Yes, it was!

"Elisabeth?" Peter whispered hoarsely. For a moment he just stared, his mouth wide open. He pinched himself as hard as he could. If this was a dream and he woke up ... Yes! He was sure that the girl was Elisabeth! Never had Peter felt so overwhelmed in his life.

"Um ... Peter. Are you well?" Andrew asked with concern. "You look like you are about to burst."

Unable to help himself, Peter let out a small cry and joyfully began to crawl on his hands and knees as fast as he could through the people's legs. Some tripped, but Peter didn't care. He was like a starving person seeking warm food. Once he finally made it to the center, after what seemed like an eternity, he gently wound his arms around his sister lovingly and squeezed her hard, as if he were afraid that she would disappear. Peter had not known that it was possible to laugh and cry at the same time, but he was doing it now. Tears were flowing down his face profusely, yet billows of laughter were rolling out of his mouth at the same time. He had never felt so much overwhelming joy before in his life, and he thought his chest might burst. Peter lifted his eyes to heaven and whispered hoarsely, "Thank you, thank you."

Everyone else, who didn't yet recognize Elisabeth, stared worryingly at Peter, as if he was insane, but Peter couldn't care less. Joy and relief continued to flood over him like a rushing river. Peter squeezed the girl as if he would never let go. He gently laid his head down on his sister's chest and wept joyfully. He could hear her gentle heart beating softly. It was at this time that Elisabeth began to awaken from her unconscious state. When her precious blue eyes fluttered open, Peter was fully sure it was really Elisabeth. Excitedly he stared down into her little face, which was still coated in dirt and grime.

"Hello," he whispered gently. Elisabeth stared up at him searchingly, as if trying to figure out whether or not this was a dream. "It's me," Peter continued. "Peter—your brother. And you are safe here now. You are home! And you're alive! Oh, thank God you're alive! They don't have you anymore. You're all right. Oh, thank God you are all right."

Then, as if suddenly recognizing who Peter was, a little ghost of a smile spread across her dirty pale face. Weakly she put her thin arms around Peter's back, and again Peter squeezed her as hard as he could, gently rocking her back and forth. He lovingly planted a kiss on her scarred neck. He didn't care who thought he was a sissy or if anyone watching him considered him overly emotional. Father, who had been very concerned about the fact that his son had apparently crawled out through a crowd of people to cry over a total stranger, walked over to Peter and tapped him on the shoulder.

"Are you all right?" he asked seriously. Peter glanced up briefly but was too overwhelmed to answer. Searchingly, Father stared into Peter's tear-streaked face. "It appears you are seriously ill, son," he declared, reaching out gently to pry him off the girl. But Peter continued to cling to her like a raft. "Did you eat anything odd after dinner tonight?"

"This is Elisabeth," Peter explained hoarsely, trying to regain his composure.

"What?"

"It's Elisabeth."

"What are you talking about?"

"This girl here is Elisabeth."

"That is impossible, son. She's dead."

"She is here, Father. Look. It is true. It is."

Hesitantly, as if afraid to be disappointed, Father glanced down at the little lump of body, dirt, and rags and suddenly realized who it was. Immediately he scooped her up in his arms, and an overwhelmed expression that Peter had never seen before spread across his face. For a moment, he just closed his eyes and cradled Elisabeth against his chest.

Confused, Mr. Winslow headed up to him. "John, what is going on?"

Father slowly brushed tears out of his eyes and replied, "This is my daughter."

Mother and Rebeccah were equally elated when Elisabeth was presented to them. The news quickly spread around, and no time was wasted in bathing, bandaging, clothing, and feeding the welcome little girl. Peter later found Elisabeth lying peacefully on a low hammock in a corner, her eyes closed in sleep, and Mother and Father lovingly watching over her like angels. Timidly Peter stood back, wondering if they would rather be alone.

"Can I come over with you?" he asked softly.

"Of course you may, son," Mother replied. "And that's *may* I come over here, by the way." Peter settled down and again stared down at her now-clean face. Most of her curly blonde hair had been hacked off, but some of it was still there. Solemnly Peter wondered what exactly they had done to his sister back when she was at the Tumitataken village. *I suppose it doesn't matter much now,* Peter thought sleepily. *We are all home now as a family. All home.* How wonderful those sweet words were! Here were Mother, Father, him, and Elisabeth. Rebeccah had curled up sleepily by her twin sister and fallen asleep.

"What time is it?" Peter asked curiously.

"Midnight," Father replied, sliding out his pocket watch.

Peter smiled happily as he offered up another silent prayer of thanks. Without question, this had been the most wonderful day of his life.

CHAPTER XIV

THE ORENEANS CONTINUED TO CELEBRATE joyously for the next fortnight. During this time, all of the humbled Tumitatakens reluctantly migrated out of the Orenean land, where they had been living for many hundreds of years. I know not where they settled after they departed. But I do know that the Oreneans rarely heard from them again. Their abandoned villages provided excellent homes for those freed slaves whose home villages had been destroyed. (The run-down village just outside of the cave also was used). Some of the Tumitataken men and women, like Ruex, who had bravely stood up for the Oreneans, were permitted to stay in their homeland. That is why to this day there still is a small population of Tumitatakens in Orenea.

Because of the many poor memories that remained there, no freed Orenean captive desired to stay in the great Tumitataken village itself, so that is where the Washingsworths and their friends and family lodged for the winter.

It snowed more than a dusting only four or five times in this part of Orenea in the winter, and Peter didn't savor the times that it did because he had to wear a bulky Orenean fur snowsuit that was twice as large as he was and made him look half his size. But when he was allowed, he played outside with the others anyway and helped teach the Orenean children to make snowmen like English children did. I should also mention briefly that Mr. Snows and Mrs. Cox were married during that happy winter in Orenea.

During the time directly following, when she was brought home, Elisabeth was still very weak and sick. The poor girl was skin and bones and covered from head to toe in sores and lice. Because she had so often faithfully sat with him when he was ill, Peter returned the favor by staying with her much of the time. Elisabeth also had a brand mark on her lower back from her former owner and suffered nightmares almost every night. She would eventually recover, though. When he was not sitting with Elisabeth, Peter enjoyed exploring the Tumitataken chief's palace with his friends and playing "fort" in the space where the agentes had hidden beneath the stage.

The news of Peter's victory quickly spread to the other tribes and soon was on the tip of every tongue within a hundred miles. The cluster of white men also attended a nearby church. Andrew, who was deathly afraid of heights, did not enjoy this because the children were seated in the rafters, and he spent most of the service fearfully clinging to whomever happened to be sitting next to him. The Orenean accents made it difficult to understand the service anyhow. Eventually, the Orenean version of English grew easier to understand for Peter and he had to work hard not to catch the accent himself!

During the winter, they decided to attempt a return to Plymouth. Mr. Winslow and Shamaro were very much in favor of this because they had left their families back there. All winter this was planned, and everyone expectantly awaited spring.

Spring in Orenea is the most glorious thing you can imagine. When the earth throws off its white winter gown and slips on it colorful spring apparel, Orenea is the most colorful jewel of all. The quimpinita trees burst open their blossoms, wildflowers paint the ground, the trees are the greenest green you can imagine, and the Fire Hills are as orange as ever. A songbird orchestra rings from the trees, and the air is perfumed with the scent of flowers.

It was time to depart. Peter was very sorry to leave his Orenean friends, but unsurely he stuffed his few belongings into a small sack, climbed onto a horse, and trotted off into the unknown with the rest of them and two Orenean guides. The treacherous journey took many months. Along the way, they lay their heads down at night in tepees, which they could easily carry with them, and ate whatever they could hunt or gather along the way. The land beyond the mountains was flat and broad, like an ever-spreading green ocean. If I were to describe to you all of the adventures that they encountered along the way, I would need to write a volume II. Therefore, I will only relay one or two.

As they were passing through near a river, they met a bright Orenean man who worked with herbs to make medicine and knew how to treat illnesses. He had been captured a few years ago and sold to this faraway tribe and was glad when he discovered the news of the tyrant Tumitataken chief's death; he begged to join the travelers so that he could return home. The Oreneans gladly agreed. After all, it *would* be handy to have someone on board who could help treat disease.

He was soon given opportunity to use his skill, for one night, Mother, who had been pregnant for a long while, discovered that she was about to give birth to her child. Restlessly Peter waited at a long distance with the others as Mother was in labor. It was soon agreed the waiting was well worth it when it was announced that Peter now had a younger brother, who was soon named Matthew. Peter was delighted with the tiny little baby—his new brother. There was much happiness and rejoicing at his birth.

The way they were travelling was mostly inhabited by friendly, welcoming tribes who often kindly fed and housed the little clan for the night as they were passing through. But the nation which owned one territory that they needed to pass through was hostile and cruel. The group tried carefully to maneuver down and around their land, which slowed down their progress of travel by a few weeks. But soon they were all back on their way again. The journey was long. One of the worst parts was that Mother, who tended to have been very paranoid about Peter's "civility" in the past, had almost never allowed

Peter to remove his shoes—even as he slept! So when the soles of his old moccasins wore through and fell off, the rough, rocky terrain was free to wreak as much havoc on his soft, tender, un-calloused feet as it wished.

While Peter was hobbling about painfully, Andrew, whose feet were rough and callused over, was breezing along. Sometimes Peter would try to wrap his blistered, bleeding feet in strips of buffalo fur to act as "shoes" until further footwear could be provided. But soon his soles callused over like Andrew's and his scarred feet healed. His legs too, which at the beginning of the journey had throbbed from the continuous trekking across the countryside, were growing tough and strong for walking.

"It do you well," commented Cakechiwa, the younger of the two original oarsmen, who was now beginning to pick up the English language. "Your legs be easy walk all life!"

But even so, the constant moving on of things, especially while caring for an infant, proved to be a challenge. Moreover, travelling was difficult and uncomfortable when Peter was ill.

Soon they began to draw nearer and nearer to home, and the excitement grew more and more. It had been almost this exact time the previous year when they had first set out on this adventure. It was a very joyful day when they finally made it home. Peter's heart could not be more happy and content. A large feast was held in their honor. The Orenean doctor and guides were welcome to stay the winter there so that they could start making their way slowly home again in the spring.

Although their old little house that Father had built so long ago had been occupied by someone else for a long while now, the Washingsworth family happily built and settled in another slightly larger cabin in the woods outside Plymouth.

The Oreneans sadly left their friends to return home in the spring. I know not whether they made it back safely (bickering as they tended to do), but I assume that they did. As for the agentes, they were allowed to return to their families to settle down. But you can be sure they visited Chief and Keoko often.

Every few years, the people in Plymouth would notice buffalo carts slowly rumbling over the horizon as the Oreneans eagerly returned to trade their gold for horses, cattle, and other things, until the route was eventually blocked by warring tribes.

Over time and generations, as the settlement of Plymouth grew, the new settlers (not the original group, of course) gradually forgot the old stories about that Indian nation nestled far in the western mountains—but the Oreneans never forgot. In fact, if you ever visit Orenea today, be sure to show up around late October or early November, which is when the Oreneans celebrate "Peter's Day"—a joyful autumn holiday to commemorate the great legend of how God can even use a boy like Peter E. Washingsworth to save a nation. And while you are at it, you may as well visit the Washingsworth family line; I am sure they would be proud to show you the very bronze sword that Peter used. Unfortunately, I do not know exactly where it is now, but I am sure you can find it with a little checking.

And so, things in Orenea returned to normal after the twelve years of horror (as they were come to be called). That is not to say there was no adventure, for there will always be plenty of adventure in Orenea. But the people were now happy and peaceful again. The crops were planted and harvested. People came and went. Autumn rolled around again and again. The sun peeked over the horizon and set again. Chiefs rose and fell, and there was nothing new under the sun.

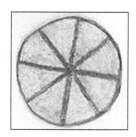

ABOUT THE AUTHOR

S. G. Muscarello is a fourteen year old author who has been writing short stories since she was eight years old. At ten she decided to graduate from short stories to something much longer – this book. It took a while but at twelve the original story was finished. After some editing, she finally submitted the manuscript at thirteen for publication. Almost all of the writing was done with just pencil and paper.

Cameron Park

CPSIA information can be obtained
at www.ICGtesting.com
Printed in the USA
FSHW022027280219
56023FS